The Echoes of Ashlington

Rowan MacKemsley

For James and Claire,

The world is a kinder place

with you in it.

And for Irene

Acknowledgments

Writing this novel would not have been possible without the love and support of my husband and children, who, on occasion, were left to the horror of fending for themselves while words flowed. My children are my inspiration. Their resilience and wonder continue to surprise me every day.

Thanks to those that read my story in its early stages and gave much needed encouragement: Vince, Samantha, Sofia, Tracy, Natalie, Cate, Jess, and Andrea. To my Vegas coffee-fuelled writing posse, Cate and Kathy, thank you for the weekly sanity.

Huge thanks to Elizabeth Garner for her professional navigation through developmental edits. It was wonderful working with you and the team at Jericho Writers.

And last, but not least, to Andrew May and the team at Spectrum Books for the perfect home for this story, their faith in me, and endless patience.

Historical note - While I have followed most movements of the 28th Regiment, artistic licence has been used in places, the most notable being their return to England.

The swim for the boats at Fort Ragusa was actually performed by grenadiers of the 92nd who were indeed rewarded with gold by Sir Rowland Hill. It seemed the sort of impulsive yet brave thing Henry would think to do.

I highly recommend Charles Cadell's *The Slashers* for anyone wanting to know more about the 28th Regiment's journey through the Napoleonic War. I was captivated by his account of a soldier saving his life by taking a 'ball' meant for him, and used it as the inspiration for a certain scene within the novel.

About the author

Having grown up in the rural Cotswolds, Rowan's love of aviation led to a private pilot's licence at seventeen, and subsequent career in the aviation industry. Marrying a military man means lots of moving around, currently in country number six (the USA), raising two amazing, resilient children she hopes the world will be a fairer and less judgemental place for.

Rowan's love for books began when introduced to The Hobbit in primary school. The combination of dragons, maps, and adventure sparking an imagination that she eventually took seriously. When not writing, she loves to travel with the family, exploring the great outdoors and history of wherever they find themselves—even better if castles and battlefields are involved. If it is race weekend for the Formula 1, then she'll be glued to the tv watching the highs and lows of her beloved scarlet team.

The Echoes of Ashlington is her debut novel.

Prologue

Bones and flesh shattered by cannon; the captain lay in the dirt shivering. Accepting the end gave little comfort; having endured so long gave no solace. Home had been months ago.

Home? He played the word on his lips, confused by its intrusion. Attempts to conjure an image of stone walls or family failed. Instead, like an old friend, he welcomed the searing memory of a stolen moment and a smile that belonged to him alone.

Startled back to alertness by the call of his name, he moaned, trying to move legs that rebelled, declining his order; each inhalation growing more resistant. He felt a hand reach into his pocket for the letter he carried—an unspoken agreement between brothers.

The captain had stood among his men in the fields close to Mont-Saint-Jean, holding their defensive square in formation against wave after wave of vicious cavalry charges. They further held in line against Napoleon Bonaparte's formidable moustached Old Guard, the taunting chorus of 'Vive la France' giving song through the smoke to their wraith-like columns. Pride for his valiant company of Slashers flooded his heart as his very life drained from it.

He looked up as the ranks closed once more, ready for

the final push forward. Someone picked up the colours; the flag whipping urgently above his head.

"It's time," a welcome voice said.

The captain turned his head to search for the man it belonged to. Denial had been a traitorous companion for many years. He lay alone. The regiment had moved on. His next visitors would be the looters with their quick fingers and resolute purpose.

With a grunt, he reached for his sword and heaved it to his chest, tightening fingers around the crest engraved on the blade.

"You promised we'd do this together," he whispered, the pain in his heart overcoming that of his broken body. He strayed once more, reaching for where he belonged and dreams of a future that, even before this day, could never have been; dry lips curling with the ghost of a smile.

His surroundings fell quiet. The indistinguishable screams of injured men and horses, the crack of muskets, and explosions of cannon fading, leaving only the echo of regret.

As the smoke dispersed, there, outlined against the blue of the clearing sky, he thought he saw a figure in red hold out his hand.

Chapter 1

London, March 2015

Lillian Durand forced her way through the crowd, some of which parted reverently for her. Those that didn't, she was happy to nudge aside. Like every Friday night, the narrow wine bar heaved; in the main with boasting colleagues from the development company Lillian worked for. Together, they congratulated themselves on being at the peak of their profitable careers with noisy enthusiasm and little regard for the outrageous prices charged.

Above the crowd, a hand commanded her to the bar.

"Here she is!" Guy Theakston, surveying the throng like a circus ringmaster lacking only the top hat, greeted her with a kiss on each cheek. "The lady of the hour."

"Of the year more like," said Marcus Johansen, Lillian's fiancé and Guy's business partner. He passed Lillian a glass of champagne and bumped it with his. Not his first if the lack of co-ordination was anything to go by. "Here's to those rules of yours. Test the boundaries, stand up for something or other, and what else was it?"

"Stand up for what you believe in and protect those you care about." Lillian drained her glass to a conqueror's adulation.

"Sentimental, but it worked this time," Guy agreed.

Lillian looked for the third partner, Claudia Poole; hopeful Marcus would rub her face in it as she would his. Claudia had told Marcus, in no uncertain terms, that they would never get the remaining families of George Street to sell. Lillian had been the keystone to making it happen. Contracts signed, they would soon begin work demolishing the street to make way for their combined development of luxury apartments and hotel complex.

"That went straight to my head," Lillian laughed, wobbling on her heels as the surrounding bodies pressed in with each opening of the door.

"You aren't twenty-one anymore," Marcus said, as if she couldn't feel the sag and drain herself.

Claudia drifted to Lillian's side, her attention on Marcus. "Congratulations," she offered in her dry scratching voice with a smile she had not been wearing when Lillian last saw her.

Reports as to Claudia's professional abilities wavered between competent and a waste of skin, depending on who you talked to. Had Claudia been male, Lillian could be sure those reports would have been fairer; they had worked on projects together and her visions could be spectacular. The older woman held herself with a compact, driven elegance Lillian envied. How she juggled her successful career and picture-perfect family remained an enigma to Lillian, who endeavoured to emulate Claudia's success.

A sought after architect herself, Lillian had the money thanks to her lineage, she had worked hard for the career, and now had the man. Everyone expected the children to come soon. Time was ticking as her future mother-in-law kept reminding her.

Claudia's astute eyes darted over Lillian as though seeing her for the first time. "Looks like your powers of persuasion did it again, Lillian."

"They merely needed what they thought was a sympathetic ear," Lillian said with a measured amount of grace she wouldn't normally bother with. "That and a deal they could not refuse."

"Champagne?" Marcus offered Claudia. Lillian knew he had enjoyed the in-house fight with Claudia almost as much as the actual winning of the contract. There were few things he enjoyed more than a prolonged battle at work, and Claudia never failed to provide a worthy opponent. She looked down her nose at Marcus, declining the drink before filtering back into the crowd.

Marcus continued filling glasses and entertaining his growing audience. They hung to his words, captivated like bees to honey. Only they were wasps and he, the chisel-jawed beekeeper, luring them into a trap. Lillian was not sure what this made her. The smoke, perhaps, that he would waft at those that did not bend to his will.

Lillian ordered two more bottles of her favourite champagne from the bar, distracting herself from the memory of the last woman to sign over her home to the development site; elderly deep-set eyes watering as she finally agreed to sign the document. "Does this taste funny to you?" Lillian asked Guy, trying to recall the old lady's name. Alice somebody.

"Oh, no you don't." Guy draped an arm across her shoulders. "No going dewy eyed on me. This is a celebration, Lillian. You won't get where you want to be if you go back to getting emotional about these things. They will have the time of their lives in the new apartments."

"I'm not emotional."

"Sometimes I think I know you better than you know yourself. Those people don't need your pity." Her mentor's mantra slipped off his tongue with authority. As he would be quick to point out, in the end, it was all just business.

"We should go home," Marcus announced an hour later, eventually bored with his little wasps. Guy had already left with a tall blonde half his age.

Arriving at their apartment, Lillian helped Marcus out of the cab; the champagne having taken a toll on his stability. The bright lights in the apartment's lobby building hurt her eyes almost as much as the gilded décor. She greeted the guard, who waved but did not look up from his screen.

At the onset of his career, Marcus had transformed what once used to be a derelict wharf-side warehouse into four unique apartments, the top of which they now called home. He bragged he put his soul into the design and Lillian couldn't agree more.

They rode the lift to the top floor, Lillian barefoot, carrying her shoes. It opened directly into the penthouse, a single room containing crisp minimalistic zones. Marcus settled onto the sofa while Lillian cracked open two of the half-barred windows before dropping her bag next to the concrete coffee-table covered in wedding magazines, gifts from the future mother-in-law. Each was well-thumbed and annotated with notes or post-its. All good willed intentions, Marcus assured her. The maternity magazine Lillian had dropped straight into the bin. Marcus had laughed when he found it and told her she would change her mind. He had said it with such certainty, as though he had their whole future mapped out.

She made coffee for them both, giving Marcus his as he sat scrolling through his phone checking news and e-mail. Without interrupting, she kissed him on the head and took her coffee to the bedroom area, pausing en route to enjoy the view across the marina.

London's sprawl had its pretty parts, the marina below the apartment being one of them, particularly at night. Lights from the surrounding buildings softened the water where small yachts and cruisers strained at their moorings, beckoned by the freedom of the river.

Woken by her alarm, Lillian found the space next to her empty. Marcus lay asleep on the sofa where she had left him, still in his suit, laptop open on plans for the development and suggestions for a chain of similar hotels ranging from cities to countryside tourist honeypots. Without a thought for breakfast, she showered and dressed. Focusing on getting to the office to finish some work without the distraction of her colleagues was as much a habit as the bar on a Friday night.

Interrupting the stillness of the apartment, her phone

rang as she reached the lift. "Lillian? I'm so sorry to be calling early in the morning like this." At first Lillian couldn't place the reluctant voice. The type that would ask next if there was anyone with you. "It's Janet—Janet Hawkins from the village."

"Is everything okay?" Lillian said, though she knew the answer to her question before she asked it. Her father's retired housekeeper never called, and there could be only one reason she would. "Is Dad all right?" She sunk down onto the sofa next to Marcus's unperturbed feet, hand gripping the telephone as though gravity itself depended on Janet's next sentence.

Lillian met Janet at the hospital in Cheltenham later that afternoon. Janet led the way to the ward with an efficient stride for such tiny legs, following a line painted on the floor through bleached corridors. She introduced Lillian to the doctor on duty. The doctor spoke in veiled sentences, Lillian's hazy concentration from the three-hour drive unable to determine the meaning behind the alien medical words or slippery evasion.

Just as clarity seemed lost forever, Janet thrust a hot vending machine coffee into her hand. "Everything will be all right."

"I know. He is a Durand. He barely catches a cold."

Apart from the feathery red lines around his nose, Alistair Durand looked pale. At Christmas, he had been his usual self. No hint of illness or the heart attack that had brought him here; but that had been months ago. A snake of guilt wound its way around the pit of Lillian's stomach. How could she have been so wrapped up in her own pressing world of finalising contracts when he was here alone? Why hadn't she called him that week?

Janet fussed, making him laugh with some inconsequential gossip from the village and a promise of smuggled contraband. How did anyone get used to seeing loved ones like this? Did it get easier with age? Experience? Her father's skin hung off his face, the dark skeletal hollows of his eyes aging him. Mortal, after all.

Lillian turned her head away, forcing herself to look at the over-bed table suspended above her father's feet.

"You shouldn't have come all this way, Lily. You are busy," he told her.

"Of course I needed to come. Protect those you care about, remember. You taught me that. I spoke to the doctor. She says you need to stay for some more tests."

"It's all they seem to do nowadays. Tests. I think they want to operate, but I'm tired. I'd rather go home."

"Well, I am staying to help, so let them do the tests, okay?" So he didn't think she had ignored his disguised plea, she added, "I have taken time off from work for a few weeks so I can look after you when you come home."

"That's nice. You can help me with my project." He tried to straighten himself in the bed, a glint of intelligence returning to his milky blue eyes. The movement made him wheeze. Both Lillian and Janet stood up. He waved off their attention, the spark snuffed. "Don't fuss, I'm fine," he insisted.

"Have some water." Lillian poured him a cup from a brown plastic jug, distracting herself once more from his decay. "Tell me about this project? Is this what you have been working on all this time, the family history thing you mentioned at Christmas?" He had become obsessed with looking back through time at Ashlington Manor's past. That much he had told her.

"I want to ask Nicholas if he would take a look and give me some expert help. I'd like to write about a character I have discovered. It is important."

"Where is Nick nowadays?" The mention of Janet's son brought an image of the face and floppy hair of her childhood friend. One she had not spoken to in years. "Deep underground in some tomb surrounded by jungle?" She gave a nervous laugh, looking from her father to Janet. "Just as well you have e-mail, or have you finally learned how to FaceTime?" She took a sip of the now lukewarm coffee.

"Nick is back in Ashlington," Janet said.

Shock sent Lillian's coffee down the wrong way. She spluttered into her elbow, struggling to disguise it.

"He has been back since the summer," Alistair added, the mischievous glimmer restored.

***

Two weeks later, were it not for his own father's hand that gripped his arm vice-like, Nick Hawkins would have been at Lillian's side when she buckled. The two men locked glares, then gradually, the elder loosened his hold. Nick returned to his previous stance; arms locked to his side, fists clenched shut, as Lillian's shiny clean-cut fiancé, Marcus Bloody Johansen, shuffled his feet and looked about him in embarrassment. No comforting arm around her shoulder, no whispered words of reassurance. Not until Nick's mother Janet emerged at Lillian's side and drew her into her arms, did Nick let out the breath he held.

Alistair Durand finished his journey into the wet earth, the funeral attendants completing their job with professional detachment. Done. Gone. Nick couldn't help but think the old man would be pleased with himself. His death in hospital had been sudden, none of this 'languishing about the place.'

At least I spared Olivia another funeral, he thought. He had sent his daughter off to school that morning, despite her assurances that she could hold his hand. She was not as strong as she pretended to be though, reminding Nick of the last time they held hands at a graveside in the rain, misery carved on her face. He would do anything to never see her like that again.

Parts of Ashlington Manor's yellow limestone walls had stood for hundreds of years, nestled against dense woodland in the folds of the Cotswold escarpment, alongside the village of the same name. Almost hidden from the narrow winding lane with its overgrown verges of cow parsley and nettles, only the tall iron gates hinted at the existence of the house beyond. There in the private graveyard within the grounds, among plenty of Durand ancestors, Alistair was now at rest with his wife. The mother Lillian had never known. To anchor himself to something solid, Nick focussed his attention on the angel statue he had loved as a child. Its stone wings were now covered with ivy and framed with a willow tree; the tangle of its branches dripping spring tears.

Nick felt his father's hand on his arm again, this time propelling him forwards. People were shuffling past the grave; steps on the wooden boardwalk punctuated by the clattering of soil thrown down. He looked. A single lily stem rested on the coffin lid. Pure white petals sullied by the blend of earth and rain coming from above.

The ambling procession back to the house picked its way through vehicles littering the driveway. Some flapped and shook umbrellas, abandoning them in the stone porch before pausing at the threshold to wipe their feet.

Stepping inside, Nick pulled at his tie (the only one he possessed) and undid the top two buttons of his shirt. He did not plan to stay for long; there was something disturbing about crowds of people. All the social graces, all the things one shouldn't say or do. Breaking away from his father's side, he slid into the dining room, searching for the safety of solitude.

The room remained how he remembered from all those years ago, calming the clenching of his belly. A long mahogany dining table surrounded by voluptuous chairs filled the room's centre, around which hung a variety of portraits. At the far end, a pair of matching sofas faced each other, like bookends, on either side of the huge fireplace. As a boy, Nick used to stare up the chimney, wondering if he could climb it like the Victorian chimney sweeps. He never tried.

The fire was lit but neglected. He shrugged off his coat, left it hanging on the back of a dining chair with his tie stuffed into the pocket, and placed another log on the fire. He stood, letting the heat soak through his soggy trousers before his attention moved upwards to the painting above the mantle.

"Hello, old friend."

The painting of a Durand ancestor, dressed in the uniform of a British army captain from the Peninsula War, had always looked at odds with those keeping it company. This canvas dared whoever viewed it to enquire beyond the brush strokes of a classically posed portrait. Nick found himself still in awe of the scruffy figure and his horse, despite the frown of anger carried on his features. Impossibly young, he stood with one hand resting on the horse's neck, red coat unbuttoned, hat missing and fair Durand hair an unruly mess. Behind him, in the distance, lay a city.

"I always wondered what he called the horse."

"Hello Lily," Nick said without turning.

"Hi Nick."

They stood in front of the painting; their silence marked by the dependable tick of the grandfather clock at the opposite end of the room. "He always looks so uncomfortable," Lillian said, voice a whisper.

Unsure if she talked about him or the painting, Nick stole a sideways glance. She may have changed the clothes muddied at the graveside but hadn't changed a drop in twenty years. Blonde hair wrapped up at her neck, arms pulling her jacket around her middle despite the warmth of the fire. Nick looked back at the painting, silently asking it for help.

"Sad, even."

"Angry," Nick replied. "I always thought he looked angry." Enveloped by silence once more, Nick searched for some way to tell her how sorry he was. As he drew breath to speak again, a voice from the hallway called her name.

She moved towards the door, brushing his arm as she passed. "Thanks for coming, I know it would have meant a lot to Dad."

Nick spent a further half hour in the kitchen, working his way through two beers before he felt ready to join his parents in the large reception room that had once been a ballroom.

"Okay, son?" Jack Hawkins frowned at the bottle Nick held. Nick's father stood close to the door that led out into the garden. Propped ajar by Jack's foot, it let in a welcoming damp breeze. Jack looked as uncomfortable as Nick felt.

"You?"

Jack made a grumbling noise. "Your mother is putting on a brave face."

Janet worked the room offering comfort with chit-chat or a pat on the arm. It felt like the entire village had turned out to pay their respects. In any other village there may have been an intrusive motive to this, but this was Ashlington, and the number of people packed into the ballroom only proved how well the Durands were thought of. His mother would not be alone hurting today.

Nick caught sight of Lillian stood next to Marcus Johansen, who waved his arms around as he talked. A glass of something clear, likely a fashionable gin, dangerously sloshing. Johansen had lost Lillian's attention. She had drifted far away. Why didn't she just ask everyone to go home and leave her in peace?

"Nicholas, you remember Reverend Attwood?" His father nudged his elbow, returning Nick to his immediate surroundings.

"It was a lovely service," Nick said. That's what people were meant to say at funerals. It made him wonder if anyone ever admitted to the awful ones he knew existed. Ones in which twelve-year-old girls lost their innocence as they watched a mother's casket descend where they cannot follow.

With a firm handshake, the reverend embarked upon an explanation of hymn choices. Nick bit at an unbidden inappropriate snigger threatening to escape. Reverend Attwood wore round steel-rimmed glasses which together with his white fluffy hair gave him an uncanny resemblance to the vicar in the children's tv programme, *Postman Pat*. The emotional gymnastics caught Nick off guard. He put it down to being back in this house and seeing Lillian again.

"I read your book on the tomb you found in Columbia. Fascinating stuff. Your mother has kept me up to date on your career. You have been very successful." Had there been any surprise in the reverend's statement, he hid it well. "So, what is next? Your work always sounds so adventurous I

15

can't imagine there is much to keep you here in sleepy Gloucestershire?"

"I don't know about that," Nick shrugged. "My daughter is studying for her A-Levels—"

"She's a pretty good historian herself," Jack interjected.

"So, we are here for now. Then we'll see."

"Ah, a stable base," Attwood nodded. "I understand."

Nick found that hard to believe. The reverend had lived in the area his entire life. How could he understand what life had been like for Olivia, moving from country to country, dig to dig?

"So, more books in the meantime?"

"A bit of lecturing and helping an old colleague."

"Call by the vicarage sometime. I would love to talk more. I don't suppose you would sign my copy of *Teyuna's Mummies*?"

"Sure."

"Splendid." Attwood patted him on the back as though Nick were a boy again, then looked at his watch. "If you will excuse me, I should catch up with your mother. Good to talk to you both. Keep up the wonderful work, Nicholas."

Like his father, Nick found himself reluctant to move away from the fresh breeze of the side door and they were largely left alone, neither having a reputation for being sociable. With the notable exception of Johansen's brash baritone, conversations were quiet; the house soaking up any suffering.

"Did you talk to her yet?" Jack asked, fracturing their

silence. He looked in Lillian's direction.

"Sort of. Do you want another drink?"

"I've had enough." His father had barely touched what was in his glass. Nick was on his third, enjoying—until that moment and his father's masked message—the familiar fuzz that blurred his edges and made socialising tolerable.

"I think I will go home then. Want to come?" Nick leaned his head toward the open door through which the fresh scent of the recent rain and a non-judgemental bottle of single malt called.

"I'll wait for your Mum."

Nick slid away, escaping the crowd once more, collected his coat from the dining room and, with a nod to the soldier in the painting, made his way to the front door.

He almost made it.

"Nick? Are you leaving?"

He paused for a moment with his hand on the doorknob before forcing a smile to turn and greet Lillian again.

"I—if you have a minute, I need your help with something."

What could she, Lillian Durand, possibly need me for? He thought as she made a sideways motion with her head. He found himself compelled to follow her back into the dining room. She always had been good at getting what she wanted.

"My father would have wished he could have talked to you before—you know." She swallowed and jutted out her chin. That proud Durand chin stuck in the air, telling Nick she was doing everything in her power not to cry. "He had spent months working on a project, rifling through old letters and diaries of ancestors, trying to put them together in some sort of order. It obsessed him. One of the last conversations I had with him was about you funnily enough." She rubbed at the back of her long neck where strands of gold had broken free.

Nick looked away, the soldier in the painting a safer place to settle his gaze.

"He said you were back in Ashlington and he was going to ask if you would help him, see if there is anything worth writing about. You know what he is—was like; he would have hated to leave anything unfinished."

She had always stirred conflicting emotions within him, and this was no exception. Although touched that Alistair would want him to look at the work, researching the family history of the upper classes was far from his field of expertise. That said, their family was unique, having been in Ashlington since actual archers drank at the village pub as its name suggested. It could prove to be a fascinating distraction. But then there was his history with the woman that stood before him asking for his help.

History, Nick decided, best left entombed.

"I'm sorry Lily; it is not exactly my area of specialty."

"Oh."

He had surprised her. There was a time he used to do everything she asked of him. For a moment, he felt smug about it.

"I suppose I should have expected that," she said, and

before he could murmur anything else, he found himself alone.

Nick retreated to the fireplace and stared up at the soldier. Darker than when he had stood there earlier, the sun had now moved around the house; the shadows on the youthful face now giving the distinct impression of disapproval.

He took the shortest route back to his cottage, through the rose garden to the moon gate. Alistair had built the moon gate himself, a circular opening in the stone wall with a wrought-iron gate dressing the lower half. The top half, overhung with ivy, forced Nick to stoop and curse Alistair as he walked through. Being back in Ashlington at the same time as Lillian felt exactly like something the old man would have planned.

Chapter 2

A week following the funeral, Lillian stood with her hand on the door to her father's study and glanced at his dog. Holly, the liver and white springer spaniel, wagged her tail and cocked her head. The day Lillian's father died, she had shut the study door and not allowed anyone in since. Though she had dealt with the more immediate of his affairs, she knew much of him waited on the other side of that door, including the project he wanted finished.

With Marcus back in London, she had been alone for the week; the stream of well-wishers, offerings of sympathy, soups and shepherd's pie, now dried up. His return looming, she decided she could put it off no more, or he would rightly question what she had been doing with her time. Wandering the halls of Ashlington in a reminiscent daze hardly seemed something he would understand.

She squared her shoulders and pushed the door open.

Floor to ceiling bookshelves lined two of the walls which linked above the door. There seemed no order to them. Books or magazines crammed any available gap like the cardboard boxes on the floor she had to traverse. Holly hurried around the boxes and sniffed at the chair behind the desk before settling herself next to it with a low moan Lillian felt in her ribs.

Her father's desk remained covered with paperwork

requiring her attention, or at the very least, organising. A cobweb, stretched between the desk lamp and pen pot, reminded Lillian to let the cleaner back in. Flecked with spreading mirror rot, the mirror above the fireplace had hung there for as long as she could remember. Below it, on the dusty mantelpiece, stood cherished items like sentries guarding the memories they marked. A wedding photo in a silver frame—her favourite photograph of her father. With her mother stood beside him, he looked different from the man Lillian knew; lighter, invincible. Then her mother's tin box that Lillian knew contained a seashell from the beach where her father had proposed. The flintlock pistol at the centre of the shelf seemed out of place among the romantic items. But her father had treasured it. A long-lost belonging of an ancestor. Finally, a simple owl made from clay. Swallowing a sob, Lillian picked up the owl. It had lost its tail, but she could still make out the indentations of the tiny fingers that had moulded the clay. Her fingers. A Father's Day gift from long ago. She returned the owl to the mantelpiece and turned her back on the memories.

Fuelled by a mug of strong coffee, Lillian worked her way through phone calls with her father's solicitor, and paperwork for a few hours, until the doorbell made Holly bark and rush to the entrance hall. Lillian followed her, glad of the interruption.

When she slid out of the heavy studded oak front door, leaving the barking dog inside, a hand thrust towards her in greeting. "Louis Varnal, from Dawson and Varnal."

The name was unfamiliar. The man's car matched his

suit; beige and expensive. Neither held any clue as to the business of Dawson and Varnal.

"Yes?" she said, inviting him to elaborate.

"I have an appointment with Mrs Johansen for a valuation." He paused and slowly looked her over, beady eyes lingering in places they shouldn't, before he whisked a business card from his pocket.

Unimpressed, Lillian took the card which announced what he had already told her but with the addition of the word "auctioneers" embossed in gold letters.

Varnal continued talking as he scrolled through his iPad. "Paintings, furniture and several antique collectables—"

"There must be some mistake. I have not arranged for any valuation."

"I beg your pardon?"

"Like I said, I am not selling anything yet." She handed him back the business card which he took with a look of bewilderment. "It looks as though you have had a wasted journey."

Varnal made a derisive noise in his throat. "I don't think you understand, young lady," he said, causing Lillian to sigh loudly and fold her arms. "Mr Johansen has arranged—"

"Mr Johansen has nothing to sell here," she said as calmly as she could. Marcus had organised this? Admittedly, she had mentioned selling the house, but there was much to do before that stage. "This house and everything in it belongs to me, not to him." Varnal's patriarchal attitude

22

made her defensive. She was sure if and when she sold anything, house or contents, he would be the last man she would want handling it.

"You're not Mrs Johansen?" The swiping on the iPad reached a fraught level as he double checked his facts. "But I have my instructions from Mr Johansen to—"

"Mr Varnal!" Lillian felt her nose wrinkle with annoyance. "You seem to have difficulty, so I will explain it to you again. I made no appointment with you or your office. Nothing here is for sale." As her volume got louder, Varnal backed himself out of the porch. "Now get the hell off my property before I have you forcibly removed!" The thought of vigorously expelling him, preferably at gunpoint, rather appealed. She thought of the flintlock pistol in the study, a sudden temptation of how the weight of it might feel in her hand. The reality was setting an elderly flatulent spaniel after him.

"But—"

"Do you want me to call my security? I doubt that very much." She pulled her phone out of her back pocket and pretended to dial. It was a big house. Having security was not unheard of.

Varnal promptly got into his car and reversed. Through the windscreen, Lillian could see him scowling while holding his phone to his ear. No doubt calling Marcus. She would need to set him straight; it will take more time to go through everything and decide whether to sell it outright or develop it? Were she her own client, then she would convince herself selling was in the best interest of everyone;

the owner, the village, the community. First, she needed to get through a day without crying.

When Marcus arrived that night, the dinner Lillian cooked had not sat well in the oven waiting for him, so she suggested meeting him at the village pub. Many said The Archer was older than the manor. Lillian had no proof of this, though it was evident to anyone that stepped over the threshold stone, worn concave from decades of passing feet, that the endearing public house had been at the heart of the village for hundreds of years. Black and white photographs of villagers and cricket teams (many including a Durand) adorned the walls, and tankards belonging to loyal locals hung above the bar where the landlord greeted Lillian with a sympathetic smile of recognition.

"Bit chintz, isn't it?" Marcus said, giving someone's hand-crocheted doily a depreciating scowl.

"It's a village pub. What did you expect?"

"They could make a fortune here if they updated it. Knock some of these walls down, put in a new fireplace. Lighten it all up. More tables for dining, a decent kitchen."

"There is nothing wrong with the kitchen. The food takes a while because they make it fresh. Dad used to love it. He would always have his Sunday roast here." She pictured him sat by the fire (normally lit nine months of the year) surrounded by horse brasses reading the newspaper, or nursing a pint while playing chess with Jack Hawkins.

"I'm sorry about Varnal," Marcus said, oblivious that in her thoughts she remained with her father. "I did not expect him to come straight down. I just want you to know I am ready to help you get this all sorted."

"You think I should sell it?"

"That was always the plan, wasn't it? I think it will be a burden to us. It's not like this is your home anymore."

"I know, but I need more time though to finish going through all of Dad's things."

"I can help for the weekends, but I need to be in London during the week, especially with you not at the office."

They ate quietly, Marcus stopping every so often to check his phone and answer messages. Lillian forcing herself to eat, though she did not feel the slightest bit hungry.

"How is Guy? I haven't heard much from him."

"He and Claudia are trying to find something to keep the banks happy. You know Guy, he moans about missing you. You are better with the clients."

"The banks? Is the company in trouble?"

"No. The company will be fine. None of us want to be in a position where it is not, that's all. We worked too hard to get where we are." Working too hard referred to the fact that neither Marcus, Guy or Claudia came from wealthy backgrounds. The company was the result of their blood, sweat and tears. Something Marcus liked to remind Lillian about often. He looked down at his plate. "This is awful, I'm not going to pay for this," he said, clicking his fingers impatiently at the passing teenage server.

"It's fine, Marcus. Don't make a fuss."

"Any dessert or coffee?" the server asked. She looked

too young to be working tables in a pub; full of hope and itching to get out of the tiny village and discover the world. Lillian had been the same.

"No, I don't think so," Marcus said with a snort.

"It was lovely," Lillian told her. "I'll come settle the bill at the bar."

Marcus drove them back to the manor, where light from the windows leaked onto the brick work, giving the Cotswold stone a toasty orange hue. Were it not for Marcus grumbling as he drove up the beech-lined driveway, it might look romantic.

"It's a shame," he mumbled. "It could make a lovely wedding venue."

Marcus never seemed comfortable at the manor. Lillian was unsure if it was because the history surrounding him made him feel agitated, or the fact her father disliked him. Either way, any stay in the old house with Marcus was fraught with restlessness and foul mood. Whenever they visited her father, she would spend the entire time wanting to be back in London to escape the resentment between the two men. Her father had never been that way about Nick. If anything, he positively encouraged Nick being around. She caught him once teaching Nick how to fish in the lake, like one might teach a son. Nick had hated it but went along with it because he liked to keep everyone happy. Why she had thought of him, she did not know; likely the fact that most of her childhood memories were wrapped with him as much as they were with her father.

"Did your father never get the heating replaced?"

Marcus shivered, inspecting the lounge thermostat, twisting the dial back-and-forth as though the room's temperature would respond immediately to his demand.

"It's an old house, the heating has a mind of its own."

"One less thing to worry about when you sell it."

A draught slammed the lounge door shut. She must have left a window open upstairs.

"Marcus!"

He held his hands up in mock surrender. "Okay, I won't bring it up again."

"What are we doing for Guy's birthday this year?"

Marcus, engrossed in his phone once more, looked up with a blank expression. "He doesn't want a fuss this time. Dinner party?"

"We could do it here."

Marcus groaned. "Fine, but get some caterers to do the food."

"My cooking is not that bad."

"But why not just pay someone else to sort it out? Not that bunch from the pub, though. Their funeral sandwiches were abysmal. Get someone good. It is his birthday, after all. Did I mention I am going to drive back home on Sunday afternoon?" The phone scrolling resumed.

"Busy morning on Monday?"

"Early meeting with the contractors. We break ground on the George Street development on Tuesday. Why don't you come along? Get you away from this place for a day?"

"I'll think about it."

By Sunday night Lillian sat alone on the sofa with a glass of wine, Marcus having left to fight his way through the traffic back to the city. Holly trotted towards her, tail wagging. Both dog and human knew full well that Alistair Durand had never allowed Holly onto the furniture. Without him there to disapprove and as they were both missing him, Lillian gave the space next to her a pat.

By her side lay a box file she had found on her father's desk, labelled in his hand with the name Henry Durand. The soldier in the painting in the dining room was a Henry. Is he the character her father had mentioned? Inside the box, on top of a stack of notebooks and documents, was a letter.

She unfolded the small package, being careful of the crumbling snapped wax seal. Stained by the passage of time, the paper crackled at her touch and brought with it the impression of dutiful monks scratching on parchment. She sighed at the beautiful penmanship of the handwriting. No one wrote letters like this anymore.

To Henry Durand, Ashlington Manor, Ashlington, Gloucestershire

It has come to my attention that you would find use of an introduction for commission into His Majesty's Army. As captain commanding a company within the 1st Battalion of the 28th (North Gloucestershire) Regiment, it would be my honour to provide this for you. I have space for an ensign and you have come highly recommended by a loyal man of the 28th, a friend, and one to whom I owe a great debt.

Should you wish to make use of this introduction then reply with your intentions and further so, report to me at barracks in Colchester on the 10th July.

T Sinclair

Captain, 28th Regiment

Chapter 3

Ashlington, June 1807

"How?" Christopher asked, laughing as he gave Henry a shove. "You are sixteen, for pity's sake. Come on Danny, enlighten our fair, innocent brother. When did you first kiss a girl?"

"Fourteen."

Christopher smirked as though he caught the whiff of victory for once. "My point exactly. I am quite sure I was ten. How have you not, Henry? Not even Louisa?"

Why his two brothers found his inexperience such a source of hilarity and insisted on teasing him about it as they made their way to the lake, Henry could only guess. A swim had been his older brother Danny's idea to follow an exerting afternoon helping with the haymaking. Although Henry found himself covered in more filth than his brothers, he felt reluctant to join in; his own relationship with the lake being a precarious one.

"Never mind, Henry, father has found someone for you to marry so you'll know what to do soon," Danny teased.

"We could always send you to one of the ladies in town, you know, to make sure you know what goes where before your wedding night." Despite being the youngest brother by a year, Christopher offered this with all the experience of one whose visits to the doctor for repeated bouts of uncomfortable itching remained something no one could tell their mother about.

"Shut up, both of you!" Henry grumbled. "What do you mean father has found someone for me to marry?" His slowly dawning alarm brought Henry to a curt halt, his brothers erupting with laughter at his expense once more. The two of them stripped completely, continuing their mocking as they jumped in, splashing frigid water Henry's way.

"You will find out soon enough," Danny told him, surfacing with a chilled gasp. "Father says the Smalleys are breaking their journey to Malvern here next week, in time for the ball."

Henry felt his mouth flap open.

"It is how the world works, Henry. They expect men from families like ours to marry well and produce heirs."

"At least you don't have to marry Ursula," Christopher offered. That was some consolation, Henry supposed, but then Ursula Chilton was Danny's fate.

"Coming in?" Danny asked, pushing Christopher underwater as punishment.

"I don't think I'll bother," Henry said, unable to shake the growing urge to run away; that his role lay somewhere outside Ashlington, that stepping towards it would take more courage than he had. He kicked out angrily at a lump of stone, hurting his toe in the process, and left his brothers for the woods. It was hard work being a Durand sometimes.

The rich canopy gave some shade and relief from the clammy heat, with dappled bursts of light filtering through to the path. Disturbed by his footfall, a pheasant clattered out of the undergrowth with squawks of alarm. He wished he could launch himself into the air with it. Resigned to a life on the ground, he aimed himself at the tree house he had built with his friend Louisa. They called it a tree house. No one else did. The gamekeeper referred to it as 'that monstrosity.'

Louisa, the innkeeper's daughter, had been an unlikely friend for a boy of Henry's social standing. Not that it had deterred either of them. Together they found themselves kindred free spirits playing among the woods and the stream, getting filthy (Henry often getting confused for a village boy on account of his untidy appearance), and coming home late for supper. They spent so much of their childhood together, many in the village gossiped about their friendship, which confused Henry. He had never felt that way about her.

Approaching the tree house, he heard sobbing. "Louisa?"

"Up here," she sniffed.

He climbed the dubious ladder to find her curled up in the corner of the wooden platform. The surface groaned with his added weight as he shifted onto it. It could probably do with additional support now, he mused. Their ten-year-old selves did not know when they built it, they would still use it six years later to escape the world.

"What's wrong?" he asked, keeping his distance on account of the perilous angle he found himself in.

She looked up from where her head lay in her arms,

revealing red angry marks along them.

"Did he hit you again?"

"No. Just hurt me. You know how he gets. It was my fault."

Henry doubted that very much. All Louisa did was try to please her father. "I am sorry, Louisa. I wish I could make it better for you." She shuffled over to him and lay in his lap while he stroked her dark hair, making what he hoped were comforting noises. He never knew what to say, preferring action to words, but whenever her father lashed out, Louisa would seek comfort from him. It always seemed to help, just being there for her. On any other day she was measurably stronger than anyone Henry knew.

When the tears receded, she looked up and wiped her nose on her sleeve. Henry would have offered a handkerchief, but he always forgot to carry one. "Thank you," she said. "Sorry to be such a bore."

"Hardly."

A strand of hair fell in front of her face, so he brushed it aside for her. Then a thought, a ridiculous impetuous thought, took hold and he kissed her. At least that is what he intended, but having never done it before, he did not know if he did it right. He kept his eyes open and watched her own paler blue orbs widen in shock.

She certainly did not kiss him back.

There was no lingering or soft, wet opening, like his experienced brothers had described in vivid detail. Instead, she recoiled in astonishment. The following blow to his cheek sent Henry reeling backwards, his breath caught in his throat with the shock of it.

"Henry!" she yelled, standing up to add a forceful kick to her retaliation. Luckily, it missed anything precious.

Falling from him in a chaotic jumble, his apologies fell on deaf ears.

"Don't you get it?" she bawled. "You are different from all the other boys. With you, I always felt safe. Now you have gone and ruined it!" She jumped out of the tree house, not bothering with the ladder; landed like a cat and ran deeper into the lush woodland.

With their swim finished his brothers lounged in the sun to dry while Henry pushed a wheelbarrow for the gardener, Jones. No one knew his first name, but there was something about him Henry liked. Weathered, craggy, and with a permanent trace of pipe tobacco about him, Jones held himself as though he knew much of the world. He certainly knew much of Ashlington. He was clearing weeds in the kitchen garden, stopping every so often to bend over and pull at young shoots that, left to their own devices, would overrun the vegetables. The more stubborn among them faced his hoe.

"Much on your mind, Master Henry?" the old man said after Henry gave a third particularly wretched sigh.

"Just the usual really."

"Ah, don't tell me. Your father wants you to get married and run the estate with Mister Danny."

Henry narrowed his eyes at him. "That and I kissed my closest friend and now she hates me."

"You kissed Louisa Dale?" Jones's tangled eyebrows disappeared into his hat.

Henry nodded and looked to his feet. There ants darted in and out of a crack in the dry earth. Unable to flee like the pheasant, perhaps he could be as tiny as the ants; give himself to the ground and disappear along a dark tunnel to the comfort of anonymity.

"Brave man," Jones said with a whistle through stained teeth. Henry did not know if this referred to Louisa's own fierce reputation or that of her father. "So, you don't want to get married? It's not all that bad, you know."

"I don't suppose I would make anyone a good husband."

"Master Henry, you have always been your own man. There is nothing wrong with wanting your own path," Jones said, gesturing for Henry to follow him further up the garden. Henry pushed the wheelbarrow behind him, bringing it to a halt again when Jones bent to pluck at some obstinate groundsel.

"Don't let my father hear you say that."

"Fathers try to do the best by their sons."

Henry thought this a curious thing for a man with no children to say. "Is it so wrong for me to want to escape this place?"

"I would not know of such things." Jones turned to face Henry and leant on the hoe. "I suspect what I ran from is different to what you want to run from."

The statement smarted. One thing Henry did know about Jones was that he had come from a miserable background before finding shelter in the army and later Ashlington. "I know I should be grateful for all this, but sometimes I think I should just run away, join the navy, sail off to sea and the New World."

"No need to be so dramatic," Jones grimaced. "The navy? Heavens no. I know a man who can help—a soldier—if you want to serve your country?"

The army? What better way to prove himself? Was there any better judge of a man than how he faces battle? And death? The only question remaining was why it had never occurred to him before.

"I'd be glad of your help, Jones. If it is of no trouble."

"I can make enquires on your behalf, but would need to know you are serious first. My captain is intolerant of hogwash."

"I am serious." Escape could have taken many forms, but the army could be the answer to many of his problems. Admittedly, he could be squeamish about blood, but he imagined were he lucky enough to see action and prove himself on the field of battle, then blood was something he would get used to. He shrugged any remaining doubt away.

"Then, provided we keep my involvement between the two of us, it is of no trouble at all, Master Henry." Jones tugged his hat at Henry, who took charge of the wheelbarrow once more. His imagination already at work, reshaping him into the man he longed to be.

Four weeks later, following an exchange of correspondence with a Captain Theodore Sinclair, Henry left

Ashlington without telling his parents. This served two purposes. It allowed him to get far enough away from his father before he wrote to announce his commission, and it prevented Henry from having to see the inevitable disappointment on his face.

He arrived in a dreary Colchester, searching the grey streets for supper before reporting to the barracks. No sooner had Henry chosen the inn emitting the most mouth-watering aroma and seen to his horse, than a commotion in the adjacent yard caught his attention. A soldier on the ground, hissing and spitting like a tomcat, was being kicked by two thugs. A third lay alongside moaning, holding his groin, while a fourth was getting to his feet wiping a fountain of blood from his nose.

"You there!" The call left Henry's mouth before he had chance to assess the situation and make any decision as to his involvement. To him it simply looked like four against one, and though the one had done damage, he was losing.

Distracted by Henry's shout, those dealing out kicks paused, giving the soldier the opportunity to grab at a pair of legs. He pulled the man backwards, the resulting fall and elbow to the throat rendering him out of action. "Thieves," the young soldier said in explanation, getting to his feet.

The man with the bloody nose squared up to Henry, who found himself back-to-back with the soldier. Henry's work was short; his opponent already had a broken nose. Thankfully, a smart jab to it again sent him running. Henry wheeled around to find his new friend had taken care of the last man.

With a personable dimpled grin, the soldier wiped his hand on his red uniform coat then offered it to Henry. "Robert Westbrook, much obliged."

"Henry Durand," Henry took the hand and laughed. "Though I don't think I made much of a difference." He glanced at the three remaining thieves nursing their injuries. It was hard not to be impressed. "Are you hurt?"

Westbrook patted himself down, taking inventory. "Nothing that won't mend."

"I have just arrived to take my commission," Henry said. "This was not quite the welcome I had expected."

"Under Sinclair?" Westbrook asked, bending to pick up his scattered belongings, which included a beautiful engraved sword that Westbrook took a moment to sheath back at his side before he took Henry by the elbow and steered him back to the front of the inn. Henry wondered why the sword had been discarded in the fight. "We are expecting someone new." Westbrook added.

"Yes, Captain Sinclair."

"What luck!" Westbrook continued. "We Slashers will be lucky to have you, Henry."

"Slashers?"

"The 28th Regiment, it is what they called themselves back when they all carried swords. I suppose it stuck. Let me buy you a drink now that I have retrieved my coin."

When they later arrived at Colchester barracks, not only were they late but somewhat inebriated and in denial about both. The guard at the gate eyed Westbrook's bruises and split lip suspiciously. Upon checking his list for Henry's name, he invited them in, directing Henry to the office of Captain Sinclair. Westbrook offered to show him the way.

The captain found them bumping their way down the corridor, humming to a tune Westbrook was trying to teach Henry. "I should have guessed," he said, striding towards them and his office, unyielding eyes fixed on Westbrook. "Good God, Robert, have you been in another brawl?"

"Thieves, sir," Westbrook hiccupped.

Sinclair eyed him with the same suspicion the guard at the gate had, leading Henry to conclude that Westbrook liked a fight, and thieves were often an excuse.

"And who is this?"

"Henry Durand, sir," Henry said. "You wrote and—"

"You're late, Durand. It won't do." Sinclair led them into his office. "Do you always appear so untidy?"

Henry tugged at the waist of his coat and ran a self-conscious hand through his hair.

"That was my fault, were it not for Durand, I—" Westbrook's voice trailed away as Sinclair slammed his hand down on the desk, causing both young men to jump.

"Wait outside, Robert," he said, lowering his voice, which had the bizarre effect of making him more intimidating. "My officers are not meant to be brawling in the streets, Durand. It is not the gentlemanly thing to do. You would do well to remember that." Sinclair's cross expression changed in an instant once Westbrook left the room, surprising Henry with a burst of clemency. "I trust the rogues came off worse?" He shuffled some papers on his desk and scratched at his chin as though the answer were not of importance.

"My assistance was barely needed."

"Is that so?" Sinclair said, sitting down. Henry noticed a variety of pencil sketches among the written paperwork. They were good. Sinclair was quite the artist. Though he looked nothing like what Henry imagined an artist to look like. In his mind's eye, artists looked more like his brother Christopher; a clean-shaven vision of style and extravagant smelling cologne. This man was none of those things.

"It appears I get to keep all the trouble in the one company," Sinclair surmised, looking Henry up and down. "You'll do." He nodded slowly, as though in only a glance he could weigh not only Henry's soldiering potential, but his soul. "Westbrook will show you around. Make sure you see the quartermaster about your uniform in the morning."

"Yes, sir."

Henry found Westbrook waiting outside the door, leaning against the wall, fully engaged in an inspection of his grazed knuckles.

"Robert!" Sinclair yelled.

Giving him a sympathetic wince, Henry waited for his new friend, doing his best not to hear the exchange that followed.

"I have told you time and time again, stop looking for a fight. They will find you soon enough."

"They set upon me and took my purse!" Westbrook whined.

"So let them have it. Likely they have more need of

your purse than you. You don't have to fight everyone, Robert. You have to know when to walk away, when you don't have to prove yourself."

"I have to prove myself here every day. To you, to everyone."

"You are so like him," Sinclair said, his voice softer again. "But that is what got him killed. I promised your mother that—"

"I know, and I am grateful."

"So, help me keep that promise, will you, my boy— dismissed—see to that bruised eye and find Durand a decent bed."

"Sir. Goodnight, sir."

Chapter 4

Lillian folded the letter and, with great care, slipped it back into the plastic envelope. She took a long sip of wine; an uneasy sensation settling on her, as though reading the letter had opened a window to the past. Judging by the date, the recipient could easily have been the Henry from the painting in the dining room. According to the stories passed down through the generations, that particular ancestor had met a heroic end at the battle of Waterloo eight years after Captain Sinclair wrote the letter.

Nick would kick himself for refusing to help, she was sure. He used to have a thing about that painting. Perhaps she shouldn't have accepted his refusal so easily. Storming off the second he said no was a little childish; all it did was push him away. She shivered and glanced at the fire in the grate, far beyond resurrection. Holly snorted and jumped to her feet with surprising swiftness for a dog so elderly. Hackles ruffled, she barked, jumping down off the sofa, growling at a corner of the room.

"What are you doing, you daft dog?" she muttered, glancing down despondently at her empty wineglass. In answer, Holly rolled onto her back, tail wagging.

A quick check of her phone confirmed no messages

from Marcus. She had asked him to text when he got home. It was something her father always insisted on when she would drive back to London. "Call me, let me know you got back okay." She switched on her laptop and hit the Netflix icon, looking for something suitably diverting to take her mind off him.

She spent the hour curled on the sofa engrossed in a western show because it would have been something her father would have chosen, then returned her glass and the alarming empty wine bottle to the kitchen. Holly circled her beanbag bed in the hallway before settling down on it, the foam beads squeaking as she got comfy. Lillian gave her a rub goodnight, then checked the front door and made her way up the staircase.

Somewhere ahead a door banged shut. The lights flickered. She didn't think any windows were open. She had definitely closed her bathroom one, she remembered doing so. But then the big house contained some impressive draughts, and the wiring was older than ancient. She caught movement out of the corner of her eye and froze mid-step on the stairs. If there was someone up there, she had nothing to defend herself with. In London she kept a hockey stick under the bed.

She fought herself to calm down and think logically. If there was someone in the house, Holly would know and would be barking. As she wasn't, logic would dictate that she was alone with a combination of draught and overactive imagination courtesy of the wine, that's all. It must be. Still, she gripped the wooden banister, knuckles white where the skin stretched taut. She counted to ten and forced herself to let it go, took a breath, and continued up.

"You should tell him," a voice said in front of her, bringing with it a chill that ran down her spine. But she could see no one. Lillian span around, eyes wide with fear, daring not to breathe. She was on her own, but the voice was right next to her, this time its tone gentle and familiar, the chill a fraction warmer. "It is not too late."

"Dad?"

Hope made her call to him. The grief she was burying twirled and danced at such a thought that he might be there. When her senses caught up with her, she took a step backwards. Impossible. He couldn't be here. She only wants him to be, desperately; to hold her and comfort her once more. But he couldn't.

The chill left her. The house grew warm and settled once more.

Home.

Although her surroundings felt at peace and she saw or heard nothing else unusual, she couldn't help feeling nervous as she brushed her teeth, not daring to take her eyes off the mirror. She called Marcus, acknowledging that she only did so in the hope it would make her feel better.

"Oh shit, I was supposed to call, wasn't I?"

"You are home then?"

"Yeah, I got back hours ago. Did you need anything?"

A hug. Someone to tell her everything would be alright. But that was not the sort of thing she could say to Marcus. She had to be strong. "No. It's okay. Night."

Once settled in bed, she found sleep elusive; tossing and turning for over half an hour before switching on the light and resorting to the book on the bedside table. Losing track of time reading of the architectural highlights of Florence, she fell asleep with the book in her hands, and the light on.

***

Nick rented Gatehouse Cottage rather than bought somewhere; all part of his plan built around not staying long. As its name suggested, the thatched cottage used to be a gatehouse for the manor. In matching mellow stone, it stood alongside an ornate gate, now only used by the farmer for access to the fields that had once been parkland of the Ashlington estate.

A low, dry stone wall surrounded the front lawn with a straight path leading to the front door. Lavender, in need of trimming, engulfed the path from both sides, brushing against Nick's legs as he passed. They did not build Cotswold cottages for men of his height, and he had to stoop twice; once as he entered the timber porch, and again as he went through the front door. It groaned tortuously on its hinges, assisted by a bump of the shoulder.

The last thing he expected to see was Olivia, home from school early. She lay huddled on the sofa, with the tv on, crisp and chocolate packets strewn about the floor, watching *Star Trek: the Next Generation*. Nick immediately recognised the signs of his daughter dealing with internal struggle. She used the coping mechanism he had honed himself.

"I could have come picked you up," he said, lowering himself beside her. She snuggled against him.

"You should really start grounding me, you know."

"Chance would be a fine thing." He pointed at the tv screen, recognising the episode. "*Best of Both Worlds*? Are you planning a battle?"

"Nah, just a rubbish day at school. Why do they have to be so childish?"

"You are too used to spending your time with adults. That's the problem. Have you contacted Demetrio?" The son of Nick's right-hand man at any dig he led, Demetrio had provided at least one constant for Olivia growing up.

"Hearing from him just makes it worse," she paused, and Nick spent that time wrestling with his guilt for taking her away from her only friend. "I have a tough choice to make."

"What would Picard do?"

"Well, in this case, what would Riker do?" she said.

Which explained the choice of episode, Nick concluded.""And it ca"t be what Picard would do, right""

"Riker has to figure it out for himself."

"Did you figure it out?"

"Not yet."

"Boy involved?"

"Dad!" She rolled her eyes, looking more like her mother than she could ever possibly know. "Trust me, if you met the lot at school, you would not bother asking that

46

question."

"Good. That's good then," he said, relaxing. "So, how did you get home? Cycle?"

"I called Granddad."

That figured, Nick thought. "Hungry? Sandwich?" Nick looked about the floor at the discarded wrappers, marvelling at the wonder that was the teenage metabolism.

"I'm starving. Thanks."

He made a stack of Olivia's favourite sandwiches, avocado and beetroot, and added a sliced apple on the side of her plate to limit the damage of the consumed junk food. He joined her back on the sofa in time to watch one of his favourite cliff-hanging episodes; Olivia groaning at him when he quoted along with the dialogue.

"Grandma has invited Lillian from the big house for supper tomorrow," Olivia said as the chirpy credits rolled, and she reached for her second sandwich. Until that moment, Nick had been looking forward to their weekly dinner with his parents.

"Did she?"

"She is the one, isn't she?"

"Hmm?"

"Lillian—Lily. Grandma says you had a thing for her years ago." She took a bite of sandwich and watched him, blinking, waiting for an answer as she chewed.

"Grandma is an old gossip."

"But usually right. Well? Did you?"

Nick spent longer than he should have wondering how best to answer. "Lily was my best friend. That's all there was to it," he said, deciding on nonchalance.

"I'm looking forward to meeting her. I am only surprised it has taken this long. So, what about now?" Olivia asked, her words impeded by another mouthful of sandwich, the beetroot staining her lips.

"You want to meet her now?"

"You know that's not what I mean? Do you still like her now? Is that why you have been in a funny mood since the funeral?"

"I have not been in a funny mood and no, I hardly know her anymore." Even Nick heard his defensiveness. It was why he hadn't wanted to go to the funeral. He knew seeing her would complicate things even more.

"It is okay with me if you like her. You can admit it." Olivia stared at him. Not a challenge. Nick ran the date in his head. It was tomorrow, the anniversary of her mother's death.

"Beach day tomorrow?" he said. It is how they liked to remember Taylor. Being Californian, she had loved the sea. "It's all right, lass," he said, mindful of her watering eyes, the Yorkshire accent an echo of his father's. He pulled her in for a hug, resting his chin in her hair. "Your Mum would be so proud of you."

"Mom," she corrected. "She hasn't spoken to me in a long time. Do you think that is because we are here? That we are too far away?"

That was his baby girl. Sensitive yet direct. With everything she had endured, it amazed him time and time again how she dealt with the things she experienced.

Moments like these, though, he knew she needed a hand on hers, a gentle reminder of how much she was loved, especially by her mother. "You think distance would keep your Mom away from you? No, I am sure she still watches over you. You are older now, though. Finding your own way. It's what we parents have to do. Let you go, you know?"

"Yeah, I know."

They finished their sandwiches in silence. Nick noticed it had begun to drizzle; racing lines of moisture dripping down the windows like the tears of rain on the day they had buried Alistair.

***

Although Lillian loved Ashlington Manor, there was something about Janet and Jack's terraced cottage on the village green that felt equally comforting. The gate squeaked as she pushed it open, answered by a deep bark from within the cottage. She made her way up the flagstone path, the stout painted door opening before she could knock.

"You must be Lillian?" said a girl with a flawless bronzed glow that made Lillian feel every one of her forty years. Olivia was tall for her age, like her father, and Lillian couldn't help thinking, not built for small cottages with their low beams and crowded thresholds.

"And you must be Olivia," she replied. "Nice to meet you." Janet appeared at the girl's shoulder restraining two golden retrievers, all wags and excited slobber. "Haven't seen you boys in a while," Lillian said, trying to share the fuss between them one handed as she passed Janet a bunch of flowers.

"You shouldn't have. It's only supper," Janet said. "Olivia, are you going to let Lillian in?" she gave Olivia a tug on her sweater.

Olivia gave way, herding the retrievers along the hallway to the kitchen, from where the enticing scent of Janet's homemade pies emanated. Instinctively, Lillian bent down to take her shoes off lest she incur the dreaded 'boots off,' a shout that Janet would give to anyone threatening her clean floors, even Lillian's father in his own home. She arrived in the snug kitchen a few moments later, having convinced herself not to cry at the thought of her father unable to enjoy the company of the Hawkins family any more.

She greeted Jack, who rose from his seat. "I found this in Dad's drinks cabinet and thought you might enjoy it more than me?" She handed him an unopened bottle of Aberlour Scotch.

His face lit up, but the smile vanished as he gripped the bottle. "Thank you, Lillian. Happen we shared a few glasses of this over the years, aye"" he said, his accent gruffer than normal.

"Tea, Lillian?" Janet asked.

"Please." Lillian sat down next to Olivia and looked around for Nick, relieved that she could settle in without having to deal with any moody brooding he might direct her way.

"Dad has been lecturing today," Olivia said, as if

reading her thoughts.

"Is he still always late for everything?"

Jack grunted the affirmative and took a large slurp of his tea.

"No!" Janet replied with maternal defence, at the same time as Olivia mouthed the words 'all the time.'

Lillian laughed, enjoying the mischief in the girl's otherwise amiable expression. Lillian had looked up the late Taylor Beckley, Olivia's mother, out of curiosity. She needn't have bothered. The legacy of the beautiful American actress sat before her. Olivia's skin tone was a rich blend of her parents', eyes and hair jet like her mother. Other than the height, at first glance Lillian could not see much of Nick, but then Olivia smiled again.

"Talk of the devil," Janet said to the sound of wheels on gravel and a chugging diesel engine.

"That sounds like that old Land Rover he had," Lillian said, recalling Nick's first vehicle when he passed his driving test; a rusty Land Rover with fading blue paint. The type that carried a bale of straw in the back for no other reason than it could, and a dubious looking spare wheel bolted to the bonnet.

"It is the same one. Granddad kept it for him. Could it be any more embarrassing?" Olivia said as Nick burst through the back door, got tangled in the golden retrievers and banged his head on the door lintel.

"Sorry I'm late," he said, rubbing his head and sending the dogs outside. He took a step closer to Olivia and kissed her on the cheek. "Good day?"

"Algebra homework."

Nick grimaced, then noticed his mother looking at him with her hands on her hips. "Bloody hell," he mumbled, kicking off his boots.

Lillian stifled a smile with her hand.

Supper was exactly how she imagined the Hawkins to still be; relaxed, noisy in their own funny way, and precisely what she needed to take her mind off the voice she had heard. It had spoken to her again that morning as she had opened the door to her father's bedroom, ready to pack up his clothing for charity. "You are not alone, Lillian," it had said gently, yet bringing a chill that had fogged her breath. She had shut the door on the room without stepping inside.

Sat at the kitchen table with the Hawkins family, passing dishes around and listening to their easy banter, felt reassuring. Least of all, because if she were going crazy, either Janet or Nick would notice and tell her.

"When do you start with Alistair's family history project?" Janet asked Nick.

"Oh, he said he couldn't help. Not his area," Lillian said, fully aware she was throwing Nick to the wolves and fairly convinced he deserved it. "I am at a bit of a loss on where to start myself. There is so much of Henry's stuff to go through."

Janet slapped her son on the arm. "Nicholas! Why won't you help?"

"Henry? Not the soldier in the painting?" Nick asked, ignoring his mother's protest.

"Yes, shame really," Lillian continued, hoping he

would take the bait. "He is the character Dad was interested in."

"You always had a thing about that painting," Janet said.

"He used to talk to it," Lillian added.

"No, I didn't."

"Yes, you did," Janet said.

Lillian had seen it for herself. He would tell Lillian that all the children at his school thought he was weird. She always found this hard to believe. To her, he was interesting and knowledgeable. If Nick was interested in something, he would research it thoroughly, filing away facts and figures in that huge brain of his. He never went into detail about what would happen at school with her, but she had heard him telling the soldier, as if the fact he did not talk back made communicating with him easier. She supposed digging or lecturing might hold a similar appeal.

"Probably the only way I could get a word in edgeways," Nick huffed, looking to his father for moral support.

"You don't seem to have that problem now," Lillian said.

"A lot can change in twenty years. Other things remain exactly the same." He narrowed his eyes with a look Lillian had not seen in years. Did he think she had changed that much?

Jack shifted in his chair, while Olivia looked from Lillian to Nick and back again with wide eyes that made Lillian wonder what was so entertaining.

"So you'll help her then? It's not like you have anything else to do," Olivia said in a surprising assertion of allegiance to team Lillian.

"I have lectures..."

"Once a week. One lecture."

"Then there is the dig..."

"That does not start until the summer."

A private, silent communication between father and daughter followed, all raised eyebrows and tilted heads that may have included a kick under the table. Lillian could not be sure.

"I guess I can help you make a start, get things organised at least," Nick said eventually, after a particularly pained look to his daughter. "I could come over Monday morning."

"Really?" Despite everything, Lillian wanted to hug him. Finishing her father's project was important to her. She should have told her father over the years how much she loved him. How she only stayed away working so hard because she wanted to make him proud.

"I have to warn you, these things do not happen overnight. If you want him researched properly, then it will take time."

"It is what Dad wanted. Thanks, Nick." She reached into her bag and handed him the letter inviting Henry to the regiment. "He seemed to think this kicked it all off for Henry." Lillian had kept it in the plastic wallet and labelled it 'Invitation.'

Chapter 5

Portugal, September 1808

"We shouldn't be looting, West."

"We are not looting—technically—consider this borrowing."

Henry shook his head. Finding himself an accomplice to breaking into a bookshop (of all things) on the backstreets of Lisbon was not exactly what he had imagined when Westbrook dragged him away from the fire that night. He thought they would raid Sinclair's billet for wine, like they had the previous week. Unless robbing his godfather blind of supplies, Westbrook was normally reluctant to take advantage of his relationship with their captain. If Sinclair knew the culprit behind the regular missing items, he kept that knowledge to himself and patiently maintained a regular re-stock.

"We'll get ourselves shot. As officers, we should set an example," Henry complained, crouching against the wall. Though they both wore long, dark cloaks over their scarlet uniforms, he couldn't help but feel exposed in the wide, empty street.

Westbrook stopped working on the lock and looked up from where he knelt on the step in the dark. "You aren't scared of being shot. You fear being sent home," he declared with a side stare in that annoying way of his where he seemed to know exactly what was going through Henry's mind. "Did you never get into trouble as a child?"

"Plenty." It seemed important that Westbrook think he was just as brave as he was. "My friend Louisa and I were always getting into trouble and I have two brothers."

"Ah, Louisa!"

"Like I keep telling you, it was never like that with her."

"She sure writes you plenty of letters."

It had been a year since Henry had left Ashlington and despite the circumstances in which he had last seen Louisa, and though it had taken several months for her to forgive him, she now wrote often. Crouched next to Westbrook, still struggling with the lock, Henry wiggled his jaw, recalling how much it had hurt when she hit him. How much he had hurt her.

Westbrook glanced his way. "You never stole anything though?"

"No, unless food from the pantry counts?"

"Not really." Westbrook grinned as though amused by Henry's innocence. It made Henry want to wipe the stupid dimpled grin off his face. "Well, I suppose you are from a prominent family. That explains it. You never needed to."

"And you did? You are a gentleman too."

"Not in the same way as you, Henry. My family is not from some fancy house of ancient lineage in the country with sheltered lives and—"

"I didn't have a sheltered life." The last thing he

wanted was for folk to think he was some soft country dandy. Turning himself into the complete opposite was a work in progress, admittedly, oft aided by the intrepid imagination and experience of his friend. Westbrook's additional year in age seemed to be of great advantage.

"Well, we can agree that my childhood was very different to yours." Westbrook was an army brat through and through. That much, Henry knew. "While you were being schooled by your expensive tutors, I was scratching around the tents and billets of whatever barracks we found ourselves in. At least until he left." He being his father. Westbrook did not talk of him much.

"What is it with books anyway?" Henry asked, trying to deflect the conversation. He much preferred cheery Westbrook to the brooding one.

"Books are everything," Westbrook said, smiling once more. "The very best of distractions. They allow you to journey away to any realm you could imagine. You can ask anything of them and they always have a reply."

"Is that why you read so much? You want to escape?"

Westbrook paused again in his work of the lock. He had now spent over five minutes trying to pick the thing. It made Henry consider if a great deal of Westbrook's confidence in such matters was only bluster. "I hadn't thought of it quite like that. I suppose so. Don't you?"

Henry blew the air from his cheeks. "It's why I am here, not sitting on a fat horse riding around my fancy estate in the country," he said with equal degrees of truth and sarcasm, accompanied by a shrug. "Here I am not a Durand of Ashlington, I am just another officer of the 28th, judged on my actions with the regiment." In some respects, he felt disappointed that Westbrook had a way of wheedling the truth from him. Perhaps that is what the uncomfortable feeling was. Perhaps that was part of why they got on so well. Rather like Louisa, he considered Westbrook to be all the things he was not.

The lock clicked. "Shall we?" Westbrook asked.

"Just don't get us killed for a bloody book," Henry grumbled, stepping past him through the open door.

It amused Henry to observe the transformation in his friend. Like an excited child in a room of new toys, Westbrook hurried up and down the dusty aisles, searching. As far as Henry could tell, the chase held an equal delight to the capture, Westbrook dragging his hand along the books as though collectively they held the secrets to all his questions at his fingertips.

"Tell me again how this is not stealing?" Henry said, taking a collection of Shakespeare's *Sonnets* off the shelf to admire the binding.

"Because of these," Westbrook answered, undoing his coat, spilling five books onto the floor.

Henry recognised the titles as those Westbrook had been recently reading. "You're an idiot, West," he said, giving him a nudge, then bent to help pick the books up. "Half of these aren't even Portuguese, and I am quite sure this mouldy one belongs to Sinclair."

"Five books in—five books out seems fair," Westbrook said with his dimpled grin, patting Henry on the shoulder. "What have you got there?"

"This one is mine." Henry tucked the book of sonnets out of sight under his cloak. "So, you get four. An acceptable deal for being your lookout?"

Westbrook narrowed his eyes at him. "Am I corrupting you, Henry Durand?"

"Probably," Henry grumbled, though not altogether upset at the idea. "Get a move on, will you, before we are found."

Henry positioned himself at the window to check the street; empty but for the steam rising from a pile of horse muck, and a pair of rats skulking in the shadows off to commit their nocturnal business. His attention turned back to Westbrook, now on his knees checking the lower shelves.

A larger sudden movement outside of the window caught Henry's eye. He whistled and signalled for his friend to get down out of sight. Westbrook did so with a thud and what sounded like a bemused chuckle. Henry pressed himself flat against the wall next to the window where two dark shapes stood, the light from a lantern bobbing in query. He screwed his eyes shut, shaking his head again, ruing the day he found Westbrook. Things had never quite been the same since.

I knew you'd get me killed. He threw Westbrook a cross glare.

Don't be such a milkmaid, Westbrook's eye roll told him from where he lay prone on the floor and began calmly flicking through a book assisted by the glow from the window. Henry cursed under his breath, then did so again with a wry smile. His friend had even corrupted his use of language.

As the shapes at the window diminished with fading footsteps, Henry let out his breath. Westbrook stood up, moving to the window to observe the missed danger for himself. "Patrol," he grimaced. "That was close. Come along, Henry. Stop dawdling." He left his contribution to the bookshop neatly stacked on the table, together with some coins Henry was sure he was not supposed to notice.

The following evening, a group of officers poised themselves for dispersal among the locals in one of Lisbon's market squares. One gave a low whistle of appreciation as a woman walked past. Hair piled high, exposing a long neck above slender shoulders, nose in the air with a confident, almost disdainful awareness of her admirers. No shawl. No gloves. No doubt fully aware of the hungry eyes ravishing her. With the exception of Henry, the officers tracked her movement through the crowd. Henry's attention was elsewhere, fixed on the delicious smell of hot pastry.

"I wish they wouldn't do that," Westbrook mumbled. "I'm sure the women here have had enough to deal with recently." He tugged smooth his uniform coat with a grumble then ran a hand through his collar-length dark curls.

Henry tilted his head to where several of their fellow soldiers had joined the crowd with boisterous enthusiasm. "You aren't…?"

"No, I'll come help you find some dinner. No doubt you are hungry by now?"

"I'm always hungry, West," Henry teased, grateful that his friend had chosen to stay. "We can't all survive on wine alone."

"Think you're so funny?" Westbrook jeered, grabbing Henry in a high-spirited headlock and rubbing at his hair.

"Don't! You'll make it even worse," Henry moaned. Sinclair already gave him a daily talking to for the state of his hair, and his uniform. Henry tried, but both hair and uniform proved mutinous.

He escaped Westbrook's clutches as he loosened his grip to stand. "Can we please find some dinner now? I'm starving."

"Hardly," Westbrook snorted. "You have become quite portly this summer."

"Portly? Are you saying I am fat?" He struck, but Westbrook anticipated it, twisting away and taking off. Henry pursued him, determined to prove any additional summer padding had not slowed him down. They rounded a corner where Henry pounced, catching Westbrook around the legs, bringing him down like a felled tree.

"Bloody hell, Henry!" Westbrook squirmed face down in the dirt with Henry sat on him, holding his arm behind his back.

"Tell me I am not fat."

"The weight on my back would beg to differ!" Westbrook said with a strained exhalation.

Henry twisted the arm higher.

"No, no, you aren't fat!"

Henry let him go with the smug satisfaction of having

proved his point; getting to his feet with a knee in Westbrook's spine, that caused his friend to make a noise like a pair of forge bellows.

Westbrook rolled over. "Just pudgier."

"What kind of word is that?" Henry asked, laughing again, pulling Westbrook to his feet. "I am quite sure that is not even a word."

"It means that you are a fraction squishier this year than the last." He prodded at Henry's waist with a finger, more tickle than poke.

"Doesn't slow me down though," Henry said, despite the self-conscious hand he rubbed on his belly, which was not shy in reminding him it still needed feeding.

"By winter we'll have lost it all again anyway," Westbrook said in a more serious tone, brushing himself down. They both fell quiet, Henry remembering the pangs of hunger that ate at his belly the previous winter. Hiding stale bread to share with Westbrook, the temptation to steal from others testing his honour. Days where grown men would weep with how hungry they were.

Henry gave Westbrook a nudge. "Look! Pie!"

Having finally found the source of the delicious aroma wafting through the streets of Lisbon, he purchased two meat pies, thick with golden pastry, from a street vendor. Westbrook tasked himself into the closest inn for a bottle of something to share. While Henry could sniff out the best food in town, Westbrook's nose for a good bottle of liquor was unmatched.

"I have a surprise for your birthday. Come on, if we

hurry, we won't miss the start," Henry told him when he returned with a bottle of something stashed in his coat. "You did pay for that, didn't you?"

"Yes, I paid for it." Westbrook sighed. "Where are we going?"

"Do you trust me?"

"You know I do."

"Then wait and see." Henry led Westbrook uphill through the streets, avoiding any with crowds just in case his friend caught the whiff of a distraction. With the French force now gone, Lisbon was trying to get back to some sense of normality and the warmth of the autumn evening had brought everyone outdoors.

"Ah! Here it is." He found the tunnel in the bushes he had been looking for and took Westbrook's hand, pulling him through after him.

"What are we—"

"Shush!" Henry crouched and swatted at Westbrook to do the same. They crept forward and as they approached the rise, Henry lay flat on his belly. Westbrook muttered something about the state his uniform would get into, but shuffled on knees and elbows to Henry's side. Henry watched, enthralled, as the dimples in Westbrook's cheeks deepened with his growing smile.

They lay on a step in the hillside that rose above a garden belonging to a large house. Not the vastness of Ashlington Manor, but large enough for a wooden platform to be constructed on the open lawn. Chairs, filled with Lisbon's remaining aristocracy, had been arranged around it, lanterns surrounding the ghostly outlines of the audience. The stage was lit and rich cloth had been draped over the wall to the rear, where props of various kinds awaited the thespians.

"A play!" Westbrook gasped. "Henry! I don't know—no one has ever—this is magnificent!"

"I was talking with a chap about the Roman amphitheatre here in the city. It got buried in the earthquake, apparently. He told me about this place. I saw them building the stage yesterday. We could have got in for the rehearsals, but you were too busy—"

"They are starting," Westbrook said with a squeak of excitement, tilting his head to the stage where actors were filing to take their places. In all the turmoil, the family who owned this house, in the small act of putting on a play, had packed their garden with those wanting to escape and travel to another place. If only for an hour or so.

"Happy birthday, West." Henry passed him the book of sonnets he had taken from the bookshop on their morally questionable excursion the night before.

Westbrook read the message inside the cover, erupting into laughter. Henry put his hand over his mouth, reminding him to be quiet. Still chuckling, Westbrook tucked the book into his inner pocket, then bumped Henry with his shoulder.

Hidden from the audience, they lay in the dust, Westbrook's green eyes widening with wonder as a powerful voice filled the still air.

"Two households, both alike in dignity, in fair Verona, where we lay our scene..."

Chapter 6

Ashlington, April 2015

"Nick!" Although she expected him, seeing him on the doorstep felt oddly surreal. He gave her a lopsided smile and for a split second she thought she could smell freshly mown hay.

"Reporting for duty," he declared with a sarcasm he must have perfected in the last twenty years. He never used to understand it.

"Tea first?"

"Okay."

As she led him through the stone porch, Holly leapt about to greet him, tail wagging in recognition. "I almost thought Mum wouldn't give her back to you," he said, giving the dog plenty of fuss.

"I don't know whose heart I was breaking more bringing her back here, your Mum's or Holly's." She had half-thought about asking Janet to keep her. "Janet has been amazing."

"She thought a lot of your dad," Nick replied, looking up at her from where he crouched on the floor, scratching Holly's belly. "We all did."

Lillian inhaled deeply. "I just realised I've known you for all these years and have no idea how you take your tea."

She laughed, hoping it didn't sound too forced as her emotions swirled. She hadn't expected them to. The day had started so well.

"Just black is fine."

She led him into the kitchen where Holly trotted through their legs and out of the door leading to the garden. She gestured for Nick to take a seat at the table and dragged the kettle onto the Aga's hotspot.

"I always loved this thing," he said, smoothing his hands over the tabletop. "Wasn't it a hatch from a freight ship?"

"I think so."

"Does it still have—" He bent down, looking underneath it, then chuckled. "Yep, still there."

"What?" Then she remembered. Although there were now chairs around the table, when they were little there used to be a bench along one side. She and Nick had laid on it head-to-head one day, drawing on the underneath of the table with permanent marker pens. Nick had drawn a wild zig-zaggy letter N and Lillian an intertwining L. It had not been the most rebellious thing they had ever done together, but at the time, it certainly felt like it. She bent down to look for herself. "Good grief." She laughed again, then felt guilty for it, though she did not know why.

"How have you been?" Nick asked. He dropped it casually like his mother would; the talk of the table a gentle lead in.

"I'm fine," she bristled. "Really."

"You said you had more research material here?"

Lillian took clean mugs out of the dishwasher and nodded; glad he had accepted her word for it. "Seriously, Nick, there is so much of it. Not just about Henry, either. I am just beginning to realise the enormity of the task. Thanks for agreeing to help. I did not want to do it alone," she said, surprising herself with her honesty.

Nick did not comment. It reminded her of the time they found a dead bird. They must have been around ten. The bird, a sparrow, had crashed into a window, the impact killing it. Lillian talked about nothing but death for days while Nick patiently listened.

"Do you think you will sell it? This place?"

"It's not my home anymore."

"Sounds like a very un-Durand thing to say. There has been a Durand in Ashlington for hundreds of years."

"But I'm the last one." She set his tea down in front of him with a thud, sending it sloshing over the rim of the stoneware mug. Nick reached for some kitchen paper to mop it up with. "Sorry," she said, sliding into the chair opposite, trying to regain some degree of the composure she felt close to losing, having thought of her father and his disappointment he did not have any grandchildren. How her stubbornness risked the line of Durand. "So how much do you charge for your time?"

Nick blew at his tea. "There is no charge." He smiled, then looked away quickly. "It is a favour for a friend." Returned from the garden, Holly shoved her nose onto Nick's lap and left it there. Nick obliged and fussed her behind the ears.

"Thanks Nick, I can't tell you how much that means. I liked Olivia. You did a good job."

He looked surprised at the subject change.

"Your mum is very proud of you both."

Nick made a deep, throaty noise that may have been a cough. "Do you remember what we were like at sixteen?"

Lillian did. That was half the problem.

"Olivia is desperate to find her place in the world. She has never really known a home. She'll be okay, she has been through worse."

Lillian studied her old friend as he finished his drink. She could no more reconcile Nick being a grownup, let alone him being a father. His hair had become lighter around the temples, and he had collected lines at the corners of his eyes, clues to a happy existence. His cheeks were still ruddy, and despite the greying stubble, he still had a scent of adventure about him. It made Lillian wonder just how much she had missed out on.

She used to share all his adventures. Coming home from boarding school to spend a summer or Christmas holiday with Nick, hanging around while his mother cleaned, highlighted each year. He always had a gift for her, some treasure he would find during term time. A special stone from the river, an interesting feather, one year the skull of a fox. It was still here on the bookshelf in her room. The next men in her life—culminating in Marcus—had given gifts of flowers, daring underwear and expensive jewellery. Marcus had even taken her on luxury holidays. She had missed nothing, she reminded herself.

"Are you still vegan?" she asked, deciding that was a far safer subject. It had been something he had started in his teens, having devoured facts about animal welfare. To his mother, he had declared that eating animals while loving them was simply not logical.

He nodded. "Olivia too, though she makes a better advocate than me. She is way better with people."

Lillian's phone rang, vibrating its way across the table before she could give a sarcastic answer. "It's Marcus, sorry I need to take this." She stood up, swiped the phone and motioned for Nick to help himself to another cup of tea before moving out of the kitchen.

"Good morning," Marcus chirped.

"You sound happy this morning," she said, but then Marcus always sounded more content back in London.

"I am getting ready for tomorrow."

"Tomorrow?"

"Breaking ground on the George Street development. Did you forget? You are still coming?"

Lillian peered back into the kitchen, where Nick was pouring more tea. "I'm sorry. Something has come up. I won't be able to make it."

"Oh. I thought by now you would have been ready to come back."

"There is still too much to do and sort out here. I'll tell you more about it later."

"Why, you have to go?" Marcus asked.

"Nick is here."

"Nick?"

"Janet's son, you remember, you must have met him at the funeral."

"The cleaner's son?" he scoffed.

"Don't say it like that."

"I thought you were *busy* sorting the house out for sale, not socialising with—"

"He is an old friend, Marcus, and he is helping me with something for Dad. Look, I have to go, I'll call you later."

"Fine."

Nick stood outside on the patio with his back to the house, mug in hand, Holly at his feet, the two of them watching a pair of blackbirds plucking at bugs on the lawn. He had refilled her mug and left it on the counter. Leaving it there, she joined him outside.

"Do you remember how your dad used to tell us off for riding our bikes around the tennis court?" Nick said with a chuckle. "And the hay den we built one summer?"

His grin fell lopsided again, and Lillian felt her cheeks flush. She looked away, remembering that summer all too well; being an awkward fifteen-year-old reunited with her best friend, startled that she suddenly found him attractive. That summer had been long and hot. They had spent much of it unnecessarily squashed together in that den. Her thumb flicked at the band of her engagement ring. She suddenly felt old, the impression of fresh hay fading.

"I miss him, Nick," she said with a catch in her throat. The stirring of memories brought with them the veritable truth of change, that her father would no longer be a part of her life. She turned to seek refuge in the house so Nick would not see the tears she couldn't hold back any more, but he caught her.

"It's okay," he told her and held out his arms. An invitation totally on her terms. She accepted and the squeeze he gave released a wave of grief. One she had been holding on to for weeks. Without even trying to repress it anymore, she cried until the tissue she wiped her face with was reduced to a snotty mess, and she had left a significant wet patch on his checked shirt. Nick remained stoic, holding her and his mug, until Holly jumped up at his legs, demanding some attention, too.

"Shall we see what secrets we can find?" he breathed.

With stiff cheeks, Lillian nodded and tried her best to make it convincing.

***

"Most of Dad's work is in his study," Lillian told him, composed again, having washed her face, as they followed Holly through the hall. "I have no idea where to start. Most of this stuff mentions Henry in some way. There are diaries, letters, newspaper cuttings."

"So we take it box by box and work out what we are dealing with. Then we work on Henry's timeline and see what we find. You said your father already made some notes?"

"At his desk, in a box file. He did it all by hand."

Nick looked at the desk and the chair behind it. He

remembered Alistair sitting there chain-smoking cigarettes as vividly as he could see Lillian. "I would offer you one," Alistair would say. "But I know you'd only say no, and your mother would kill me!" He would laugh, and Nick often wondered what Alistair would have done had he accepted.

Lillian looked as reluctant to take the chair as he felt. He took the box file off the desk and lowered himself onto the floor cross-legged.

The numbness of his rear hours later informed Nick he had sat on the floor in the study, surrounded by Durand history for too long. He found himself fascinated by how much stuff the family kept, practically on the verge of hoarding. Did Durands throw nothing away?

With Lillian's help, he had spent the morning skimming through files to discover what pile of journals and letters went where on Ashlington's extensive time line, and which related to Henry. She seemed glad of the distraction and had been content to keep any conversation to the topic at hand. The letter from Captain Sinclair had set things in motion for Henry. Who the original recommendation to Sinclair came from remained to be seen. Nick could feel himself falling for the work and pleased he had given in and agreed to help.

Then there was the trunk.

Tucked up against one side of the desk, it supported a substantial stack of magazines. "Lily, what is this?"

"That old thing? It has always been there."

He removed the magazines and brushed off the

remaining layer of dust. The trunk half of a campaign chest; it called to him like a siren to a sailor across the waves. Years of polishing had preserved the shine of the lid, though it bent in the middle as though it had endured a significant weight upon it. Only the scratched brass corners and worn oval name plaque hinted at its age.

H Durand 1/28

"It's his! Henry's," Lillian gasped.

Nick rather liked the sound. He also rather liked the fact she knelt on the floor next to him. Close enough that he became intensely aware of each breath she took.

"Shall we open it?" she whispered.

"Do you want to?"

She nudged him. "Open it."

"What if it needs a key?" he whispered back, stalling.

"We won't know unless you try it."

Nick took a deep breath and tried the lid. It opened. The inside of the lid cradled a round mirror and two candle holders caked in wax. The left half of the main compartment held small drawers and partitioned sections. Of the items contained within, he selected a book. A small collection of Shakespeare's *Sonnets*, Nick ran a finger down the book's spine and opened it. The inside cover held a message scratched in untidy, yet charming, loopy handwriting.

Your corrupted friend,
HD

Nick returned it to its place. He tried to ignore the folded red uniform jacket, the very scent of which evoked a time of danger and adventure. His heart wanted to pull it out and find what else it buried, but his professional reasoning told him the contents needed careful handling and, if he were honest, expert advice.

"We need to be careful with all of this."

"Is that his jacket?"

"Probably. It has the rank epaulettes of a captain, like the painting."

"How did it get here?"

"What do you mean?"

"If he was killed at Waterloo. Who brought his trunk back?"

"That is the type of thing we will find out, hopefully, if all this proves as promising as it looks. Someone brought it back here so part of him could get home, maybe." It made Nick consider that he would want the same. Some part of him to come back to the place where he had always felt himself.

"You still like the mystery?" she asked.

"Don't you?" She was still in close proximity and his brain was struggling to stay on task. She was studying him again, like she had earlier in the kitchen.

She stood up and gave her legs a rub, then offered to make coffee. After stretching and moving about the room to get the blood to re-circulate through his limbs, Nick propped open the glass-paned door to the garden. He returned to his spot cross-legged on the floor, the dog returning its nose to his knee, a breeze turning the pages of one of the open notebooks. He placed his hand on it, arresting the movement on a page that Alistair had annotated with red ink.

Henry died at Waterloo.
Why do we still have so many of his personal effects?
Who couldn't let go?

Chapter 7

Spain, March 1811

"What do we fight for, then?" Private Young asked, pushing another stick into the brazier, sending embers floating upwards in the heat like heaven-bound fireflies.

"Because Napoleon Bonaparte wants all of Europe. If we stand together, he can't have it," Henry said. It was a much watered-down version of what Sinclair had said at dinner one night. Henry didn't really care what Bonaparte wanted. He was not in Spain out of loyalty to his country.

"If you really want to know what you fight for, Young, look at the man next to you," Adams said, surprising everyone. A veteran of the Egypt campaign like Sinclair, the older man never spoke much. What little he had to say, Henry had learned, was worth listening to. Judging by the faces around the fire, all focussed his way, he was not the only one.

"That's what I fight for," Adams continued. "I fight for the captain. Sinclair is the best I have served under, and I don't mind telling you, I have served under many. I fight for the lieutenants," he nodded at Henry and Westbrook, "and I fight for my brothers." He used the chewed stem of his pipe to gesture at the other men.

There followed a silence in which those gathered

regarded each other. Westbrook glanced Henry's way and winked. Henry decided he would commit those words to memory. Even though it seemed at odds with the red-blooded persona he strived to embody, he felt much affection for his company.

Young broke the silence with mood-splitting humour. "Blimey Adams, that is the most I have ever heard you say. You'll be needing a lie down?"

Everyone chuckled, their jocular ease restored.

"Cheeky whippersnapper," Adams said, giving Young a parental slap to the back of his head.

"Good coffee that was, Lieutenant," Jackson said to Westbrook, gesturing at the pot on the grate.

"Compliments of the captain," Westbrook told them cheerfully. Henry suspected Captain Sinclair knew nothing of his coffee donation.

Henry took this as their cue to leave the ranks to their evening. "Don't stay up too late," he said with a meaningful glance to Adams, who knew what the veiled statement meant. Likely there would be action tomorrow.

"Good night, sirs," came the chorus as they left the fire.

The following morning, the 28th threaded their way through a dense forest of pine at Barossa on the left flank of the force raiding the French siege works of Cadiz. When they finally emerged from the gloom, they faced a brigade of French in chaos, sporadically firing cannons at them. To Henry, it looked as though they could easily outflank the

French, and he felt optimistic about their chances.

Sinclair ordered the company to form line. Henry repeating the order, encouraging the men to do so quickly. He noticed that they had gained men from other regiments; their meandering through the forest having mixed them up. No time to sort it out. They would work with who they had. He instinctively checked for Westbrook, identifying him further down the line, brandishing his sword.

Sinclair marched them forward a few steps, assessing the range. The closest cannon, no doubt a worry. A grape shot shell fell short, thudding into the ground, sending dirt and wicked shards of metal skyward adding to the smoke. Sinclair looked impatient, waiting for the order to charge. If they didn't move soon, the cannon would have their range. It fired again, a shadow chasing the round over the ground.

Henry knew it would hit their ranks. The noise as it did so a splintering sound followed by the cry of injured men and Sinclair's call to, "Steady the line!"

Henry checked for his friend. "Where are you, West?" he asked aloud, searching. Only half a thought now on his duty. He'd feel better if he could find Westbrook's figure among the men. But he couldn't. The growing dawning that he might be injured felt like someone had punched Henry deep in the gut, winding him. He isn't dead. He told himself. I won't believe it.

With a glance to Sinclair, Henry ran from his post, adding to Sinclair's shouts of "Steady!" with his own. The words in his head 'don't be dead' echoing with each heavy footstep.

He found Westbrook face down, glorious sword still in his hand, on top of the broken body of the soldier who had stood next to him. Henry took a breath and rolled him over. "You better not be dead!" he told Westbrook, then gasped when he saw him, swallowing hard, wishing he had not tempted fate so blatantly. Half of Westbrook's face was gone. It caused a surprising sharp pain in Henry's chest.

"Not dead, but that really hurt!" Westbrook mumbled.

Henry looked to the sky and closed his eyes, exhaling a long breath. He suddenly felt like throttling his friend for worrying him so. "Can you stand?"

"I can stand," Westbrook said, the shake to his voice betraying him. "I can't see very well, though." He raised a hand to his face, but Henry stopped him, the worry returning. Not gone after all, but gravely damaged, the source of the all the blood a swollen wound to his left eye. Feeling a little lightheaded from the sight of it, Henry glanced from Westbrook to the line.

"They're moving forward, West. Let me get you to the rear."

"I'm quite alright." Still clinging to his sword, Westbrook braced himself around Henry's shoulders as he picked him up and got him back to his feet. "Get me back to the line, Henry, I want that blasted cannon."

With Westbrook at his side, three times they followed Sinclair to charge the opposing French regiment, Sinclair taking the cannon team ruthlessly. When the field erupted into the final mêlée, the close combat that often never happened at all given a good rout of the enemy, Westbrook looked like Death himself had joined them on the battlefield. He blocked a bayonet strike that would have hit Henry. Henry hacked at the enemy with his sword, stepping over another fallen body to face the next. Only aware of Sinclair ahead, leading with shouts of encouragement; Westbrook on his left cutting and slashing, moving as one with Henry; and Young, who had gravitated to his right, using his bayonet to devastating effect.

Henry heard someone whoop with the joy of it, realising seconds later that the noise had come from him; a spark of giddiness not from the act of killing men, but from not having a chance to feel anything else but alive.

As shouts of "Parole!" went up, the remaining French dropped their weapons and held up their hands.

Henry looked to his friend. "You are a mess, West," Henry told him. Fully aware it was how his friend would usually greet him.

"That's what I normally say to you," Westbrook replied with a laugh that sounded eerily demonic given his grim appearance; face and neck now wet with blood. His voice then fell to a more serious tone. "Henry, I'm not sure I can stand up much longer."

Henry caught him as he staggered and looped Westbrook's arm over his shoulder to pull him to the side of where Sinclair had regrouped his force. Sinclair looked their way and waved, acknowledging their predicament. Henry sat Westbrook down on a handy fallen log, quickly taking off his neckcloth to wipe away some of the blood and assess the damage.

"Anyone got any water?" he asked the column of the living, making their way back to the city of Cadiz. Weary, yet heads held high, the soldiers filed past with the whisper of a sad song murmured through the ranks. Victory could feel like defeat when brothers were lost.

"Here, sir!" someone called back, throwing Henry a canteen. He knelt next to Westbrook, wet the cloth and began wiping away the blood, some of which had dried into lumps. Westbrook's left eye was a mess. It might even be gone, Henry couldn't tell yet.

"You will need to see the surgeon. You know I thought you were dead." Henry said, half concern, half scolding. He wondered how Westbrook managed to still smile his ridiculous dimpled smile, considering the pain he must be in.

"I promise you Henry, I won't go without you."

"Well, make sure you don't. We'll die gloriously in battle together." It seemed a reasonable thing to agree on. "Now, the surgeon?"

"There are others that have more need of Mr Evans right now. Just shove something on it, would you?"

Henry shook his head. It looked bad. He held Westbrook's chin, tilting his head upwards, trying to be gentle with him as he worked.

"You are a most contradictory fellow, Henry," Westbrook continued. "Only moments ago, you were cutting and hacking at the French like a barbarian. Now you are caring for me with all the tenderness of a lov—ouch!"

"Sorry. I don't want to hurt you, but there is a piece of metal or something sticking out of your face. I don't know what to do with it."

"Pull it out."

Henry frowned and looked to his friend in all seriousness. "If I do that, I will be sick on you."

"Just pull it out, Henry, I'll take my—"

Henry did so before Westbrook finished his sentence. Surprisingly, he kept his stomach and, as directed, shoved a wad of cloth on his friend's ruined eye socket and wound his neckcloth around Westbrook's head to hold it in place. To do this, Henry had to pull his friend's head forward, resting it against his shoulder so that he may reach behind the dark curls to tie it up.

"What's the damage?" Westbrook asked, voice muffled by Henry's coat. His weight had significantly increased as he rested there. Henry likened it to holding a child when they fall asleep, suddenly becoming heavier.

"I think it is permanent," Henry said, righting him again to inspect his work.

"I dare say," Westbrook replied with a brave grin.

"Will he live?" Young asked from close behind, peering over Henry's shoulder, startling him. Young gave Henry a nod of begrudging approval at his bandaging efforts.

"Only half as handsome for now, Young," Westbrook teased through gritted teeth, putting his arm around Henry for balance as Henry lifted him to his feet again. "Give the rest of you a chance with the ladies."

"Thank God!" Young laughed before joining the column.

Once prisoners were secure and the men settled into their billets, Henry escorted Westbrook to the regimental surgeon, now occupying a series of vaulted underground rooms in the city.

"Two of yours over there, Lieutenant Durand," Mr Evans said, with a casual glance at Henry. "If you are going to vomit this time, be a good chap and use the bucket, not my floor."

Henry looked down at the grim mixture of straw and liquids of undetermined origins on the cobbles, wondering why it would make any difference where he threw up. He felt Westbrook tense under his touch and look curiously at him. Henry had never liked to make a big deal of the fact he would visit their injured men following a battle, despite loathing the very thought of their Welsh surgeon more than he did the sight of blood, so had told no one. Without comment, he sat Westbrook down on a table, maintaining a hand on his shoulder, equally for his own comfort as Westbrook's.

Evans took one look at Westbrook and threw his hands in the air. "How long has he been like this?" he asked crossly, untying Henry's makeshift bandage, pulling the now congealed wounds making them bleed again. "You should have got yourself to the rear when it happened, Lieutenant. I might have been able to do more." He glanced behind him where his assistant twisted at a tourniquet on some poor soul's arm, the boy's eyes white with fear. It was coming off. No question about it.

"You should deal with him first," Westbrook

suggested, the surgeon's stained hands already probing his face.

"No, that will take me some time. I think getting Durand out of here before that happens is better for all."

Henry agreed wholeheartedly.

"I will stitch what I can," Evans continued with a murmur of disapproval over the eyeglasses perched on the end of his nose, angling Westbrook's head downwards.

"Stitch?"

"You do know you lost the eye, don't you?"

"Lost it?" Any good humour Westbrook had been holding on to dissolved in an instant. "Are you saying I'm going to be blind? I thought I could not see from it because it is bruised shut! I took some grape shot, that is all. I have had plenty a black eye before."

"There is little left of it, Lieutenant. You won't see out of it again. Now, there is still some metal in there that needs to come out. I'm afraid you won't be pretty when I'm finished. Want some brandy?" Evans picked up some menacing looking forceps Henry had last seen employed in extracting rotten teeth. Westbrook took the offered bottle within which there remained hardly two mouthfuls, glanced back to the lad with the tattered arm, then gave it back to Evans without drinking a drop. Instead, he gritted his teeth and gripped the table's edge as Henry drifted towards the back of the room to a figure struggling to sit up in his bed.

"Hallo, sir."

"As you were, Private."

"I'm sorry." The lad gestured at his surroundings, as

bleak as his milky face.

"I saw you fight, Peter. Made me proud. Loaded that musket quicker than any other man in the front rank."

"I did?"

"You did. Now get some rest so you can get back to the lads. They are saving you some supper. I heard a rumour of rabbit stew." Henry doubted Peter, a wheelwright's boy from Oxford, would ever see the outside of Cadiz again. The smell of death lingered over him like the clawing hands of the reaper himself.

"I will, sir."

"Dear Lord, Stephens, the French got you too? Whatever will we do with two of our finest lying here taking in the sweet air?" Henry made a show of coughing and flapped a hand in front of his face. The older soldier chuckled. The air underground far from sweet, and as they both knew, sickness had a greedy, cunning habit of taking more men than battle.

"I won't stay long, sir."

"I am counting on it." Henry knew from experience that Stephens would be out within a few hours, providing he could walk on his own two legs and give the surgeon the slip.

"Lieutenant?" He overheard Evans trying to get Westbrook's attention and glanced their way.

"What?" Westbrook said, flinching at the surgeon's heavy probing, as though only just noticing the pain. What Henry thought must be a slither of bone dropped into a jar with an unpleasant rattling sound.

"That is all of it out. You are lucky, there is some flesh left, so I'll stitch up what I can, rather than leave you with a gaping hole, but I was not exaggerating when I said it would not be pretty."

Henry had already resigned himself to the fact that his friend would carry wearing an eyepatch off in perfect roguish form. It would be Westbrook's luck that it would likely make him more attractive and, at the same time, more terrifying. Though how the man himself, now unusually quiet, was taking the news remained to be seen.

"It helps, what he does," Evans continued, chatting as he worked.

"Hmm?"

"Lieutenant Durand. He comes and jokes with the men. Raises their spirits. The men from your company never stay with me long."

"They don't want to let him down," Henry heard Westbrook say.

Daring to glance their way again, Henry observed the surgeon pulling thread back from Westbrook's head then plunging the needle back at his eye socket. The stitching must have hurt like hell. Westbrook made no noise.

"I have done as much as I can, gentlemen. Now, I have to take this boy's arm off," Evans declared with the relish of a man whose skill with a saw was known throughout the entire army.

"We shall excuse ourselves then." Henry put his hand on Westbrook's shoulder. No chance he wanted to be around for an amputation. Westbrook shrugged him off.

"There are some patches over there in a box," Evans told Henry. "Leave the bandages on a day or two," this he said to Westbrook. "Then I want to see you again. Sooner if anything goes juicy or starts to smell."

That nearly sealed the fate for Henry's stomach, but he managed to swallow what he heaved, and divert himself by seeking out the eyepatches. He found them next to an ominous crate of crutches and pocketed two. Henry helped Westbrook to the door, then into the stone tunnel where the cooler air, by contrast, tasted delicious.

"See you next time, Durand!" the surgeon called behind them. Henry shuddered.

"I can manage, Henry," Westbrook growled after a few steps, shaking him off once more and turning away. "Will you just leave me alone!"

"No. I won't."

"I mean it!" With a sudden burst of anger, he pushed Henry away. "Don't make me hit you."

"You wouldn't," Henry snorted.

"Try me."

Henry thought about it. He wanted to grab Westbrook by the collar and bang his head against the wall for being a stubborn stewed prune.

"I don't want your help and I don't want you anywhere near me."

"You vain bastard," Henry countered and stormed ahead. He immediately regretted calling him that. Still, Westbrook's distemper occurred the moment the surgeon told him he lost the eye. Did it really matter that much to him? There were plenty of decent soldiers with one eye. When he looked back, Westbrook was making slow progress along the tunnel, albeit guiding himself with one hand. His head turned so his remaining eye, the right one, led.

"How is he?" Sinclair asked, hurrying through the tunnel towards them. "I only just got away from the colonel. Is it bad?"

"He is moody and petulant," Henry said, folding his arms and glaring back Westbrook's way. Sinclair accepted this description as nothing to be too alarmed about, and relaxed his shoulders with a sigh of relief.

Westbrook stopped at the sight of his godfather and set off in the opposite direction, muttering something they could not hear.

"So I see," Sinclair said.

"Mr Evans has stitched him up. The shot took his eye, but he won't accept my help," Henry explained with the hint of a whine, fully expecting Sinclair to bark an order at his godson to accept the offered assistance.

"Nor mine, by the looks of it," Sinclair said. "Well, carry on, Durand." Sinclair patted Henry on the back, then turned on his heel and departed the way he came, leaving Henry both disappointed and at a loss as to what the hell he should do next.

Should he follow his friend and make sure he makes it to his bed, or does he follow Sinclair's example and leave the stubborn idiot to it? Letting out a large, resigned sigh that echoed through the tunnel to mix with the distant cacophony of the arm amputation, he followed Westbrook.

Westbrook stumbled on the stairs to their shared billet and groaned in pain. Henry remained in the shadows and let his friend pick himself up, though it hurt to watch such a thing.

"I know you are there," Westbrook growled as he reached the door.

"Where else would I be?" Henry replied, pushing past him. He began to undress, pretending to ignore Westbrook, who now struggled to hide the agony. Such ignorance proved increasingly difficult, so only minutes later, with a further dramatic sigh, this time of surrender, Henry dug in his trunk for a bottle of port he had hidden from his friend for such an emergency.

"Why don't you hate me?" Westbrook asked, uncorking the bottle with his teeth then sitting on his bed where he proceeded to drink half the bottle in rapid gulps; sounding not unlike a drain in a storm.

"You are the only idiot that will put up with me," Henry said.

"I'm sorry. I didn't mean it. What I said earlier."

"Nor I. Does it hurt much?"

Westbrook nodded.

"Still think you can read with just the one eye?"

He nodded again.

"Good." Henry threw Westbrook the new book he had bought from a corporal of the Rifles two days earlier. It had caught his eye not only because it was Shakespeare but because of its title. *Henry IV*. It had been in his inner pocket for the entire battle.

Westbrook relinquished the bottle to cradle the book. "Before you go to bed, would you take the rest of the bottle to that lad whose arm they were taking? Evans was fair out of brandy."

Chapter 8

Ashlington, April 2015

Lillian swept the dead petals off the headstone, the eroded letters of her mother's name now joined by the freshly carved name of her father. "There. That's better."

Satisfied with her work of clearing away the faded flowers and arranging fresh ones into the pot, she stood and said goodbye. The goodbyes always felt inadequate now. How had she not known that the last time she saw him would be her last chance to make a proper job of it?

"I miss you, Dad. I wish I had spent more time here with you before—and I wish—I had so much I wanted to tell you. Am I going crazy or are you trying to tell me something? Have you been trying to talk to me? Warn me of something? If only you could give me some sign."

It was Thursday and Marcus had called to say he would arrive that evening for a long weekend, so she wanted to get some extra groceries from the village shop. She made her way back to the house to collect her purse, only to find Marcus's black BMW already on the driveway, together with a familiar Mercedes. Beige.

She tracked their voices to the dining room. "Yes, it is a Sinclair. He was a decorated officer in Wellington's army and, during his time in Spain, sketched his officers. It is reported he lost his leg during the battle of Toulouse, returned to England and spent his convalescence painting from those very sketches. His collection is rather sought after in particular circles. I might know of a buyer that would be interested if you wanted to come to a private arrangement for the piece."

"Marcus?"

Both men turned around, Marcus at least with the decency to appear surprised to see her, whereas Varnal ran his eyes up and down her in that condescending way of his.

Lillian's eyes were drawn to the painting they discussed. Illuminated by a shaft of light from the window that caught the blue of Henry's eyes, she felt like he stared straight back at her, angrier than before.

"Lillian, I didn't expect you to be here."

"Obviously."

"We could be talking this sort of figure." Varnal ignored her interruption and scribbled something in a notepad, tore out the page, and passed it to Marcus. His rubbery nose twitched.

Marcus's lips formed a perfect O. "Really?"

Varnal nodded.

"But the painting is not—"

Marcus raised his voice, cutting Lillian off. "Would you excuse us? My fiancée has been through a tough time with the passing of her father. It has put her under a lot of strain." He steered Lillian out of the room.

"What are you doing?" she said, trying to shake off his hold on her.

In the hallway, he closed the door behind them and pulled her into him so that his face was close enough to hers that she could feel the warmth of his breath. "Do you have any idea what this could mean?" he spoke harshly, then closed his eyes as though calming himself. "Our dream, Lillian. The apartment in Barcelona, the family. There is nothing tying us to this place anymore." He let go of her and she rubbed at her arms where he had been holding them. "You're tired. Why don't you go lie down? I'll get rid of Varnal."

"This is your home," said the voice. Part statement, part plea.

Later, over dinner, Lillian broached the subject of the voice with Marcus.

"I think it is about time you saw a doctor." Marcus said matter-of-factly. "You aren't sleeping much, are you? That is probably why you are hearing voices."

"Not voices. I'm not going mad, Marcus. It is one voice, and it sounds like my father."

Did he think she was going crazy? He could be hard to read sometimes. He steepled his fingers, elbows propped on the table, before pointing her way as though he had a revelation.

"You *think* you are hearing your father. That is how grief works, darling. You hardly saw him in the year before he died, so naturally you are feeling guilty about it. You are here in this creepy house by yourself—lonely—so your brain is conjuring your father. See a doctor. He'll give you something to help you sleep."

Marcus never doubted himself. It was part of what attracted her to him in the first place. There was some truth to what he had said. She had not been sleeping well. Her mind was playing tricks on her, that's all.

"I am real, Lillian," insisted the voice as she cleared dinner away. Which is precisely what a voice conjured from her imagination would say.

***

Finding Bloody Johansen sat having breakfast when he arrived at the manor Friday morning caught Nick off guard.

"Marcus Johansen," Marcus said, offering a handshake above his bowl of Weetabix. "Lillian's fiancé. We never got a chance to meet at the funeral."

"Nick Hawkins," Nick said, suddenly feeling like a stranger in the house.

"Hawkins? Oh yes, your mother used to help about the place."

"Tea, Nick?" Lillian asked before Nick could answer.

"Ah—no—I'm okay. I'll go make a start."

Holly followed him and settled on Nick's feet when he sat down at the desk in the study. He stared at his blank laptop screen, wondering what it was Lillian saw in Marcus. Other than the bank balance, washboard physique and chiselled jaw, of course.

Lillian came in shortly after and placed a mug of tea

on the desk. She then leant against it; her bottom perched on the edge. "Sorry about Marcus. He can be insensitive sometimes."

"He doesn't like me being here."

"No, it's not that—"

"You never used to lie to me, Lily."

"What do you want me to say? That he is threatened by you because all I used to do was talk about how you broke my heart?"

"I broke *your* heart?"

"Shush!"

"I broke *your* heart?" he repeated in a shrill whisper.

"You are so frustrating sometimes, Nick Hawkins."

She walked out, giving the door a slam on her way, leaving Nick utterly confused. It also appeared she would not be helping with the research today, after all. He sneaked into the dining room and stood in front of Henry's painting. "What was all that about?" he whispered. "Why does she keep closing down on me like that, and what the hell am I supposed to do to tell her she doesn't have to?" He had asked the painting the same thing years ago. And just like back then, the painted figure looked down at him with a wistful sadness and said nothing.

Even the old house seemed to feel Marcus as a disruption, sympathising with groaning floorboards and whispered gusts throughout the morning. The study door creaked open in a draught several times until Nick slammed it shut. Nick stayed, admittedly in hiding, in the study.

Lillian entered at around ten thirty, scowled at him, and left again, taking the stack of letters she had been working on.

Nearer to lunchtime, Marcus stuck his head around the study door. "Hawkins."

"Johansen." Nick couldn't work him out. His mother didn't like him either, but then he doubted anyone was good enough for Lillian in his mother's eyes. "I'm just on my way out."

Marcus nodded, and his eyes glanced around the room. "How is it going, then? The family tree stuff? Surely you have better things to be doing with your time? Lillian says you have quite the reputation in the archaeology world."

Busy analysing to what degree Marcus would escalate his hostility, Nick didn't reply. He continued to stack letters, close his laptop, and then pushed his chair back, standing up. Marcus took a step backwards. People that didn't know he hated conflict often did when confronted with Nick's height.

"Don't suppose you have much more to do, what, a few more days?" Marcus asked.

"A little longer than that. This character Alistair found has a past worth writing about. Would you like to read some of what we have discovered?"

"No, I don't think so. I don't think all this talk of the past is good for Lillian. Not when she needs to move on." Marcus picked up the silver wedding-photo frame on the mantle, studied it, and put it down again. "Having you here spewing stories of whatever it is, whoever, is stopping her from doing that. It's unhealthy."

"I don't spew," Nick said. "She asked for my help. I am happy to give it until she says otherwise. Seems like someone should listen to what she wants." He tucked his laptop under his arm, walked around the desk, and stood in front of Johansen.

"Oh, that's what you're doing," Marcus said. "Listening?" He chuckled, a cold sound.

"Have a pleasant weekend," Nick said, and left with a new opinion of Marcus Johansen.

Nick did not make a habit of taking source material back to the cottage, but the less time spent around Bloody Johansen, the better. He hated to admit it, but he had been getting used to working at the manor and as the weeks passed even resented Fridays and the impending break of the weekend. *You are in too deep now*, he told himself, already further than simply helping Lillian make a start. *You are your own worst enemy, but then Ashlington Manor always did have a way of getting into your bones.*

The stack of papers he brought back with him also contained the book from Henry's trunk. It fell out of the pile onto the floor, dropping a letter. He picked it up and held his breath. Not only was the letter addressed to Henry, but it remained unopened.

Lillian's answer to his text came quickly.

Are you kidding? Open it. Just make sure you tell me all about it on Monday.

Have a great weekend x

He stared at the kiss. A dramatic shift in how she had been with him all morning after she had accused him of breaking her heart. Was she messing with him? Trying to score a point? He shook the notion away. Lillian didn't play games.

He made a coffee. Took it black, hoping the caffeine kick would get his mind back on track. Then he stared at the letter on the counter. "Will you forgive me if I open it, Henry?" he asked, thinking of how downcast the painting had looked that morning. The letter stirred in a breeze from the open kitchen window. Nick picked it up and snapped the seal carefully.

The first eyes to see the message in two hundred years.

Dated weeks before Waterloo, Nick could only speculate on why it had not been opened. Had it arrived the night before the battle? Had it arrived after and got tucked away with Henry's belongings? Had it not arrived at all and got placed in his trunk when it returned to Ashlington after he died?

Dearest Henry,

How I wish you would write. Your mother rarely smiles with abandon now, but a letter from you, were it possible, would make all the difference.

I wrote to Robert yesterday. Though I fear my concern will go unnoticed. I sent him a package of willow bark to ease his knee (my grandmother swore by it for her joints) and, yes, a new book. No doubt he will roll his eyes at the choice, but I rather enjoyed reading about the Dashwood sisters and their sensibilities. It occurred to me I should ask him to write a list of what he has already read, though he would likely reply that he has not the time. I worry that drinking liquor in the quantities he does will only serve to mask the pain he is in rather than confront it. Were you able, then I would encourage you to search his billet and remove that particular temptation.

I love you dearly, but Robert makes a far better correspondent, I only wish I had known this earlier. Indeed, he wrote in his last letter (an actual letter, not the few lines you would write), that in his experience reading aloud could calm the darkest Durand tempest (how I laughed). Having resorted to testing this by reading the front page of the Cheltenham Chronicle to Teddy in the small hours of the morning, I can confirm this minor miracle to be effective on even the youngest Durand boy.

Teddy has grown you would not believe how much. He feeds well and has such a smile I often think my heart will burst for the love of him. Your father has taken to spending at least an hour with him each day, carrying him off to the study. Your mother jokes he is teaching him the books already. Teddy has given him a second chance at love. He is endeavouring to get it right this time.

The letter smudged.

I met an interesting family (a brother and sister) last

week. Anthony and Lucy Rundell from Woodcombe Hall. Do you remember them? She is a lovely vibrant soul that reminds me of how we were all those years ago. The brother is undoubtedly a rake.

I have also seen Ursula Chilton. That woman's greed is as plain as the nose on her face, and our family needs no more of that evil. Fear not. I made you a promise and I intend to see it through.

It ended with a declaration of continued prayers and signed off simply with the name Louisa. Interesting how fondly she wrote of Westbrook, Nick thought; how her love for her child shone through her writing and how heartbreaking it was to think that Henry never met his son.

Chapter 9

Spain, June 1811

The convent stood in solitude. An ominous plume of smoke rising from the chapel reduced their march to a shuffle as the men squinted into the distance, hopeful for some sign that the fire was intentional.

"We were here just a few days ago, Lieutenant. It's full of children," Jackson said, his hand on Henry's sleeve. He removed it quickly. "Beggin' your pardon, sir."

Henry slid out his telescope to rest it on Young's shoulder and studied the hillside, the narrow field of view concentrating his choices.

"Come along, Durand, we have reports to make," Roylance said, marching on past. A stickler for protocol, the captain commanding their patrol had led a blistering pace back to camp. Even so, they had barely a few hours of daylight remaining. Any delay and they would march not only into darkness but also the wrath of Major Sinclair.

"We should check the convent," Henry said.

Roylance made a smart about turn and took Henry aside with a jerk of his head. "We don't have the time, Durand, you know it as well as I."

"You worry about the deserters?" Henry did not intend the question as an insult. Local reports of a violent band of deserters had them all on edge. The leader had been described in detail, a foul beast of a man that left death in his path. Henry also knew it was not only the deserters Roylance feared, but the word whipping from Sinclair that might put a stop to his recommendation for promotion.

"We can send the provosts back tomorrow. It's their job after all," Roylance said.

A scream carried on the wind begged for help at the same time Henry's belly grumbled. Breakfast had been long ago, and he knew Sinclair's table waited for them. His stomach would not be happy, but he decided it could wait. "I'm volunteering to confirm all is well at the convent, sir," he said.

Roylance sighed. "You can't very well go on your own."

"He won't be on his own," Westbrook said from Henry's side. He nodded solemnly at Henry, then turned his remaining eye to Roylance. Young, Jackson and Adams stepped forward as Henry knew they would.

"But Sinclair—"

"I shall take full responsibility as far as Sinclair is concerned," Henry replied.

Roylance shuffled his feet, still yet to be convinced.

"Shall I write him a note to that effect?" The folded note he passed Roylance was blunt, even by Henry's standards, but then he wrote it more for Roylance's benefit than Sinclair's.

Heard a scream. Investigating.

HD

With Roylance mollified, they parted ways, Henry promising to be back in camp by morning. He signalled for Westbrook and the others to follow him down into the valley, weapons drawn.

Trouble met them at the convent walls in the form of a turncoat, thankfully too drunk to raise the alarm. Young dealt with him silently. The body of an old man, buzzing with flies, lay in the dust of the gateway, as though interrupted trying to close the gate. Jackson checked for signs of life, looked at Henry, and shook his head.

"There are more," Young said, wiping his knife on the deserter's coat. He pointed to two more bodies, both nuns. "That lady brought food out to us three days ago."

A thin dog trotted towards them. Someone kicked a stone at it, causing the dog to veer away. In pairs, they checked each building as they advanced silently towards the burning chapel.

Henry heard a gunshot and was halfway across the cloisters in support when Adams and Jackson emerged. Adams mumbling an apology for the noise when stealth was called for. The shot, he explained, being from a drunken deserter harmlessly missing his target. They would not be of any more trouble, he assured.

Movement to his right caught Henry's attention, Westbrook diving onto a man through the doorway of a storeroom. Henry could make out more shapes in the shadows, drew his knife, and went in after his friend.

On the floor, Westbrook was dealing out blows to the man he had tackled. Henry lashed out at another, taking aim at his friend with a pistol. The man was bigger than Henry but Henry proved quicker, slashing him on the arm with the knife then landing a series of explosive jabs to the man's jaw hinge, nose and throat alternately with his left fist and the butt of the knife.

Someone else grabbed at Henry from behind, smashing his knife hand against the wall. The knife dropped. The side of Henry's head banged into the wall, ears ringing with the impact. From such a position, he could see that Westbrook was fairing no better. Westbrook's larger assailant had turned him over and held him down with hands around his throat. Henry kicked his fallen knife backwards. Westbrook grasped it and plunged it into the man's neck.

While ramming his elbow backwards and doing his best to save his head from further assault, Henry heard a crash directly behind him. Suddenly released from the force holding him, he turned to see the gap-toothed smile of Jackson; the handle of the jug he had just smashed over the head of the man, now slumped on the floor, still in his hand.

Holding his hands on his knees, Henry caught his breath. "Better late than never, Jackson!"

Jackson grinned at him in the way he did whenever his officers threw themselves at danger. He then helped Westbrook, who was rubbing deserter's blood from his face with the crook of his arm, to his feet before making quick work of tying up the two injured men.

The one with the bleeding nose and crooked jaw

looked at Henry, pallor and twitching betraying his fear. "You are all deserters?" Henry asked.

The man nodded, eyes to the floor in shame about the situation he now found himself in. "We only wanted feeding proper. What the others are doing is nuffin' to do with us," he said nasally before discharging a glob of red snot.

"What others? How many of you are there?"

"Nine."

Which by Henry's reckoning left three unaccounted for.

Back outside, Henry beckoned Young for a report. Young crossed the street, hunched over, and thudded his back into the wall next to Henry. "Roof of the chapel is a goner, sir; nothing we can do." It was some consolation it stood out of reach of the other buildings, the flames unlikely to spread in the still night.

Alerted by a noise, an untamed cry like a wounded animal, Henry put a finger to his lips for quiet. He signalled for the others to remain outside, as Westbrook readied himself and his weapons next to a pair of double doors.

It took a few seconds for Henry's eyes to adjust to the dimmer light inside. Wooden benches lay on their sides in disarray around a long refectory table with broken plates, scattered food, and fallen candles. Another scream, higher pitched, followed by a deep laugh, came from above them.

Westbrook pointed at the staircase in the corner.

Henry led, since Barossa he always did, the hair on the back of his neck prickling.

"Cut it off, Tom," a voice snarled. "She'll talk!"

Henry put a tentative foot on the bottom step of the steep wooden staircase. It climbed to the frightened faces of several young girls cowering on the landing. They studied him as he crept up the stairs with a finger on his lips and Westbrook so close behind him he could feel his breath tickling his ear.

One child held up her hand.

Henry froze.

A man lurched in front of the children, thankfully facing them, so he didn't see the men paused on the stairs. There was no mistaking the description of the huge deserter they had been warned about, nor what remained of his British uniform. The soldier growled at the children before stepping out of view again. The girl peered down at Henry, one eye purple with bruising, and blood trickling from the corner of her tiny mouth. She met his eyes with an inquisitive stare.

"Cuantos?" he mouthed.

She held up three fingers.

The scene that met them beyond the landing cooked Henry's blood to a boil; all possibility of giving the remaining deserters fair warning lost in that second of comprehension. He thrust forward, plunging his sword into the enormous man. It met flesh, plenty of it, Henry ensuring it went in deep before the effort of jerking it free. The man fell to his knees, clutching his belly.

A girl struggled, hands tied with cord, blood dripping from cuts on her arms. The man stood behind the girl— frozen with the girl's hand braced on a table, knife poised to cut off a second finger—met his end at Westbrook's hand. His pistol cracking loudly in the enclosed space.

At the noise, the third man dropped his grip from around the throat of a young woman. She fell to the floor, habit torn, and bruised head rolled to one side; the degree of consciousness unknown. Her attacker turned to meet Henry who, striding across the room, threw down his sword and drew his pistol, eyes narrowing as he aimed at the man's head, the weapon holding equal menace to Henry's grim countenance.

The deserter raised his hands. "All right officers, no 'arm done, she says there is no gold here, but she'll talk soon enough, just takes the right motivation. Plenty to share," he said, wiping his mouth with the back of his grubby sleeve.

Westbrook uttered something that should never come from the mouth of a gentleman and lunged towards him. Henry took a step forward to thump the man hard, sending him crashing through the window backwards; a satisfying thud punctuating his grunt of surprise. Henry lent out of the window and watched as the man twitched a while then stopped moving; a warped halo of blood circling his head.

Henry fought to re-bury his temper and regret the loss of life instead. He should have arrested them and let the army judge their crimes. Death had let them off easy. The girl that Henry had seen from the stairs ran into the room with a blanket. Henry helped her tuck it around the nun's battered body, questioning what type of God would allow this to happen to his flock. Across the landing, Westbrook cut the tied girl free and fell to his knees. She accepted the offered comfort readily. As he whispered to her in Spanish, checking her wounds, she sobbed and shook against him. He had a younger sister back home. Henry knew she would be on his friend's mind as he comforted the girl, as much as Louisa was on his, no doubt reminded of the danger he could not be there to protect her against.

The bloody scene confronting them now forced Henry to swallow hard. The last thing he wanted to do was drag the bodies down the stairs, leaving more evidence of horror for the children to endure. He glanced at the girls again and made his decision. Grabbing the man he had killed first by the ankles, he began dragging him toward the window. It was hard work; he was a heavy fellow. Westbrook saw what he was about and sat the girl down with the others, then lifted the body by the wrists. Together they man-handled him out of the window, the last deserter landing on top moments later.

The injured nun muttered something to Westbrook, pulling on his sleeve urgently. He asked her to repeat it. "She is saying something about finding the little ones. I don't know what she means."

"More children?"

"Niños?" Westbrook asked her.

The nun nodded.

"You go, I'll take care of them," Westbrook said. Henry was sure he saw the track of a tear through the dust on his friend's cheek. He squeezed Westbrook's shoulder before banging his way down the stairs.

"Jackson!"

"Yes, sir," Jackson answered from the doorway. "We have searched this side, all clear. No more deserters other than the men you chucked out the window?" he said this with a tone that asked a question. A question Henry did not have the time or inclination to answer.

"You said the place was full of children last time we came this way. There are only four girls upstairs."

Jackson frowned, then the implication hit home.

"Take that side," Henry ordered. "I'll re-search over here. They will be scared." He did not need to add what they both dreaded.

As a child, he had been hopeless at hide-and-seek. Louisa preferred to do the seeking and found him first every time, usually sat in the pantry with an uncontrollable urge to pee, stuffing his face with treats. Christopher would give himself away with noisy giggling or mid-game change of hiding spot. Danny excelled at the game. Some days they would simply give up and he would appear hours later, declaring victory.

The third room Henry searched sent him backing out again. He recognised the early stench of death confined by the small space; the pungent mixture of faeces and urine that clenched his stomach and forced him to cover his nose and mouth with his sleeve as he gagged.

The body was small.

A child.

The boy lay on his back, arms outstretched as though he had been protecting something—or someone. A single shot to his chest and an astonished look of betrayal on his face.

Beyond him stood a large wooden wardrobe that had likely been there for years, now spattered with blood. A decent enough, if not original, hiding place. Henry took off his coat and placed it over the body.

"I won't hurt you," he said softly, admittedly in English, but he hoped his tone would calm any remaining frightened children. "My friends and I have sent the bad men away. They won't be of any more harm." He waited for a moment, listening, then continued. "Your revered sister is very worried about you. Why don't you come on out, you must be hungry?" The door of the wardrobe shook ever so slightly, as though a small hand held it from inside. Henry reached forward and opened it.

How so many children had squashed inside he did not know, but the largest one stepped out and held up his fists. Part of Henry, the part that could not handle any more horror, wanted to laugh. But the boy must have only been six. At six Henry had been terribly serious, so he treated him as such and took a knee.

"Lieutenant Henry Durand of His Britannic Majesty's 28th Regiment of Foot," he told the boy with as much ceremony as he could. He reversed his sword, noting belatedly that the blade still dripped blood, so wiped it on his trouser leg before resting it on his arm in surrender. The sword was a standard issue officer's sabre, the guard nearly broken. Nothing like the quality of steel Westbrook carried. The boy puffed out his chest and took it, leaving Henry wondering what to do next. He hadn't thought that far ahead.

"Parole?" he asked, unable to recall the appropriate Spanish phrase.

The boy seemed to understand and nodded solemnly, handing Henry his sword back. The son of a long dead soldier, perhaps. He didn't think the boy would have run him through. His gangly arms had struggled to keep the sword aloft, still Henry was glad that particular skirmish was over. The boy beckoned the others out of the wardrobe as Young and Jackson entered the room.

"Blimey!" Young said. "Where'd you find this little lot?"

Thankful he did not have to explain his surrender to a six-year-old to his men, Henry set Jackson as first picquet and gave instructions for Young and Adams to bury the old man and women in the churchyard. The deserters, undeserving of burial on sacred ground, were to be thrown into a communal grave outside the convent, no more than a dusty pit. Their shamefaced prisoners promised to be of no bother tied in the storeroom.

The child's body Henry carried himself, with the group of smaller children following him like a pack of motherless puppies. When his contrary stomach rumbled again, he requested, via sign language, if they had any food for his men. Given purpose, the children left him.

Alone, he searched for another shovel and went to dig a tiny grave.

He returned later, dusty and furious once more, to the refectory to find Westbrook washing his face. Henry's arrival sparked a hasty replacement of his eyepatch. Despite being the one that bandaged it for him on that day at Barossa, a sober Westbrook never let Henry see beneath it. Roaring drunk was another matter, and the reason Henry carried a spare patch for his friend.

"I don't think it was just about gold. Their torment was entertainment." Westbrook hung his head as he spoke. The words 'if only we had got here quicker,' left unsaid, but they haunted Henry too. "I have dealt with their wounds as best I could." Westbrook then looked up at Henry, single eye creased with concern. "I hear you buried a child?"

Henry didn't trust himself to answer. The sadness he knew he should feel had become entangled and swallowed by straightforward fury. "Who was the old man?" he asked, taking his turn to wash the death off his hands.

"A labourer. Mother Elvira runs the orphanage. She and two other sisters had travelled into town. They keep busy now with more children on account of the war, you understand. They are due to return tomorrow."

"We can send the provosts here in the morning, to be sure. Get the Spanish to send a guard."

"Señor," a boy said, tugging at Henry's sleeve. He gestured to his mouth before pulling Henry towards the kitchen.

As darkness fell, Henry, the men, and the children had eaten a veritable feast of bread and cheese, figs, and some salted pork. The children warmed to their new friends, particularly Westbrook who, having entertained them with a story and song, dozed in a chair with the smallest girl from the wardrobe asleep on his lap; her chubby little fists gripping tightly to his shirt.

Henry could hardly blame her.

"You are still angry?" Westbrook asked later when Henry joined him at the gate to relieve him of sentry duty. The fire from the chapel had long since gone out, the skinny dog wandering across the cloistered quadrangle the only movement in a starless night.

"I don't want to talk about it."

"No, you want to thump something because you think that is how best to deal with what you feel inside."

"I hate you sometimes."

"No, you don't."

"Do you want to talk about it?" Henry asked.

"I'm not the one pacing up and down."

"I always pace."

Westbrook mumbled something unintelligible, then handed Henry the musket, and with it the responsibility of guard.

"Why would a man do that to children?" Henry asked some time later, not really knowing whom he asked, or expecting an answer.

"Real men don't."

"Is what I did any better? I killed two men in cold blood."

"You forced the issue with Roylance to come here. Had we not, all of those children might be dead now. You think leaving those disgusting beasts alive would have been justice for what they did? They don't deserve a second thought from either of us."

Despite his bluster, Henry knew it would eat at Westbrook's loyal heart that they were British turncoats, and was likely the reason Westbrook still stood at the gate with him, instead of finding sleep.

"You are a good man, Henry. You doubt that? Still?"

"I doubt it every day." Least of all because of the violence, he thought. "You were just as angry as I was up there, West. How are you so calm already?"

"I am not. Not really. But it isn't the first time I have seen something like that. I have been around the army for longer than you. Part of that is seeing men at their best and at their worst."

"It made you cry."

"You say that like it is a bad thing."

"I just—"

"You think I am weak?" Westbrook scratched under his eyepatch, and Henry immediately regretted bringing it up. "I know I am no longer as brave as I once pretended to be, but—"

"That's not what I meant. I don't think you are weak, not for a single minute, West. You actually make it look so easy dealing with it, is what I meant."

"It feels better to let it out on occasion, that's all. That said, I would not have done such a thing in front of the men."

Henry tried to weigh up what that meant. He let the silence grow between them and once more scanned the shadows for any sign they were not alone before speaking again. "Your godfather wants you to take the captaincy when Roylance moves."

"I don't want it."

"Why not? You deserve it."

"I used to want it. Before this." Westbrook pointed to his eyepatch. "I'm not able to be what the men need now, you know that. I second guess everything."

"There is no one else I would want at my side in a fight, West."

"Which is where I am happy to be. Leading them, though, that is your job. If you hadn't noticed by now, Henry, the men would follow you anywhere. You should tell Sinclair you want it."

"But Sinclair—"

"You know him almost as well as I do. He is not only this hard scarred warrior, the best major in the whole damn army, but also the man that just wants to give his heart to the two children he inherited from my father. Away from all this—" Westbrook waved a hand which Henry took to indicate the entirety of the Iberian Peninsula, "he is different, softer. He won't make me take it if I don't want to. No matter what they have taught you to believe, I don't think his compassion makes him any less of a man."

"You are more like him than you know."

"Durand, my boy, button your coat, there's a good fellow," Westbrook rumbled in perfect imitation as he flicked at Henry's open coat. Henry laughed. Westbrook looked pleased to have evoked a smile finally and leant against the wall. Henry came to rest next to him.

"If you don't take it, the promotion, you'll end up having to move to another company or regiment eventually," Westbrook said, his tone serious once more.

"Well, that's settled then, I shall have to take it."

"So we can stay together? You'd do that?"

Henry could not imagine being anywhere different. "Who else would read all the books I buy?"

Later, when he pulled himself next to Young on a bench in the refectory following his turn at watch, Henry sank into a disturbing dream. Stood in a room that looked like the ballroom of Ashlington Manor, he talked with a girl as tall as him. She wore the most outrageous clothing and her forced smile mirrored his own. Family surrounded him, celebrating something. It felt far from a celebration for Henry. He couldn't help feel he had made a huge mistake, or worse, that one cage had been swapped for another. Overwhelmingly, something was missing; a part of him, perhaps, a sense of loss and loneliness that physically hurt.

"Don't go!" the girl said, gripping his wrists. He felt himself fall as she said his name.

He awoke with a jerk that almost shook him off the bench. Haunted by the sadness of the dream, he rose slowly and stretched. His muscles stiff and head aching.

"Sunrise, sir." Young tapped Henry's shoulder.

"Get em' up, Corporal."

"You heard the lieutenant, up and at em' lads!" Young yelled with an enthusiasm loud enough to wake the dead but not a slumbering Lieutenant Westbrook, who groaned and covered his head with his blanket before Henry gave him a kick with the toe of his boot.

Sister Francis greeted them with warm water with which to wash and offered fresh bread. Her steps were awkward, her face bruised and split. Henry did not need a translation for what she told Westbrook before they left. Her message was obvious.

"We will pray for you all, Lieutenant. And shall never forget what you did here."

Chapter 10

Ashlington, April 2015

By early afternoon, with hours of research behind him, Nick stretched and, with a groan of protest from his knees, got off the floor. Lillian had set herself up in the lounge with her laptop to complete some work commitments, leaving him taking notes from Henry's journal. Even though he preferred working on the floor like he was still twenty, his forty-year-old body complained. His coffee cold, he wandered to the kitchen, thankful for the excuse to stretch his legs.

Lillian had left him a note on the fridge.

Made you a sandwich x

Why did she insist on taunting him with the kiss? The question transported him back to a summer long ago. They had taken it in turns to choose a Friday night movie together, usually in her room. Sometimes Alistair was there, sometimes he was out at some dinner party or business event.

"What are we watching?" the then sixteen-year-old Lillian had said one night.

"*Raiders of the Lost Ark*," Nick told her, waving the VHS videotape. Not his prized possession, but close.

"Again?"

"It's a good film."

"You have already made me watch it twice."

"You want to put something else on?"

"No. It's fine. I swear if you quote or talk through the whole damn thing, then next week I will choose *ET* and make you sob through that again."

"You are all talk sometimes, Lily."

"But I have popcorn and cider."

"Your Dad will kill us."

"He won't be back until midnight, so he won't know. Besides, he thinks because you are here I can't possibly get into trouble."

"How is Cameron?" Some rich bloke with amazing hair and a bright red Golf GTI.

"No idea. I don't see anything of him."

"You two fall out?"

"He just wasn't..."

Nick waited.

"He was all show. You know?"

"I told you."

She glared at him.

"Cameron had a lucky escape if you ask me."

"I didn't."

They propped themselves up with her pillows and before long she had nestled against him, like she always did. He liked to think it made him feel grown up, as though he was defending her from all that scared her. All it really did was make his heart race and his voice squeak. Whether it

119

was the cider or the fact she was bored with the movie, she kept giving him strange looks.

Most looks of hers he had catalogued in his memory, tagged with their meanings. This one seemed dangerous and gave him the impulse to run. An impulse that made him jolt, knocking her arm, spilling her drink.

"Nick!"

"Sorry." He leapt off her bed.

"I'm soaked." The drink had thoroughly wet her t-shirt, which now clung to her. The t-shirt she now pulled off in front of him.

He turned away quickly, willing himself to think of anything but her. On the tv screen the ark had opened, releasing a host of beautiful ghostly angels. "Shut your eyes, Marion, don't look at it!" Indiana Jones instructed. "No matter what happens!"

Nick thought it good advice.

"I should go," he said, scratching at his neck. When he plucked up courage to peek behind him, he found her wearing a clean t-shirt, standing with her hands on her hips.

"Why?" she asked with a tilt of the head.

He wanted to tell her. Wanted to say that she was breaking his heart. His fragile glass teenage heart that felt fit to burst with her.

"Nick."

"Yes?" he squeaked.

"Don't go yet," she said this quietly, the strange look back. What on earth did it mean? He was so fixed on working it out that he hadn't noticed she had stepped forward. Then she pressed her lips onto his.

Overwhelmed by the warmth and sudden taste of sweet fermented apples, he was barely aware of the melting Gestapo officer in the movie (normally his favourite part). They were still kissing when the end credits rolled, though they had moved onto her bed, lying side by side. They fell asleep there, his arms wrapped around her.

Nick woke what must have been an hour later to the noise of a vehicle on the gravel outside and a churning panic. Alistair. Lillian remained asleep, looking both peaceful and utterly dangerous at the same time. He glanced at the cider bottle. It easily explained her affectionate advances. He should have stopped her. How could he face her father now? They had only been kissing. Nevertheless, Alistair possessed a shotgun.

He ran a hand through his hair and checked he did not look too dishevelled in the mirror, wiping hard at his cheek to rub away the sticky trace of what she had told him was bubble-gum flavoured lip-gloss. Then he slipped out of her room, tiptoeing down the stairs, hoping to creep out undetected.

"Good night?" Alistair asked from the dark of the hallway. He stepped into the shaft of moonlight from the window above the door, like a menacing villain.

Nick swallowed. No sign of the shotgun. "Yes, thank you," he said honestly.

"Don't tell me, Indiana Jones again?"

Nick nodded. Rapidly.

"She thought so. Thanks for keeping her company,

Nicholas. You can always stay, you know, instead of walking home. Take one of the spare rooms."

"Okay, I think I—right—I'll umm, g'night, Mr Durand."

"Night, Nick."

Nick left the manor to walk back into the village in the dark, wishing for two things. The first that he could learn to string a sentence together under pressure and the second that Lillian would not hate him tomorrow. She hadn't. In fact, they never spoke of it. Not until a few years later, when it was time to leave. Too late.

Nick let the memory go with an audible exhalation, then opened the fridge and retrieved the sandwich, an enormous pile of salad and hummus between two slices of wholemeal bread. No cheese, no meat, just how he liked it. He poured a fresh mug of coffee, made Lillian a green tea, and wandered down the hall through to the lounge, trying not to think about cider.

"Tea's up."

"You're a life saver," she replied from behind her laptop, evidence of her own lunch crumbled on an empty plate next to her, her hair twisted up and balanced on the top of her head with the aid of—*were those pencils?* Uninvited memories of sitting close to her at the kitchen table doing homework together encroached. She would write messages in his exercise books he would later find in class.

The fox skull looks so serious I have called him Nick!

or

4 weeks and counting until the summer!

And then his particular favourite, a quote from Marion in *Raiders of the Lost Ark* ...

Well Jones, at least you still know how to show a lady a good time

The kid he sat next to in maths would tease him about all the hearts and snakes she had drawn.

She accepted the steaming mug and leant back on the sofa. Nick dropped himself into an armchair off to one side, out of reach.

Out of danger.

"How is the world of architecture this afternoon?" he enquired.

"You know it makes me wonder what would I do if I kept this place?" She tapped her pen at her notebook as though adding ideas to a mental list.

"What would you want to do?"

"Have my own business. Restorations and helping people build their dream homes."

"I thought that's what you did?"

She gave him a sideways look. "No. Not really."

"So what is stopping you?"

"It sounds nice, but I have responsibilities elsewhere." She twisted the engagement ring on her finger. A huge rock, glinting in the light like a balefire; reminding him her heart also belonged elsewhere. "What about Durand ancestry? What have I missed?"

"Well, I have put together some highlights for you on what I found today. I e-mailed them over. A few examples from Henry's journal of some action they saw. I would be interested to see what you think when you get the chance."

"Sounds intriguing. Is there something I should look for?" Lillian asked, blowing on her tea.

"I don't know. I might be reading more in to it, which is why I'd like your opinion. A fresh pair of eyes." Hers were a steely blue that still made him hot under the collar. "Better crack on," he said and leant across to retrieve her plate. When he got to the door, he turned to find her watching him. "I'm having trouble finding the record of Henry's death at Waterloo, so I thought I'd visit the Soldiers of Gloucestershire museum tomorrow. Want to come?" She didn't answer straight away, causing him to wish he had said nothing at all. He had not meant it to sound like a date. "It's okay, you are busy, it was just—"

"I'd love to."

"Oh, great. Okay."

Holly chose that moment to announce a new visitor seconds before Nick heard an approaching car with a throaty roar. He glimpsed it through the window. A beautiful Morgan sports car in British racing green.

"Good grief, it's Lady Sylvia." Lillian said from over his shoulder.

"Not *the* Lady Sylvia?"

"You remember her?"

"Fairly eccentric friend of your dad's?"

"He preferred to describe her as dependable, wickedly intelligent, and of her own person. Come on, I might need backup."

Lady Sylvia unfolded herself from the low car with a groan Nick heard from the front door. "They say I should trade it in for a Range Rover," she declared, "but I can't bear to part with it."

"Lady Sylvia, it is good to see you." Lillian met her outside, leaning forward to kiss her cheeks, but Lady Sylvia grabbed her in what Nick could only describe as a skinny bear hug.

"I am so sorry about your father, dear girl. Would have been here for the funeral, but I was stuck in New York with *them*. Can't stay long, only I wanted to bring you this..." She dashed back to the car and retrieved a basket containing an earthenware lidded dish. Delft Blue. "A casserole!" she announced proudly. Then she looked at Nick with a narrow raised eyebrow of approval. "On other thoughts, perhaps I have time for tea." She dangled her arm into his and dragged him into the house. He glanced back at Lillian, who clearly found the situation hilarious, a broad smile on her face, the casserole in her arms.

He mouthed the word "help!"

Traitor that she was, she ignored him.

Settled with tea, Nick asked Lady Sylvia about her trip to New York. "Frightfully dull and sadly only two theatre visits," she informed them. "Do come see me now I am home, Lillian. Bring your handsome friend here with you. I could do with some intelligent company and a pretty face about the place." Nick got the distinct impression he only qualified as the later in Lady Sylvia's opinion.

"I can't remember the last time I was at Woodcombe Hall," Lillian said. Nick remembered his. He had taken Olivia there during a visit to his parents one summer. The grounds were spectacular.

"Place needs some love and care. I have ideas for some building work, but finding someone to share my vision has been difficult," she said.

"Something you could help with?" Nick asked Lillian.

"Of course!" Lady Sylvia went wide eyed. "Your father always boasted about how you were the best architect in the country! Say you will come take a look for me?"

"She *is* the best," Nick agreed. He didn't know if this was strictly true, but a sudden part of him would be happy for any excuse to have Lillian stay longer.

"Well, I don't know about that," she gave Nick a glare, cheeks reddening in a humble way he found charming. "But I would be happy to come discuss your ideas."

He could tell the idea was growing on her. Nearby Woodcombe Hall was the largest stately home for miles. Getting her hands on it, in the architectural sense, he was sure would be not only an honour, but a treat.

"Fabulous!" Lady Sylvia exclaimed with a cheeky wink at Nick, which he didn't know whether to label as flirtatious or conspiring. "Now, sadly I must dash, I'm playing golf with that bozo Ambrose at three."

Lillian gave a nod of sympathetic understanding.

Outside, Lady Sylvia lowered herself into the car and gave them a wave, spinning the wheels on the gravel as she left.

"Your father has interesting taste in friends," Nick said.

"Like father, like daughter," Lillian said, waving as the car disappeared out of sight.

Returning to the study, Nick scratched his head, trying to find the journal he had been working on. He was sure he had placed it right in front of him on the desk. He searched under stacks of documents, finding a note of Alistair's that caught his eye.

Diary of my grandfather c1944 - I fell from the window. Angel?

Nick shivered. This was why he loved the past. What did Alistair mean by angel? What happened? Accepting the sidetrack, he searched for the journals covering 1944 and an hour of reading later found the page he was looking for.

The house, at times, bustles and rings with the noise of Alistair playing. Other times it is stark, bare, and lonely. I find myself thinking of Jonathan and what horrors he must have faced on the continent. They must surely echo those I experienced myself in the last war. The newspapers are full of stories of the courageous men and the battles they endure.

With Helena and little Alistair, one has to put on a

brave face. Some days I find this easy, other days when the house is quiet, it is the hardest thing to do. If I do not keep busy, then I see that telegram boy making his way up the driveway again, like the day he brought us news of Jonathan, those lines of beech heralding death.

Once again, war has taken so many of Ashlington's boys from us. Mrs Hopkins lost both her sons, and the very thought of the Taylor girl out there working in the nursing stations is almost incomprehensible.

Alistair is truly his father's boy, intelligent and brave. Only yesterday he fell from the nursery window. I was in the garden and saw him fall. Fearing the worst, I rushed over to the boy, who was, by some miracle, unharmed. "The red angel caught me, Grampy," he said.

Like an actual angel? Whatever—whoever—it was, had caught adult Alistair's attention, too. Had he remembered the incident, and this sparked his interest in the research?

***

Marcus showed little interest in how Lillian spent her days at Ashlington while he remained in London. It came as a surprise, therefore, when he called on the only day she didn't want him to know what she was doing. Not that there was anything wrong with accompanying Nick to the museum in Gloucester. Even so, she told Marcus she was going shopping with a friend. He had replied with a predictable comment about how it might be good for her to get out and about, moving on and all that.

She glanced across to the passenger seat of her Mini where Nick sat, fists clenched on his knees. "You could have driven."

"It's fine," he said with a sharp intake of breath at a late lane change she made approaching a roundabout. "Just how many speeding fines have you had?"

Lillian happily contemplated leaning over, opening his door, and pushing him out. "There was plenty of room."

"Erm Lily," he pointed out of the window to their missed exit. "That was the exit. Back there."

She orbited the roundabout, finding the correct exit, and two junctions later took another wrong turn, which led them through a slow moving traffic jam. Ten minutes of Nick sighing and judging her navigation skills later, they arrived at the docks. Lillian reversed at speed into a narrow parking spot and glared at him.

He smiled, disarming her completely.

Two white sphinx statues guarded the entrance to the museum, which occupied the old red-brick customs house. Nick gave one a pat on the head as they passed. Lillian expected he would have some magic archaeologist's pass that would allow him free access to museums, like a Blue Peter badge, but he paid the entrance fee for them both. She took a ten-pound note from her purse and shoved it deep into the pocket of his jeans, unsure what the resulting expression on his face meant, but she rather enjoyed the squeak he emitted.

She followed Nick at a slow pace, getting equally lost in the stories on display ranging from the present day and service in Afghanistan to the roots of the regiments, including Henry's 28th, in their many forms.

"It makes me wonder what Henry would think, if it were his thoughts on display for the world to read?" Nick said, peering into a display case of donated Victorian items. "When you think about it, he was writing for himself, making sense of things, you know. He didn't write of regimental manoeuvres or the intricacies of battles, he wrote about what he found important, his friends. How could any of them imagine their letters to loved ones or journal entries would end up here?"

It seemed a gentle thing for a man that dug up dead bodies for a living to think. Lillian wondered if he made this sort of connection with them too, or was it just Henry and his attachment to Ashlington that stirred the sensitive side of Nick? "Are you having second thoughts?"

"No, I only hope I do them justice. It's not just his story, is it? The others he writes about, it is their story too."

"You don't think he would want us to know about Westbrook, Sinclair, and the others? If you ask me, I think he would be proud to see their deeds and stories told. Agreed he would be thoroughly embarrassed having himself described as a hero, but not Westbrook and his men. I think he would want everyone to know about them. I, for one, want to hear more of their exploits. They bring him to life, you know?"

Nick looked unconvinced.

"I trust you, Nick. I'm sure if he knew you, Henry

would too." They had paused their meanderings to look into a glass case showcasing medals from the campaign in Egypt. "What is it with Egypt, anyway? You said the battle cry of Henry's regiment mention it?"

"That battle—in 1801—is why the 28th wear a back badge. The only regiment to do so. The rear rank were told to about face and fire volleys at the cavalry that had broken through the line and come at them from the rear during the Battle of Alexandria," Nick explained. "Here." He pointed her towards a plaque that explained the regiment's part in the battle and went back to taking photographs. "It was quite the unique manoeuvre."

Something else had caught Lillian's eye. A beautiful gold pocket-watch with a large white dial. The curators of the museum had placed a mirror behind it so guests could view the front of the case and the intricate worn engraving of a leopard's head with leaves coming out of its mouth. "Nick, there is mention of Sinclair here."

Nick remained engrossed in photographing. The card explaining the next display led Lillian's eyes up to the wall, upon which hung the unmistakable brush strokes of Major Theodore Sinclair. It was a far smaller painting than the one of Henry that hung in Ashlington, but similar in composition. More like a photograph of the subject; an image captured in time and mood.

The officer looked like he had shared a joke with Sinclair. A friendly smile, the deep dimples giving him a boyish cheekiness. But there was something else there to— pride. He fit the uniform well, the shallow slope of his shoulders hinting that he carried responsibility, but did so with confidence. Or was it contentment? A man who had everything he needed. She wondered if he knew he would end up hung in a museum for all to see such an intimate bond between artist and subject. Would she want to be immortalised in such a way? She supposed it would depend on who was doing the immortalising.

This character looked comfortable being drawn, unlike Henry in his painting, who looked decidedly distressed about the ordeal. Did this man have a different relationship with Sinclair? It was hard to draw her attention away from him, but when she did, she noticed displayed below more sketches of the same officer and others, in differing circumstances, dating back to beyond the campaign in Egypt.

She grabbed at Nick's sleeve, pulling him towards her. "I didn't realise Sinclair was in Egypt."

"Yes, Henry wrote of it. Adams was there too, remember. And Westbrook's father."

"He was talented with oils, that's for sure, but I almost prefer the sketches. They are rawer," she said. More intimate, she thought. "My grandfather and my great grandfather served. Dad always said Henry inspired them to answer the call. I guess it is why the painting has hung at Ashlington for so long."

When she emerged from the museum some hours later, the sun had warmed, yet the world seemed noisier and brasher than she had left it. People darted along the footpaths, going about their business, ignorant of the sacrifices detailed within the stone walls of the museum.

She took out her phone and began searching for restaurants with vegan options on the menu, waiting for Nick, who had begun a conversation with the lady on the till.

"Sorry, I got talking with the curator about records," he said when he emerged ten minutes later. "I told them what we were doing, mentioned the Sinclair. It's only of a James Westbrook. That's Robert Westbrook's father."

"No!"

"He died in Egypt during that campaign. They have some of Sinclair's letters and agreed to send me copies. I know it is a bit of a sidestep, but there might be mention of Henry too."

He looked so excited that Lillian put her arm around him and told him to smile for a selfie with the museum as a backdrop. "We haven't changed a bit," she said, reviewing the image. They had, of course. Not the smiles or the eyes, but everything else showed the 'mileage' as Indiana Jones would put it. Had she wasted all that time?

He leaned towards her so he could see the screen. "Not in the slightest," he agreed with equal sarcasm, linking his arm into hers. "Now, I know you are dying to take me to lunch. I presume you have found somewhere suitably expensive? That Greek place looked promising."

"Dream on, Hawkins. I thought we'd share a cone of chips," she teased.

The meal she shared two days later with a different

man did not start as relaxed. Lillian and Guy met halfway, her suggestion of Guy visiting Ashlington declined. He offered brunch in Oxford as a compromise to coincide with an appointment with the client they had been working for when her father died.

She arrived late and found Guy drumming his fingers on the table. Thankfully, the restaurant he had chosen seemed quiet. Too early for lunch goers and what few were there for brunch, ate and drank quietly around them, locked in their own conversations.

"Sorry, finding a parking spot was horrendous," she said, taking the seat opposite. He took off his glasses, folded the arms with care and placed them next to his wallet, giving Lillian the impression she was in trouble. He had dressed casually for him; bright checked trousers and a black turtleneck that suited his long sideburns. It made him look younger than ten years her senior.

"I've only been here five minutes, it's fine." He handed Lillian a menu and, without giving her time to peruse it in any detail, beckoned the server. She made a pressured decision and ordered a safe sounding salad.

"I didn't mind covering you for a few weeks Lillian, but really, isn't it time you came back and got on with your life again? We have missed you," Guy said as soon as the server turned away.

"You sound like Marcus," she told him, straightening the cutlery of her place setting for want of something to do with her hands.

"That is because, for once, Marcus is on to

something."

"I'm not ready."

He studied her down his long nose, then his attention turned to the returning server who offered a bottle of white wine. Despite Lillian's insistence that she wouldn't drink because she was driving, Guy made a show of sucking in air as he tasted it, nodded with approval, then told the server to charge both glasses. The bottle was left close by in an ice bucket.

"Have you considered that you never will be ready if you keep hiding in the country?"

"You think I'm hiding?"

"It's the easy thing to do, isn't it? The sentimental thing." He picked up the small jar containing a tea light from the centre of the table. A simple decoration, out of place in the bold, brightly coloured seventies aesthetic of the restaurant. He tipped the jar from side to side, causing the tea light to slip and spill its wax.

Lillian considered his question and concluded that she did not entertain it at all. The easy thing would be to return to London and her predictable routine. Deep inside her, though, something sparked. A surprising flame of desire to stay at Ashlington that she hadn't realised was there until now.

"I need to do what is right for me, and at the moment that is to continue taking the leave I have booked until I am ready to come back or to take another route."

"What other route? Have you been talking to Colin? That slimy—"

"No! It's nothing to do with Warrilow." She hadn't wanted to broach the subject with him yet, but the last thing she needed was him assuming Colin Warrilow from a rival firm was poaching employees. "I was thinking of setting up my own business back at Ashlington and having local clients in the Cotswolds." She felt Guy watching her as she pushed away the glass of wine she had not asked for.

"Sure, we could ponder adding a rustic branch to the company, but I didn't spend all those years developing your talent for you to waste it on barn conversions."

"It's not about barn conversions, it is about having my own business. A friend of my father's has asked me to look at some work on her property. It is something I would love to get involved with."

Colour drained from his face, which looked on blankly as the server delivered their meals. Eventually, with slow deliberate moves, Guy unfolded his napkin and draped it across his lap before acknowledging Lillian again. "Your own business?" His very tone suggested the ridiculous.

She nodded, unable to help the nervous churn of her stomach. Guy had been her mentor from the minute she arrived at the firm, even before she had got involved with Marcus. It made her feel special to have the boss take a particular interest in her work and in her as a person. She allowed Guy to mould her in to the creative talent she became. His shock was understandable and made her feel disloyal.

"Where is this coming from, Lillian?" he said. "You can't just walk away after all that I have done for you. You have responsibilities to the company. What does Marcus think of all this?"

"He doesn't know yet."

The following silence only served to make her want to prove to him that she was perfectly capable of deciding her own path.

"He wants me to sell Ashlington," she continued. "The week after I buried my dad, he sent an auctioneer to the house, calling me Mrs Johansen with a list of things to value. He wants me to deal with my father's death in the same way he would. He does not seem to understand I am not the same as him."

"You know Marcus," Guy laughed. "He would have just been trying to help. He wants you to move on, get back to London and put all this behind you. Get on with that wedding you have been avoiding. He is just being protective."

"I've not been avoiding it."

"The two long years you have been engaged for might disagree with you. If you stopped being so sickeningly compassionate about it, you would ditch him. I love Marcus like a brother, but he is not what you need, and you know that deep down or you would have a wedding ring on that finger. But he is right about getting back to London."

London, where she was a mere buoy on the ocean, slave to the tether beneath. It had been her drive to prove herself to her father that kept her in London. Now he was gone. "I'd never expect you to understand."

Guy dropped his knife and fork down on his plate with

a clatter and pushed it away.

"You think you are the only one to lose someone? You have no idea, Lillian." His words stung like a whip. His wife had left him. Hardly the same thing.

She glanced around the restaurant, relieved that the other diners, sat engrossed in their own conversations, paid their raised voices no attention. Guy wiped his mouth with his napkin, slapped it down next to his glass and took a breath which seemed to suck the air from the room.

"I'm sorry, Guy," she said, defending her insensitivity. He looked hurt. Guy stared into the tea light flame. It flickered and faltered, its life almost extinguished.

"I never told you what happened to my sister, did I? It was a long time ago," he said, blowing the candle out. "A home fire. She was eight. It killed her. My point is that you have to carry on and get back to your life." For a moment she allowed him to draw her in, a vulnerable moment shared over the spiralling grey wisps of candle smoke. Then she remembered how he always used a brief story, true or otherwise, a nugget of wise experience to get a point across and guide her towards a different outcome.

"Marcus told you Warrilow is interested in your house, didn't he?"

"He did."

"It is a sound business proposition. I have looked at it myself. You'd be a fool not to consider it."

The main course arrived, the large plate placed in front of her like a challenge. The challenge she needed to focus on, however, was getting Guy back on side.

"I will look at it. I have been a bit distracted by this project of my father's."

"Your inheritance tax won't pay itself, Lillian. But, consider this instead. You say you want your own business. Did Marcus mention Claudia is leaving? Selling out."

"Claudia's selling her share in the business? What on earth for? She has it all."

"Something to do with family, blah blah, but that's not what matters. What matters is you could buy her stake. I know you, Lillian, better than you know yourself. You are smart and ambitious. Think on it. A partnership with Marcus and I. It is what you dreamed of."

"I don't know what to say." Filling Claudia's shoes, having more say over the direction of the company, her name on the letter head and the construction signage. It *was* what she had always wanted.

"Just say you will think about it."

It began raining as Lillian pulled into the village of Ashlington. By the time she drove up the driveway, large puddles had formed in the gravel and the windscreen wipers were barely coping with the intensity.

She parked as close to the door as she could and, with her jacket over her head, made a dash for the porch. As she turned to close the heavy front door behind her, she felt the cold gather around her shoulders, the damp mist of longing. "I only want my home," the voice said. She banged the door shut on the lines of the plunging deluge, wishing she could shut the voice out too.

She made her way directly to the kitchen, where she searched the drawer for the number of her father's local doctor. Whatever she decided about the house, it was time to ask for help.

Chapter 11

Spain, July 1811

It has been four years, Henry. Do you not think that is long enough? I have spoken to Mr Smalley and discovered that the youngest Smalley girl is still available. If you come home this summer, then I can still salvage a decent marriage for you.

I have written to your commanding officer informing him of the situation. There should be no loss of whatever honour you think you owe your regiment by resigning.

It would also make your mother happy.

I expect your next communication with news of your return at the earliest.

Your father,

ND

A string of lewd words left the newly promoted Captain Henry Durand's mouth.

"Hmm?" Westbrook enquired from where he lay contorted on his bed with one leg propped up against the wall, the other crossed over it; frozen in the bizarre position, utterly lost to the contents of Henry's latest gift, Shakespeare's *Julius Caesar.*

Billeted on the top floor of a farmhouse within a

village now home to two regiments, the two officers had retreated to their room to escape the heat of the midday sun. Having read his father's letter, the attic felt oppressive and pungent, despite the holes in the roofing.

"Read that." Henry snatched the book off his friend, replacing it with the letter. Westbrook's eye scanned the ink as Henry resumed pacing.

"For the love of God, will you sit down for one minute," Westbrook said, arranging himself to a regular sitting position to give the letter his full attention.

Henry sat as directed, leg bouncing with frustration.

"You would prefer to marry Louisa?"

"Louisa? No!" Henry snatched the letter back. "Don't you see?" he exploded. "I don't want to marry any of them!"

He fled the attic, boots clattering down the stairs, disturbing the officers slumbering below. Someone slung a tankard at him.

"Corporal Young!" he bellowed once outside.

"Sir?" Young said from behind him.

"I want the men formed up for an inspection in five minutes. Here in the yard."

Overflowing with impatience, Henry paced while he waited for them, then proceeded to pick fault in every man as they stood sweating in the prickly heat reflected by the pale walls of the farm. He even picked fault in Adams, with whom he actually found none.

About to launch into a tirade about how they were the lousiest company in the regiment he felt, rather than saw, Westbrook appear at his side.

"Shall I take the company for musket drill?"

Young practically sighed with relief. Private Cotton looked close to passing out.

"Yes, Lieutenant," Henry said, voice hoarse with all the shouting and feeling somewhat relieved himself. "I want every man firing three rounds to the minute," he added to save face. "Not two. Not two and a half-cocked ram-rod. I want a steady three."

"Yes, sir," Westbrook said calmly. "The shady spot we used yesterday, Corporal."

Young gave orders for the company to march, and they left the square with the rhythmic pounding of well-drilled boots.

Henry shook his head and ran a hand through his hair, disappointed at his lack of self-control, more so for taking out his frustrations on his company. Westbrook said nothing. He took a spare musket from a stack and followed the men. Henry went in search of Sinclair and damage limitation.

He found the major behind a desk of paperwork in the farmhouse, looking as miserable about it as Henry would be to find himself desk bound.

"I have received a letter from your father, Durand. He wants you home to be married."

Henry swallowed a colourful response that questioned his father's paternity. To Sinclair he said, "I will not be going home, Major."

"Splendid. Glad to hear it," Sinclair said. "Easy enough to put your wife on a boat, get her rooms in Lisbon, perhaps."

"What? No, there will be no wife. I am not going home, nor am I getting married." He added a further "sir," belatedly.

"I get the impression that will not please your father. He has hopes for you." Sinclair's blue eyes studied him.

Hopes that do not take into consideration what I want, Henry thought. "His hopes are—just that. They are his hopes." The hopes of one that might cage a wild animal and take joy in its confined misery.

"A good marriage might be just what you need."

"I don't see your wife here," Henry snapped, then immediately wished he had learnt to shut the hell up.

Sinclair stood.

There was no wife. There never had been. Only his duty to his regiment and his dead friend's children. Henry braced himself, but the deserved word whipping did not occur. Instead, Sinclair growled a low, "Get out!"

Henry found the company by following the noise. He snatched a musket and fistful of cartridges from Young, who had been timing the rounds shot. He gave Young a nod, bit at a cartridge, loaded and fired, repeating the process twice more before Young declared the minute. Not bad for a first effort, considering it had been several weeks since he had fired a musket. The act of loading calmed his temper. There were nods of approval among the ranks. Then he handed Westbrook the weapon.

Westbrook took it reluctantly. "Are you trying to embarrass me?" he asked Henry with his back to the company. "I'm too slow since I lost my eye."

"Missing eye or not, I know you are more than capable of firing four in the dark with your arms tied behind your back. Show them."

Westbrook stared at him, then stripped off his coat and rolled up his sleeves.

"The lieutenant means business," someone joked.

"Ready with the time, Corporal?" Henry asked cheerfully.

"Ready, Captain."

Westbrook took a breath, nodded to Young, and began. He fired four rounds and had just spat a fifth ball into the muzzle when Young called time, just as Henry knew he would.

Henry led the cheer for their one-eyed lieutenant, patted him on the back, then went to write a reply to his father.

Staying with the regiment.
Apologies to Mr Smalley.
HD

Seeing the words on paper finally, felt like a weight had been lifted. Staying with the regiment felt right. He had made his decision and his father, no matter how enraged, would have to deal with it.

In contrast, that winter in the peninsula began cruelly. Officers and ranks alike felt its bitter fingers clutching at them and their empty bellies. Food had been scarce the last few weeks for the Slashers as they moved towards French held territory. Their march slowed and spirits were low. At night, they huddled in groups with simple bivouacs made from their packs and blankets.

One such night, despite his tendency to run hot, even Westbrook's teeth chattered in his head where he sat sandwiched between Henry and Corporal Young, the trio doing their best to share their collective warmth.

"If you could be anywhere else right now, where would you be?" Westbrook mumbled, in Henry's opinion sounding most unimpressed that he too felt the cold for once.

"Nestled in the ample bosoms of Nelly O'Connell," Young said before Henry could answer the question he presumed Westbrook aimed at him. Henry leaned forward to see a look of satisfied recollection on Young's dirt-smudged face.

"Is she your girl, Young?" he asked before blowing into his cupped hands, then shoving them under his armpits again.

"From back home, aye, I have a mind to ask her to wed me when this is all done."

Henry admired his optimism.

"And you, sir?"

"Me? A girl? No."

This prompted a strange noise from Westbrook.

"Louisa is not my girl. How many times do I have to tell you?" Henry complained. Then continued louder for Young's benefit. "As to where I would rather be right now, why just sat here with you two fine gentlemen. What more could a man wish for?" This caused Westbrook to shake with suppressed laughter. But Henry did not intend it to be so amusing. He meant it.

Sat here on the freezing cold ground with those he trusted his life to was far preferable to being at Ashlington with his family. "Glorious weather, a blanket fit for a king, strong chance of lice, and a diet that ensures I need a new belt hole each year. No, you can keep your warm comfortable beds," Westbrook groaned as Henry continued, "your pheasant in port sauce and my particular favourite, potatoes mashed in butter. Our cook back at Ashlington, makes it the best, always puts in melted—"

"Oh Christ, stop!" Westbrook complained, giving Henry a jab in the ribs. "Wish I'd never asked."

They fell silent again, Henry's thoughts tumbling to Ashlington and Louisa. What would she be doing now? She had mentioned Danny many times, so she still spent time at the manor. Had she found someone to make her happy? The rumble of Young's snoring, no doubt dreaming of Nelly O'Connell, brought Henry back to the freezing reality he sat in.

"What about you, West?" Henry whispered, so not to disturb their sleeping corporal.

"I'm right where I belong," Westbrook said, leaning his head back against the tree.

Henry pulled the blanket tighter and rested his head on Westbrook, allowing the gentle rise and fall of his friend's shoulder to lull him to sleep.

The following morning, they rejoined the main column as it swung towards Almendralejo with orders for a small force to detach and take a seemingly insignificant town to the south. Perched on a low rocky outcrop, the town held a small garrison of French. The cannons were an unexpected welcome. Henry counted two, but for their minor attack, any dalliance could prove fatal. It was why getting to the guns quickly would be critical. Controlling the attack from the ridge, Sinclair gave Henry the left flank. A test Henry relished.

"Private Jackson, did I tell you about the time the lieutenant lost his eye?" Henry asked as he weaved between the two lines of soldiers.

"Amorous gypsy lady, wasn't it?" Jackson replied.

"Nah, I heard it was one of them big black crows," Adams offered. "Flew right up to him and pecked it out."

Henry had to admit that was one of his favourite versions of the tall tales he span at Westbrook's expense. "And what did the lieutenant do?" Henry asked, putting his hand on the shoulder of the most nervous looking boy.

"He held the line, sir," the boy said, straightening his shoulders.

"He held the line," Henry agreed. "Gentlemen, let's get this over with." The company received his words with an impatient jeer, the boy now joining in enthusiastically. "Hold the line like you always do, and 28th..."

"Remember Egypt!" the men cheered their battle cry with gusto as smoke from the guns filled the air.

"We'll hold, sir," Young confirmed, speaking for them

all.

Henry grinned down the line at Westbrook.

But would the right? Westbrook's tilt of head asked.

The company holding the right flank, with their new captain, the aptly named Newton, was untested. Rumour had it the well-connected Newton purchased his way quickly up the promotional ladder and before setting foot in the Peninsula had never held a sword. Newton's men looked jittery at best.

The bugle sounded the advance. Henry sent a silent prayer aimed between Westbrook's shoulders, that his friend would be protected through whatever came next, and stepped in front of the line to lead the march forward.

The Slashers proved time and time again that they would hold no matter what the French threw at them, but only a hundred yards in to the advance the right flank's hesitancy became a problem. When a well-aimed cannon-shot hit their front rank, tearing a hole through to the rear as it bounced through the men, they didn't close up. They stupidly stood staring at the destruction while musket fire picked them off.

"Get your bloody men moving!" Henry shouted across to Newton, who had turned his back to the town and inexplicably dropped his sword.

He heard Westbrook call out to his own men out on the far left, releasing sharpshooters to take care of the French skirmishers taking potshots from the woodland. Without doubt Henry knew that as long as he had air in his lungs, Westbrook and the left would hold.

Which was more than could be said for the right flank by then in tatters, their line broken with a handful of men running back towards the ridge. One of Newton's sergeants waved at their men frantically, trying his best to rally them as he pushed and shoved them back into formation. Newton himself stood still, confused by the whole affair.

"Damn him!" Henry yelled with frustration as Sinclair's bugle urgently repeated the advance. Leaving his position, Henry ran for Newton, picked up his sword and forced him to grip it.

"Forward!" he called over his shoulder at the shrivelling ranks. Then shouted it again, together with a great deal of spittle, in Newton's face to prevent himself from punching the fool. He roared once more, encouragement this time, at the sergeant doing his utmost to keep control of Newton's men, only for the man to jerk backwards and fall dead in the dirt. This released the rear rank to run.

Henry looked down the line to Westbrook. *It's over,* Henry's shake of the head said. *We have to retreat.*

The bugle agreed.

Not your fault, Westbrook's small shoulder raise replied.

He didn't like it, but with the right flank reduced to a bumbling mess and their already impossibly small numbers halved, there was nothing to be done. They began their slow march backwards, rewarded with more cannon fire and taunting from the French at the town gate.

Henry's attention remained focused on the men and

keeping what remained of Newton's line moving. To his left he checked his own company, his head swivelling constantly, watching for signs more might run. He needn't have worried. To the man, they wore the frustration and disappointment etched on their faces, in both their fellows and the shame of retreat. Every step heavy with reluctance.

Henry felt the mortification down to his core. More than anything, he wanted to prove to Sinclair that his faith had been justified. He dreaded seeing the same disappointment on Sinclair's face as his father would wear.

Something stung Henry's thigh, causing him to stumble. He reached for the wound, felt the heat and wetness of blood. No sooner had he congratulated himself on his good fortune for only taking a leg wound than he fell backwards; punched by an explosion of earth sods and stone. His head hit something hard.

His vision blurred, and a distinct whine in his ears made him blink his eyes and shake his head repeatedly. Had that been a cannon shot? Everything hurt. Was this the end? he thought with a sudden sense of dread. Henry's concern rapidly shifted to Westbrook, and how his friend would handle his demise. Would he be angry that Henry had left him alone? Who would buy his books now? He hadn't managed to find him a copy of *Hamlet* yet!

Newton's face stared at him in slack surprise before darkness seeped into the edges of what little Henry could see and the world collapsed.

When Henry opened his eyes again, Newton was moaning. Henry shifted to find he had hit his own head on a rock in the fall. The back of his neck felt wet and sticky. He reached for Newton, the other captain in a far worse condition having received a massive open wound to the bowels.

Henry heaved, spitting out yellow bile.

Unaware of how long he had been on the ground for, as he crawled to help Newton, he checked on the progress of the line looking for Westbrook's outline. He found him, unmistakable in his stance on the skyline, amongst a faltering retreat. He watched as Westbrook and Young flailed, looking around them. What could they be searching for?

"Go!" Henry bellowed, scrambling to his feet. He fell, his leg unable to support his weight, so resorted to waving his sword at the idiots. The surrounding ground erupted in musket fire, attracted by his movement. "Retreat God damn it, West!" *What the bloody hell was he doing?* To make things worse, another pack of French voltigeurs had emerged from the gate, no doubt the talented devils the source of the wound to his leg.

In an act of incomprehensible dumb foolhardery, Westbrook began running forwards. Henry collapsed, flabbergasted as the whole God damned line came running after him, roaring collectively like a hoard of savages. Westbrook arrived alongside with an idiotic look of pride on his face. The men overtook them and charged the French like the devil and his hell hounds were after them. Following them came a great deal of Newton's men joining in with the battle cry of the Slashers.

"What the hell are you doing, West?" Henry asked, angrily trying to shake off his help.

"You should know full well by now—" Westbrook said, heaving Henry up off the ground, "if our captain doesn't retreat—neither do we."

Westbrook reached out, stopping a lad slowed by a leg wound he received during their last skirmish. Cotton was also the youngest in the company, having just turned fifteen. "Cotton. Take the captain to the rear. Ensure Mr Evans sees to him. You make sure he does, got that?"

"Yes, sir," Cotton stuttered.

Westbrook shifted Henry's weight onto the boy before straightening his eyepatch and retrieving his sword, then set off after the company; any loss of confidence since losing his eye forgotten.

Henry resisted leaving without Newton. With Henry's own injuries rendering carrying the man impossible, they dragged him hideously. It would have been more merciful to shoot him. Once out of range of enemy fire, Henry turned and refused to move any further, much to the horror of Cotton, who might have feared his one-eyed lieutenant more than the French.

Henry watched, gripping tightly to his sword hilt. Westbrook had already caught up to the company and forced his way to the front. The sudden rush of the British took the French by surprise and though they tried to close the gate, by the time they realised what was happening they had not only lost their plucky voltigeurs but were too slow to get the gate closed. A strange mixture of regret, pride, but mostly helplessness overcame Henry as he watched his company pour into the town. Shortly after, the guns ceased firing.

"Be safe," Henry mumbled.

A low grumble of approval made him aware of the major, who watched the fight from only a few metres away. "That's my boy!" Sinclair whooped from astride his horse as the French flag lowered. He slid his telescope shut with a satisfied nod before returning to a more commanding tone to send his runner back to the regiment. "The town is ours. The 28th never forget, eh? You turned the fight Durand. Very well done," he said with a smile, then kicked back his heels, sending his mount cantering down the ridge towards the town.

"Sir?" Cotton gestured from beside Henry. "The surgeon?"

"No!" Henry snapped. "I'll wait for them. Take Newton."

Cotton didn't. Instead, he delegated the task to some walking wounded and positioned himself a few feet behind Henry, out of range of his captain's failing temper.

The ability to do anything with the good grace of patience was not something Henry ever felt equipped for, but he stood leaning on Cotton's musket on the ridge, barking orders until the sun set and they had collected the wounded from the field.

It was not until he caught sight of Westbrook emerging from the gate that he let the ground take him. Whatever force had been keeping him upright, utterly spent. Closing his eyes, he surrendered to the pounding in his head.

He woke only a few moments later to hear an indignant, deep voice chastising Cotton. "What is he still doing here? I thought I ordered you to take him to Mr Evans?"

"I tried, sir. But ..."

"Yes, I know," Westbrook said, giving Henry a side stare. "Go find Corporal Young in the town. He needs assistance with the prisoners." Westbrook gave the boy a hearty clap to the back that made him sway in his boots. Cotton left at a trot.

"As for you, you pig-headed Durand ..." he said, heaving Henry off the ground. Henry staggered as the sudden movement made his ears ring. He grabbed for the solidness of his friend. Westbrook leant his head on Henry's shoulder for a breath, then took Henry's face in his hands, moving it from side to side, inspecting him for the source of the blood matted in his hair.

"Did you see them?" he asked, apparently satisfied his captain would live after all. "They turned back for you."

"You turned them back, West. That was all you."

"It's about time you promoted Young. He'd already taken that first gun by the time I caught up." Westbrook's voice then changed. "I thought I'd lost you." The bottomless single eye scanned Henry for an instant, then with a grunt he lifted Henry off the ground and over his shoulder.

"I don't need the bloody surgeon," Henry groaned as the blood rushed to his head.

Westbrook deposited him minutes later in the surgeon's stinking excuse for a tent, angry, squirming, and threatening disciplinary action for Westbrook's blatant defiance of orders. Having poked at Henry's scalp and held his eyelids open forever, the surgeon did nothing more than wrap his throbbing head in bandages to match his leg and order him to lie down.

Henry did no such thing. He paced, offering what little comfort he could. Newton did not last the hour and died holding on to Henry's hand, whimpering about home and duty. Shortly after, Henry deemed it prudent to slip away, lest he lose an appendage to the surgeon's enthusiastic sawing. He dismissed the open tent flap where Mr Evans lurked, instead wriggling under the edge nearest to him.

There he found Westbrook curled asleep on the cold ground. Arms wrapped around Henry's hat and sword, an unopened bottle of port he likely liberated from the town still stuffed inside his bloodstained coat.

Chapter 12

Ashlington, April 2015

"Tell me about the voices."

"Just one. It sounds like my father. Is that normal?"

"More common than you would think, subconscious manifestation," the doctor said. "Our brains are very good at protecting us. Think of it as a defensive mechanism."

"So I'm not schizophrenic then?"

"Have you had anything like this happen before?"

"No, never."

"Then I am sure, under the circumstances, we can rule that out. I'll take your blood pressure while you are here. Losing someone can be stressful."

The cuff squeezed Lillian's arm painfully. Hardly comfortable, it always felt a contradictory process.

"Yes, a little high. I can prescribe you something to help with sleeping. That will help with everything else. Rest is important. Let's see how you get on for a couple of weeks." She typed on her keyboard, and the printer next to her sprang into life. "Here are some resources that might help, but know that it will be hard work before it gets easier." She handed Lillian a list of websites. As Lillian looked down the list, the doctor continued with talk of the effectiveness of breathing exercises and a strong suggestion to try meditation.

Was this it? Lillian thought, disappointed there was not some magic bereavement pill she could take to make it all go away. She walked out with the prescription for the sleeping pills and a follow- up appointment, feeling rather underwhelmed.

Old houses like Ashlington Manor creak and groan with the slightest of draughts. Floorboards moaning as the temperature changed, while the ancient oil central heating system bangs and clatters in league with the plumbing. During the day Lillian hardly noticed, but at night she slept, fidgeting with troubled dreams, the noises of the house brought to life by its past. Footsteps along the hall, the creak of a floorboard, the low moan of sorrow shared.

She woke abruptly as though arrested from a fall, in the early hours of the morning, to the call of her name. Her hand shook as she reached for the bedside lamp, knocking off the bottle of sleeping pills she had been reluctant to use, and switched it on, heart thumping. Again, logic told her she was alone. The illumination of the room confirmed the fact. Her subconscious, however, would not let go of the icy belief there was a presence in the house. A flicker of movement by the window caught her eye, only to be the curtains rippling in the draught from the ill-fitting window frame.

"I won't hurt you," a close voice said, cracking Lillian's nerves.

"That's it!" The doctor's mention of subconscious

manifestation worrying at her.

She didn't want to be hurt.

Picking up her mobile, she dialled the first person she thought of, fighting off the dread of impending descent into the more unstable corners of her mind. What she needed now was an anchor.

Lillian opened the door to him, wrapped in a blanket. He had dressed; jeans and a threadbare grey sweatshirt with a faded Latin logo she recognised from one of his favourite tv shows. He was out of breath as though he had run, but his arrival instantly put her at ease.

"I'm such a berk. Sorry Nick, you shouldn't have to babysit me. I guess I got myself a little freaked out," she said, letting him in. He brushed past her. She caught the scent of mint and, disturbingly, fresh hay.

"Lily, your father died a few weeks ago. Give yourself a break. There was a time you would always ask me for help."

She wanted him to hug her. To hold her in his arms again and whisper into her hair that everything would be okay, but he didn't. He stood there with that awkward teenage look of his. The one she had last seen the day she received her university offer

"What you need is hot chocolate," he did say, striding off to the kitchen. Like mother, like son, Lillian thought, and highly practical. Hot chocolate had always been Janet's answer to a crisis. Peering into the fridge, he gave a whistle. "Oat milk? Am I rubbing off on you?"

"Doesn't seem to do you any harm."

Nick smiled and poured it into two mugs. She passed him the cocoa powder, which he added before warming them in the microwave. With the drinks made, she suggested they move to comfier seating in the lounge. Nick sat down on the opposite end of the sofa, lifting his bare feet onto the centre cushion. She mirrored him and they sat in silence. Which was fine, she decided, since she didn't need conversation. She just wanted him there. She let her body relax, legs tilting to touch his. He didn't move.

"Thanks, Nick, for being here," she said sometime later, reaching behind her to place the empty mug on the side table.

"Any time."

"You might regret saying that." She smiled, sinking deeper into the warm blanket around her shoulders. "It's weird, isn't it? Being back. I spent most of my teenage years desperate to grow up and leave. I don't think I appreciated it back then."

"We were kids," he said with a shrug. "Do kids ever appreciate anything?" He hesitated and shifted in his seat. "It is strange being back. You know, at your father's funeral, I didn't want to talk to you. I had it in my head that things would never be as they used to be, that I wouldn't belong here anymore and that seeing you would make that feel worse."

"So what made you say yes to the project in the end? It wasn't all Olivia's powers of persuasion?"

"I was wrong."

"I'm glad you are back too, Nick."

"You have never asked me about Taylor," he said some time later.

"I never liked to bring it up. I am sorry. I heard about the accident." Who hadn't? The newspapers and internet had been full of the news that Taylor had been killed in a car accident on the way to her latest film premiere. "I sometimes forget you have been through all this." By all this, she meant losing a loved one. She could hardly imagine the beautiful actor sat about in pyjamas with her feet up on the furniture.

"I lost my friend and the mother of my daughter that day."

"Friend?"

"We were never in love, Lily. Olivia was not exactly planned."

"Why did you never marry?" She winced. This was definitely prying territory.

But Nick smiled, as though glad she had asked the question. "Because it was never like that. For either of us."

Lillian could not decide if she felt happier about this revelation or not.

"It was an enormous shock to Taylor, getting pregnant. She thought it would be the end of her career, so I took Olivia to live with me. I even got to hold her first when she was born." He smiled, the corners of his eyes creasing with the movement. "I knew then that she was the most precious thing. That I would do anything to keep her safe."

"That's why you are here?"

"It seemed the best for her education to come back to the UK."

"What about you? When she is settled into uni, or whatever, what will you do then?"

"You know the lecturing I have been doing, well, I have been offered a full-time position."

"That's amazing. Congratulations."

"Let's not get ahead of ourselves. I'm not sure. It would mean less opportunity to work in the field, but I do quite like teaching. Either way, I don't have to decide yet."

But he might stay, Lillian thought. He hadn't said he wouldn't, and she couldn't help wonder if that made things clearer or more complicated.

When Lillian woke around seven, Nick had gone. A lecturing day. He had sent a text message.

N - Hope it goes well with your meeting today. See you tomorrow.

She had a lazy breakfast and walked Holly around the garden before getting ready. Lady Sylvia had invited her to Woodcombe Hall to discuss the restorations. A flood of butterflies clattered around her stomach. She had not felt so excited about a potential design project since her first ever pitch.

Chapter 13

Spain, April 1812

"I told them they had twenty minutes, then we are drilling some musket practice," Westbrook said. He lay on his back, shirtless, on the riverbank, one arm in the air, holding a book above his head. The rest of the company splashed in the river or lay sunning themselves while drying uniforms, in various states of undress scattered along the riverbank.

Twenty minutes of tranquillity it would be then, Henry thought. "How's the water?" he asked, shirking off his coat and shirt.

"Bloody freezing."

He did not exaggerate. Henry washed himself quickly, enjoying the opportunity to rid himself of the grime that had accumulated since the last time he had washed so thoroughly. He could not recall when that had been.

"Good book?" he asked Westbrook, lowering himself down perpendicular to him, the spring sun already drying the water from his skin. Henry shut his eyes, not only on account of the brightness but because they were becoming increasingly untrustworthy around his friend.

"It's the one you found me last week, *Henry V.* I read it years ago when Sinclair first took me in. Always was my favourite." Westbrook turned the page. "Listen to this, it's from where Henry is wooing Katherine," he said, tapping Henry on his chest to get his attention. Then he left his hand there, moving it absently as he read the passage, each circle of a finger a collection of words, the words themselves equally torturous.

"A speaker is but a prater, a rhyme is but a ballad, a good leg will fall, a straight back will stoop, a black beard will turn white, a curled pate will grow bald, a fair face will wither, a full eye will wax hollow, but a good heart, Kate, is the sun and moon, or rather the sun and not the moon, for it shines bright and never changes but keeps his course truly."

Henry opened one eye, checking for dark clouds that might accompany a smiting from God. There were none; just the relentless sun drenching his skin, Westbrook dragging heat through his fingertips, and Henry's increasingly shallow breath. Part of him hoped Westbrook wouldn't notice what he was doing, but someone else might notice, his head—rapidly losing any authority—told him.

"If thou would have such a one, take me..." Westbrook continued, lowering his voice to a gravelly whisper. "And take me, take a soldier. Take a soldier, take a king."

Did he have any idea what he was saying? Henry wanted to ask him. Let alone the horrifying effect it was having? But he asked nothing, only pushed Westbrook's hand away and got to his feet, all but running back to the river, submerging himself this time. The icy swirl around his ears brings with it the sound of his brother's voice telling him, "It is how the world works. They expect men from families like ours to marry well and produce heirs."

He stayed underwater for as long as he could, waiting for the current to wash his soul clean again, then re-surfaced and ordered everyone out with a bad-tempered snarl. Oblivious to his plight the men complained, their promised twenty minutes cut short; being his, they obeyed.

Westbrook had propped himself on his elbow, tapping the book against his chin, watching on with an inquisitive tilt of the head, looking like a hairier, sun-kissed, one-eyed version of a rippling marble statue they had seen in Lisbon.

It is the heat, Henry told himself. The damned Spanish spring heat, luring him out of winter with the sweet song of a trap. What he needed, he decided, was distance from his friend.

"A transfer?" Sinclair laughed, fanning himself with a sketch of what looked like a cannon team. "Good God, Durand, have you had too much sun?"

Henry had left Westbrook in charge of the musket drill. He expected Sinclair would be pleased to see the back of him, given all the names he called him. For his own part, he could not imagine serving under any other officer, but it seemed the only course of action that made sense. Henry now shuffled his feet, feeling quite preposterous under Sinclair's confused scrutiny.

"What makes you think I would let you go?"

"Westbrook can handle the company, sir."

"And what makes you think anyone else would have you?"

Henry's mouth flapped. He honestly hadn't thought

that through.

"Does Robert know you are here?"

"No."

Sinclair sighed and sat back down at his desk. He flicked through some documents, leaving Henry stood there waiting with a bead of sweat tickling its way down his back. Henry was sure Sinclair did it on purpose.

"My problem, Henry, is this," he said finally, leaning back in his chair, the wood creaking with the strain. "Together, you and Robert make a whole decent officer. He is no longer hell-bent on self-destruction, and you have proved yourself as a leader with him at your side repeatedly. If I take one of you away, the other will fall apart. His Majesty's Army needs you two together. We need all the decent officers we can get. You have seen for yourself what happens when they send those milkmaids direct from Horse Guards. So no, I want no more talk of a transfer."

Henry glared at Sinclair, holding in everything he wanted to say, racking his brain in desperation for some other solution. "I heard they need officers to assist the engineers prepare for the storming of the city?" he said eventually when he trusted his voice not to crack. He had not really thought this option through either, but any action felt preferable to more lying around in the sun despising himself. "I'd rather be doing something useful."

Sinclair eyed him for a moment, then said, "go and see Colonel Fletcher. If he wants your assistance before the main event, then he can have it. Otherwise, like the rest of us, you will have to wait until it is our turn. You are dismissed,

Durand."

"Thank you, sir."

He felt Sinclair's disappointment boring into his back.

Wood smoke and darkness shrouded the camp the night of the attack on Badajos. Henry sat by the fire with Young, taking a moment to enjoy a coffee, though it hardly tasted of coffee anymore. He had his suspicions it contained more hare dung than coffee now, but it was hot and wet, and likely his last.

A figure loomed up on them in the gloom, causing Young to take one look at the storm of the approaching Lieutenant Westbrook and clear his throat. "Night, sir," Young said, and before Henry could reply, he had disappeared into the camp.

Henry braced himself.

"Were you even going to tell me?" Without breaking his stride, Westbrook negotiated the camp fire and lifted Henry clean off his stool by the coat collar. "Or were you just going to go off and get yourself killed?" Westbrook's face was less than an inch from Henry's, making him intensely aware of the different shades to the flecks of green in his remaining eye, and how the soul inside was screaming at him.

"Is this about my going with the attack?" Henry forced a smile of innocence. Of course, Westbrook would find out. British soldiers were frightful gossips. The colonel in charge of the engineers had accepted Henry's search for distance. He didn't feel it prudent to tell Sinclair that this involved placement of the ladders during the first wave against the walls. Not as suicidal as volunteering for the forlorn hope itself, but close. As the 28th were held in reserve, Henry thought it the perfect opportunity to go alone and prove several things to himself, not least the type of man he was.

"Well, I'm going with you," Westbrook said matter-of-factly, releasing his hold on Henry but maintaining the proximity and ferocity.

And he wonders why I didn't tell him, Henry thought. Then he used what he considered his most commanding voice. "I need you to remain with the company, West."

"Did I do something wrong?" Westbrook's eye creased. "You have been acting strange for weeks." He grabbed Henry by the elbow which felt like lighting the fuse to a keg of powder.

Henry put all his force, deep from within the swing of his hips, into his fist and sent Westbrook flailing backwards, staggering against the tent. He punched him again in the stomach. Westbrook crumpled, then stood straight and spat blood from his cut lip before looking at Henry, poised to hit him again. Not once did he raise his own arms to defend himself or strike back. Had he done either, Henry would have happily continued.

"Stop pushing me away!"

Henry released the fist he had made and with it the rage of holding himself in check all the God damn while. He placed his other hand on Westbrook's shoulder, left it there for a beat, then turned his back on him.

Two hours later, on the outskirts of the city, the columns gathered, crouched in their trenches with the ladders they would use to scale rubble and walls. Henry instinctively looked for Westbrook. Not having him there felt as strange as he imagined going into battle without a sword might feel. But at least his friend was safe. His own safety was of no matter.

It would not be a straightforward attack, and if the men later went berserk like those that stormed Ciudad Rodrigo, then he was glad Westbrook and the 28th would be out of it. If Henry did not come back, then at least no one would ever know what burned inside. There would be no shame. He would have to hate himself no longer.

Double checking his loaded pistol and grip on the ladder, he looked out towards the wall once more; concentrating on each breath, trying to calm himself, waiting for the call that would propel him forward. He fell inwards, fighting off the fear of what might come.

Piercing this steady absorption, he heard a familiar deep voice say his name. "Durand of the 28th?"

For the love of all things holy, what was he doing here? Henry shut his eyes, hoping he had imagined it.

"He's over there with the ladders," someone said.

Then he was there with a hand on Henry's shoulder, lighting the dark as sure as the sun rose every morning. "You shouldn't be here, West," Henry said, shaking his head.

"I'm right where I belong, remember. Are you going to tell me why you are here? Or is this about your damned stubborn pride again?" Westbrook hissed.

Because I need to prove myself worthy? Because I hoped I wouldn't come back so you never know my secret? "I'm sorry, West," Henry settled for. "What about Sinclair? I cannot believe for a minute he let you come too."

"What he doesn't know won't hurt him. Henry, everyone leaves me. You—"

Someone called for quiet. Westbrook patted Henry's shoulder, then settled himself behind him, one hand on the ladder, his beautiful sword drawn.

Moments later they surged towards the city along their trench, ready to throw themselves against the wall. A hail of fire from the woken French greeted them. They slung everything at the storming British, tearing them apart. Bodies littered the route already, and they hadn't even got the ladders up yet.

With no expertise available to mine under the city, Wellesley was throwing his army against the walls in a brutal battle of attrition. Henry's task was to ensure the ladders among his section of wall remained in place as the force used them to scale the walls. He called out to the men, giving some a helpful push as they set feet on the rungs. Those that fell back down, either repelled by waiting bayonets or muskets, Henry and Westbrook pulled grimly out of the way.

The ladders had to stand. To Henry, it felt like forcing men through the gates of hell itself, only for them to drop at his feet dead, with open eyes asking, 'Why?' One lad, even younger than Cotton, shook as he climbed the ladder so close to the man in front that his head rested on the man's back, blue eyes looking down at Henry like a mirror. A mirror of dread. Another fellow, not much older, had pissed himself; the dark stain down the leg of his trousers clear for all to see as he took his turn. He would not be the last adding to the stench of the attack.

A barrel dropped in front of Henry, its lit fuse spluttering. He didn't see it explode, only the rush of black sky as it flung him through the air like a discarded child's doll. He landed on something soft and staggered to his feet, ears ringing with the ghastly keening of injured soldiers. Reaching to his left where Westbrook should have been, Henry grasped at empty air. A shove from behind pressed him against the wall as more men surged forward to the ladders.

Henry's lungs heaved as he drew breath to call for his friend. Though his lips formed the name, he heard nothing above the buzzing of his ears and the clatter of the surrounding swell. He swiped at his eyes with his sleeve, blinking rapidly to rid himself of the stinging sweat, dust, and smoke that swam in the air. Moving sideways along the wall, he searched for Westbrook, reaching to pick up a struggling fallen soldier by his cross straps only to find him to be Corporal Young. Henry could not fathom what Young thought he was doing with the attack, but dragged the errant corporal to his feet.

"Stand sure, Young!"

Young took station on Henry's right, the gap on his left like an ache in his side.

Where the ladders were placed caused a bottleneck. A narrowing in which men had piled up where they fell, forcing those alive to climb over the wounded and dead just to make ground. It was at the bottom of such a mass of terror that Henry stepped on the hilt of a unique yet familiar sword, illuminated by a burning bale of hay.

He howled; the noise erupting from a guttural place within himself he never knew existed. Dropping to his knees, he began heaving bodies off Westbrook. There must have been six, perhaps ten. Henry wasn't counting. He heard Young grunting with effort next to him as he tried to deflect more from falling on them, but Henry could only focus on his task.

A gruesome task.

Tearing at the men, some of which were still alive, their gaping wounds or partially severed limbs making them scream and fight back, Henry pulled in the sheer desperation of getting to Westbrook before the weight of the fallen overcame him.

The excrement and guts of the dead covered Westbrook. His face, still bruised from where Henry punched him just hours earlier, had swollen and gone a hideous shade of death. His fingers were bloody and gashed where he had lost nails from tearing at the ground. Any lesser man would have given up.

Henry pulled Westbrook free and rolled him over, unsure if he breathed at all. "Don't you dare leave me!" Henry shouted, shaking him. *You promised.*

Hopeless. He was gone.

The darkness blanketed Henry once more.

Then Westbrook gasped like a man that had been underwater for too long, sucking on the free air with an enormous scouring breath—a glorious sound. He clawed at Henry's wrists, each new breath returning a flicker of life.

A flicker of light.

Henry was unaware that the surge had moved up and beyond the walls until Young bent over his bayoneted musket and threw up. The sound of retching, not his own, penetrated Henry's daze, bringing him back to the business at hand. Someone called his name with urgency, ordering him into the fray.

Duty.

"Are you hurt, Young?" Henry called.

"It's nothing." The corporal clasped the top of his arm, blood pouring through his fingers.

"You're a brave man," Henry said, "But I need you to look after Westbrook."

"I can fight!" Young began in protest, attempting to raise his musket. Unable to maintain his grip, it clattered to the ground.

"I know you'd fight with your bare teeth if you had to, but your arm is no good. He has more need of you."

Henry knew sitting out of the action would be the last thing Young would want to do, but he also knew the loyal corporal would not leave Westbrook if he needed him, and that there was no one else Henry would trust with such a precious undertaking. Extracting himself with care from under his friend, Henry pulled his neckcloth off and tightened it around Young's arm, trying hard not to vomit on him.

"I'll see he gets taken to the rear, sir," Young told him.

With duty wrenching at him, Henry picked up his sword, took a deep breath, and scrambled up the closest ladder.

Henry fought his way through the town in a haze, certain his friend would be dead before daylight. Surely no man could survive such a thing. One moment he led a ragtag group of whoever he could find to take a barricaded street, the next he ferociously entered a house to pull pillaging British soldiers out. Much later, he found himself inside a small dwelling, on his knees, in a patch of his own vomit. In spasm next to him lay a French soldier, not yet a man, whose guts were spilling in a shiny pile over his legs. Henry's hands were trying in vain to push the quivering mass back into the wound as the boy groaned for "*Maman*."

"We're going home, West," Henry told the boy in a delirious fog.

Something grabbed at Henry's arm, shaking him. A green-jacketed private of the 95th Rifles, trying to pull him off the Frenchman. Henry refused to let go, so the private shoved him hard, knocking him over. The rifleman then stabbed the French boy in the throat and began pilfering his pockets, the sight of pulsing blood causing Henry to heave again.

He tried to protest, but his bile burnt throat would not allow his voice to work. He tried to follow the private out of the house, but couldn't get to his feet. His legs refused to hold his weight and skittered in the pool of hellbroth, so he slid back down the wall and noticed the seeds of a tremor in his right hand.

Was Westbrook dead now?

The body on the floor had long since stopped moving. Screams from the street penetrated the room, forcing Henry to cover his ears. He watched a shaft of light track along the floor until it was in his eyes. Daylight? Morning? His legs worked this time, though they ached, and he had a cut to his thigh, now scabbed dry, matted with his trousers.

"West?" he called. Only it was not Westbrook but the French boy dead on the floor. *I have to find him*, Henry thought, staggering out of the dwelling into the street onto the blood-soaked cobbles. There were still screams, just fainter now.

"Don't be dead," he said aloud. "We are meant to die together."

Chapter 14

Ashlington, April 2015

Lillian shut her laptop and switched off the tv she had been using as background noise; a repeat of a war film, a favourite of her father's. Until then, she had been unaware of the storm brewing outside but could now hear the battering of the trees, and rain beating the glass of the windows as though many hands demanded entry.

"Bed time," she said to Holly, who didn't look pleased at the prospect. Holly then barked and rushed off to the front door. Lillian followed, not to the door, it being too late for callers, but to the kitchen to put the dishwasher on. In the relative dark, without the kitchen spotlights on, the house felt cold and sad.

In the hall, Holly whined and circled the mat at the front door the way she would wait for Nick to arrive. Pining. That's what the house felt like, as though it had lost something.

It had lost something. Her thoughts rapidly spiralled. It had lost her father. She forced herself to take a deep breath. The doctor had said something about fear being our opposite. "It needs breath to die. Deep breaths. Take a few." Maybe I should also take a pill tonight to help me sleep, she thought.

She showered and had just pulled her pyjamas on when the doorbell rang. Holly barking at the door, this time with excitable urgency.

She checked from the landing to see that the porch light was now on and a familiar tall figure looked up at her, then disappeared into the porch and rang the doorbell again—and again.

"Nick. Stop ringing the flipping bell! Come in out of the rain, is everything all right?" Lillian belatedly tied her dressing gown around her middle, not wanting him to see her comfortable nightwear underneath as she pulled him inside.

"Shhh!" he said, putting a finger on her lips. He swayed. "Don't want Bloody Johan—Mister—What's His Name to hear." He leant his head on the wall and knocked on it as though trying to summon Marcus from the fabric of the house.

"Oh my God, you're plastered!" she said, suddenly unsure of what to do with him.

Luckily, a soft knock at the door and desperate call of, "Dad?" meant she did not have to deal with him alone. Drenched through, Olivia looked devastated. "I'm so sorry, Lillian. Come on, Dad. We need to go home," she said, taking her father in hand.

"I am home!" Nick declared, bending over her as though he were talking to a small child.

"Er, no you aren't, Dad." She looked at Lillian again and mouthed the words, 'I'm so sorry'. Then took her father firmly by the elbow, muttering, "I swear to God, you are so embarrassing," under her breath, steering him back to the door.

Lillian stopped her. "Olivia, it is pouring with rain. You're soaked." She gestured at Nick. "And he looks like he won't make it down the driveway." She helped Olivia steer him around. "We can put him on the sofa and you can take a spare room."

"Are you sure? I don't want to be any bother."

"No bother at all," Lillian said as Nick got increasingly heavy. "Come on, you, to the sofa. That's it."

He fell onto it, curling himself around a cushion, and Olivia covered him with the throw, cuffing tears from her eyes. "Can we leave a light on for him?" she asked. "In case he needs the bathroom."

"Good idea," Lillian said and switched on a lamp. Holly jumped onto the sofa, settling alongside Nick, giving him a peaceful domesticated look, rather than the drunk-on-a-park-bench he had sailed perilously close to.

Olivia shivered.

"I can lend you some dry clothes," Lillian said, inviting her upstairs.

"I'm so sorry, Lillian. He'll hate that you saw him like this."

"Does it happen often?"

"No. Not really. Not to this extent." She looked at the ceiling and corrected herself. "Like this, about once a year."

"That is rather specific. Is it about your mother?"

"You'll have to ask him. He pretends it hasn't happened the following day, though he has never wandered off before."

"He only came here. It's okay." She handed Olivia a choice of t-shirts and jogging bottoms with a towel. "Will these do?"

"Sure, thanks."

"There is a bed made up in this room," she said, gesturing across the hall from her own. "Have a hot shower if you need to warm up. Bring me your pyjamas, I'll put them in the drier."

Olivia lingered by the door and it suddenly struck Lillian how much in common they had, and possibly what the girl needed right now. With Lillian there, she didn't need to be the adult anymore.

"Come here," Lillian said and held her arms out like Nick had done for her. Olivia accepted, and held on to Lillian as though if she didn't, she might blow away.

Lillian made small noises of comfort, then gave up and cried with her; for her father, for Olivia's mother, for Henry, and for Nick in a drunken coma downstairs on the sofa.

"I miss my Mom."

"I know, Olivia, I know."

"I don't want Dad to feel bad about this in the morning. He deals with everything on his own. He gave up so much for me." She kneaded her eyes with the base of her palms and gave a loud sniff.

"I'm sure he wouldn't have it any other way. He told me he got to hold you first when you were born. That he decided there in that moment he would do anything to keep you safe. Don't tell him I said this but, from what I can tell, he has done exactly that. Maybe he deserves a night off every so often?"

"It is hard to stay mad at him."

"Yes, I know."

"Thanks Lillian. I mean it. That was kinda nice." She gave a small shrug and left Lillian stood in the doorway in shock. It had been 'Kinda' nice. And she felt warm, like something else had shifted around her. A sense of comfort and hope.

***

"Well, this is awkward," Nick mumbled to the dog at the door of the kitchen, unsure whether to brave the interior and the combined female wrath he could imagine waited for him. They sat at the counter eating fresh croissants, the pair of them looking like they would be more at home in a glamorous Parisian cafe. He had woken up on Lillian's sofa with Holly lay on top of him licking his face. The only troubling thing about this was that it had been the best night's sleep he had in years. Four, to be precise.

"Tea or coffee?" Lillian asked him, a teapot in one hand, the other gesturing at the coffee machine.

"Either way, better make it black," Olivia said, just as the clamour in Nick's head reached a crescendo.

"Looks like I owe an apology," he said with a grimace.

"Not at all," Lillian said sweetly. Too sweetly. She looked away from him, back to Olivia, as Nick lowered himself gingerly onto a stool at the counter.

"School bus is in half an hour, Olivia," Lillian said.

Olivia checked her phone. "Thanks. I better get home to get ready." She took a final slurp of tea, then gave Lillian a hug. Since when did she hug Lillian? "Bye, Dad. Ah, have a good day." She gave Nick a kiss on the cheek and whispered, "good luck!"

Lillian saw Olivia out, then slammed a black coffee in front of Nick and tapped her foot. He took a mouthful of the coffee. It was good. Strong. Just what he needed. The foot tapping increased in frequency. She was waiting for him to say something. He had already apologised. What more should he be saying? He searched the index cards in his head for the appropriate action and drew a blank. So he studied her face. She displayed all the classic I am mad with you signs and the unique Lillian wrinkle on her nose that used to foretell an explosion of Durand temper.

"I'm sorry," he said. Deciding two apologies were likely better than one, after all.

"I think you owe that to your teenage daughter. She came looking for you in a storm, in her pyjamas, Nick. Your teenage daughter."

"Don't you think I feel awful that I put her through that?" He rested his cheek on the counter top, wishing for the sake of his head that she wouldn't yell at him anymore.

"I just don't understand why," she said. "What did you need?"

How could he possibly answer? Did he even know himself? "I think I came here because—" He stopped, unsure of how to say it. But then this was Lillian. She had that built-in Nick interpretation thing that meant even when he screwed it up, she got the gist. "I needed to feel safe," he said, head now buried in his arms.

He heard her move, then felt her arms around him from behind. She pressed her face against his back, and he wished they were sixteen again without the baggage. He shifted and turned, meeting her with his own arms, wondering if she needed him just as much too. How did she manage to make him feel safe and off balance at the same time?

They pulled away, her steely blue eyes flicking to his mouth, and before he registered what was happening his lips were on hers. Lillian kissing him back with equal enthusiasm.

When his brain caught up with him, he pulled away.

"I'm sorry!" she said, holding her hand to her mouth. The hand with the huge engagement ring glinting at him.

"No, I'm sorry. I didn't mean for—"

"We probably shouldn't do that again," she told him, taking the stool next to his at the counter, cheeks flushed pink. "The kiss. Not the coming here. That was fine, you can do that any time. Just ..." she sighed. "You don't have to get drunk to seek comfort from me, Nick."

Chapter 15

Henry couldn't be sure if he found Westbrook or if Westbrook found him. Their eyes met in recognition at the same time and they collided, having steered their individual courses across the square still littered with the evidence of the slaughter both had witnessed during the night.

"I have been looking for you," Westbrook said, trying to straighten his shoulders despite the sniff. "I feared you were—" He looked back at the bodies.

Henry embraced him tighter, too exhausted to fight the tears that rolled down his cheeks, too exhausted for once to care who watched. "How are you even here?" he asked.

"Harder to kill than you think," Westbrook replied, his voice gruff and own fierce grip on Henry, causing him to wheeze sporadically. "Besides, we have an agreement."

Henry released him, relief flooding his bones for the second time since their night's work had begun. Discretion was catching up with him. He didn't want Westbrook to see it, any of it, so he kept his gaze on the bloodstained ground. Not daring to look into the eye that had the ability to penetrate deep into his soul and read his very thoughts. He doubted Westbrook would like what he saw there.

"Are you hurt?" Westbrook asked. Even without

looking, Henry felt the weight of his appraisal run over him, assessing what blood was Henry's own.

"The sick is mine, majority of the blood is not. What did Mr Evans say?" Guilt forced Henry to look up. "You weren't supposed to be there, West. I nearly got you killed."

"And I keep telling you, at your side is where I belong. Anyway, it only hurts when I breathe, cough or laugh." He gave a nonchalant wave to a bandage on his knee, the source of his limp. "Henry, if you hadn't found me under—"

Henry swallowed at the dry air and gripped Westbrook's wrist. "Don't say it," he said, even though he had thought it. "And Young?"

"Little idiot. Got a nice slice in his arm," Westbrook coughed, guarding his ribs as he did so. "He got stitched up, and I made him run messages ever since. They are pulling the officers out of the city. They say it's all gone to hell again."

"It has," Henry said, shaking away an uninvited image of a hanging man, his uniform so covered in blood Henry did not know to which army he belonged. "As for Young, he is a loyal little idiot. He was there simply because we were." Henry squeezed Westbrook's wrist again. "Will you accept my apology, West? About pushing you away before—and for hitting you. I regret my actions most—" Westbrook suddenly seemed closer. Henry swallowed, aware of a thirst and dryness in his throat threatening to crack his voice. "And I promise I will make it up to you. It is because I—" *No, that wouldn't do,* he sighed. "I can't do any of this—" He waved vaguely at the city, "without you." It was part of the truth, at least. Sinclair had said it himself. Henry needed Westbrook at his side.

Westbrook grinned. "We keep fighting and do what we must, together?" he said with a solemn nod. "That's the only other promise I need from you, Henry."

"Always, West."

Chapter 16

Olivia called Nick later that morning, asking if she could stay at a friend's for the night. "An actual friend!" he said to Lillian when the call ended. "How about that!"

"Good for her," Lillian said. "She's settling down."

Nick wondered if he was doing the same thing, roots being sent out to take hold. Was that what the kiss was about?

They worked through the accounts of Badajos late into the night, only stopping for a quick dinner. The kiss not mentioned. Thankfully.

"Here is Henry's entry about finding Westbrook," he said as they settled into the study once more. Nick on the floor, back against the bookcase, Lillian curled in the armchair by the fire. He passed her the journal. "Or would you prefer the typed version? I just finished it."

"No, the journal is fine." She said, far from fine if the signs of moisture in her eyes were anything to go by. He let it go. Trusting her to tell him if she needed him.

"I can't!" she declared moments later, dropping the journal on the desk and rushing out of the room. He heard her footsteps hurrying up the stairs.

You're a complete jerk, Nicholas, Nick told himself.

186

Should have called it a night earlier, before getting to how mortified Henry had been at the prospect of finding Westbrook dead. She had only just lost her father. Of course it would upset her. He rubbed his hands over his face, noticing that it felt as though even the house seeped grief through its walls. He rested his hand on the wall for a moment, like he might on the wall of a tomb, trying to connect with the soul it contained. Ashlington Manor felt only cold and sad.

Ten minutes later Lillian still had not emerged, and he began to worry.

"Lily?" he called from the hallway. Holly set a foot on the bottom step. "Stay there, Holly. I've got her," he told the dog. "Lily? Everything okay?" he called, climbing the stairs.

He found her on the floor of her bedroom. Knees drawn up to her chest, arms wrapped around her middle, back against her bed. It felt cold in there.

"Go away."

"Okay," Nick said, but he didn't. He lowered himself next to her.

"It was supposed to get better," she sniffed, leaning her head on his arm.

"That's what they tell you."

"Is that why you drink? Because you still mourn Taylor?"

Had anyone else asked the question, he would not have answered. But this was Lily and when he turned up on her doorstep in a drunken mess, she had lain him on her couch with her dog. She deserved an answer. An honest one.

"Probably. But I feel guilty too. And Angry. That's the thing they don't tell you about. How angry you feel at them for leaving. I think—most of all—I'm angry with her for leaving Olivia."

"We're supposed to be okay, aren't we? I mean, we have everything we need. No money worries, careers, I am engaged, for heaven's sake. Why am I on the floor of my bedroom in pieces?"

"You can have all of that and still hurt, I guess. I don't know. Let me know when you figure it out." He nudged her.

She took another big sniff, then wiped her nose on her sleeve. "Will you stay with me tonight?" she asked.

"Sure. I'll go make sure everything is locked up." He made his way downstairs, double checked the doors, then cleared away their dinner and set the dishwasher going. He gave Holly some fuss, then climbed the stairs once more.

When he put his head around Lillian's door, she had got into bed. "Night then."

"Where are you going?"

"Spare room." He gestured down the hallway.

"Nick, I meant stay with me. In here," she said, flapping the duvet open.

Nick swallowed.

"I don't want to be on my own," she said.

He moved inside and shut the door behind him, discarded his jeans and climbed into bed. She wiggled closer. Digging deep for fortitude, he held out his arm so she could cuddle up the way they did years ago.

"Better?"

"Much. You'll be here in the morning?"

"Yes."

***

When she woke, Lillian found her arms wrapped around Nick, cheek resting against the back of his t-shirt. It felt warm and peaceful there. She hoped he would not wake for some time so they could stay that way.

When she felt him stir, she pretended to still be asleep. He seemed surprised to find himself in her arms, and she was pretty sure he checked under the covers to confirm his state of undress. She felt his shoulders relax afterwards. Probably relieved. He had bedded a movie star. How in the hell could she compete with that? He did a funny wiggle that pressed back against her. She increased her grip on him ever so slightly. They dozed together for what the clock on her dresser told her was fifteen minutes before she felt Nick ease her arm off him. He got out of the bed and went into the en-suite. She heard the toilet, then the shower.

She stared at the fox skull on her bookshelf, the one Nick had given her one summer long ago, a million things running through her head. Did sleeping in the same bed as Nick mean she had been unfaithful to Marcus? She decided no, but it left her feeling uncomfortable. Her thoughts when she woke had certainly been unfaithful, even if her actions were not. Apart from the kiss. She had forgotten about that. Yesterday, she had most definitely enjoyed kissing him, even though she had pretended she didn't. In her book, that qualified.

She rolled onto the warm patch of the bed Nick had left, wrapping herself in his scent, which served only to increase the guilt. From there, she looked to the door of the en-suite bathroom. It never shut properly, the door being slightly too big for the frame and the heavy Georgian door handle meant it always swung open an inch if you didn't slam it shut in the first place. She didn't mean to look, but he was there in her shower, quite naked, clothes in a pile on the floor.

She climbed out of bed with all the good intentions of getting dressed, fighting an overwhelming urge to do as her imagination suggested. Shy of the door, she could still see through the gap, the glass of the shower now covered in steam, where Nick did something most un-Nick like. He wiped a circle of the shower door clear of condensation and beckoned her with a finger.

When his phone bleeped over an hour later he mumbled something with a chuckle, that shook her in his arms, about it probably being his teenage daughter checking up on him. It brought Lillian back to reality with a bump. He was a father, and she was engaged. To be married! They both had responsibilities, and she had just slept with her childhood best friend.

"I won't say anything if that is what you are worried about," he said. "I shouldn't have let that happen. I should have been more responsible with your feelings."

"Nick, I needed you and you were here—" He tensed.

She hadn't meant it to sound like that. Now he thought she was using him. "I didn't mean it like that."

"I'll always be here for you," he said, tensing again.

"No, you won't. You'll leave me. Just like last time."

"I didn't leave you. You were going to university and so was I." He loosened his arms from around her and sat up, warmth and comfort removed.

"You left the country afterwards." She sat up next to him, pulling up the covers to save whatever modesty remained. It sounded like she was trying to score a point against him and she hated herself for it, but she found herself suddenly angry with him again.

"Only because you didn't come back for the summer," he said, as though her absence had hurt him more. The summer she had graduated and begun her career in London, eager to leave the tiny village behind and prove herself. Back then, it had felt like there was no time to waste. Now she wondered if she had done exactly that.

His phone bleeped again. He looked towards the pile of clothes on the floor where she knew it lay in the back pocket of his jeans. "I should get that. It might be Olivia."

He swung himself out of bed and walked to the bathroom, picking up his jeans on the way, where he shut the door firmly this time, leaving Lillian considering if she had come back to Ashlington that summer from university, would he have stayed? Would everything have been different?

"You okay, Ollie?" She heard him say. "I'm at the manor ... no, it's not that early." She could imagine him cringing with the possibility of being found out. "Seriously?" There was a pause. "Sure, I'll bring it. Where is it? Okay, I'll leave it with the front office. Love you."

He came back into the bedroom doing up the flies of his jeans, looking for his t-shirt. "She forgot her PE kit. I need to go drop it off at school."

"Here." Lillian threw his t-shirt at him.

"Will you be okay?"

Did he mean would she fall apart without him? "I think I can manage, Nick," she snapped.

"That's not what I—" He pulled his t-shirt on. "I'll be about an hour. I want to research more about Badajos today. If that's okay?"

"Sure," she said, trying to be blasé, but realising too late that it made her sound cold.

She listened to his footfall along the hallway, then the rapid descent down the staircase. The front door slammed, and she heard Holly whine. She sympathised. She couldn't help feel abandoned too.

Then she thought of Westbrook losing one parent and the other sending him away to his godfather. Was that why Sinclair mentioned his self-destruction to Henry, and why Westbrook had followed Henry to Badajos? Henry kept pushing Westbrook away, only to regret it. Is this what she was doing with Nick? Should she be more open with him?

She pulled at the bedsheets, emptied the pillow cases and bundled the bedding into her arms for the washing machine. She added extra detergent and a large handful of the fragrant beads that would melt in the hot water, determined to erase any trace of him.

She felt the small laundry room chill and shivered, bracing herself, listening. "You should tell him," the voice said.

She took her deep breaths. One, two, three. "It is merely your sub-conscious, Lillian," she told herself. "You are fretting about Nick, that's all."

Wasn't it?

"So tell him."

"Go away!"

She skipped breakfast and took Holly for a quick amble about the garden. Then made a coffee and took it to the study. Without Nick sat on the floor taking up all that space his limbs tended to, the room felt empty. Cold.

"Don't leave it too late," the voice said insistently.

"I am not listening to you," she said, wishing she could have control of at least one thing that day. Didn't she have enough on her plate without her stupid sub-conscious nagging at her? I can ignore it, she thought. Busy myself with other things.

Holly sniffed at Nick's chair and whined again. "Don't you start," she told the dog and patted her leg. Holly refused to budge and settled under the desk. Then her phone rang.

Marcus calling to say he would not make it to Ashlington after all that weekend. As if she even cared at this stage. "You'll be okay?" he asked, though it was not said with the concern that Nick had used. More like Marcus was telling her she would be okay. She had to be, had to put on that stiff upper lip and get on with it.

"Of course. I have plenty to keep me busy," she told him. If she hadn't felt so guilty about sleeping with Nick, then she might have continued to feel cross with Marcus. She would tell him, but not over the phone. She couldn't help the selfish relief that she would at least have another week before she had to face his—what would it be? Hurt, disappointment or dent of pride? What she didn't know was if it would force him to break up with her. Let alone what she thought of that possibility.

"Really? You sound distracted. Did you see the doctor yet?"

"Yes, and like you said, she explained it is perfectly normal. All part of the process. She gave me something to help me sleep." She hadn't needed anything last night, having Nick there, which was interesting. Maybe she didn't need them after all.

"Well, that's a start. Did you look at the plans I sent you?" The plans for developing Ashlington.

"No. I'll look today." It was the least she could do. Considering. She hadn't realised she had wandered into the dining room and to the fireplace until she looked up at Henry's painting.

"Speak to you later, then," Marcus said.

"What would you do?" Lillian asked Henry after she hung up. He looked back at her, the hint of the frown he carried disapproving. "You pushed away the person you cared the most about and it almost ended in disaster. Is that what I just did with Nick? Is that what I did to him years ago?"

"Tell him before it is too late, don't make my mistake," the voice answered.

She had not expected an answer, especially having told herself to go away earlier. For a split second, his name escaped with another question, "Henry?" She reeled, taking a step backwards, hand flying to her mouth with a gasp.

Breathe.

No, it couldn't be. She had been spending too much time in the past, that is all. "Is that you?" she asked despite herself.

She shook her head. The doctor had clearly said grief can manifest into a voice of reason. This was her voice, the one that mourned her father and felt guilty she had not seen him more in the last few years. The one that defiantly felt guilty about what happened with Nick. The idea it is Henry, like he is some protector of lost souls, is as ridiculous as thinking it is her father.

Irritated to action, she moved to the study only to begin pacing up and down between the door and the glass-paned door to the garden. Why did they have to both be back here at the same time? Why did she have to do such a stupid thing like sleep with him? Even though he had been glorious, generous, and what she had said to him was true, that she had needed him. Marcus could not have given her what she needed that morning. He wouldn't have recognised that she needed anything at all, Lillian told herself. Not that she could use that as an excuse for such impulsive behaviour.

Had it been impulsive? She asked, turning to complete

another lap. They had merely picked up where they had left off all those years ago. And what the hell had got into Nick. After all, he had invited her into the shower, not the other way around. For a split second, an ounce or two of guilt lifted. Then she realised there were no excuses. She was simply a selfish, terrible person. An incoming text alert bleeped from her pocket.

N – Sorry, won't make it today. Have a good weekend with Marcus.

She had expected it. There was no chance she had lived up to the perfect Taylor. He was already regretting his actions.

L - No problem. Marcus not coming. See you Monday.
N - Will call in tomorrow then.

Did he expect a re-run? Her heart lurched—did she want a re-run? The phone pinged again.

N - Worried you might get the wrong idea. I mean, come to make up work I missed today.

Another ping.

N - If you are still talking to me?
L - Shut up, Nick. See you tomorrow. Want lunch?

N - Shutting up. Yes to lunch X.

She stared at the capitalised x. He had never done that before. She glanced at the ring on her finger. No, she convinced herself, a re-run was definitely out of the question.

Lillian sipped her coffee as she lowered herself back into the office chair, looking around her, realising that even the study had become his. Her father had faded, leaving only Nick's indelible presence. Holly looked up as if thinking the same thing, then lay her nose back on her feet with a sneeze.

She opened her laptop, looking for the plans Marcus had sent. He suggested a joint project with Colin Warrilow. Having significant experience at working on stately homes, Warrilow seemed a good choice. The figures looked interesting. Profitable. Typical Marcus, no matter that Guy hated Warrilow, the profit and the right man for the job was what mattered.

Then she pulled up the plans.

The main house would become a hotel, while they would widen the driveway to allow for delivery traffic. The northern lawn would be cleared for further parking, which would wrap around the back to the stables. They would convert these into luxury holiday cottages. A health suite with swimming pool, gym and rooms for spa treatments was proposed beyond the stables, taking up the meadow.

Marcus had looked at the interior. She recognised his style. Ripping down walls and making the place look more of a barren showroom than an ancient Cotswold home.

She closed the file, unwilling to look at it any more. Instead, she opened her own designs for Lady Sylvia. Similar to many of the larger stately homes, Lady Sylvia had been forced to open nearby Woodcombe Hall to the public to maintain its upkeep. Tastefully, she had concentrated on opening the gardens for leisure and the first floor of the house for weddings and filming. With its increasing popularity, Lady Sylvia wanted to offer a wedding-night suite and use the coach house for four small, inexpensive apartments, affordable for local professionals to rent. "I want it to remain as faithful to the house as possible," Lady Sylvia had said. "That is the most important thing to me, maintaining the heritage."

As Lillian recalled those words, an email alert from Guy popped onto the screen. She opened it and read aloud.

This is a great opportunity, Lily. You get rid of the eyesore, make a tidy profit, and in doing so, sort out any inheritance tax problems. The company benefits from the cash flow, which keeps the banks off our backs and everything goes back to normal. All the worries go away. You said it yourself about how stressed Marcus has been. What's that motto of yours again? Protect those you care about? That's what I am doing. I'm looking out for you. Like I always have done.

Her coffee mug fell off the desk and smashed to the floor. Holly barked, giving it a good telling off. Lillian hadn't knocked it, she was sure. It had not even been on the edge of the desk.

"Don't do it!" said the voice.

Chapter 17

Spain, May 1812

To keep them out of further trouble, Major Sinclair volunteered the reconnaissance services of Henry and Westbrook to Sir Rowland Hill. It is how they found themselves lay on their stomachs with telescopes drawn, looking down at the river Tagus and the pontoon bridge the French had built to connect the two forts either side.

"Strange looking bloody bridge," Young muttered.

"You're not even supposed to be here," Henry hissed crossly. "Either of you."

He looked over his shoulder, where Jackson gave him a defiant, gappy grin. Young and Jackson had followed them out of camp, jogging after the horses. Westbrook had mutinously pointed at his eyepatch and denied all knowledge of their stealthy shadows by the time Henry noticed the two insubordinate rascals.

"The Tagus divides the enemy. Soult to the South and Marmont near Salamanca," he explained with a patience he dug deep to find, before returning his attention back to the forts.

"We take the bridge and the forts, then we keep them apart," Young responded with a shiver of excitement in his voice. Corporal Ernest Young, a carpenter's son, despite being only eighteen, had already proven himself on the field with a sharp intellect that betrayed the poverty of his past. He had taken the King's shilling following his arrest for poaching. How he ever got caught astonished Henry on account of Young sneaking about as his perpetual shadow, appearing when needed, as if out of nowhere.

"The centre of the bridge is just boats," Westbrook said with a nudge.

"All they have to do is cut the boats free and they stop us crossing," Henry agreed, finishing his sketch. Buildings he could draw. It was no Sinclair, but it was accurate. "What do you think, West? Two hundred metres?"

"Looks like. The earthworks are a problem."

"Fort Napoleon shouldn't be too difficult. See the slopes, how they step up."

"Ladders will help."

Henry nodded.

"And the other? How high would you say the tower is, twenty foot?"

"Ragusa. More like twenty-five." Henry licked his pencil and scribbled. "What worries me is getting there. The terrain around here will slow us down, and getting any guns there may prove impossible. Ready?"

Westbrook slid his telescope shut and tucked it back into his belt. "Ready."

They crawled backwards, sliding down the dusty bank back into cover where Jackson waited, protecting their rear, spinning his bayonet in his hand to pass the time.

Brushing at his coat, Henry tried to rid himself of at

least a little of the dust that seemed to infiltrate every seam and had turned even his underwear a shade of orange. Westbrook patted him on the back only to send a cloud of dust into his own face, earning him a violent cough that, if the way he held his arm across his middle was anything to go by, still hurt his ribs. They found their hobbled horses munching on the dry brush, swishing their tails at troublesome flies.

Following their trail back to camp, they grew more cheerful the further from the French and site of the impending battle they got. The promise of action affected men in different ways. Westbrook would typically share a coffee with the ranks, then bury his head in a book as the hour approached. Henry would walk around the camp too restless to sit still. He'd pretend to check the mens' equipment, but in truth it was an excuse to assess the mood, give encouragement where needed and settle his own nerves.

"You seem quiet today, Jackson?" Henry said from where he and Westbrook, making the most of the opportunity to stretch their legs, walked shoulder to shoulder on the narrow road behind Jackson and Young, leading their horses.

"He got a letter from home," Young volunteered. Jackson gave him a grumpy shove. Usually vocal about whatever was causing his sullenness, the fact he was keeping it to himself was no doubt of concern to his friend.

"Bad news?" Westbrook enquired.

"My girl is getting married," Jackson said. "My Ma wrote and told me."

"You did not have an understanding?" Henry asked

with all the sympathy of one who knew love that could not be.

"I thought we did."

"I keep telling him that there are plenty more out there," Young offered. "He'll meet some comely Spanish wench—"

"Like Nelly O'Connell!" Westbrook gave an exaggerated sigh, causing Young to turn about. Westbrook cupped at an imaginary pair of breasts with an impressive leer for a man with one eye.

"Oi!" Young responded with a look of incredulous shock. "Sir!"

Westbrook laughed, a deep bellied sound, the first since Badajos, which caused even Jackson to break into a smile.

Henry gave Westbrook a shove with his elbow. "Don't torment the lad, West, he has no idea just how many in the company keep warm at night thinking of Nelly O'Connell and her..."

"Ample bosoms!" Jackson finished, enjoying the joke at his friend's expense.

"You'll be all right, Sid," Young chuckled, blushing. "The girls will line up for a hero like you when we get home."

If I'm good enough to get you all home, Henry thought.

At the edge of the camp, the officers re-mounted, parting ways with Young and Jackson, to whom Henry gave orders to find some supper. He wouldn't have given the cart full of ladders a second glance, but Westbrook had halted his horse alongside.

"West?"

Westbrook didn't answer, but pulled at his neckcloth and tugged at the top of his shirt with a desperate clawing that made his horse startle backwards, ears pricked and nostrils flaring, looking for danger. Westbrook brushed an arm across his forehead. He looked at Henry, face drained of colour.

"West?"

"They didn't clean the ladders," Westbrook said, the words almost lost on the breeze.

Henry looked inside the cart, his mood plummeting with the realisation that they were the same ladders used weeks earlier for the storming of Badajos, alarmingly still covered in the blood and brains of men. His stomach lurched before he could do anything to help it, and he had to spit out what little contents it contained. He dismounted, took Westbrook's horse by the bit and led them through the camp to give their report to Sir Rowland, in the firm knowledge that the demons would visit both of them that night. It had been only a few weeks since Badajos, and neither of them slept well anymore.

He hated it when he was right. The demons found Westbrook at the bottom of a port bottle around three hours later, one he had helped himself to out of Sinclair's trunk. Henry found him staggering through the camp without his eyepatch, doing his best to pick a fight with a much bigger lieutenant of the 4th company.

"Just bloody hit me!" he yelled at the man.

"No! Don't do that," Henry shouted, pushing past the few that had formed a ring around them, ready to provide assistance to their man or make wagers on the impending entertainment. "For God's sake, don't encourage him, he is still injured," he told them, putting himself in front of Westbrook, pushing his friend backwards.

In Henry's experience, there were two ways a drunken Westbrook could go. Since Badajos, the first (his favourite) became a most wobbly, affectionate fellow with lingering embraces and the intense desire to break into song. The second was at war with himself. The one Henry had first met in Colchester and the one he was dealing with now. The one that hurt deep inside so sought external pain, usually in its largest form, to numb it. Henry had much sympathy with that Westbrook.

"You were there, weren't you, Durand?" one of them said. "Badajos?"

"We both were."

The huge lieutenant let out a breath. He knew. The 28th had watched on in horror at the storming of Badajos.

"Were he anyone else, he would be up on charge in front of the colonel. You should keep a closer rein on him. His name will only get him so far," someone else said.

"Be careful who you make threats to," Henry prickled, steering Westbrook away. He would have thumped the man himself were it not for having to support the growing weight of his friend about his shoulders.

"I only wanted them to go away, Henry," Westbrook

sniffed as they moved through the camp. "They come at me in the dark, always when it is dark."

"Who do, West?" Although no larger than Henry, he was a solid fellow. Henry stopped them so he could redistribute Westbrook's weight. He used the pause to take the spare eyepatch out of his pocket and tie it around Westbrook's head. "That's better, eh?" Westbrook would hate waking in the morning without it.

"The faces—the men I killed—the men I lost because I was not good enough." He stared out into the night over Henry's shoulder. Henry checked but could see no one. "They are all here, hiding in the shadows. Will *you* hit me, my Henry?" Westbrook hiccupped. Henry did not dwell on his choice of words. "Make them go away?"

"I will not hit you, my friend. When you see those faces again, tell me. I'll chase them away for you."

"You would?"

"You fight my demon for me all the time, West. Trust me with yours."

He settled Westbrook in his hazy state of drunken terror into his bed within their tent and wrapped all the blankets he could find around him in lieu of his arms. He left the candle burning so Westbrook would not find himself in the dark if he woke.

As if to prove his point all over again, Henry's own demon found him in his sleep—a pack of bodies suffocating him. His calls for Westbrook unanswered.

Lost.

Alone.

Alone under the tremendous weight of all the things he wanted to do, all the things he wanted to say, but could not.

Westbrook would never come. Henry would be lost forever.

The weight pressed at him further, sinking into the mud.

The bodies that he tore at, that night at Badajos to reach his friend, tore back at him. Ripping Henry open, releasing a devilled creature that climbed out of him with horns and tail.

His true self screaming to be let free.

Then Westbrook was there, after all. Strong arms holding Henry. Pulling him up out of the sea of bodies. "I've got you."

Henry woke to find Westbrook holding him, stroking his hair, singing the soft Spanish lullaby he had sung to the children in the convent. Warm and safe, Henry leant back against him, wishing morning wouldn't come, so he never had to let go.

Two nights later, the march to the river took Henry's company along winding goat paths which they used to traverse the woodland in an effort to remain unseen by the Castle of Marabita controlling the road leading to the bridge. Major Sinclair had given specific orders for Henry's company, while offering support to the forlorn hope, to avoid joining it at all costs.

"You support! Do you hear me, Durand?"

"Yes, sir."

"Westbrook? I'm not even sure you should be going. Do I make myself understood? Absolutely no repeat of last time. I can find other officers who would actually obey—"

"I think we understand your meaning, sir," Westbrook told his godfather, who had been turning his pocket watch over in his hand before returning it to his pocket. The major had been writing letters. Henry had written enough of his own to the mothers or wives of his fallen brothers to know of the weight the major was carrying. Sinclair would have no desire to write to his good friend Kitty Westbrook, informing her he had lost her only son. The great man had been close to tears himself when Henry and Westbrook had finally reported back to him after Badajos. If the horror of that night still showed in their eyes, then Sinclair had seen and recognised it.

That night, the men were quiet, each locked away in his own thoughts, heads down, following the goat tracks. To Henry's dismay and despite his report, the route proved so circuitous that they did not arrive at the bottom of the hill under cover of darkness, but as the first light of the day shone on them like a beacon. The fort's many cannons began firing, all hope of surprise dashed.

A further two nights later, a fresh approach left Sinclair's force at Marabita as part of the decoy to keep the castle by the road busy as others attacked the twin forts by the bridge. A frustrated Henry and his company missed most of the action, the first fort captured by the time they reached it.

It was approaching along the river that Henry shouted, "The boats!"

The panicking occupants of Fort Ragusa, on the far bank of the river, had cut the centre boats free from the pontoon. Henry watched as they drifted downstream, where they got caught in an eddy on the opposite bank. He pulled off his coat and undid his belt, allowing sword, pistol and knife to drop to the ground. Then he hopped on one leg, pulling at a boot, all the while watching the boats. Getting into water, especially deep water where he could not touch the bottom, was the last thing he wanted to do, but he also made a point of leading by example.

"We are not?" Westbrook said, despite shrugging off his own coat and belt. "We are," he muttered. "Of course we bloody are. Because you will jump into that river like a lunatic and swim for the boats, so naturally I'm going to have to bloody follow you, because that is what I do!"

"Are you—" Young had pulled up next to Westbrook, assessing the situation with a quick eye. "Oh!" he said, and calling for Jackson, he too began undressing, accompanied by the more colourful language of the ranks.

Henry was already running the last few metres to the shore, where he dived into the dark water. The cold took his breath away with burning urgency, but he resisted the impulse to draw air until he had swum a few strokes. Although a competent swimmer on account of summers spent in the lake at Ashlington, he had to force himself to continue as he felt the river bottom drop away below him.

Westbrook entered the water with more noise and less

grace, then caught him up and leaned on the side of the first boat, panting, dark hair plastered to his face.

"Take this one," Henry told him. "I'll swim for the next." He felt something whip past his head and a musket ball embedded itself into the boat next to his hand. A second splintered the wood on the other side of Westbrook who cursed with some new obscene words he had picked up from Young. Henry pushed away and swam hard for the second boat, doing his best to ignore the streams of bubbles where musket fire tried to catch him.

The four men paddled the boats back upstream towards the bridge under constant fire, where they were used to repair the pontoon. This would allow Sir Rowland's force to cross the river and seize Fort Ragusta.

The weight of the water that dripped from his soaked shirt and trousers slowed Henry's scramble up the riverbank. "That was refreshing!"

"You enjoyed that, didn't you?" Westbrook shook his head vigorously like a dog, the curled ends of his hair tightening.

"It was fun."

"Fun?" he said, wagging a finger at Henry. "Most men of breeding, Henry Durand, have *fun* playing cards, riding with hounds, drinking a fine brandy whilst smoking cigars. There was a time you were the voice of reason, now your twisted idea of fun has me—"

Henry bent over at the waist, hands on his knees, laughing. Not only in agreement that times had indeed changed, but at the spectacle before him.

"What?" Westbrook asked with a deep dimpled smile that turned to a look of horror as he patted at his shirt. "What on God's—" He pulled his shirttails loose and a fair sized fish fell to the floor.

Westbrook shrieked.

Henry collapsed to the ground.

Young and Jackson looked on, trying not to laugh at their lieutenant but doing so anyway with the spluttering relief and release of having cheated death once more. The three offered commentary as Westbrook chased the fish despite its flapping efforts at escape. After a lengthy pursuit, he succeeded and chucked it, without ceremony, back into the river.

"Waste of a good supper, that," Jackson said with a disappointed shake of the head.

Having recomposed himself, Henry took off his shirt and wrung it out. Someone brought them their coats, belts and boots back and they witnessed the storming of Fort Ragusta which put up little resistance once Sir Rowland Hill's men surged across the bridge.

The remaining Slashers with Major Sinclair joined them shortly after, the major making it known what he thought of the exploits of his wet wayward men with his hands on his hips and a stern glare he aimed at Henry. A glare that disappeared when Sir Rowland Hill himself marched up and presented him with a small bag of gold coins.

"Quick thinking that!" Hill said. "Would have been tricky if we had lost those boats. Share that among the swimmers, Sinclair."

Sinclair muttered something about 'Not wanting to encourage the idiots any further,' but Hill did not hear him, having already turned and walked back towards the fort. Henry, Westbrook, Young and Jackson grinned like soggy loons at the major. He tossed the bag to Henry.

"Well done," he said. "Very well done."

Chapter 18

Ashlington, April 2015

Confident Nick had gone. He was back to looking like an awkward teenager in a forty-year-old man's skin. Not that Lillian minded. She was not altogether sure if she would have survived confident Nick again.

"You didn't have to check on me," she said.

"If I leave it until Monday, it would be even more awkward," he said.

She sighed with relief, thankful he felt the same way and appreciating his honesty. "Did you mean what you said yesterday?" she asked.

"About always being here for you?"

She nodded.

"Yes, I rarely say anything I do not mean."

"I know." She drew breath to say more, but he said it for her.

"And I know you are engaged. We both have our reasons for what happened yesterday; let's just get your dad's project finished. Then everything can go back to normal."

Normal? What was normal anymore? Was normal not having Nick breeze into Ashlington Manor every day, moulding himself to it like part of the furniture? Was normal convincing old ladies like Alice Prescott to let go of everything they held dear? Alice Prescott. Why did the name come so easily now?

Nick flashed a lopsided smile that reminded her of stepping into the shower with him. She shoved the recollection aside and followed him to the study, where she picked up the first journal she came across, happy to distract herself with Henry's story once more.

"They all wrote, you know, their thoughts and secrets. It is all here. I wonder what imprint we will leave for future generations?" Nick said.

She moved to the fireplace, drawn to the clay owl, and gave it a stroke. Then she turned to face Nick. "I was thinking about Henry. How he refers to keeping so much of himself hidden. Can I tell you something? You'll think I am crazy—jeez—I am probably crazy." She immediately regretted saying anything and thought about walking out. But Nick put down the pile of letters he was sifting through and stood up. Without comment, he held out a hand. She took it.

"Coffee?" he suggested.

Still holding her hand, he led her to the kitchen. She wasn't sure what it meant; the hand holding. Was it because they slept together or did it just feel comfortable, like friends?

"Why do you assume I would think you are crazy?" he asked, giving her hand a small shake while depositing her at the kitchen table. She shivered with an unexpected chill, making her wish she had thought to put on a sweater that morning.

"Tell him. Before it is too late!" the voice insisted, it almost sounded cross at her.

Lillian froze and put her hands over her ears. Then she felt Nick's cool hands on hers. He tugged them down from her head. She opened her eyes to find him very close.

"Tell me."

She trusted him. She could tell him. "I keep hearing a voice. I thought it was my dad."

"Okay."

"I'm serious. You know what it is like here, the house feels like—oh, I don't know."

"It feels like it carries all that history in its walls? All those vibrations of the past?"

"Yes—that—whatever that means."

"So tell me about the voice."

"You don't think I'm crazy? Marcus told me I should see the doctor, but it hasn't helped. I still hear it and things keep happening."

"And now you don't think it is your dad?"

"I think—I think it might be Henry."

Nick sat down at the table, so she did likewise. "Our Henry?"

"I knew you'd think I had lost the plot."

"No, Lily. Carry on. What makes you think it is Henry?"

"Do you remember that journal entry from my great grandfather, Dad had found. The one about the angel?"

"You think that was Henry?"

"My Dad had just lost his father. I have just lost mine."

Nick nodded thoughtfully.

"Marcus said I was probably manifesting it. Wanting some kind of protector figure now my father had gone."

"I don't think Marcus understands Ashlington," Nick huffed.

"No, he doesn't," she agreed.

"So if it is Henry, you think he is here because you are grieving? And that is what he does? He offers comfort?"

"I don't know. He certainly dealt with his fair share of loss throughout the war."

Nick titled his head, considering this.

"You don't believe me, do you?"

"I believe you. I just think there must be more to his reasoning than what he experienced in the war. It is almost not personal enough, like he would be there haunting Spain or Waterloo with his men, not here."

That made sense. Lillian couldn't help feel a wave of relief. He hadn't dismissed her like Marcus; he trusted her and wanted to understand. "I think you and Henry would have got on like a house on fire."

Nick put his hands in his pockets and leant back in the chair. "I like him. His sense of honour drove him in everything he did. You have to respect that in a man, particularly one so young. Did you hear the voice the night you called me?"

"Yes, it's what scared me. But now, I don't think it is coming from a place of malevolence; there is more of a sadness to it. I don't *think* I need to be scared. You're not scared of being here, are you?"

"Oh, I am scared about plenty of things. Large groups of people, small talk, spiders—the cottage is full of the blighters." He shuddered. "But no, I'm not scared here. I have been to many places where the spirits let you know they don't want you there. This is not one of them."

The revelation he had experienced something like this was not only surprising, but reassuring. "You have encountered something like this before? In your work? Well, I guess that would make sense if ghosts were real considering what you do."

"It's never been exactly like this. I'm not sure I can describe it. Doing what I do, I ... disturb things; remains, resting places, and what I now believe is that not all rest in peace. But ..."

He bit on the inside of his cheek. Weighing up whether to continue, she supposed. She didn't want to push, so gave an encouraging nod instead.

Nick took a deep breath. "More than that, Olivia says she has heard her mum."

Olivia had been through the same thing? But she always seemed so well put together. So innocent. "Did it scare her?"

Nick laughed. "Not in the slightest. Olivia has this— hmm—how to describe it? Digging makes me feel connected to the earth, to something old and powerful that binds me to whoever I would find, but Olivia has always experienced it deeper. She is extremely sensitive to her surroundings. Do you know what she says about this place?"

"What?"

"That it is full of hope."

***

On Monday morning, to make the most of a surprisingly sunny start to the day, Nick left the cottage early, having first ensured Olivia ate a healthy breakfast. He walked the long way, dropping further off the escarpment, following the border of the village along its length over the fields.

Nick felt like he wanted to crawl out of his skin. Lines had been crossed, and the more he thought about it, the more ashamed he felt. How could he have treated Lillian like that? All she wanted was comfort from him. He couldn't help feeling like he had taken advantage of her vulnerability to get into her bed. What kind of friend had he become?

The village convenience store disguised among a row of slate roofed cottages provided an offering for lunch with some locally grown produce. As he carried his decent camera and the light was favourable, he made the Norman church with its round blue clock-face his next stop.

Inside, he placed his grocery bag on the floor by the stone font and stood appreciating the tall stained-glass window above the altar. He remembered sitting in the pews for Sunday services, watching shafts of colour move across the flagstone floor as the reverend's voice sent him into a state of bored listlessness.

To his right were memorial stones for various village family members set into the wall. He sought the plaque he knew to contain mention of the Durands.

"I don't see you in here often," said a voice behind him. Nick turned to find the Reverend Attwood stood in the centre of the isle, black cassock brushing the flagstones, hands interlocked, resting on his belly.

"Hello, Reverend."

"Ah, so you came to see about the Durands? I heard you were researching one of them. Henry, isn't it? The soldier from that painting? Another book?"

"You know of him?"

"Rumour has it he died at Waterloo." Attwood took a seat in the nearest pew.

Nick was not sure why, but he sat down next to him. The church felt full to the rafters with calm. He regretted not appreciating that as a child when his mother had dragged him there with wet combed hair, wearing his smartest outfit for the monthly family services.

"It is so peaceful in here." He closed his eyes and tilted back his head.

"We try."

"We?" Nick realised a fraction of a second later who the "we" referred to.

Attwood pointed upwards, confirming this. "I see a look of scepticism. You used to have the same look as a boy. Always questioning. Do you remember?"

"I do." Nick smiled. His mother used to give him a right talking to on the way home afterwards.

"It is hardly surprising you found yourself seeking truth for a living."

Nick thought this incredibly perceptive of the older man. But then he did have that calm, all knowing look about him. Perhaps that was just the clothing, though.

"Not sure it brought me any closer to finding out what I believe."

"Believing in something is the important thing. It gives us hope. It gives us a code to live by. Your god—" he raised a hand in anticipation of Nick's objection. "Let's just call it that for ease of conversation. Your god might be different to mine, but faith is the door to hope, and with that we can set out to discover where we belong and what our purpose there is."

Before he could think any further on that matter, the next quandary crowding his thoughts escaped his lips. "What are your thoughts on ghosts?"

"You've been spending a lot of time at the manor," the reverend replied, surprising Nick once more. Did he know?

"Have you spent much time there?"

"Some of it is older than the church is. But you'd know that, given your field of work. Do you encounter many lost souls doing what you do?"

There was no humour in Attwood's tone. Nick glanced his way; the reverend met his eyes openly, curious. "Some," Nick said honestly. "You?"

"Some." Attwood nodded.

"But surely you believe in the afterlife? Heaven and harps?"

"I do. But what if they don't want to go? What if there is something keeping them here?"

"Unfinished business? Isn't that fiction or wishful thinking?" Nick said.

"Some might argue, the whole thing is. Until we have evidence to the contrary, it can still be a possibility, can it not?"

Despite his experiences in cultures with ancient beliefs, Nick felt unqualified to answer, yet he longed to understand more. Far from what he had expected when he had stepped into the church and far from any conversation he had ever had with a member of the clergy before, Nick found it oddly refreshing and quite possibly what he needed to organise his thoughts on Henry. Had he known this before stepping in to the church?

"Take your Henry, for example. What if he had a task to finish before he felt he could move on? Something at the very root of what made him who he was. He would not rest in peace until it was done, would he not?"

Nick said nothing. He did not recall mentioning Henry in direct relation to ghosts.

"When Alistair's wife died, Alistair talked about a presence in the house."

"The manor is like that," Nick said with a shrug. "What sort of presence?"

"A friendly one. Comforting. He told me that without it he would never have got through that year, dealing with Rose's death and Lillian as a baby." The silence grew between them again before Attwood spoke again. "How is

Lillian? I think she has been avoiding me."

"She..." Nick stopped, considering if this broke the code of friendship. Didn't the clergy have a confidentiality pact, or was that solely for catholic confession? Reverend Attwood said nothing, just gave a small inclination of his head, inviting Nick to continue. "She thinks she has heard things."

"Things?"

"The message is not clear."

"Tell her to ask him to be more precise then?"

"You mean have a conversation?" Nick didn't know why the idea surprised him so much. He talked to the painting all the time. Was it even possible that Henry could hear him? Was this even what Attwood meant?

"Has she tried to talk back?"

Nick didn't have time to answer. The door to the church creaked open and a hefty floral arrangement bustled in, a pair of stout legs sticking out of the bottom. "Am I disturbing you?" said a familiar voice from behind the foliage. "Hello, love," Nick's mother said. "This is the last place I would expect to bump into you." She looked at Attwood and mouthed the words 'No offence.'

Nick and the reverend both got to their feet. "We have been enjoying the light," Attwood said, gesturing at the glass as Janet deposited the flower arrangement on the wooden lid of the font, then twisted it, finding the best angle with an experienced eye.

"Thank you for listening," Nick said.

"All in a day's work. Think about what I said."

His mother walked out with him, shuttling home for the next flower arrangement. "How is it going up at the big house? You will be careful, won't you, love?"

"Careful?"

"You fell for her before. I would hate to see her— either of you—hurt."

"I think she will end up selling the manor." He immediately kicked himself for saying anything, but his conversation with Attwood had stirred something a bit desperate inside him.

Janet gasped. "Has it come to that?"

"For God's sake, don't say anything," Nick said with a glance back at the church.

"Of course I won't. I am not the village gossip you know, Nick."

Nick bit back a wheeze of disagreement.

"Will you be all right?"

"I don't know, Mum. I honestly don't know."

"Well, give your old Mum a hug, then go get to work." She put her arms around him, releasing the scent of her preferred laundry softener. "Enjoy it while you can."

"Thanks Mum."

***

"I didn't expect this," Lillian told Nick as she brought him a coffee that afternoon. "I am not sure what I expected, but it is really getting to me reading Henry's journal entries. He seems so at odds with himself unable to deal with his

223

emotions, yet writing, like you said at the museum, he uses his writing to make sense of it all."

"Even out there in the war, miles away from home, he kept having to deal with the expectation of his family."

"It also surprised me how devoted they were to each other, the soldiers. I guess that's a foxhole thing?"

Nick raised an eyebrow.

"What?" Lillian said. "That thing with the eyebrow." She wagged a finger at him. "What does that mean?"

"Friendship is complicated."

"You are being very cryptic, Nick. I'm not sure it suits you," she said dryly. It made him laugh, and she smiled back. "You were the one that said you didn't think any of that was personal enough to give him a reason to still be here."

"It might surprise you to learn that I am wrong sometimes."

Lillian snorted.

"Henry's time in the war is interesting enough," Nick continued, "but things really get shaken up when he gets back here."

"Have you been peeping ahead without me?"

Nick chuckled.

"And to think there was a time I used to think Ashlington was dull. Well, stop sitting about drinking coffee. Let's get to it, Hawkins." Lillian relieved him of his mug and shooed him out of the kitchen.

The following morning, among a late spring frost that

etched the lawn with feathers of silver, she found him in the graveyard on his hands and knees next to the angel statue.

"Nick!"

He jumped out of his skin, making Lillian laugh, a reaction she decided she rather liked. One she hadn't felt in a while.

"Bloody hell, Lily. You know it's not nice creeping up on people in a graveyard," he said, hand on his heart as though trying to restart it through will alone, breath steaming in the cold like a train.

"Sorry." She couldn't help herself but continue laughing. His face, a mixture of bewilderment and umbrage, just made her laugh harder. He folded his arms, waiting for her to finish, even though his mouth had slipped into that lopsided smile of his.

"Are you quite done?"

"Oh, I think so," she said, wiping her eyes, taking a deep breath. "I needed that. Sorry."

"Evidently," he huffed.

"What are you doing, anyway?" she asked, stroking the head of the angel statue. He must have cleared it. Yesterday, ivy had covered it from halo to toe.

"This is a grave marker for Henry's sister. I used to love looking at it as a child. Thought it magical, you know."

Lillian nodded.

"But now I know it is hers, that of a child, it seems rather tragic."

"I don't remember much mention of her."

"She was the firstborn but died when she was about

three. I found this." He handed her a blue glass bead. "Thought you might like it. It is not very old, Victorian."

She turned it over in her hand, then held it to the light. She did like it. All the more because he had found it. "Is that why you do it? Archaeology—the whole history thing. Is it about feeling close to those that have gone?" she grimaced, hoping it didn't seem like she was prying about Taylor again.

Nick's head tilted in thought, and his eyes looked out over her shoulder. "It's the stories I love. Entire lifetimes lived and passed. Like Henry, there is more to him than a heroic figure in a priceless painting. He had doubts, regrets, joys, scars—both physical and emotional. Above all, he wrestled with finding where he belonged. I enjoy finding out what made them real. I suppose the fact that they are dead makes that easier for me. The living are a whole different ball game." He shrugged, and finally his amber eyes came to rest on hers. "You need to talk to him."

"Who?"

"Henry."

"Don't be ridiculous. I am not talking to him. You do it."

"I do. He doesn't talk back. Not to me."

She refused. If she could be honest with Nick, she would tell him it was because she was scared. Not of Henry or having a ghost in the house, but of the other possibility. That this was still all in her mind. Not to mention that being that honest with Nick would only lead her to tell him other truths. Truths that would ruin everything.

An hour later, he brought her a cup of tea perched on a

plate. She had answered a call from Lady Sylvia in the lounge. Lady Sylvia had been excited about Lillian's plans and asked if she would pitch them in person to her and the builder she would want to use. Lillian waved Nick in. He set the tea in front of her, twisting the cup handle to reveal a hidden biscuit.

"If you do decide to talk to Henry, I'll be there with you," he said with no pre-amble, once she finished the call.

She looked at the biscuit. Perhaps this was the only way to confirm one way or the other. Either this was all like the doctor had said, or it was actually Henry. She nodded and said, "okay then."

It is why they both stood in front of Henry's painting in the dining room ten minutes later, looking up at him in his unbuttoned red uniform coat. She tilted her head and peered forward, scrutinising it. She hadn't really noticed it before, but most portraits, certainly the others in the room, looked directly out in that creepy 'Always following you about the room" way. Henry's didn't. He looked off to the side ever so slightly, as though his thoughts lay elsewhere. Not far. Somewhere close by.

Here goes nothing.

"Henry?" Lillian looked to Nick. He nodded in reassurance, so she continued. "Can you hear me? We wanted you to tell us more about why you are here." She paused, but the only answer was from the ticking of the grandfather clock at the other end of the room. "This is hopeless." She could not shake the consideration that even if their theory was true, that the voice belonged to Henry, letting herself believe it might throw herself open to the craziness.

"Wait," Nick said, gazing at the painting, a deep crease in his forehead and eyes narrowed. Lillian giggled. He put his hands on his hips. "You're not taking this seriously."

"I am, of course I am Nick, I'm sorry you just looked hilarious." She sucked in her lips, trying to suppress any further laughter, but her sense of resolute unravelled into one of those occasions where no matter how serious the situation, she couldn't stop laughing. Perhaps the madness had caught her after all.

"He won't talk to us if we are messing about."

"How do you know? He might actually have a sense of humour."

"What's that supposed to mean?"

"Are you two listening?"

Lillian watched Nick's eyes widen. They both turned to look behind them. There was no one there.

"Henry?" Lillian said.

"Yes."

"So, it is you?"

"Yes. I'm here." He made a noise like a broken-hearted sigh. "I have always been here."

Lillian glanced at Nick, relieved. She had not been crazy after all. Nick looked ghostly white. "Are you okay?" she whispered to him.

His focus remaining on the painting, he nodded.

"You hear him?"

Nick nodded again and took a step back. He looked

unsure of himself. Like he did the night she kissed him for the first time.

"Nicholas, Ashlington is your home too," Henry said.

"Why are you here, Henry? What is it you need?" Lillian asked.

"No one has ever asked me that." He sounded surprised. "Not for a long time, anyway."

"Well, I am asking now."

"I need my home and I don't want you to make my mistake."

"That's what you kept saying. What mistake Henry?"

Henry didn't answer.

"Henry?"

"I think he is gone," Nick said. "It must take considerable energy to reach us. Maybe he's out of juice."

"Juice?" Lillian put a hand to her head. The temperature in the room had dropped with Henry's presence, but her forehead felt hot.

"I have no other way to even contemplate what is happening. If you have a better suggestion, be my guest. Theorise away." Nick flapped his arms.

"Nope. Juice is good," she said. "Perhaps I will sleep better now." She shrugged, unconvinced. Contacting a spirit was unsettling. Had Nick not been there experiencing the same thing, she would have called the doctor again and offered herself up for committal. "You want to hit the books, I can tell." She gave Nick a pat on the arm, hand hesitating once in contact, reluctant to let him go.

"No, I want to go back to my quaint, spider infested

cottage, pour myself a large whisky and put *Star Trek* on the tv while my brain catches up with what just happened."

"Disconcerting, isn't it?"

"It's one thing believing you, it is another thing experiencing it for myself."

"What else? There is something else. You do that thing with your lip when you want to say something but are busy weighing up whether or not to say it."

"I am not sure he was being totally honest with us."

"You think he is hiding something? I felt it too," she whispered this in case Henry could hear.

"He said he needed his home. But he hated it here. What changed?"

"Other than me selling it?"

"So, you are then?"

"I don't think I have any choice. Don't look so shocked. The inheritance tax is enormous, and my life is in London." They were her words, but somehow, she didn't believe them.

"You'll be leaving."

"I'm getting married, Nick. You know that. Nothing has changed. The hotel will probably bring in—"

"A hotel? You are going to let someone turn this place into a hotel? Some city boy's idea of what Ashlington should be? The Lily I grew up with would be horrified!"

"But that's it, Nick. I grew up."

Nick rubbed his hand through his hair and stared at her for a moment. "I'm sorry, I shouldn't have said that. I understand why you would want to get back to your life.

When Taylor died, I couldn't wait to get Olivia out of Los Angeles and back to ours."

"I find it hard to imagine you somewhere like LA."

"That's exactly why I spent little time there. It was hardest for Olivia, of course. Stuck between two parents who tried their best but were far better off in their separate lives."

Lillian said nothing about what Henry had said about Ashlington being Nick's home, too. If she were honest with herself, she would agree.

Chapter 19

Spain, 1812

A week after they crossed the river Tagus, an unusually quiet, recently promoted Sergeant Young caught Henry's attention in camp.

"Sir?" Young shuffled his feet, refusing to look Henry in the eye.

"What is it, Ernest?" There was something about how the lad approached him that made Henry use his first name, something he rarely did.

"I wanted to ask if you would take my last letter, Captain. It is to Nelly. I want you to make sure she gets it. Only I feel like today is my day." He offered a piece of paper to Henry, who waved it away with a laugh. Young was the most optimistic man in the entire regiment and a superb practical joker. Henry's smile quickly fell when he studied him. Eyes heavy with lack of sleep were enough to tell Henry that all was not well with the soldier. Young had the envious ability to lay his head and find sleep anywhere.

"Nonsense." Henry put a hand on his shoulder and gave it a friendly squeeze. "You are a fine soldier, one of the best. You will chase the French with me all the way back to Paris, and then you're going home. Back to Nelly O'Connell and her—"

"No, I'm certain. Please take it."

Henry reached slowly and took the paper with a frown before pushing it into his coat pocket. "I shall return it later, you'll see."

Young threw him a smart salute, which Henry returned together with a smile of encouragement, but could do nothing about the tightness in his belly and sense of foreboding.

Many had commented over the years on how Young looked like a younger version of Henry. Both blonde and blue-eyed, they also shared a similar aversion to blood despite their competence and experience in battle. Assuming not only a captain's responsibility but that of an older sibling, he decided he would keep an extra eye on Young that day and keep him close.

Henry watched Young steady the square with his normal cool head, making Henry forget all about their conversation until later in the afternoon as the French were retreating. Their casualties had been few, so Henry felt in good spirits when he gathered the company together. He gave Young a slap on the back.

"See! What did I tell you?" he said, retrieving the letter and pulling Young's coat open, scrunched it into his inner pocket.

Young had been organising the men back into line, ready to re-join the regiment, but Henry's intervention had turned him towards a copse of trees at the base of the slope. "Captain!" Young shouted, alerting Henry to a Frenchman loading his rifle in the trees. Young stepped in front of Henry and presented his musket.

He fell before he fired; a shot passing straight through his neck at the same time Henry, behind him, received a punch to the chest that knocked him off his feet. He fell behind Young, whose blood gushed from his throat like a dam breached. Too stunned to be sick, Henry crawled down the slope to where the life rushed from his friend.

"Sorry Cap—"

Tears ran freely down Henry's cheeks as his efforts to contain the bleeding became increasingly futile, unable to help the feeling that he was undeserving of such devotion.

"Why did you do that, Young?" Henry felt a knot in his throat. "Time to go rest now, eh?"

Young clutched his hand, and Henry squeezed back.

"I'll make sure your letter gets home, lad. I shall write and make sure they all know how bravely you fought. How you were my brother and the best sergeant in the entire army." He rested his forehead on Young's, holding his attention as the life faded.

"Ernest?" Exactly when Jackson had arrived next to them, Henry did not know.

Henry wiped his eyes and squeezed Jackson's shoulder, suddenly realising that his chest still burnt like it was on fire. "I'm sorry, Jackson."

"You took the same shot, let me see." With a shake of his head, Jackson transferred his concern to his captain. "You are bleeding."

"No, I think it's Young's blood. I am not harmed badly." Twisting onto his back, Henry undid his coat buttons.

The spent musket ball fell to the dirt, revealing a round red spot in the centre of Henry's chest where it had hit him with force, but not enough to cause anything more than a winding and bruise. The realisation that not only had Young been right about the day, but had saved Henry with his actions, made his heart ache. He would have willingly traded places with the lad if it meant Young could have seen home again.

Westbrook slid through the dirt, attracting more gunfire from the trees, landing next to Henry and Jackson. "Henry?" he said, voice pitched high with concern.

"The blood is Young's."

Westbrook reached for Young, but Henry grasped his arm.

He's gone.

The loss that registered over Westbrook's features only added a furious weight to Henry's own.

"Fucking frog bastard!" Jackson yelled, perfectly articulating how they all felt. He attempted to get to his feet as he caved to the anger, but Westbrook grabbed his ankle and held it tight as Jackson struggled.

"Wait!" Westbrook growled.

"We do this properly," Henry said. "West, take a few of the men and make your way down and round to the left. Tell Adams the company are to fix bayonets, give two ranks of fire on my signal, then they follow me."

Taking charge and taking action had the effect of calming Henry. He concentrated on giving orders and trusting his friends. Westbrook nodded and shuffled backwards. Henry watched his progress over his shoulder.

Once out of range, Westbrook passed the instructions to Adams, who, Henry noticed, already had the company formed up into two ranks with muskets aimed.

"Jackson."

Jackson remained looking at Young's body blankly.

"Sergeant Jackson!"

Jackson blinked rapidly, then gave Henry a nod, acknowledgement of the field promotion but without celebration. Filling a dead man's shoes had that effect.

"Take three others and bend right."

Jackson slid backwards, face creased in concentration, eyes black with the promise of vengeance. With Westbrook covering the left and Jackson the right, Henry waited, muscles coiled, sword drawn, for the next shot.

It struck the ground next to Young's head. He raised his sword. The company gave their volleys, then Henry ran.

He felt another shot zip past him, but he was throwing himself forwards down the slope, screaming at the French in the trees with Westbrook and Jackson rushing them from the sides. It was not a wise thing to do, running into cover like that, the enemy being already in retreat. Henry told himself it was all about Young, but he was all too aware of the part of him that still needed to prove himself, though to whom he no longer knew.

Henry bent the truth of it during his later report to Sinclair, knowing that Sinclair would have done the same were it his godson who lay dead. As it was, they caught the French by surprise and left none alive with no damage to themselves, bar Private Cotton with an egg sized bruise to his head where the clot had run into a low branch and knocked himself out.

Later, Henry retrieved the scribbled letter from Young's pocket, together with a tiny wooden angel he had been carving. They buried their friend in the dirt with a hastily fashioned wooden cross.

"It feels different this time," Westbrook said, as the last of the men shuffled away to catch up to the column.

"He was a brother."

They stood close to each other. Close enough that Henry wanted to reach out, to brush Westbrook's knuckles with his fingers in comfort. The shackles of guilt tightened. Young was in his care. He was the captain. How long before he lost everyone he cared about? Who would he get killed next?

"I know what you are doing. Stop it."

Henry jerked his hand away. Had he reached for him without releasing?

"You are blaming yourself. It was not your fault." Westbrook placed a heavy hand on Henry's shoulder. "Young would do it again, even if he knew how it would end. You're his captain."

After losing Young, Henry's mood did little to improve over the next weeks as the regiment wallowed in camp with no sign of action. He checked in with Jackson each day. Some days under the guise of needing help with something, other days to listen to Jackson tell stories of his friend.

The only brightness had been finding a series of plays to buy Westbrook. He presented Westbrook with one, *Antony and Cleopatra,* then hid the other two, *Coriolanus* and *Richard III*, in their tent for him to stumble across. Each discovery causing a bright moment of delight.

In contrast, Henry's melancholy grew, knitting together with his guilt, and the ever-growing feeling that eventually what he hid would be flayed bare for all to see.

At the end of the week, Sinclair invited his officers and several spares to dine at his table in celebration of his birthday. The inside of the dining tent was cramped and boisterous as they greeted each other and socialised with drinks before Sinclair asked them to be seated.

"What happened to you?" Sinclair asked Westbrook, eyeing a fresh bruise on his cheek.

"That was me," Henry said.

"The nightmares?" Sinclair asked in a low tone, not to draw attention to them. Henry nodded. Westbrook always offered the comfort no matter how much it hurt him when Henry lashed out while still asleep, not knowing against whom he fought. The only consolation was that he was not the only one in the regiment to cry out at night, and that no one would mention it the next day.

Henry took his seat at the table, removing himself from Sinclair's proximity before Sinclair thought he had to say anything more on the matter. It would be well-intended, but Henry would receive it as pity and the fact that he had no control of it, that it only highlighted his weakness, made him hate himself almost as much as did for hurting Westbrook.

Henry knew all present around the table that night, except for an older captain of the 34th called Hughes, and a gaunt, sickly looking lieutenant dripping snot, who clung to his every word. Henry found himself not the only one frustrated by Hughes's insistence to trample over any story, adding his own anecdotes before the speaker had finished. Henry heard plenty of murmurs of disapproval from the opposite side of the table. The man was damn impolite, but finally Henry had found somewhere to direct his agitation. He simmered, waiting.

"Robert, I hear Cotton has become a fearful shot," Sinclair said, from where he sketched on the paper next to his plate. "Henry, more potato?" Obedient hands passed the dish Henry's way.

"Jackson would beg to differ, but yes, I'd say Cotton is our best," Westbrook agreed. "Yesterday he managed to—" Westbrook's tale, a good one too, Henry thought, having heard it earlier, got cut short loudly by Hughes at the other end of the table with an altogether different topic.

"Avery of the 50th? Terrible state of affairs, but they would have hanged him, anyway."

The mention of hanging transported Henry back to Badajos, watching the swinging feet of a man whose bloody body dangled from a rope tightened about his neck. Ashen face bulging like Westbrook's had when he found him under the dead. Then he was back at Sinclair's table with his hand shaking so much it spilt his wine. He put the glass down and tucked his hand under his leg, out of sight.

Westbrook dropped his napkin over the red stain

blotting into the tablecloth.

"Scandal?" the sickly lieutenant asked.

"I will ask you to not blacken a man's reputation when all the facts are not known," Sinclair growled. Henry knew the tone well. One a dog would give to another about to steal its bone. Normally most effective. Hackles up, if such a thing was possible, Henry thought Sinclair might have doubled in size. "The man had a wife and children."

They had all heard the rumour; it was not to be spoken of. Hughes paid the warning no heed. "They found him in his billet, trousers around his ankles, having a go with some ensign. The beating the two of them received went overlooked, as it should, though Avery died during it. They hanged the ensign. If you ask me, they got everything they deserved the dirty—"

Sinclair slammed his hand on the table, jolting the silverware. "Damn it, man, I will not have such talk at my table!"

Henry stood up. He felt the air on his left move as Westbrook tried to stop him, but missed his target. "Leave it, Henry."

"The major gave you a warning, sir, refrain or step out," Henry told Hughes, moving around the table, altogether hoping the man did neither.

"What's it to you, Durand? You have sympathy with such a man?"

Henry heard Westbrook's groan as his fist made contact with Hughes's face. Someone wisely grabbed the port decanter, rescuing it from the man's frantic windmilling as he tried to remain on his feet, and Henry grabbed him by the throat.

"Enough!" Sinclair bellowed and, with a remarkable swiftness, moved around the table to wrench Henry away and growl in his ear. "You will not call him out, you hear me, or I will flog you myself and put you on the next boat home. Honour is intact." He then raised his voice again for the benefit of the others present. "I don't want to see you until morning, Durand." He gave Henry a shove towards the tent flap, then bellowed, "Someone remove Hughes from my sight! Next time a senior officer tells you to shut up—you bloody shut up, man!" The last thing Henry heard was Sinclair levelling his temper at Westbrook. "Sit down, Robert, before I make you. And finish your dinner!"

Henry waited in the shadows for Hughes to pass. Because of the staggering, it took some time. Henry followed him, his current state of emotion not helped by the fact men sat around the table had laughed at the revelation. Men who, Henry knew, Avery had considered friends. Twice, Henry got close enough to take Hughes down. Twice, he stopped himself. Sinclair's threat of flogging was of no matter. Being sent home was. That and the fact Hughes was unarmed.

He let Hughes go and returned to his tent where he fell face down onto his bed in the dark, boots and all, contemplating why it bothered him so much.

That he had instinctively reacted to what Hughes had said told him more than any soul searching did. The truth being it had always been part of him. Louisa had said it herself years ago. "You are different from the other boys." One of the fallen. The only thing separating him from Avery was that Henry had not acted on his desires.

"Henry?" a voice said minutes later, accompanied by the groan of Henry's trunk at the foot of his bed as Westbrook sat on it.

"What?"

"You still have your boots on."

"I know."

Like the weeks before Badajos all over again, Henry wished he felt numb rather than the overwhelming burden of pretence and guilt. Could he just feel nothing for once? Could he cut it out? He pushed himself up, hand on the knife at his hip. He should take himself off into the dark to save himself from an end like Avery. The ever present 'Young should be alive, not me,' a heavy burden.

"I have to go—"

"You will not leave this tent tonight," Westbrook growled, pushing him back down. "I will not allow it. We do this together, always. You gave me your word."

A fool's hope. There never could be a 'Together, always,' for men like Henry. No matter how earnest Westbrook had looked when he first said it that awful night at Badajos, the words did not mean the same to him. He was sure of that much. Westbrook, for his part, was simply a man free with his affection. Any touch, just that, a touch. No matter how it burnt.

Henry felt Westbrook's fingers at his waist undoing his belt and stopped breathing, only to realise he was being relieved of knife and sword. He heard the scrape as Westbrook shoved them under his bed opposite. No doubt together with his own weapons. Out of Henry's reach. He heard the thump of boots as Westbrook discarded his own, then a tugging at his feet as he pulled Henry's off.

"Shall I read to you?" Westbrook asked in a cheerier manner Henry saw straight through. "I have just the thing somewhere, you should recognise it—"

"Forgive me, West. I shouldn't have—"

"Hush now." He felt Westbrook's hand run through his hair, like he would calm a horse. Henry hoped he would leave it there. He didn't. The touch left his head but took some of Henry's desolation with it.

Westbrook pulled the blanket off his bed and covered Henry with it, Henry drawing it up high around himself because it smelt of his friend. Feeling rather like a caterpillar in a chrysalis, he rolled onto his side. Perhaps if he stayed inside long enough, he would emerge as someone else.

Something else.

Westbrook lit a candle and took off his uniform coat, which he lay neatly on his own trunk at the foot of his bed. He then shrugged his arms out of his braces and untucked his shirt. Henry recognised it as one of his own, embroidered with HD at the hem, which explained the irregularities with his laundry. He had been meaning to ask the company wives about it, if only they didn't terrify him so much.

Henry continued to watch from his chrysalis, his soul noting every curve and every line his friend created as he moved, searching for the book.

"Shall I begin?" Westbrook asked, the book found, settling on his bed propped on one elbow facing Henry, legs crossed at the ankles. Westbrook reading to him was a light in the dark, when all Henry wanted to do was cling to him and cry like a child.

"Go ahead."

"Two households, both alike in dignity, in fair Verona, where we lay our scene..."

Henry felt the effect immediately, smiling at the recollection of their secret view of the play in Lisbon. The meaning in his world returning.

Westbrook played the words on his lips, cascading them, until he paused to lower the book and smile back, the candlelight softening his outline.

He can never know how you feel about him, Henry's guilt tormented. You'll get him killed too.

Chapter 20

Lillian stared at the inviting corporate logo-covered boarding around the site. Sunny artist's impressions of the new hotel complex and apartments on large billboards implied a happy existence for those bold enough to reach deep into their pockets for their dreams. She felt proud that not only were Theakston, Johansen and Poole proving themselves a force to be reckoned with for high-end property development, but that her designs and business efforts had been part of it. It was not difficult to imagine the addition of her own name to the signage.

"Finally," Guy said, greeting her by the gate as she opened the boot of her car to retrieve her hard hat and high-viz jacket. "As you can see, we have made excellent progress. You should have been here for the groundbreaking, quite the celebration. Did Marcus not insist?"

Inside the chipboard perimeter, most of the street had been cleared. The derelict factory, the terraced housing demolished. All signs of the lives that had lived and worked there for generations, wiped out. It made Lillian slow, her confident pace lost to a thought for the bent figure of Alice Prescott stood on the northern boundary of the site. Where the wooden boarding became a chain fence negotiating a protected oak tree, wrinkled fingers clutched the wire. Lillian felt a heave in her heart. What memories haunted Alice Prescott? Did she feel the weight of regret like Henry, or did she see the faces of those lost, like Westbrook?

Who was left to comfort her now she had lost her home? That tiny two-up, two-down terraced house that smelt of cat litter and chicken-barley soup on a constant simmer; the threadbare carpet at the front door, the sunken arm chair in which her husband passed away peacefully that winter, and the photographs.

Lillian had not been aware of them the first few times she visited. During the visit where the old lady finally agreed to sign the sale papers, she had insisted on making tea, leaving Lillian and the lawyer in the front room. The best room, Alice Prescott had called it. Lillian noticed the photographs then. Some hung by ruthless nails on the wall, some propped on the mantelpiece or on the dresser. There had been no dust. The pictures cared for daily, Lillian supposed.

Were the tears on that woman's face today the true price of Lillian's ruthless pursuit of what she thought she needed to be successful, the top of her game, the unbending drive to prove her worth? Or was it the almost audible breaking of the old lady's heart as the bulldozers shoved and rammed at the rubble that was once her home?

Parts of the houses were still recognisable in the debris. A splintered banister, an avocado coloured kitchen cupboard door, a chipped porcelain sink.

A picture frame.

"Wait!" Lillian shouted. She ran forwards waving her arms in front of the bulldozer. "Wait, please!" she called to the driver.

The banksman, the person in charge of making sure reckless people like Lillian did not impede the machinery, tried to stop her, signalling frantically to the bulldozer driver who halted his machine. The driver threw his hands in the air, stood up and shouted something rude at both Lillian and the banksman. She ignored their protests and climbed into the rubble, soon to be sorted for recycling.

"Lillian? What the hell are you doing?" Marcus called.

She ignored him too and pulled at a wooden floorboard. It gave way, and she found what had caught her attention. The frame was destroyed, but, miraculously; the photograph held within had survived. She pulled it out and shook off broken glass and dust.

"Sorry. Thanks!" she called to the bulldozer driver, who sat back in his seat still cursing and waited for her to move out of the way.

"You can't go doing that on site Lillian, you'll get yourself killed or we'll get shut down if the health and safety lot see you," Marcus said, stilling the banksman, preventing him adding his angry berating. Lillian was under no illusion which would be worse in Marcus's opinion.

She walked over to the chain fence and met the old lady's eyes with hers. "I'm sorry," she said with a frown and handed her the photograph. It fell woefully short of what she should say.

"The moving people said they had boxed everything,"

Alice Prescott said. It had been part of the deal Lillian had negotiated. They had offered the reluctant sellers of homes on George Street moving services and new apartments in the complex at a reduced price. Lillian had been the one that convinced them all it was the best thing for them. "I have missed this one. Thank you."

"Lillian?" Marcus called from behind her. She turned, realising then how angry he looked. "Is this what that was all about? You risked the whole site for some picture?"

Not a picture. A memory.

Lillian looked back to the old woman to offer further apology, but she had gone. Already across the street, the photograph clutched to her chest.

"I need to go home," Lillian said, suddenly claustrophobic with the lofty buildings of the city leaning over her. Raptors circling a carcass they recognised. "Sorry Marcus, I can't stay. I need to get back to Ashlington."

"But I made a dinner reservation with my parents to talk about the wedding. Mum thinks she has found the perfect venue. One night, Lillian. Is that so much to ask?"

She left him holding his hands up in despair rather like the bulldozer driver had, and an equally confused expression on the face of Guy.

Though still cross with her for leaving the building site the way she did, Marcus drove down to Ashlington the following night and surprised Lillian with a crate of expensive champagne for Guy's birthday dinner.

"Have you seen my phone?" he called from Lillian's

bedroom. She stood in the en-suite bathroom guiltily brushing her teeth, calculating when to tell Marcus about the last man that had been in her bedroom.

"I left it right here on the dresser." Marcus was silent for a moment, then swore. "How did it get there? Bloody hell, the screen is smashed. And you wonder why I hate this place."

I don't think it is particularly fond of you either, Lillian thought. There was always more door slamming, and yesterday he lost his car keys only to find them on the doormat. Lillian had convinced him he had dropped them there himself, but she had seen him put them on the hall table. Henry, like the house, preferred it when Marcus was in London.

He fell silent, so Lillian leaned to the side, allowing her a view through the doorway of Marcus inspecting his broken phone. She returned to the sink spitting out the toothpaste and rinsed with mouthwash.

"What if I don't want to go back?"

She heard his footfall on the bare floorboards, and he appeared in the doorway. "You can't be serious. Our lives are in London, the business, your career. I thought that's what you wanted?" He shook his head, as though disappointed by her lack of understanding. "Selling this place is the only thing that makes sense. It is tired, sooner or later it will start falling down around you. We have an excellent offer, one I worked hard to get. You know Warrilow, he can be an old goat but he will pay well over market value to develop this place so he can link it to his hotel in Stratford."

Lillian thought of Henry and what he said about needing his home. What would happen to him if Ashlington Manor became a hotel?

"We'd be free of it then," Marcus continued. "If you don't like the hotel idea, then we could do it ourselves, convert it into luxury apartments. In stately homes they fetch quite a profit—what's the matter?"

"What if I want to stay, keep it, live here, start my own business?"

"You can't mean that?" Marcus looked confused, as though her having her own mind about the subject had not occurred to him, let alone her following it through.

She watched him weigh up what to do next.

"Maybe Saturday will help. Having our friends here will make you feel better, remind you what you left behind and where you belong. Maybe Guy can talk some sense in to you. He seems to be the only one that you listen to. Did you mention this idea to him?"

She nodded.

"What did he say?"

"Only something about moving on."

He gave a look that said, 'See, it's not just me,' all self importance and told you so. "Yes, the dinner party will do you some good."

"I was looking forward to having the house full."

"So you don't have to listen to your voices?" he said as though it were all some joke, that she hadn't worried for her sanity. It broke any sincerity like a soap bubble, and with it, any chance of her telling him about Nick that night. How could he possibly understand?

The insincerity also reminded her of the letter she had read earlier. Buried in Henry's trunk, it was one of many letters from his mother.

I wish you would write more. A one-line message of the nature 'I am still alive' is not the type of correspondence to prevent your father from sailing to Spain and dragging you home himself.

I have done my best to placate him about your refusal to return and marry the Smalley girl, but there is still time. Indeed, I approve of the union myself, as does she. She remembers you from the ball before you left, and if I am any judge of character, then I think what she saw pleased her very much. When you make an effort, you can look more dashing than Christopher and, despite what your father might say, I know you to be Danny's match intellectually.

I urge you to act fast, Henry. She is of the looks and connections that will be taken up soon.

Enclosed is the book you asked for. Is it for your friend or have you taken to reading again? You have not read Gulliver's Travels *since you were a boy, though I remember it was your favourite, a little rebellious for my tastes.*

We pray for your continued safety and most expeditious return.

Chapter 21

Spain, June 1813

Henry growled with frustration, then began pacing the floor, waiting for the shaking to stop.

"What is it?"

"My hand, sometimes it shakes so much I can't do anything with it."

"Here, let me." Westbrook took over tying Henry's neckcloth for him. "It happens when you are anxious. It is a dance, not a battle. There," he said, tucking the ends into Henry's shirt, a stray finger grazing his skin. He then began work on Henry's coat buttons. A task he managed without looking. Instead, the attention of his single eye darted between Henry's two. "Better?"

Most of the time, proximity to Westbrook was perfectly manageable. Reassuring, in fact. Other times, like this, when all around them was still and quiet and they stood eye to eye, close enough that Henry could tune himself to the thrum of Westbrook's heart beating, he thought it might all be too much.

They were preparing for a ball. A ball! Whoever dreamed these things up? Good for morale, they had been told, and (in Sinclair's opinion) an opportunity for the Spanish general to show off. The alarming shake of Henry's hand, the relic of the horror of Badajos that haunted him regularly, a trusted sign of misgiving.

He had attempted to comb his hair into a neat parting, but had quickly given up. It preferred to fall forwards in an untidy fashion, and there was little he could do to convince it otherwise. He'd also cut himself shaving, something Westbrook, now finished with the buttons, noticed, and dabbed at with his thumb.

It occurred to Henry that if loving Westbrook made him a bad person, perhaps he should resign himself to the fact he didn't want to be good after all. As if agreeing with him, the tremor in his hand stopped.

They arrived at the ball on horseback, Sinclair having declined the use of a carriage. Inside the grand house they skilfully dodged prowling women looking for suitors for their daughters; with such choice before the ladies, the atmosphere fizzed with possibility. Henry and Westbrook prioritised drinks, followed by refuge in a corner where they could watch the proceedings from behind the cover of several eager junior officers.

The last ball of this size Henry had attended had been at Ashlington six years ago. One in which his parents introduced him to Erica Smalley, their idea of what Henry's future would look like. Delicate, mouse-like and irritatingly repellent, she only confirmed his need to flee. Henry spent most of that ball being poked and prodded to his parents' will until Danny took pity on him, running interference so Henry could escape. He had slept in the tree house that night, lost and alone.

Sinclair soon found Henry and Westbrook, routing them out of their defensive position to introduce them to a colonel of the 95th, his wife and, predictably, their unmarried daughter.

"You like to dance?" the daughter, whose eyes darted to their rank insignia with a practised evaluation, asked both of them, before her attention came to rest on the higher ranked Henry. Thankfully, a well-aimed glare from Sinclair told his godson to be a gentleman and dance with her.

Westbrook straightened his back. "It would be my honour," he said with a fixed smile that Henry knew meant he did not mean it, and offered the girl his arm. Still, at least Sinclair had not picked on him, Henry thought, taking a shifty step backwards in case his matchmaking major found an unfortunate daughter to send his way too.

Westbrook made a reasonable job at dancing once he got into it, only standing on the woman's foot twice as far as Henry could tell, though he lacked the pomp and seriousness of his fellows. Henry thought of his brother Christopher, an excellent dancer, light on his feet, who would happily dance all night to find a girl willing to give him a kiss. The colonel's daughter certainly looked willing enough as she gazed up at Westbrook with long darting eyelashes and menacing low-cut dress-line. Uncharitably, Henry hoped she might catch a cramp and have to sit the next dance out.

He was vaguely aware of his friend Major Roylance, now a more confident man than the one that had dithered about the convent, stood next to him talking about storming a French cannon position with his new command. A subject which would normally have Henry captivated, but Henry's attention was elsewhere. Fixed on Westbrook; on his innocent oblivion that he shone more than any other. As if to add to Henry's growing madness, Westbrook kept looking his way, giving Henry the same smile he would when he read at night; the smile that melted Henry's heart every damn time.

Henry tracked him for a while through the reels then, deciding he had put himself through enough torture, excused himself from Roylance. He sought the fresh air of the terrace, exchanging his empty wineglass for a full one on the way.

He undid his coat and pulled his smartly tied neckcloth loose, enjoying the night breeze tapping at him. A welcome change from the suffocating presumptions inside the house. He settled by the railing, looking out over the rear of the house and its garden. A newer estate than Ashlington, the trees were not as large or established. The perfectly manicured lawn led to a maze of tightly cut high hedges where guests wandered, disappearing past lanterns into the dark in pairs. A footman attempted to offer something to eat from a tray balanced expertly on stretched fingers, only to veer away when Henry glowered at him.

Moments later, he felt a touch at his shoulder; the gentle press and warmth of a familiar form. "You hate these things," Westbrook said, his back leaning against the rail.

"I hate having to pretend." Henry passed him the wineglass, wondering why he didn't think more before speaking.

Westbrook gulped some wine and passed it back. "What if we didn't have to?"

"That's the place I dream of."

Westbrook bumped him with a lean. "You'd have to take me with you, to look after you, make sure you don't do anything stupid."

Henry laughed, not altogether sure they were talking of the same thing. "Of course. I wouldn't get far without you, West."

"What would we call it? Such a place?"

Henry considered this. Home? He did not get time to answer.

"Psst! Westbrook. Durand," a voice came from behind them. Recognising it, Henry turned to greet Roylance, and leant back on the rail like Westbrook was, both now facing the house, shoulders touching. Like a pair of laid-back, red-coated sentinels.

"She asked me to take a turn about the garden," Roylance said with what was almost an excitable hop, and a nod behind him to where the Colonel's daughter Westbrook had been dancing with waited. Fast work indeed. "Can't thank you enough for the introduction, Robert. If anyone asks—you have not seen us."

"Major Roylance?" she enquired with a glance back at the house. Time was of an essence. How long before her father noticed her absence? Roylance jigged his weight from one foot to the other.

Westbrook gave him an encouraging slap on the arm.

"Just Remember Egypt, Seymour, you'll be fine," he told him with a wink.

"Egypt—of course—that's the spirit." Roylance swallowed again, hand darting to his sword hilt. With a smart turn, he marched bravely, Henry thought, to the woman waiting for him.

Westbrook nudged Henry with a conspirative snigger, and they both turned to look out over the garden, elbows propped on the rail, shoulders in contact once more. Henry passed him the drink again and caught sight of Roylance with his lady walking towards the maze, envious of their comparative freedom.

"Wasn't that the colonel's daughter you were dancing with? You don't mind?" he said.

"Mind what?"

"That Roylance gets to take her into the garden?"

"Not at all. She is attractive enough—pleasant enough for conversation, but not the type I could fall in love or share a life with." Westbrook passed the glass back to Henry, who finished the contents.

"What is?" It suddenly seemed strange that they had never talked of such things; Henry unable to decide if he wanted to hear the answer.

Westbrook turned his attention back to the garden and scratched beneath his eyepatch. Henry expected him to ponder such a question for a while, but he seemed to have his answer at hand. "I admire bravery and honour. Apparently, I also find an impulsive countenance attractive. You know, the sort that doesn't always think things through, yet always has the ability to put others first, often to a fault." He shook his head and chuckled as though fondly remembering such a moment. He then gave Henry a hard stare. "Someone that needs me as much as I need them."

Henry stared back into the pool of green, trying to recall if they had come across such a woman.

"They'd also buy me lots of books," Westbrook added with a raised eyebrow.

"Naturally, they'd be a fool not to." Henry fell quiet and looked out to the garden, twisting the empty wineglass, mulling over the part about books.

"I would spend forever with that person," Westbrook sighed.

He said it so quietly Henry was sure he had imagined it. Even so, the garden beckoned. It pulled at him like an irresistible purr. Were he immeasurably braver, he would reach for Westbrook's hand and lead him to their doom.

The sad reality would, he had no doubt, be a broken nose and knee to the groin, punctuating the loss of his closest friend. What if, in some other realm, like one of his books, Westbrook felt the same? Would he follow Henry into the dark this night, and light it for him?

He dared to look at his friend and found him staring at Henry's hand where it gripped the rail.

"There you are!" boomed a voice as a heavy weight fell on Henry's shoulder. At the same time, he felt Westbrook jolt next to him. "I have been looking for you two. What the devil are you doing out here in the cold?" Sinclair enquired. "There is someone I'd like to introduce you to, Robert.

Come along, Durand, you too."

They followed him, like two young children following their father ready for a beating, heads down, hands behind backs. Henry could feel himself falling to the lost place again, but then Westbrook bumped him with his shoulder.

Toulouse, France, 1814

I write once more despite having not having received reply since Christmas. We pray you are safe and your lack of communication is because of the complicated nature of having mail reach you on the march and not a sign you are injured. Mama is so wrought with worry for you, I fear it is making her sick. If you can find the time to write a brief note or send word that you are indeed well, it would be received most fervently by all of us here at Ashlington.

Life here continues in its monotonous routine, nothing like the excitement you must experience. The newspapers are full of news of your victories.

The estate takes most of my time, but the tenants are behaving themselves and spring has been adequately productive. A date has set for the wedding. In a few months I shall be a married man. I'm thrilled; a family of my own is what I have longed for but, ~~if only.~~ It does not matter, things have to happen a certain way and I have a duty to our name and the estate.

The disapproval in your last letter was blunt, little brother, but that is a luxury you can afford. I cannot. Marriage to Ursula will secure this place for generations to come, and in return her father gets the land he wanted to quarry.

I saw Louisa yesterday; she sends her fondest regards.

Henry threw the letter on his bed, leaving the rest unread. Danny didn't even love Ursula Chilton, he mused. How predictable for his brother to take the weight of the entire family on his shoulders. But then, Danny was the dependable one. Henry had only run from his family. The army may have changed him, but he doubted it would ever be enough for them. He rubbed his face with both hands, coarse whiskers scratching at his fingers. Perhaps he should shave before the assault? A thought he soon dismissed.

"Henry?" a deep voice from beyond the tent flap enquired.

"In here, West." Henry tucked the letter away into his journal, then grabbed for his coat. Typically covered in dust, fraying around the yellow cuffs and with a growing hole in one elbow, it was overdue for laundering. As it was his comfortable one, he was reluctant to give it up. A nearby cannon fired. "They're early."

"Actually, you are late," Westbrook said, picking up an apple from the table and rubbing it on his sleeve. "The old man gives his compliments and asks if you will get a bloody move on." Westbrook perched himself on the trunk at the foot of Henry's bed, causing it to creak, adding to the dent he had created in the lid. In all the years they had shared a billet or tent, Westbrook never sat on his own trunk, wore Henry's shirts more than his own, and now stored his overflowing collection of books in Henry's trunk, increasing its weight significantly.

"I had hoped he'd get bored and go do something else," Henry said.

Most of the officers had posed for Sinclair, though it was something Henry had, until now, avoided. He eyed Westbrook dubiously, convinced the major would have forgotten had Westbrook not mentioned it at dinner last night.

"He says he will use the sketches to paint from and sell them to our families after the war."

"I find it hard to imagine my father paying anyone for a painting of me," Henry snorted.

"I'm not sure who is more fed up, him or that monster of a horse of yours," Westbrook said, leaning out of the tent flap. He took a noisy bite of the apple, his grin suggesting he knew full well it would irritate Henry into action.

Henry sighed. For the sake of his favourite horse, if no one else, he would get on with it.

"Will I do?" he asked.

Westbrook narrowed his remaining eye. "Honestly? It's your particularly dishevelled look, but at least the drawing will be an accurate representation." He dodged the apple thrown in his direction and Henry stalked out of the tent, taking the last with him.

Holding a hand up to shield his eyes from the glare, Henry found what he was looking for as the major arranged his considerable bulk onto a small wooden stool that hardly looked up to the task. Behind him lounged three of Henry's company, taunting an unwitting private they had coerced into holding Henry's new horse. Though lighter than the usual male horses favoured for war, the chestnut mare, rescued from a breeder, was faster and had a reputation similar to her owner.

"Sergeant Jackson, I can find you something to do!" Henry shouted.

"You heard the cap'n!" the sergeant yelled to the others, returning promptly to a vertical position. "Stop your gawking!"

To his credit, the young private maintained his grip on the end of Whisper's reins as the horse stamped her hooves in the dust and tried to take a bite out of him. Henry relieved him and fed the horse the apple as a peace offering. She munched happily and calmed under Henry's hand, leaving him her own heartfelt gift—a trail of slobber—down his left trouser leg.

"Durand! Thought I'd lost you, my boy," Major Sinclair said, looking up from his sketch. He gestured to Henry with a frown. "Shall we button the coat?"

Henry pretended not to hear.

"Never mind. As you were, not like we have much time now."

With his tongue sticking out of the side of his mouth, Sinclair began scratching at his paper, his eyes darting between Henry and the drawing.

Henry stood staring towards the city of Toulouse, patting Whisper who had long since ceased to flinch at the sound of cannon. The breeze tugged at his open coat and hair, while his thoughts returned to Danny's news and, inevitably, the man he had left inside the tent.

Chapter 22

Guy Theakston arrived at Ashlington Manor that evening unannounced.

"Guy, you should have called. I already had dinner but would much rather have had company." Lillian stepped to the side to let her friend in, then led him towards the lounge. "Tea, coffee—or something stronger?" she added, noticing the strain in his movements.

"You on your own?"

"Just me. I was reading some notes about the battle of Toulouse, of all things. You know the whole family tree stuff, it's pretty gripping. Henry called the horse Whisper," she said, amused. "I always expected something more befitting a war horse, something more menacing."

"I'll take a gin then," Guy replied, ignoring her enthusiasm. He didn't sit, but wandered about the room.

"You won't talk me out of it, Guy. You know that, don't you," she told him, handing him a tumbler with a double gin and not much tonic. "I know I can do a good job on Lady Sylvia's project. It is not a huge profit margin, but it is something I really have a passion for."

Passion. When had she last felt that way about her work? Not the glory of bagging a lucrative contract, but the

264

visceral thrill of the design and creativity.

"That's not why I'm here." He sunk into an armchair and for a few minutes the silence grew as he stared into his glass before sipping slowly at the contents. "Do you remember when you first joined the company, Lillian? We were all so young and full of hope."

"Is everything okay?" Lillian placed a hand on his arm. He had always been thin and wiry, but now, as she studied him closely, she noticed how sunken and hooded his eyes had become. Atlas, with the world pressing down on him.

"It will be," he said. "Everything will be fine. I'm going to make sure of it." He patted her hand, letting her know she wore her concern. "Mind if I use the loo?"

She contemplated pouring him another drink, but thought better of it. He would not find the answer to whatever troubled him at the bottom of a gin glass. After being gone a while, Lillian wondered if he was ill. Truly ill. It might explain the recent weight loss and pallor. Was he here to tell her sad news?

"Remind me of those rules of yours again?" he said when he returned.

"Test the boundaries, stand up for what you believe in and protect those you care about?"

"Protect those you care about. That's it. We really need you to buy in, Lillian. We over extended on the George Street project."

"Over extended? Marcus said everything was okay."

"That's Marcus for you. Proud. Of course he would

say that. Truth is, the company is in trouble. If we don't get a quick cash injection to pay off what we borrowed, then we lose everything. Everything Marcus and I built. He won't say it, so I will. Forget Warrilow, sell this place directly to our company, we develop it, develop the surrounding land and we all come up on top. Where we belong. The three of us. If you don't, then Marcus and I are finished. The damage to our reputations would be too great."

How could they have been so stupid? "I'm your quick fix?"

"You do care about us, don't you? I can't bear to think what this would do to Marcus. We really need this, especially with Claudia leaving the sinking ship. You wouldn't do that, would you Lillian?"

Of course she cared about Marcus and Guy. How could he even ask such a thing? She owed them so much. They had so much to lose, not only reputations. The past was exactly that, the past. She had the living to care for now.

A crashing noise from the hallway made Holly bark, interrupting Lillian's consideration of her values. She followed the spaniel to investigate. The carriage clock, a wedding gift to her parents, from the hallway table had smashed on the floor. The broken glass and cogs scattered in a shiver of time. "Sorry Guy, I'll just be a moment picking this up."

"He is using you," Henry said, confirming her suspicion that no draughts were involved in the breaking of the clock. Likely not her coffee cup the other day, either.

"There are easier, less destructive ways to get my

attention, Henry," she hissed, retrieving a dustpan and brush. Her father had loved that clock.

"I'm going to go," Guy said with a shiver. Lillian could feel it, too. The house felt inhospitable and biting. It wanted him gone.

"You don't want to stay?"

He glanced around him as though feeling it himself. "No, I need to be in Oxford early in the morning. I have a hotel room booked. Call me tomorrow. Let me know what you think."

She was not sure why Henry was being so destructive. He ran away from his duty to this place. He ran to the army so he did not have to marry like his father wanted him to, and now he is telling her to stay? He turned his back on Ashlington. Why shouldn't she do the same? If doing so protected those she cared about, surely she had more of a right? Not to mention there was no way she was going to get pushed around by a ghost throwing a tantrum.

"Cut Warrilow out, Guy. Send me your proposal," she said, sounding every bit as hard as she used to, as she let him out.

Opening the front door caused several more, somewhere inside the house, to slam shut.

Chapter 23

England, September 1814

When news of Napoleon's abdication reached the 28th on the 14th April 1814 the regiment sailed home to England. Henry had not called the walls of Ashlington home for many years so while other officers made the most of the opportunity to visit families, Henry (and therefore Westbrook) remained at barracks until autumn lengthened the shadows and brought rain to the drill square.

Under pressure from the insistent correspondence of both retired Major Sinclair and Henry's father, the colonel ordered them home while he made fresh plans for embarkation to America. Having not seen Sinclair since the surgeon removed him from France following his injury at Toulouse, they made him their first stop.

Turning into the driveway of Sinclair's home Trewsbury Park near the Roman town of Cirencester, Henry couldn't help think of that day in Toulouse. Sinclair knocked off his feet by rifle shot. Not wishing to believe it, nothing could hurt Sinclair. Steadying the line, stepping forward to take his major's place. "Hold!" he called out, facing down the oncoming French column. "Front rank ... fire!" Ordering two men to get the major rear. Looking for Westbrook, finding him wiping his sleeve across his face, watching his godfather's progress to safety. Then the shell hit Sinclair, and Westbrook ran.

"My boys!" Sinclair greeted them limping, in a shuffling hurry that employed the use of a single crutch, from his front door. Sinclair's father had built the house with a three-story square facade, a symmetrical neatness Henry admired, and a sweeping double stone staircase covering the porte-cochere that allowed dry entry to the house from a coach.

Sinclair pulled Westbrook down from his horse to embrace him with a strength that lifted the younger man clean off his feet. Henry dismounted and gave Whisper's reins to the stable boy who led the horses away, unperturbed by the exuberant parental show of affection.

"Aren't they feeding you any more, Robert?" Sinclair held Westbrook at arm's length to study him. Satisfied with what he saw, he turned to Henry. "Why Henry, you look positively smart today!" he said. Henry began to button his coat, but Sinclair laughed. "I am not your commanding officer anymore."

"I beg to differ," Henry replied. In his heart, Sinclair would always be his major. He offered his hand, but Sinclair ignored it, instead drawing him into his arms. "Good to see you, Major," Henry said, wondering if he would ever breathe again.

"So, they let you two out, did they?"

"A little over two weeks," Westbrook said.

"Two weeks? Good Lord, the colonel clearly has no idea of the trouble you two could do with such time. Come along inside, boys. I want to hear everything. He thinks they are finally getting you to America?"

Wooden leg and crutch tapping on the flooring, Sinclair led them inside. Henry reached out to offer his help with the steps, but Westbrook stopped him. He was right. Sinclair would have hated it. Westbrook clenched his jaw and kept his head down, refusing to look at his godfather's decline as they followed him through the large hall to the drawing room with painfully slow progress.

It had been Westbrook that held Sinclair down in Toulouse as the surgeon cut. Later on that awful night, Henry found his friend trying to pick a fight with several bottles of port. The liquor, until that point, had been winning. "He'll hate me for it, Henry," Westbrook had slurred, the scarring of his eye socket red and angry as he cried in Henry's arms. "He will never forgive me."

Sinclair had done no such thing.

Upon reaching the drawing room, Sinclair sat them down, ordered tea, then interrogated them for information from the regiment. They gave it willingly and, by the time dinner was served, had him up to speed on all accounts. At Whisper's expense, Westbrook took much enjoyment in the recounting of their sailing.

"In his defective wisdom, he brought the little brute up topside where she promptly pinned him against the rail, stood on the bosun's foot and crapped all over the deck. I had been retching over the side when all this began and had to find a moment to stop for long enough so I could push her off Henry."

"She wouldn't let anyone else near," Henry laughed.

"Always was a bad tempered old nag," Sinclair offered, which Henry thought was hardly fair.

"Once we got him back on the ship—"

"She didn't push me off," Henry objected. "I still had one foot on deck."

"He had to feed her treats for the rest of the crossing. The Channel and I have never heaved so much, nor one horse demanded quite so much attention."

"Your father never liked the boats either, Robert," Sinclair said, chuckling. "Spent many a sailing with his head in a bucket."

"Are they very much alike?" Henry asked. "West and his father?"

"Come see for yourself." Sinclair scrapped back his chair. "Potts! Don't you get clearing away, we aren't finished yet," he called to the cook, who turned on her heels, retreating to the kitchen.

He led them into the library where, judging by the worn seat and scattered sketches, easel and paints, Sinclair spent much of his time. The long window beyond the easel let in blotches of light from the garden, a wide view stretching beyond a fountain to the horizon. A small portrait hung next to the window. Sinclair and Westbrook took up position in front of it.

"One of yours?" Henry asked, joining them. "It's remarkably lifelike." The painting was of a smiling younger Westbrook, though Sinclair had painted the nose a fraction too long, the eyes a shade too dark, and there was something

271

wrong about the uniform. "How old were you when he did this?" Henry asked.

"That's James, not Robert," Sinclair said, "he was nineteen."

"Really? Well, that answers my question then. His father was all dimples and curls too!" Henry immediately chastised himself for such an unguarded comment. He blamed it on Sinclair. Away from the army, there was something gentler and open about his major.

It struck Henry that while he looked like a mirror of his father, Westbrook had all the mannerisms of his godfather. Even now, the two of them stood looking at James with the same pensive stance; weight on one side, one arm folded, the other bent at the elbow supporting chins deep in thought. Westbrook had lost one father but gained another, not of blood but something deeper. In some respects, Henry considered, so had he.

"I always wondered what you had said to make him smile so," Westbrook said.

Sinclair chuckled. "He had just received news he was to be a father. It was you that made him smile."

Westbrook beamed.

"What are you working on now?" Henry asked.

Westbrook moved to the easel where he peeked under the cloth covering it. "My word, it is genius!"

"It isn't finished yet, Robert," Sinclair scolded.

"You have really captured his essence," Westbrook said, sucking in his cheeks to prevent himself from smiling.

They were acting most suspiciously.

"I shall let you see it when it is completed, Henry," Sinclair informed him, adjusting the cloth and herded them both out of the room.

As evening fell, with bellies full and glasses charged with Sinclair's finest brandy, they sat comfortably by the fire until Westbrook announced his intention to raid the library. He left the room singing a French song Henry was sure he would not get away with in any other company.

"How is he doing since you have been back?" Sinclair asked once they were alone.

"Haunted."

"You both are."

Henry nodded. Silence fell around them again. There was much Henry wanted to tell him, much he wished Sinclair would say. "I do try to take care of him."

"He does not always make it easy. Exhausting, isn't it?"

"He takes care of me, too. Far more than I deserve."

"That's not what I meant. I refer to the fitting in."

Henry said nothing.

"In a fairer world, Henry, we could all be who we are without fear. Don't let the expectation of society make the real you disappear altogether."

The real me? Henry wasn't sure he knew who that was anymore.

"Mind if I borrow these?" Westbrook asked, entering the room carrying a precarious pile of books he could hardly see over.

"Not at all, my boy," Sinclair said, all hint of his

conversation with Henry erased.

When Henry woke in the morning, the world had tilted, putting everything on its side. For his head to feel normal again would take a miracle. Or breakfast.

Sinclair lay slumped in his armchair with his remaining foot on a footrest, his detached wooden leg leaning against the fireplace. Someone had covered him with a blanket. Westbrook emitted a muffled purr from where he lay face up on the settee, head under an open book, one arm dangling next to a fallen glass.

Henry peeled his face off the rug, not entirely sure of how he got there. He recalled the three of them sharing stories around the fire and, though he was unlikely to admit to such a thing, as they became more intoxicated and talked of who they had lost, each shed tears. Sinclair and Westbrook openly. Henry doing his utmost to hide his own. The last thing he remembered was closing his eyes, listening to talk of James and a warm, soft peace brushing at him.

Sinclair's valet stepped over Henry to open the curtains, letting in a thunderous shaft of light.

"Someone tell the drummer boy to stop making such a din," Sinclair mumbled.

"That'll be your head, Father. Don't mind me if I stay here a while." Westbrook told him from under his book. Whether either of them registered his use of the word father, Henry did not know. Stretching and mindful of the throbbing in his skull, he went in search of something with which to line his stomach.

Hours later they ate breakfast (Henry's second), the conversation comparatively stilted. Westbrook was to stay a few more days with his godfather before riding on to Bath, to his mother and sister. It had come to the moment Henry dreaded; having to say goodbye to them. Eventually, Henry stood and thanked Sinclair formally for the hospitality.

"Is it that time already?" Sinclair said, looking at his pocket watch in as much denial as Henry was about the hour. "Don't make me have to write to the colonel again to get a visit, eh?"

"Of course."

"I shall ask Mr Collins to call for your horse to be made ready."

"He already has," Westbrook said, looking out of the window. His voice wavered, barely at all, but then Henry knew where to look. Sinclair's shoulders slumped, aging him once more. Henry turned his back on them both so they didn't see his hand shaking.

Outside, Whisper stood with her ears back, making Sinclair's stable boy work for his keep with her bad tempered nipping. Westbrook descended the steps to take over, Whisper greeting him with a nudge and nibbling investigation of his pockets.

"Henry."

This time, Henry allowed himself to enjoy the reassuring sensation of Sinclair's arms around him. Is this what a father should feel like? He wasn't even sure his own father had ever embraced him. "I don't want to go. I would much rather stay here," Henry whispered. He suddenly felt very young. Too young.

Sinclair rubbed him on the back. "They are your family, Henry. Just remember, home isn't always a place."

Henry joined Westbrook, who had busied himself adjusting Whisper's bridle. He needn't have. Henry could see the stable boy had done a fine job.

"See you in two weeks," Westbrook said, looking at his feet. It would be the longest they had been apart. Then, as though he threw all caution to the wind, he took hold of Henry. "Don't do anything stupid without me."

Henry rested his face against the warm fold between Westbrook's neck and shoulder, hoping that from where Sinclair stood, it might look like a regular fraternal embrace. Had Westbrook not had a considerable amount to drink the night before, his fingers working their way from the base of Henry's neck into his hair, may have spoken otherwise.

"I promise," Henry said, and Westbrook let go.

From the gate, Henry looked back before taking his path north to Ashlington. Sinclair stood in the doorway, one hand supporting himself on the door frame, the other waving him off. Westbrook had gone.

Henry reached Ashlington late in the afternoon. He stopped first at Ashlington's village inn, The Archer, hoping to surprise Louisa, she being the one thing that might make returning home bearable. As she was not home, it was Louisa's mother that greeted him. "You can't go home to your mother looking like that," she told him, taking an aggressive clothes-brush to his coat. "You always could find the puddle on a perfectly dry road." She stood back and looked up at his hair with a tut. "Perhaps if we—" She ran a hand over it. "No, perhaps not," she said, frowning, recognising an impossible task when she saw it. "I shall tell Louisa you called."

He halted Whisper by Ashlington's gate house cottage, pausing for a moment, concerned by the disturbing tang of smoke that filled his nostrils and caused his stomach to lurch; the thick pungent smoke of a fire out of control, like the chapel in the convent or homes in Badajos. He turned, searching for the source, his hand shaking as it did before battle. Then, as quickly as the impression came, it was gone. Whisper tossed her head and gave a buck to admonish him for his momentary panic. There is no smoke. No fire.

Henry realised then how tired and leaden he felt and dismounted lazily, swinging his leg over the neck of the horse to slide down out of the saddle. He ambled up the beech-lined driveway towards the house, savouring the approach; letting it imprint on his soul before dealing with what storms waited inside.

The lowering temperatures had transformed the garden into a display of red and gold where he found Jones the gardener busy clearing fallen leaves, his worn frame bent over the rake like the curve of a snail's shell.

"Master Henry? Is that you?" he called, raising his hand to his forehead. "Captain, I should say by the looks of it."

"Lovely day, Jones, how is the missus?"

Jones leant on the rake and gave Henry a grin that

tugged at the corners of a splendid moustache. "Well enough to still be nagging, thank you for asking."

Henry smiled. Everything was as it should be.

"Shall I find Mr Samuels for you?"

Handing the reins to the groom was appealing, but Whisper shoved at him with her nose. Henry agreed. The longer he took getting into the house, the better.

"I'll see to her. I'm sure Mr Samuels has his hands full."

"House is full, Captain, with no doubt. The Chiltons are visiting."

"Oh God, really?" The words escaped before Henry could stop them. No matter. By the look of the smirk, Jones despised them as much as Henry did.

"Wedding talk."

"Nothing escapes you, does it, Jones?"

"Something I picked up in the army. Always does well to mind your surroundings. You have learnt that too, by the looks of you."

"He still talks of you. Sinclair."

"Does he?"

"You saved his life."

"Did he tell you that?"

"Yes, though he gave little detail."

Jones smirked again. "That is how it shall be then."

Henry left Jones to his work and secrets. He settled Whisper into a stable, and promised to turn her out into the paddock if she behaved herself for one night, leaving her tucking into hay and oats with contented snorts.

The front of the predominantly Elizabethan house, a hodgepodge of gables and stone buttresses, welcomed Henry with its gaping porch. Henry had spent many a lazy hour as a child lay on the lawn watching Louisa threading daisies and counting the chimneys, of which there were twelve. Unlike the gardener, the house revealed its secrets if you knew where to search for the evidence of its past. He sought the concave hole under one of the upstairs windows from a 17th century cannonball and looked for the stone owl at the base of his parents' bedroom.

Unable to delay any further, he braced himself and entered with a feather's weight of hope that maybe this time his father might look upon him with something close to pride.

Bradley, Ashlington's sour butler, took his hat from him. "Master Henry, your parents are in the drawing room with guests." Henry made for the stairs, but Bradley stopped him with an added, "Your approach was noticed, they are expecting you directly."

Henry straightened his shoulders and re-buttoned his uniform coat, then outstretched his hands in a gesture of will I do?

The butler shook his head and rolled his eyes, then marched towards the drawing-room door where he knocked and announced Henry's arrival.

"Took your time," his father, Nathaniel, said from his chair.

Henry's older brother Danny stood, the only person to greet Henry with a welcoming smile and an enthusiastic handshake. "You've grown!" Danny exclaimed. "Broader now and in need of a shave, whoever would have thought it of my little brother."

"You look well, Danny, I'm glad to see you."

Henry's mother, Elinor, waited her turn with a tapping foot. Henry took her hand and bowed formally. Durands, unlike Sinclairs, were not known to throw aside decorum in displays of affection, even behind closed doors. When he looked up, he watched her eyes evaluate him, acknowledging the changes from the last seven years. He used the time to register her own. Her hair had whitened since he saw her last, and she had lost significant weight in her face.

"You need a bath, Henry," she said under her breath, giving Bradley a nod. He left the room to bark orders at the staff. "You remember Mr and Mrs Chilton," Elinor continued formally. "And Miss Chilton, Danny's betrothed."

"Your servant sir, ma'am." Henry bowed and then addressed Ursula, the force of nature he would soon, reluctantly, have to call sister. "Congratulations, Danny wrote of the news." He glanced at his brother, whose smiling expression had become neutral again.

"Thank you Mr Durand, I am looking forward to making Ashlington my home. Naturally, we have some changes to make here and there." Ursula Chilton cast an insensitive eye around the drawing room, the decor of which had not changed since Henry's childhood.

"Are you home long?" Mr Chilton asked. "What are you now, major?"

Henry's father harrumphed with contempt.

"Captain," Henry answered before his father added further noises of disappointment from his vast arsenal.

"Oh," Chilton said, surprised. "My nephew is a colonel already!" he told Nathaniel, puffing out his chest like a pigeon, unaware that in Henry's experience, quick promotion was not necessarily a good thing.

"Henry has the means," Nathaniel answered, more in his own defence rather than Henry's. "Out of some, what would you call it, Henry? Sense of loyalty? Not only would he not come home to his duty here, he refuses to move from the regiment so will probably remain as a captain until someone talks some sense into him or he gets himself killed."

"Father!" Danny protested.

"Henry knows I am right," Nathaniel said with a flick of the wrist.

Henry held his father's stare before answering by withdrawing. He bowed. "If you will excuse me," he said to the guests, "I shall change for dinner and rejoin you presently." He fled the room with both fists clenched and the strong urge to throttle something.

Later that night, Henry pulled off his boots and stretched. His backside sunk into the mattress of his bed and he wondered if he would ever get to sleep in such comparative luxury. He was used to finding sleep where he could, on a stone floor, or a rocky outcrop propped against Westbrook, surrounded by snoring men. If he were lucky, he would get to sleep in camp, in his officer's cot within a tent only vaguely warmer than the night's air, or a billet overrun with mice. Tonight he was home and scared the soft bed might envelop him and never let him go.

Tightness gnawed at his belly. Desperately needing fresh air, he fought to get up off the bed, won, then opened the window and drank the damp British air like a thirsty man given a tankard of ale. The grounds were quiet and blanketed in darkness but for the flickering candlelight from one or two of Ashlington's rooms. From his, he could see out across the vale towards the dark hump of Bredon Hill. A knock at the door disturbed thoughts of other landscapes, special because they had been shared.

"Where did you disappear to?" Danny asked, helping himself to the chair near the fireplace.

"Fresh air."

"For two hours?"

Henry shrugged.

"I suppose it is strange being back here after so long? Was it very horrible out there, the fighting?"

"It could be."

"You seem different now." Danny looked Henry over, probing with blue eyes identical to his brother's. Calculating. "Did you find what you were looking for?"

"I found ... much more," Henry said. "And you? You are going through with it, marrying her?"

"It is my duty."

They both watched the flames of the fire, both lost to their cages of duty.

"Good night then," Danny said eventually, getting to his feet. "I am so very glad to see you, little brother."

"You too, Danny."

With Danny gone, Henry searched his saddlebag for his journal.

He had brought little back with him. No sword, having broken the guard again, and the blade being beyond repair. The quartermaster refused to issue Henry with another until he was back safely in barracks, which left him with his knife, his pistol with a fistful of cartridges, a spare shirt that might have been Westbrook's, his journal, quill and ink. There was something about writing his thoughts down that gave him some relief from the flashes of memory ambushing him when he least expected it.

Two weeks is unreasonably long. What were we thinking?

It has only been a few hours and I am already stifled. Were he here, West would tell me to be patient, then he would read to me so I would, "kindly stop pacing the bloody floor for five minutes." He seems fond of poetry recently. I should find him something new to smuggle into his trunk.

Avoiding my father (and his nauseating cigar smoke) after supper, I visited Mrs Melton in the kitchen and talked her out of an apple pie. Jones and his wife were very grateful. I confess I enjoyed their smiles and hospitality. How fascinating that you can feel so out of place in your own home, but a man like Jones who has little, not even a child of his own, can make you so welcome. Perhaps that is the old soldier in him?

I walked back the long way through the graveyard, the angel that keeps watch over my sister's grave covered in ivy. It only took a few moments to clear it again, her solemn face and hands at prayer free once more. After all, tethered angels cannot fly.

Chapter 24

Gloucestershire, May 2015

"Don't give me that look."

"What look?"

"That knight-in-shining-armour smugness."

"I don't do smug, Lily."

"And I don't need rescuing. Let's just get that clear."

"I know. I learnt that a long time ago. But I'm glad you called me."

"Well, you were my third choice actually," Lillian said, retying her hair into a hasty ponytail, aware that she most likely had black brake dust on her cheeks from the punctured wheel.

"Third?"

"The RAC said they'd be two hours and your dad said he was in Cheltenham. You were the closest."

Nick put his hands on his hips and gave her an outraged stare. "Charming. Just bloody charming."

"I can change a wheel. I'm not completely hopeless. It's just the locking nuts. They use those air tools at the garage that are impossible to undo."

Nick cast a critical eye around her jacked Mini.

She'd read the manual was what she meant by being capable of changing a wheel. She had got halfway there, at least. Stranded in a field gateway was far from ideal, no matter how good the view was, or how good it had just got. "If you can undo the nuts for me, I'll buy you dinner," she added, hoping it might seal the deal.

"Dinner? Well, for dinner, I'll change the whole thing for you." He laughed as he stepped onto the wrench. It turned.

He gave her a smug look.

"I *am* selling the house," she announced. It was not exactly how she thought she would tell him. Why she even thought she owed him an explanation she did not know, but it tumbled out of her unbidden. "Don't hate me. I have a life back in London. I can't keep both."

"Lily, I don't hate you. Come on—you know I—look, do what is right for you. If that is selling and going back to London, then don't allow anyone else to tell you otherwise."

It was the right thing, she thought. The company would be safe, reputations would be safe, and she would get the life she wanted. All the boxes ticked. Everyone happy.

"It is the right thing to do," she said.

"That's all that matters then," he replied, wheeling the punctured tyre to the back of the car. "Spare is on; I'll just put this one in the boot for you."

The Land Rover coughed and spluttered. She pulled alongside and undid her window. "Need a jump start?" she laughed.

Nick lent his head on the steering wheel, muttering something, a prayer to the Land Rover gods perhaps, and turned the key again. It started.

"See you at home!" she called and pulled away, watching him follow in the rear-view mirror.

Home?

Why had she called it that?

Chapter 25

Ashlington, September 1814

The drizzle was the devious type that got you thoroughly soaked before you noticed it. Henry wished he were indoors, chatting to Danny by the fire with a decent brandy. It being his first full day at Ashlington; he endeavoured to make himself useful and avoid his father, so had walked to the farm to collect paperwork at Danny's behest. The hour grew late, and during the walk home, the deluge increased. About to cut his losses and take the longer route through the woods to see if the tree house still stood, he noticed a figure carrying a bag struggling through the ruts of mud.

"Louisa? What are you doing out here in the rain?" He paused, the significance of her heavy bag and proximity to the coach stop dawning on him. She muttered under her breath, but by now Henry had closed the distance between them and heard her curse. "Where are you going?"

"I see you're back. After seven years, I thought you might have called on me." She pushed past him. "It's of no matter, I'm leaving."

"Visiting you was the first stop I made. You were not at home. Wait, you can't just leave!" The very idea of Ashlington without Louisa scared him as though he were seventeen again. A distinct ball of panic churned in his stomach.

"I can. I have to. You don't understand, Henry." She turned round to face him. Lost. Her face held none of its usual light and determination.

"Do you remember pulling me out of the lake?" he asked, clutching for any subject to prevent her from walking on. She shrugged without care, but he knew she remembered.

It had been the same summer they built the tree house. The Montegue family were staying, and though Henry didn't realise it at the time, the Montegue boys were hateful brats. Being stupidly young and impressionable, he thought the older boys were fascinating, so followed them around naively trying to join in with their antics. That was until the day they held him on his back under the water in the lake.

"You appeared from nowhere and pushed one of them away. I saw you through the water. You were like an angel. The big one holding me down. Well, you thumped him in the face. He didn't know what hit him. You grabbed me by the collar and hauled me up the bank. I was coughing and spluttering, but you weren't finished. You stood wagging your finger at Danny, cussing him with words even he hadn't heard, telling him he should be ashamed of himself for allowing it to happen. That oldest Montegue boy sported the biggest black eye I have ever seen for weeks."

"He told everyone a horse kicked him," she mumbled with a hint of pleasure at the memory.

"I promise, whatever has happened, I will help you. But you need to talk to me."

289

"I don't know where to start, Henry. No one can help me. I have to leave." She pushed past him and began walking again, the hem of her dress dragging in the mud. "You need to let me go."

"But you belong here." Henry recognised the commotion of the stage coach approaching and snatched her bag out of her hands, pulling her back off the lane.

"You don't understand!" she yelled, trying to wrestle her bag free.

"Everything all right, miss?" the driver asked, waving his lamp in the darkening gloom. Louisa thumped Henry on the arm. Hard.

"We shall not be travelling, sir," Henry said, rubbing his arm, glaring at her.

The driver looked from one to the other. Another man might have seen the terror in Louisa's eyes and her struggle to free herself from a dangerous man's grasp. But the stage driver was probably running late and no doubt hungry for his supper.

"Suit yourselves," he said, and with a click of the tongue and flick of the reins, commanded the horses to heave. They trotted away, the laden coach swaying and rattling behind them.

"Now look what you have done!" Louisa screamed, pushing Henry in the chest, almost knocking him over. Then she sank into the mud.

"Bloody hell." Henry frowned and scratched at the back of his neck. He had never seen her like this. Defeated. He held out his hand. "Let's get out of the rain," he suggested. "I am sure I smelt scones earlier. We can raid the kitchen like we used to, find a drink and something to eat." It felt like coaxing a child, but it seemed to work. Reluctantly, she took his hand, and he hauled her to her feet. She linked her arm in his and they walked back to the manor, the silence between them disturbed only by her sniffs and the rain pattering on his sodden coat.

"Mrs Melton is like a magician—saw one once in Lisbon—I swear she hides them on purpose," Henry said later, scouring the kitchen for the cook's baked goods. "Ah ha!" He rummaged in the tin and selected the two largest scones, his mouth watering with anticipation. Many a day he had gone without food on campaign, even as an officer. There had been days where he had handed his last morsels to one of the men, pretending that his own stomach was not aching with emptiness. It made stolen feasts like these all the more special. He found some of Mrs Melton's jams on the shelf, and arranged them in front of Louisa, who had taken off her cloak and was wringing her bonnet out. She smiled when she saw the treats and sat herself down.

As he poured some wine, a thought struck him. "Does Danny know you were planning to leave?"

She shook her head. He said no more and turned his attention back to his task.

She sighed behind him. "Do you have any idea how frustrating you can be, Henry Durand?"

"I'm right then. This is something to do with Danny?"

"You are the brother I never had, you know that. I love

you dearly but there has never been any—attraction between us."

Henry nodded. He regarded her like a sister. Being anything more was too ridiculous to comprehend.

"But with Danny it is different?"

"Oh, God!" she buried her head in her hands.

"You understand he is betrothed?" Henry said, placing a hand on top of hers. She took a deep breath, then nodded and removed her hand from under his to fiddle with the cuffs on her sleeves, refusing to meet his eyes. "Our parents have planned it for years," he continued. "It's to be the wedding of the county and her fortune is supposed to keep Ashlington going for the rest of its days, or at least that is what father would have us all believe."

He regretted those last words the very second Louisa sobbed again, but this time with a long drawn anguish that shocked him. Like a man approaching a temperamental fuse attached to a keg of black powder, he moved seats to sit next to her, straddling the bench.

"I am with child," she said, her words barely audible. She raised her head to look at him with red, swollen eyes.

Henry's first thought was what an amazing thing to hear. She would be a wonderful mother. A little Louisa with long dark hair running around putting everyone in their places would give so much joy. But half a second later, the implication of her words hit home.

"You are not married!" The fear he had seen back in the lane now made sense. Silent, hot tears rolled down her cheeks. "And who the bloody hell is the father?" he asked, his concern for her virtue turning rapidly to anger.

"Danny."

Henry felt his eyes bulge in their sockets and his mouth hang open, so he snapped it shut. She tried to stand up, but he grabbed her arm again and forced her to sit back down.

"Did he—ah?"

"No! Danny would never—I knew you wouldn't understand. I love him and I think he loves me too. We didn't mean for this to happen. I never meant to hurt him. It's why I have to go. No one can find out." She gripped at his wrists, digging her nails in, making him wince. "Promise me, Henry. You can't tell anyone."

"Does he know?"

She shook her head. "I can't get in the way of what his marriage means to this place, to your family. The daughter of an innkeeper shouldn't be involved in such a way with the gentlefolk."

"Stuff that!" Henry said. "Tell him. You have to. He will see everything right. That's what Danny does. He will be thrilled. He has always wanted a family. It is what he wants more than anything. My mother would rejoice to the heavens with a grandchild to spoil finally, and she already loves you like a daughter. None of the other stuff matters to her." He was not entirely sure of that last statement, but it seemed the right thing to say at such a time.

"He has to marry Ursula. Your father would never forgive him."

She was right. Louisa usually was. Danny had been

reckless and misplaced his duty to his betrothal. But there was no way on God's earth Henry would let Louisa suffer for that.

"You promise me two things," he said, drawing her in to his arms, wishing he could right everything in her world again. "Tell him and stay. We will make everything work, but you have to stay."

He watched Louisa talking to Danny in the garden the following morning, praying aloud that his brother would scoop her up in his arms, call the stupid Chilton wedding off and live happily ever after with the woman he loved. But Louisa's slumped shoulders and dejected posture as she walked away from Ashlington, and the father of her child, told Henry all he needed to know.

The punch was a swift one Henry's brother did not see coming.

"You bastard!" Henry spat, wrenching him up by the front of his shirt. "How could you do that to her?"

Danny pulled his arm free from Henry's grip, staggering backwards. Henry tried to keep his anger in check and circled away, shaking the sting from his knuckles.

"She told you?"

"Yes, she bloody told me. Why would you do a selfish thing like that?" He rounded on Danny again with a growl, forcing his brother backwards against the big oak tree.

"I love her," Danny said, the agony clear. "I always did." He slumped to the ground, the despair in his movements matching Louisa's own from the evening before.

"I was stupid."

Henry said nothing.

"And reckless. There, are you happy now I've said it? I was impulsive and risked everything father has been working towards."

"I could not care less about Father's grand plans. What I care about is that my friend thought her only option was to run away. Do you have any idea what that would do to her? I have seen what comes off the streets, Danny; you would not wish that fate upon her, let alone your own child." Henry shook his head to rid himself of the smile of the cockney turncoat he pushed out of the convent window—not worth the powder of his pistol shot. He lowered himself next to his brother, who was wiping blood from his dripping lip on his neatly folded handkerchief. "She deserves better and so does your child."

"So I hide her away somewhere? Keep her as a mistress?" Danny said, eyes wet with remorse.

"What? No! Why don't you just marry her?"

Danny sighed, the exhale slow with the consequence of legacy and responsibility. "You know I can't do that."

"It's not a matter of what you can do; it is what you should do. You talk of duty to this place, what about your duty to the mother of your unborn child, damn it! The woman you love. Do you have any idea how many people can't be with the one they love?"

The words escaped before he really contemplated them. He did so in the silence that followed. Years of repeatedly telling himself that his own love was a fantasy his imagination had come up with to comfort him in war, had him almost believing it. But his love remained as real and unwavering as the sunrise each morning.

"And what of Ursula? I have a duty to her too. I am betrothed to her," Danny said.

"Perhaps you should have remembered that before you—"

"Don't say it."

Henry didn't.

"You make love sound very easy, brother. It isn't. My duty to this place must come above all else. Ursula doesn't love me; she just knows she won't find anyone better. Her father wants to increase the size of the quarry, something he can only do by purchasing acreage off our estate. It's money Ashlington desperately needs, and she is part of the deal."

"Makes her sound like one of your prize mares. Stock."

Danny shrugged. "Whatever you think of me, Henry, I do not have the choice of whom I marry. This union was arranged years ago by our parents. I realise that is something you could never understand, responsibility never was your burden."

Henry frowned, thinking of the men he'd pushed up the ladders at Badajos.

"Louisa and I will talk further. I will make sure we provide for her and find her somewhere to go to have the child in private."

"You can't fix her reputation. You have ruined her."

"There's nothing else I can do."

Chapter 26

"So I am not his? There were no other children, which means they pretended all this time? Why would they do that? You seemed certain Henry married Louisa. That is what that family tree thing you found said, right? Who does that make me?" Lillian slapped the journal onto the floor and got up to pace in front of the fireplace. "If I'm not Henry's, then who the hell am I? They based our whole family line on a bastard child?" she asked. "What will people think?"

"You think it changes who you are?" Nick said. "Is a so called pure lineage really that important to you?"

Lillian realised then she had not only insulted her own family but Olivia, her parents not being married either, but she felt too angry to apologise. "It makes me wonder why I am so cut up about selling this place, yes. When all they did was lie, I don't owe them anything, do I?"

"That's not you talking."

"What does that mean?"

"You aren't normally so quick to dismiss someone else's story."

Someone else's story? Like what she had done to poor old Alice Prescott and plenty of others before her. "That's exactly why I am going to fight for the company. I can't let them lose everything."

Nick nodded slowly. Was he trying to be sarcastic again? It did not suit him. "Henry's story is not finished. Before you judge him, further, I think we should continue and find out what really happened."

"I'm not sure I want to now."

"Please don't say that," Henry said from across the room. She hadn't even felt his chill this time. "Don't be like them. I don't want you to be ashamed of me too."

"I didn't mean it like that, Henry."

"You are all I have left," he said, leaving Lillian on the verge of tears.

"I didn't mean to upset him."

"Why do you think he wrote about this in his journal?" Nick asked. "Why would he risk someone seeing it and questioning the child's lineage just like you did?"

"I don't know. Maybe he knew he wouldn't come back. That he would go back to the army and his time would be up. He'd be killed."

"So you think he is giving Louisa the option of telling the child the truth. That she can tell him who his actual father was? But why?"

"He never felt good enough. Didn't feel worthy of it. He did not think the child would want him as a father?"

"But why?"

She regarded the wedding photograph of her parents; their smiling, carefree faces. If only they knew their time together would get cut short. That Rose Durand would die in childbirth. Lillian's birth. That Alistair, blonde and carefree in the photograph, would have to raise a daughter on his own. He never re-married. Rose had been his world.

"Okay. You win. But I cannot face any more of this today."

"Thank you." It was said so faintly, she didn't know if it came from Nick or Henry.

Chapter 27

Ashlington, September 1814

Henry heard the commotion from the far end of the lane. The uproar came from The Archer and by the sounds of it; the crockery was airborne. He took off his hat and ran. As he arrived, sliding to a halt at the gap in the stone wall, the door of the inn flew open, spilling Louisa onto the steps.

"You bring this shame to my door, child?" her father bellowed. Walter Dale was not a small man, a fact useful for a landlord. Louisa's mother tugged at his arms, tears streaming down her face. "Stop it, Walter!"

"What will people think?" Dale spat, rounding on his wife, who cowered away.

She noticed Henry and sent him a guarded plea through a glance at Louisa. "Master Henry, good morning, please excuse the row."

Henry's attention shifted to Louisa, who remained where she fell. He bent down next to her, her face red and sore where her father had struck. He wiped Louisa's tears away with the back of his hand and rose to his feet, fed up of excuses and fed up of others feigning impotence at situations of their own making. If no one else would step in to the breach, it would be over his dead body if Louisa had to face it alone.

"Do you know?" Walter Dale launched at him. "My daughter has given away her virtue and got herself with child. We'll be the scandal of the county!" he added, as though it were the only thing at stake.

That was when Henry punched him.

It not only made a satisfying sound, but seeing the bully at his feet winded was something Henry had wanted to see for a long time. He desperately wanted to do it again, but his train of thought returned to Louisa, and doing the only thing he could think of to remove her from her father's violence once and for all.

"I know because the child is mine." Henry let that sink in to the man's leathery hide. Dale, like any bully, lost all intimidation the second Henry stood up to him. The older, much bigger man shielded his jaw with his hands should Henry strike another blow.

Mrs Dale slapped her hand over her mouth, stifling a gasp.

"We are to marry next week before I return to barracks. I presume I can rely on your blessing?" Henry tapped his foot with impatience and the rage coursing through his chafed fist.

Dale took on the appearance of a landed fish. His mouth kept flapping open and shut, unable to speak, but he gave a nod. The marriage of their daughter into the Durand family would be beyond their wildest dreams. The child an heir of Ashlington.

"Good. Louisa can stay at the manor until then, in my mother's care," Henry said to Mrs Dale, who blinked rapidly with hidden thanks. "And I promise you—" these words he directed straight at Dale with a Sinclair-like low growl, "if you ever lay another hand on her I will ensure, personally, that you never walk on your own legs again." He shoved his hat back on his head and tipped it to Mrs Dale with a brisk, "Good day, ma'am," then pulled Louisa off the ground.

Unusually for her, she too had been rendered speechless by his outburst. As they got to the road, he felt her reluctance slowing their escape.

"Henry, you can't."

"I bloody well can and will," he said and, with a firm grip on her hand, dragged her along the lane behind him to her new home. As far as he was concerned, it was the only honourable thing in his power to do.

He led her to the safety of the kitchen, explaining that he needed to speak with Danny before breaking the news to his parents. Danny was the reaction he couldn't predict and the only one he cared about. Would it please him that Louisa would be close, that his child would be under his roof, or would he be furious that Henry would marry the woman he loved?

Marry. The word he had avoided for so long came crashing down on him. If he were honest with himself, Danny's was not the only reaction he cared about.

Mrs Melton the cook took one look at Henry and backed away, putting her arms protectively around Louisa. "Come and sit here, lass."

"He thinks he is helping me," Louisa mumbled to the old lady.

"Well—let's trust him to it."

Henry found Danny in the study, sat behind the heavy walnut desk immersed in writing a letter, the scratch of the quill pausing only for a dip of fresh ink. Coming to a halt on the thick rug before the desk, Henry took a deep breath and spoke. "I'm marrying Louisa."

Danny said nothing, causing Henry to wonder if he had registered him at all. He drew breath to repeat himself, but his brother rose to his feet, the scrape of the chair slicing the tension like a sword through flesh. "You are doing what?"

"Only the three of us need know the truth about the child. As far as everyone else will be concerned, the child is mine. I landed in England in the summer. Louisa and I could have met—"

"Don't say it, Henry." Danny rubbed his hands over his face. "You mean for her to become one of those army wives following the regiment around from camp to camp?"

Henry shook his head. "No. She will remain here where she belongs. Where they will be safe."

"But you can't! She is—"

"In love with you? Yes. But you can't marry her. Or rather won't."

"That's not fair." For once in his life, Danny, who never raised his voice in anger, looked on the verge of lashing out.

Henry stood his ground. "I did what I had to. You were reckless and didn't stand up to your responsibility, so I did—so she—" Henry pointed vaguely towards where

Louisa waited in the kitchen, "wouldn't end up on the streets or her back."

"I'd have never let that happen."

"But you did, Danny. She was running away to protect you when I found her. At least this way we can be certain she will be safe, your child will be safe. She is marrying me."

"Marry? What's this? Have you finally come to your senses? Shall I contact Mr Smalley?"

Henry would have preferred to fight one battle at a time, but so be it. The sooner it was over with, the better. His father entered the study as though he had sniffed out the foreseen damage to his pride. Henry shook his head at him.

"Good God, Henry, what have you done?"

"I am not asking for your permission, Father. I have my own means and have made my decision. I asked her father, and I have asked Louisa for her hand. She accepted."

"Louisa? You cannot mean the Dale girl? The innkeeper's daughter? Are you out of your mind?" his father challenged, rounding on Henry with a scarlet tide working its way up his face. Henry held his ground. "You would give up an influential marriage to the Smalley girl for the innkeeper's daughter? Whatever will people think?"

"She is with child."

"You stupid boy!" Nathaniel turned and gripped the fireplace mantel with both hands to steady himself.

"What is going on?" Henry didn't need to take his eyes off his father to know that his mother had joined them in the study. Even had she not spoke he could smell the lavender of her perfume. "The entire house can hear you arguing," she said. "Danny?"

Danny gave no reply. He sat down behind the desk once more and stared out of the window.

"Our son managed to get the Dale girl with child," Nathaniel said, rubbing his temples as though suffering with the migraine. "And in some misplaced act of chivalry has said he will marry her. The innkeeper's daughter, for heaven's sake!"

"Oh, Danny? What about Ursula?"

"Not him—he wouldn't be so recklessly impulsive— Henry." Nathaniel gave a dismissive wave of the hand in Henry's direction.

Elinor looked confused, glancing from one brother to the other. Betraying him, Henry's eyes flicked to where Danny sat. The corner of his mother's mouth quivered, the movement almost imperceptible, but enough for Henry to realise she didn't believe the story. Little happened under Ashlington's roof that Elinor Durand did not know about.

"What else was he supposed to do?" she asked her husband tartly.

"There are things that can be done, places the girl can go to—"

"Nathaniel, this is Louisa we are talking about. She is practically family anyway. You have said yourself how like a daughter she is," Elinor said, hands on her hips. "Henry, Danny, will you excuse us?"

Danny didn't move until Henry tapped him on the shoulder, disturbing wherever he had gone in his thoughts. "Come on," he said.

Instinctively, the men wandered to the kitchen, the raised voices of their parents fading behind them. "I will say this only once, Henry, then I wish to never speak of it again," Danny said. He stopped Henry, clutching him at the elbow. "Thank you for ensuring her—their—safety."

In the kitchen, Mrs Melton sat whispering comforting noises at Louisa, who held a damp cloth to her scarlet cheek and wiped her eyes as the brothers entered.

"All is well," Henry told her cheerfully.

"See," Mrs Melton added, "what did I tell you."

Louisa looked directly at Danny, her eyes not leaving his as he crossed the tiled floor.

"Louisa, I—" Danny began, Henry sensed he was about to do something impulsive like apologise for getting her pregnant in front of Mrs Melton, so he interrupted.

"You will take care of her, won't you?" Henry said. "When I am gone?"

Danny opened his mouth to respond, but their mother walked in.

"I thought I would find you here. You are both as bad as each other, hiding where there is food whenever you are in trouble." She glared at Danny, then addressed Louisa with a sweeter whisper while Mrs Melton retrieved something from the larder. "Louisa. Is it true? I will be a grandmother?"

"Yes, ma'am."

Elinor dried Louisa's cheeks with her handkerchief, inspecting the redness from her father's hand. "Was this your father?"

Louisa nodded.

"I am happy for you. Both of you," Elinor said, reaching for Henry. She pulled at one of her fingers and passed Henry her sapphire ring. "It was my mother's. One of the few non-Durand things around here. Now ask her like a gentleman, Henry. Your father and I shall wait to receive you properly in the drawing room."

"You don't have to do this," Louisa told him as he walked her into the hallway.

"I've told you I would look after you. He can't, so I will. It is that simple. I know it is not the love story or marriage you would have dreamed of, but I will be a good husband and I won't expect anything from you other than your happiness and that of the child." He shrugged. "A father! I had never imagined it."

"It is not the marriage you dreamed of either, Henry. You are throwing away your own happiness."

"No. No, I'm not. I won't ever be able to—I can never—" He shook away the heaviness in his throat together with the image of alluring dark curls and a dimpled smile, then lowered himself onto one knee. "Louisa Dale, will you do me the honour of becoming my wife?"

She hesitated, and for a moment he thought it might all be for nothing. "Yes!" she said. "I will and I promise I won't let you down."

To get everything organised in time sent the household into a frenzy. Elinor taking control like a fierce field-general not only ensured the newspapers carried the announcement at such short notice, but she also kept her husband away from Henry. Since Louisa's arrival, the atmosphere in the house had changed for the better, with the notable exception of Danny, who hid himself away buried in work. Henry had brought up the subject of being his best man, but Danny refused. Not with words, but a look that told Henry to burn in hell.

"Thank you, Mr Samuels," Henry said the morning of his wedding day as the groom led Whisper out of the stalls tacked up, ready to go. Henry told himself that a ride would ease his nerves. Somewhere deep within, he wanted to run again. Run from the cage he had sprung himself. As he couldn't run this time, he decided on a ride to Winchcombe, the bookshop there giving him purpose.

Mr Samuels passed Henry the reins and put some weight on the opposite stirrup while Henry heaved himself in to the saddle. As though sensing his desire to flee, Whisper tossed her head impatiently and took off down the drive. Henry let her take the Southern driveway, which led to the grassy lane trailing the bottom of the escarpment and on to Winchcombe. In due course he sat deep in the saddle, reined Whisper back to a walk, forced his shoulders to relax and closed his eyes, trusting his mount to pick the way along the lane while savouring the scent of Ashlington, and the bird song from the woods.

Savouring anything that morning proved impossible after only a few minutes, unable to prevent the suffocating pressure in his chest whenever he allowed his thoughts free rein. He had to grab for Whisper's neck as she reared up, nearly sending him toppling over her rear end. He pushed his weight forward and wheeled around. Senses alert, he half expected a roaring hussar to come charging out of the bushes and instinctively reached for his missing sword. All he saw was a girl lay in the ditch, limbs tangled in some metal contraption, squirming and giggling.

He slid down to lend assistance.

"I'm terribly sorry, are you hurt?" he asked as she pushed the metal thing off herself. He stretched out his hand which she accepted, and hauled her to her feet out of the long grass and nettles.

"No, I'm fine. Bloody brakes need a tune up!" Henry froze. Seconds later, he closed his mouth. It was not only the way she talked, which was with a strange accent, nor that she was as tall as he; it was the extraordinary clothes she was wearing. Tight trousers of all things and scandalously bare arms. She appeared to be studying him with equal curiosity.

"Guess you are some kind of re-enactor? One of my teachers organises big events. You might know her, Mrs Spencer?" She gestured at his uniform.

He did not understand what this meant and could not recall being acquainted with a Mrs Spencer, so shook his head.

"Is your horse okay?"

"She is unharmed." The knot in his throat had thankfully shifted and with some effort he was working on the dizziness he felt. "I think it was that thing that surprised her," he said, pointing at the wheeled object that lay at her feet.

"What? My bike?"

"Your what?"

Her saucer-like eyes squinted at him and she put her hands on her hips. The light coloured top she wore emphasised her darker skin and black hair, of which not a single strand was tied up. She blinked and he couldn't shake the feeling that he knew her, despite having never met her before. It was like a dizzier version of déjà vu and felt most unsettling, as though she had been woven from his mood.

"Have we met?" she asked.

"Henry Durand," he said by way of introduction, realising he was still clutching her hand.

"Oh, from the big house?"

He nodded and found himself reluctant to let go of her. She forced the situation by pulling her hand away, then picking up the strange wheeled thing she had called a bike. She moved towards Whisper, who sniffed at the contraption and the girl who patted her neck.

"She likes you," he said, rubbing Whisper on the nose. "She is not usually the friendly sort."

"Well, I'm sorry for scaring her. See ya' around Henry."

To his horror, she mounted the bike like it was a horse and rode it away down the lane. Knees pumping up and down until she was out of sight. He stood there for a moment more until Whisper snorted. He shrugged his shoulders as though shaking off a dream and scolding himself for not pressing for her name so he could later make enquiries, climbed back into the saddle and turned for Winchcombe.

Only hours later, with his hands behind his back and a new book in his inner pocket, Henry paced up and down inside the church, waiting for his bride to arrive, convincing himself he had made the correct decision. Louisa and Elinor had decorated not only the manor but the village church too, with autumnal offerings and displays of coloured leaves and berries. In just a few days, they had transformed the place.

The few congregation members were muttering among themselves, no doubt questioning the unusual union. Not for the first time since having arrived back in Ashlington, he felt an empty ache at his side. The message to Westbrook should have arrived in time for him to make it to Ashlington for the wedding. Instead, Henry stood alone on the flagstones by the altar when Louisa arrived.

She wore a blue dress that Henry recognised as her best, though now with added Belgian lace around the cuffs and neckline. His mother's touch, he presumed. Louisa held her flower adorned head high as she hurried down the aisle on her father's brutal arm.

Henry's emotions tumbled as he imagined a different future, insurmountable yet iridescent. One in which another walked towards him to share a life together.

Louisa's smile brought him back to his reality with a start. Not her usual boundless smile that lit her pale eyes and showed off her neat white teeth. This smile creased at one corner where she chewed her lip and wrinkled the freckles on her nose. Henry had no doubt she felt the same way he did.

The decision made, the course set, it occurred to him

with an uncharacteristic selfishness that not only had he helped Louisa in her situation, but he had also dodged a far worse fate. His father had probably still had his own plans for Henry's marriage. He might have ended up married to one of the mouse-like Smalley girls after all, rather than a dear friend. He was the lucky one.

Henry sat down on the edge of his bed later that evening, resting his head in his hands, his body tired, the emotional toll of the day having caught up with him. He had spent most of the wedding celebrations missing Westbrook and thus refusing to dance. All of which left him with a thumping head. The house might have been quiet, but outside a storm gathered pace with the rolling thunder sounding like cannon fire gaining on them with every minute. Not that it bothered Henry. He slept restlessly even on nights without the nightmares of Badajos.

Smelling of sweet rose water and a breeze, Louisa placed a hand on his thigh. "Henry, we are husband and wife now. If you want to share the bed. If you want to—" She slid her hand higher, leant over and before he knew what was happening, she kissed him.

It felt most odd.

Worse than when he kissed her in the tree house all those years ago. A lifetime ago.

A tiny part of him wanted to lie with her as man and wife—as the world would have them. Perhaps for once not have to oppress the desire to feel something good, to not have to fight for everything. For once to lay his head on a pillow with arms around him, not because he dreamed of Badajos. But none of that was about her. Like a good soldier, he listened to his gut and stood up.

"This isn't what you need, Louisa. You are in love with Danny."

"I thought you expected to—you know—it is your wedding night."

"What? No! Louisa, I love you and would do anything for you, but you are not mine in that sense. You said it yourself. There has never been an attraction. I do not care to dwell upon how strange that would be."

"Like that kiss?" she said, wrinkling her nose.

He laughed, relieved his rejection had not hurt her. "You could always go to Danny. Everyone is in bed. No one would know."

She thought about it for a moment. Then shook her head. "I'm not his now either. She put a hand to her stomach. Neither of us are."

"I'll take the guest room next door. I don't sleep well anymore, at least you won't be disturbed that way."

"What am I going to do when you are gone?"

"Remember that you are where you belong. Build a home for you and the young one and write to me often. Promise me you will keep writing. I want to hear of everything. You deserve more than anyone to be happy."

Chapter 28

"Olivia, will you get a move on!" Nick called.

"We'll be early at this rate. You're never early!" she called back down to him. Nick spent the time waiting for his daughter, rearranging the stacks of books on the coffee table. The last thing he wanted to do that evening was go to the manor for dinner with a bunch of strangers. Lillian and Bloody Johansen were holding some birthday dinner for Lillian's mentor. A last hurrah before she sold the place, hardly cause for celebration.

She didn't want to sell, not really, he could tell. He had considered forcing the issue with her like Henry had with Louisa. But he also knew he would be the last to say it to her. She had to decide for herself. He recalled the grip of his father's hand on his arm at the graveside and the stare that told him, 'It's not your place, son.'

"There you are," he said as Olivia entered the room with a frown.

"I'm going to buy you a new tie for Christmas. Maybe a box of them," she said. "How old is that thing exactly?"

"As old as the suit," Nick shrugged and smoothed the tie against his shirt. It was comfortable, which allowed him to focus on other things than starchy collars and stiff clothing. The tie practically did itself up. Olivia looked at the empty beer bottle on the coffee table. "It was just one for the road," he insisted. Goodness knows he needed it. "You look lovely. Remind me, when did you grow up so fast?"

Olivia grinned and twirled her skirt, which flared from her waist. She looked so like her mother. It made Nick sad Taylor wasn't there to share in moments like this. A huge plaster on her ankle caught his eye.

"You okay?" he asked. "What happened to your ankle?"

"Oh, it's nothing, I bumped into someone in the lane and fell off my bike."

Nick opened his mouth to object and promise his full paternal wrath to the idiot that hurt his baby daughter when she cut him off and continued.

"Wasn't his fault. I wasn't looking where I was going, probably too fast. The brakes on that thing are useless. He was a gentleman—not too many of them around—helped me up, apologised. Done, dusted." She pulled at the plaster, which had done its job, and allowed a dark red scab to form. "See, nothing to worry about."

Nick relaxed.

"Does Lillian have a cousin that does re-enactments?"

"No idea, why?"

"No worries, forget it. Can we drive?" Olivia asked, peering through the window into the dark.

"Seriously? It's not like it's far and I will definitely need more than one drink tonight."

"It is England, it's raining!" she complained,

squeezing her enormous feet into some heeled shoes Nick did not realise she owned.

He rolled his eyes and conceded, like he always did. "Okay, we'll drive, even though we possess umbrellas and walking doesn't kill us."

It took longer to start the Land Rover than it did to drive all of four minutes to get to the front door of the manor. Nick glanced back at his shabby vehicle looking out of place on the driveway and, he had to admit, lowering the tone. He wouldn't part with it, though. It had been through the proverbial mill, showed a little rust at the sides, and drank too much. Rather like its owner.

***

Lillian and Marcus moved around the kitchen, putting the finishing touches to the canapés, and as they always seemed to whenever they were in the same room as each other, were arguing. This time about how the wedding had been delayed. Again.

"You're doing it again!" Marcus said, slamming shut the refrigerator door, having just retrieved two chilled bottles of champagne. "You're stalling. Sometimes I wonder if you even want to get married."

He had said it before, and she had always smoothly convinced both of them she did. "I have had a lot going on, Marcus."

"The sooner this place is gone, the better."

"Can I please thump him?" said a voice at Lillian's

shoulder. Lillian laughed.

"Why are you laughing?" Marcus asked, obviously appalled by her lack of poise.

The doorbell broke the silence, announcing the first guests. Lillian hurried to answer it before she said something she might regret. She used to love hosting dinner parties, but she was now dreading this one even if it was to celebrate Guy's birthday. Marcus had insisted on inviting work colleagues, surrounding her with the people from their life, when all she really wanted to do was come clean about the night with Nick. A part of her, one that was demanding more attention now, wondered if it would force Marcus's hand. That he would call everything off and finally bring an end to the talk of weddings.

She could almost feel it coming, the train that had skipped the rails, running out of control toward the inevitable topple. Something would topple tonight, but as she swung open the front door and arranged a false smile, she promised herself it would not be her.

Nick stood, with an equally strained smile, on the other side.

"Thanks so much for inviting us," a familiar voice with an American twang said, from behind a fantastic flower arrangement.

"How is school going, Olivia?"

"It's okay, I guess. I'm still the new kid," she shrugged.

"Stefan still looking after you?"

"Yeah."

"Who the hell is Stefan? What did I miss?" Nick said.

"Just a friend," Olivia said with an eye roll.

Nick glanced at Lillian. She knew what the glance meant. 'Just a friend?' They both knew how that could end up.

"Anyway, I'd much rather hear about when you two were younger. There must be plenty of dirt to spill?"

Plenty. Lillian did her best to control the flush working its way up her neck. Nick, for his part, distracted her with a bottle of wine. An expensive South American one. "Thanks, Nick."

"I was on safer ground with the wine." He tilted his head towards the flowers.

"Your work?" she asked Olivia, who nodded.

"Dad was going to get some at the gas station. Grandma helped me with these instead."

"What is wrong with petrol station flowers? You and your grandma are flower snobs," Nick retorted as Olivia accepted a glass of fizz from Marcus, who joined them, all traces of their earlier argument hidden.

"Hawkins," Marcus said.

"Johansen."

"Still listening?"

"Always."

Marcus smirked.

Nick took a glass and Lillian watched him pretend not to notice Marcus's appraisal. Nick looked dashing in jacket and tie, but despite his success maintained an off-the-peg appearance that Marcus, in a Savile Row tailored three-piece, was no doubt judging him on in the silence that followed.

***

When the doorbell rang, Marcus offered to answer it, leaving Lillian with the tray.

"Go on through." She gestured before following Marcus. Nick followed Olivia, who was leading the way into the drawing room, studying the paintings as she went.

"So much history," Olivia said, running her hand along the woodwork of the doorframe. "Some memories are new though."

"Alistair put money into renovating parts of it a few years ago, apparently. Some parts are just as I remember. Others, this room for instance, have really changed." He moved around the sofa table stacked with books on architecture at one end, and a brass telescope on a tripod at the other.

"You spent a lot of time here as a kid, didn't you?"

"Most school holidays while your grandma was working. It was like a second home."

"And you were best friends?"

"Yes." He drew the word out slowly for her. "Like I keep telling you, we were best friends once."

"Where is the painting of the guy you are researching?"

"It's over the fireplace in the dining room and probably the most valuable painting in the house. There is quite the story to go with it."

"I bet this place is full of stories. You can feel it." She nudged him on the elbow. "No digging right. I doubt Mr Bloody You Know Who would approve of you digging up the croquet lawn," she said, having flicked her accent to British. "What is going on with you and Lillian tonight?"

"What do you mean?"

"You are all—I don't know—there is some weird energy between the two of you."

Nick said nothing. The last thing he needed was for Olivia and her sixth sense to catch on to anything.

"You didn't?"

"What?"

"You did!" she gasped with a degree of accusation.

"What?"

"Oh, my god! You totally slept with her!"

Nick made a noise which was part shush and part denial. It came out more like a strangled admission of guilt.

"I mean, it's totally gross, but wow, you must still have moves, Dad. She is quite the catch. What about Mr Bloody What's His Name?"

Nick opened his mouth to assert his denial.

"He doesn't know? Blimey!" she said, suddenly sounding British again. "There is more drama here than at school."

"You have no idea," Nick said, draining his champagne glass, looking hopefully for another as other guests began filing into the drawing room.

Lillian and Marcus played the perfect hosts with trays

of canapés, and conversation. Nick stayed close to the door. He thought of Alistair, and the certainty that this was a farewell dinner struck him once more, together with an overwhelming feeling of regret.

Olivia began a friendly conversation with a woman who appeared to have arrived on her own. Typical of Olivia to make someone feel comfortable, Nick thought. He smiled and nodded in the right places, but his attention was elsewhere in the room. Lillian was handing drinks to an impeccably dressed, dark-haired man with long sideburns who stood next to a tall blonde. In looks, she could have been a younger version of Lillian.

"Dad?" Olivia tugged on his sleeve. "I was just telling Mrs Spencer about your new project."

"I never missed an episode of Sharpe," Spencer said. "Call me Ashley, please. Fascinating period. Will you make it to the big Waterloo anniversary next month?"

"We had not planned to. I hear it will be quite the spectacle." The two hundredth anniversary of Waterloo was to be marked with a huge ensemble of re-enactors to depict the battle. Two hundred years since Henry's death. Could that be significant in why he was here now? Nick thought.

"The most re-enactors ever assembled. Over six-thousand of us," Ashley said. "We are determined to give the punters their money's worth."

"Mrs Spencer is part of the organisation putting it all together."

"History teacher by day, rifleman of the 95th by night—or weekend, really; it just doesn't sound as good."

Nick liked the woman instantly, recognising someone as passionate about their interests as he was. Then he put two and two together. "Oh, *the* Mrs Spencer? Olivia's history teacher?"

Ashley nodded. "She is an exceptional student. I am trying to convince her to take history further."

"Any reluctance is my fault; it's difficult being dragged around the world."

"Well, as I have told Olivia, there is a scholarship up for grabs and I think she has more than a shot."

A scholarship?

"What would Riker do?" Nick asked, leaning in.

Olivia nodded.

Realising that made him Picard, Nick wasn't sure whether to be insulted or flattered.

"I just worry that I am not passionate enough. It's been part of my life for so long everything I have picked up seems like it was handed to me, not that I worked for it."

"You don't think climbing a mountain at fourteen in the Guatemalan rainforest to spend six months in camp and helping to move soil every day was working for it?"

She looked at her feet.

"What about the time you pulled Demetrio from the river, weren't you twelve then? I think you have more than earned anything you learnt out there, but it is your future, your decision. We won't pressure you in to anything you don't want to do. Will we?" He looked meaningfully at Ashley, who nodded with reluctance. "So how do you know—" Nick paused as he fought to drop his customary

'Bloody.'

"I'm Marcus's cousin."

Which neatly answered Olivia's question from earlier, he thought.

"I know, he's not everyone's cup of tea, but my wife and I were here for the funeral and, as we are only over in Tewkesbury, Lillian invited us tonight to catch up. Charlotte is away with work, so it is just me. Lillian told me you are researching one of her ancestors?"

Pleased to find himself sat next to Ashley Spencer, no accident if the smile Lillian flashed him had anything to do with it, Nick leant back in his chair enjoying the conversation. He found Ashley an interesting woman, who travelled extensively and wore her love for history on her sleeve. They were deep into a discussion about Waterloo and Ashley's opinion regarding how the different sides treated their casualties, when Nick noticed Olivia, seated opposite, had not taken a single bite of her food. He tried to catch her attention, but she stared into space.

"Olivia!" he said louder. "Everything okay?"

"What?"

"You haven't eaten anything."

"Oh." She looked down at her plate and picked up her fork. But to Nick's dismay, she just pushed the food around and began staring vacantly again. Nick followed her gaze. She was looking down the length of the table to the fireplace.

It was Bloody Johansen that figured out what held her

interest. "Do you like art?" he asked, glancing round at the picture of Henry. "Everyone is obsessed with this scruffy chap," he said, waving a knife in the air over his shoulder. "Lillian has her old boyfriend here researching him." He addressed the man to his right, the one with the sideburns that had been introduced as Lillian's mentor, Guy. "Everyone's imaginations are running wild."

Nick opened his mouth to protest. He had never been Lillian's boyfriend. But Olivia caught his attention with a kick under the table. Being so tall had its disadvantages. "This is who you are researching?" she asked.

Nick nodded.

"Our Lillian always did like to dabble with her sentimental side," Guy said.

Lillian glared at him. "You'll have heard of Doctor Nick Hawkins," she said, for all assembled to hear. "Probably seen him on tv or read his books. Before beginning work on a dig on the Fosseway this summer, the one the BBC are filming, he kindly agreed to help finish the project my late father had begun on a Durand ancestor, the one in the painting and his role in the Napoleonic War." She leaned back in her seat with pink cheeks and directed her glare at Marcus this time.

Nick only hoped he wasn't blushing, too.

Ashley spoke next. "If that painting is a Sinclair like I think it is, then I know you have a story on your hands. That is the battle of Toulouse, I think. What is your source material, Nick?"

"We have been really lucky. The family has kept

everything. We have many of Henry's letters and journals. He was quite the storyteller." Nick glanced at Olivia, who still looked lost to the painting.

"Dad," she said. "What did you say his name was?"

"Henry."

"Henry Durand," she repeated. She looked back at the painting and slid her chair backwards. "Please excuse me," she said, addressing Lillian, "I need the bathroom."

***

Inside the bathroom, a tiny space under the stairs that was likely a closet at one time, Olivia locked the door and gave herself a good talking to. *A weird coincidence, that's all.* She splashed her face with water, hoping it might clear the caterwauling of emotions making her head throb.

On her way back to the dining room, she heard the distinct sound of music from what her father had told her was the ballroom. Investigating, she found it empty except for the piano in the corner. The enormous room, with gilded ceilings and a fancy chandelier dangling from the centre, evoked a ball worthy of a Jane Austen novel with a stringed quartet. Ladies sat on couches fanning themselves and couples dancing.

One figure caught her eye. Not due to the fact he was the only man in a red army uniform, but because he was the only one looking directly at her. Which was absurd, because this was her imagination.

She stepped into the room and he walked towards her,

ignoring everyone else, blue eyes locked on to hers. Henry Bloody Durand, and they had most defiantly met before.

"I must have drank too much champagne," she said.

"No one else knows you are here," he replied, looking about them.

"Where I am, it is only you and I in the room."

"Are you a ghost?" he asked.

"Me? No. You?"

"Alive and well."

He clearly did not understand what was happening either, but she had the advantage of history and knew that he died at Waterloo two hundred years ago. If either of them were a ghost, it had to be him, surely. It might feel like a video call through time, but it had to be an illusion. Sure, she had heard her dead mother before, but this was a whole different level of weird.

"We met in the lane, didn't we?" he said as though he sought confirmation it was not his imagination either. "If you were really here now, I would be obliged to ask you to dance. It is my wedding day after all." His exterior might have been all confidence and stiff officer-like posture, but she could feel pain diffusing from within him.

"It's okay, I wouldn't know how."

Cute, in a kind of untidy boy-next-door way, he was no bigger than her, a suggestion of leanness like an athlete. But her overwhelming impression of him was that they were bound in some way. The conflict of knowing of the time and space between them wrung at her stomach until it made her feel sick.

"Then I would offer to teach you. Though my friend is a far better dancer than I, you might prefer—" He turned his back to her, looking for someone. "He's not here," he said with a catch in his throat. "Nor is Danny."

Olivia shivered. The room had grown colder, on his end of the call or hers she couldn't be sure. She stepped to his side and studied his face. Steely eyes, just like Lillian's, scanned the room frantically. "What is it?"

When he spoke again, it was barely a whisper. "He should be here."

"You are missing someone?"

He nodded. His cheek clenched like he was biting at it. "I think I have made a terrible mistake," he said. He reached for her hand and held it tight. She gripped back as tightly as she could, as though she could tell him he was not alone. What mistake?

"It'll be okay," she breathed, believing it, though it made no sense.

"I have to go," he said, pulling away. The music and chatter of the party dissolved. A tear tickled her cheek.

"Don't go." But he was gone, and the room dark again. "Henry?"

Chapter 29

Ashlington, September 1814

The morning after his wedding, the smell of fresh baking lured Henry to the kitchen, where he found Mrs Melton up to her elbows in dough. The sight of loaves lined up on the tabletop reminded him of a particular loaf of bread in France. Why he kept thinking of his time in France so wistfully, he tried not to admit. He closed his eyes, inhaling the warmth of the yeast, allowing it to pull him to that day by the river.

Filling his canteen, the French officer had left his weapons further up the river bank. A sitting duck. But he was also injured, likely missing an arm if his pinned coat-sleeve was any judge. His men, sat on the bank behind him, looked like they had not eaten in days. Cold, hungry and lost; a pitiful clutch of the broken, struggling to keep up with the retreat.

The officer looked directly across the river into Henry's eyes and gave a resigned nod of acknowledgment that said, "Be a gentleman and make it quick. Aim true."

Henry's pistol was loaded, sword to hand if he missed, which was unlikely at such short range. But he did not fire. He did not raise his pistol. Instead, he tucked it back into his belt and returned a cordial nod.

"Bonjour!" Henry said.

"Fine morning," the officer replied.

Henry continued to the river's edge. The men on the bank stirred, one reaching for a musket. The French officer waved his hand. They were all just men in need of water that day.

Henry bent and dipped his canteen into the flow of the cool water, then took a sip, thinking of the loaf of bread he carried in his pack. He did not know what it was exactly about the French men that made him do it. Probably how hopeless and pathetic they looked; how like his own company on a bad day, only wearing a different uniform. He took his pack off and took out the bread.

"Mon amie!" he called to the French officer and launched the loaf across the river, forgetting his target only had one hand with which to catch it.

The officer caught it with grace, his face lighting up in welcome surprise. He was a handsome man, Henry decided; smcoulderingly dark like Westbrook—but cooler. His smile pleasant enough—yet not enough.

"Merci Capitaine. Merci," he said. Then he patted his pockets as though looking for something to return in exchange. *"Un moment!"* he called, then scrambled up the bank to his men. A brief discussion took place with much approval over the bread that the officer ordered to be shared. The officer himself returned with a book. Henry shook his head and laughed.

The officer threw it across the river to Henry and they all cheered when he caught it. He held it up in salute and thanked them with a low bow.

"I would accept your parole, sir. We have a fine surgeon," Henry said once the men settled.

The officer looked over his shoulder. "*Non*, I think not. We are not done yet." He smiled again.

Proud, stubborn idiot, Henry thought, admiring his spirit. "You are only two days ahead of our column," he warned.

"*Oui*, that is all we need," the officer said with a shrug.

"*Bonne chance.*"

"*Et toi.*"

Henry never told Westbrook where he got that book, Voltaire's *Candide*, but kept a precious recollection of his delighted expression when he handed it to him. He held that recollection for longer than a married man should before opening his eyes once more, returning to Ashlington's kitchen.

"You always were my favourite," Henry told the cook as he searched in baskets and under cloths for something to ease the hole in his belly.

"And you mine, Master Henry," she replied with a crooked toothless grin, flicking at him with the cloth she drew from off her shoulder. He grinned back with what he hoped was his handsomest smile, the only thing he knew might just break her resolve. She sighed and waved her hand at the shelf below the brass jelly moulds. "There are pastries in the basket."

He kissed her floury cheek before helping himself to a jam pastry, then another. "For my brother," he told her in response to her glare. She tutted, unconvinced, and continued kneading with the strength of a wrestler.

The pastry was as good as it smelt and he savoured the sweetness of the jam, no doubt from summer strawberries in the garden, whilst on his way to the study to find Danny. Loud voices stopped him as he approached the door.

"—will be another month or so. I keep telling you." The adamant voice did not belong to Danny but Christopher, their younger brother.

"But that was not the arrangement, Mr Durand. My patron already gave you more time." The other voice was lower, without waver, in control. Henry remained where he was, listening, and made a start on the second pastry— spilling a blob of jam down his front that he had to rescue with a finger.

"And I have done everything he asked. He will get it."

"Perhaps you need some encouragement?"

"Christopher?" Upon hearing quite enough of that, Henry pushed the door open and found his brother face to face with a taller, bespectacled man. At the interruption, the man thrust a document towards Christopher, thudding it against his chest, making him tilt backwards.

"I think you should leave," Henry said, voice full of authority.

"Don't bother yourself, Henry," Christopher muttered.

The man considered Henry for a moment, then took a step backwards, allowing Christopher room to breathe again. Christopher slid behind the desk, one hand resting on the marble bust of their grandfather. The man slowly picked up his hat from the desk and turned back to Christopher.

"You have two weeks, Mr Durand. Do not disappoint." Placing his hat under one arm, he moved to the door. Henry gave way and followed him out along the hallway, tucking into step behind him. Closely.

Before the man stepped off the threshold, Henry grabbed him by the jacket lapels and forced him against the wall. "You threaten my family, you come through me." He gave him a shake for emphasis. "Do you understand?"

"Oh, I understand perfectly," the man said calmly, too calmly, as Henry released him. He straightened his jacket and smiled. It was a smile that promised something. Nothing good.

"Good day, sir." Bradley shut the door after the man and gave Henry a rare smirk.

"Are you going to tell me what all that was about?" Henry said, rounding on his brother as he stormed back into the study. "When did you get here, anyway?"

Christopher had sat himself down behind the desk with a glass of whisky, the document the man had been so determined for him to have nowhere to be seen.

"This morning."

"And that?" Henry gestured to the door.

"Is under control."

"Didn't look that way to me."

"It is nothing, Henry. I can assure you." Christopher swirled his drink around in the glass before finishing it. "Want one?" he asked, reaching for the decanter.

"No," Henry said. "I used to know when something

was bothering you, Chris." He softened his tone. Experience had taught him that once he and his younger brother began butting heads, nothing could stop them. They were as stubborn as each other, Durands to the core. "Tell me what's going on."

Christopher pointed at Henry with his glass. "You wanted nothing to do with us, remember? You left. Death or Glory, wasn't it? You didn't even tell me you were leaving. Father and Danny have been running this place perfectly well without you, so what makes you think you can waltz back in here sticking your nose in?"

"I didn't realise you felt like that."

"I did my best. I tried to be of use here, but Father and Danny—well—I don't have to explain how that works to you. Why did you leave me with them? I wanted to come find you. Join up myself."

"I'm glad you didn't."

"Seven years, Henry. You were gone for seven years." Christopher stared at him.

"Chris, I am here now. I will do whatever I can to help. I promise you." Henry grabbed a chair and dragged it over to the desk so he could sit next to his brother, putting them at the same height. Almost. "You know as well as I do I couldn't stay here. I was never cut out for this. I don't know how they do it. But I found what I am good at, and my men need me." He felt the tremor in his hand and concentrated on forcing it away. It obliged. "I have been summoned to Aunt Dot's. Do you want to come?"

"You will come home reeking of dogs, and that's if

you manage to get back on your horse at all after she has fed you. I'd rather not," Christopher said.

Aunt Dorothy, his mother's sister, was a frail lady that hated to travel. She had moved to a modest town house in Cheltenham where she could enjoy the spa waters and lived there with her beloved pack of dogs. Christopher had been correct in his prediction. She plied Henry with enough food and wine; he thought his belly would burst under the pressure. She took one look at his swaying when he got out of his chair following dinner and ordered him to stay the night.

The cake Henry had delivered had impressed her all the more because he had delivered it in person and she wanted to hear all about Louisa. It was easy to pretend he was a man in love because he felt so fond of Louisa, but it was longing for another that kept him awake that night when he searched for sleep.

When he arrived back at Ashlington late in the morning, wet from the rain, the front door had been left open. The stone entrance like an enormous maw waiting to swallow him. Inside, none of the staff would look him in the eye as they hurried back and forth across the hall. More disturbingly, there was no sign of Bradley. No direction. He thought he heard sobbing from his mother's parlour and caught the scent of soapy cleaning buckets.

Beyond them, he found Louisa pacing as he or his brothers might, wringing her hands. She turned as she heard his footsteps; face red and blotchy from hours of crying.

"What happened?" he asked, rushing to her, swearing that if her father had harmed her again he would break his neck, let alone his legs. She clutched him like a frightened child clings to a parent. "What is it?"

"Thank God you are back, Henry."

"You're scaring me, Louisa. What is wrong?"

"Danny—" Her words stumbled, and she pointed to the stairs. The dread he felt stepping into the house grew, filling him. He took the stairs two at a time.

Were it not for the large dent in his head, Henry thought his brother would look the embodiment of peace and tranquillity. The curtains of his bedroom were open, letting in a shaft of light that gave the linen on his bed a golden hue. Dried lavender sprigs lay around him, and crocuses from the garden sat in a short vase on the side table. Absent of the familiar stench of death that Henry was used to, this was almost dignified.

"Henry?" Danny said.

Only it was not Danny but Christopher, cologne rousing Henry from his shock to the reality before him. Christopher stood at his side, head hung, unwilling or unable to face their older brother's body.

"Did he fall?"

Christopher failed to respond.

Henry shook him, frustrated with the lack of information or urgency. "Chris?" But when Christopher met his eyes, Henry realised he was in some form of shock himself. Henry checked himself. Christopher had not known war. He had spent his time dancing and cavorting. He had not seen death on the scale Henry had. The un-named faces. The piles. The friends.

Their father spoke next, appearing behind them as though he had been keeping a lonely vigil in the shadows. "Someone broke into the house early this morning. Danny disturbed whoever it was. The intruder fled. There was nothing the doctor could do."

"Do you know who it was?" Henry's hand began to quake, control hanging by a thread, an explosion imminent.

"Would I be standing here if I did?"

"If only I had stayed." The rage imploded.

"Jesus, Henry!" Christopher said. "Danny was a stubborn, proud fool. If he'd just let them go, he wouldn't have got hurt."

Henry frowned.

"It's obvious, isn't it? He shouldn't have fought back. But that was Danny."

The room darkened as a cloud passed in front of the sun. "I want him buried as soon as the rain stops," their father said. "You can stay, at least for that?" he asked Henry curtly.

Henry nodded, his attention back on Danny's body. His big brother gone? How was this possible? This was Ashlington. "But I have to report to the regiment by the end of the week."

His father glanced at Danny's body, then left. Henry noticed Bradley following. On hand for anything his master might need.

"You are returning to the regiment then?" Christopher said, his hand on Henry's arm.

Henry nodded again. "You have me for a few more days."

The corners of Christopher's mouth twitched. Almost a smile. Henry may have been absent for the last few years, but for once, he was there to give his support to his younger brother.

Chapter 30

Ashlington, May 2015

Some of Olivia's body had shut down, collapsing her to the floor of the hallway. It had happened before, and didn't scare her. She knew her legs would work fine again in a moment. It was just her body's way of protecting her from the overwhelming turbulence seeping from the walls. "Something terrible happened here," she told her father as he hurried to her.

"Oh, Ollie!" he said. She felt his arms around her, picking her up with ease like she was a young child again.

"Right here. There is so much pain and anger." She looked around the hallway and shivered. "Do you feel it?" She had lost count of the times she had asked him that on a dig. Like the emotional imprint of the past reached for her, though she had never experienced such profound layers before.

"Dangerous?" he asked.

She shook her head.

"I'm going to take you home. Sit here for a moment while I tell Lillian we are leaving." He left her sat on the staircase where she stared at the floor.

She didn't startle at the presence next to her. It simply grew from nothing until he was there, sat alongside her, watching the same spot on the floor. The spot making her feel uncomfortable, like an agonizing itch under a scab.

"Hello again," he said.

"This is different."

"Yes."

"You are still sad, though. Lonely?"

"I can't find him," he said. Olivia could feel the hope draining from him with the sinking of his shoulders. "It has been too long."

Then he was gone.

***

"What do you mean you saw him?" Nick asked, closing the cottage curtains as Olivia sat on the sofa, circling her palms around her temples. She had fallen asleep in the Land Rover for the brief journey back to the cottage and woken again as he lifted her out. "Do you want something for your head? Glass of water? Bowl to throw up in?"

"Ice pack," she groaned. He fetched a bag of peas from the freezer and wrapped it in a tea towel before passing it to her.

"So?"

"It was Henry, the man in the painting. He was there in the ballroom talking with me. I don't know how. I know it sounds utterly bonkers." She gave him the look that dared him to treat her like a baby and face the consequences.

"Do you mean like when you hear your Mom?"

"It isn't like how it was with Mom. I never saw her. It

339

was more like she comforted me in here," she tapped her head. "When I see the soldier, it's like I am actually there in his time, like we have some sort of bridge between worlds. It was him I bumped into in the lane a few days ago." She rubbed at her ankle. "Exactly that guy in the painting. He was actually there in the lane, in the flesh, that chestnut horse of his too. He told me then that he was Henry Durand. I recognised the name linking it to the big house, but—not the time. When I first saw him at the manor, he was at a party—his wedding, he said—but he didn't seem happy about it. The second time, while I waited for you, was different somehow. More like he had become a permanent fixture."

Nick poured a whisky and sat down next to her, giving her a quick rundown of where they had got to with Henry returning to Ashlington.

"Henry married Louisa to save her from ruin and give the baby a name and a life. Hell of a thing to do. Think about it for a moment. If he hadn't, Lily wouldn't be here," he rubbed at his face with his hands, weighing up how much more to tell her. "We think he has some unfinished business. It sounds corny, I know, but we haven't come up with any other explanation."

Olivia frowned. "You think he haunts the house?"

"Lily hears him. I have too. Never seen him like you have."

"Voice call only?"

He hadn't thought of it like that. "And you get video? Yeah, if you like. We think it has something to do with her grieving. It all started when her father died."

"Like it did for me with Mom?"

Nick nodded.

"That would make sense. I also got the impression he was looking for someone."

"What do you mean? Like who?" Nick asked. Henry had not mentioned looking for anyone.

"I don't know."

"His brother? Someone kills Danny shortly after the wedding, but we are still wading through all that."

"Maybe that was the feeling of dread I got in the hall?" she shivered as though still wrestling it away. "He mentioned Danny. I want to help him," Olivia said with a look of determination in her eyes that reminded Nick of the birthday he had presented her with her first archaeology field kit. A canvas roll of wooden handled tools and brushes. It brought with it the crushing realisation that it would be difficult to dissuade her from anything she put her mind to. He had to tread with care.

"Look, until we work out what is going on, there is not a lot we can do." Nick put his hands on her shoulders. "I love the fact that is your first thought; to help him, not freak out or run away screaming. However, I am kind of freaking out. How is any of this possible? I can't find any logical answers. You don't even want to know where the internet has taken me."

"Ew, be careful with the internet, Dad. You know, just because we don't understand what is happening yet, it doesn't mean we won't, eventually. Will you let me help with the research at least? I could be useful."

"Only if it does not interfere with your schoolwork. That comes first. Okay?"

"Deal. Got anything I can read tonight? Catch me up?"

***

Lillian should have predicted Nick and Olivia would leave first. Marcus had been cruel and if she were in Nick's shoes, she would have left too. He had excused them, saying something about Olivia not feeling well. It wasn't until they had gone Lillian understood they were the only ones there she had any desire to hold a conversation with. It left her feeling abandoned at her own party. She sent Nick a text asking how Olivia was doing.

"Fabulous dinner, Lillian." Marcus's cousin Ashley interrupted her brooding. She hadn't been aware that she had gravitated towards the mantelpiece and Henry's painting. It was where Ashley stood, looking up with open curiosity.

"You and Nick seemed to get on well," Lillian said.

"He has promised me a look at the dig in the summer in exchange for firing some flintlocks. All in the spirit of research." Ashley gave a chuckling laugh.

"Did you have time to talk much to Marcus? I'm not sure where he is," she glanced around the room but couldn't see her fiancé.

"Only briefly when I first arrived. It's okay, I'm sure I'll catch up with him," she said.

"I'll go find him. Can I get you a top up?" She gestured at her wineglass, almost empty.

"No, it's fine, really. I am driving home."

"Coffee then?"

"Thanks, a coffee would hit the spot."

In the kitchen, Lillian set the coffee machine going and waited while it gurgled into life. Through the open door to the patio, she could hear angry voices. Curiosity getting the better of her, she made her way to the sink, where she could not only hear better but see the source of the conversation through the window.

Enough light spilt onto the patio to make out Marcus and Guy. "I told you not to do it, Guy, and now we have lost Claudia too. It will take some miracle for us to sort out your mess."

Guy made an all-encompassing gesture with his hands.

"That is why you are so keen to get your hands on this place?"

"It is a back stop. A certain profit that will fill the gap. We get Lillian on board and things go back to normal."

"That's what you wanted all along," Marcus snorted.

Guy scowled.

"Lillian! I'm not blind, Guy. There is a reason you only take home tall blondes. She has obsessed you since she came to the company."

"You are being ridiculous. Don't project your insecurities onto me. She is like a sister. That is all."

It was Lillian's turn to snort. They were both being

ridiculous.

"I am not convinced she will go through with it. She has become oddly attached to the place," Marcus said.

She felt him arrive as if summoned by mention of the sale of the house; the tingle of cold followed by what was becoming a more familiar, warmer sensation. "What are they talking about?" Henry asked near her shoulder.

"Money, Henry. It is always about money."

The coffee pot fell to the floor in a puddle of smashed glass and muddy liquid.

"Henry?"

He had gone. Out of juice, as Nick would say. Lillian bit her lip and watched, hands splayed on the edge of the sink as Marcus and Guy reacted to the noise and stared her way, guilty looks on both of their faces.

"I'm going to go," Guy said, pushing past Marcus. "Thanks for the party, Lillian. I'll call you." He kissed her on the cheek, then left.

"I can explain what that was all about," Marcus said.

Lillian bent to clear up the spilt coffee pot, easing the shards of glass out of the puddle. "Guy has already told me," she said.

"This is the first I heard of it. He says he borrowed more than we should have."

"And he thinks Ashlington is the answer."

"It would help, I suppose."

"I heard what you said about not thinking I will go through with selling." She looked up at him, challenging him to deny it.

"I am talking from experience, Lillian. The wedding. You used to act like you wanted nothing more. Do you remember when I asked you to marry me? How excited you were. The trip on the jet to Barcelona? We are supposed to be starting a family, but you can hardly cope with being in the same room as me."

This is it! Tell him now.

"I slept with Nick," she said. She wrapped the broken glass in kitchen paper and placed it into the bin. It felt symbolic.

Marcus considered her. She expected disappointment or anger. She wanted him to be angry so she could be angry back. Perhaps that would lessen the turbulent scurrying of guilt inside. All he did was give a sigh that accepted the inevitable. "I thought you had," he said. "It's not like stuff like that doesn't happen. Especially with, you know, your dad dying. You didn't really know your own mind there for a while. We can pick up and carry on when you get back—"

"There is more to it than that. I don't want to marry you, Marcus. I think I was in love with the idea of having everything. It's like those magazines your mother reads. This idea is shoved down our throats everywhere we look, that to be happy we have to have the picture perfect marriage and family."

"You don't want to marry me?"

Had she said it aloud? Did she finally tell him? She had been hiding it for so long she imagined it to feel unbearable when she told him. In actual fact it felt liberating. Henry was right.

"No, Marcus. I'm sorry."

"So, this is about having children? Because of how your mother died?"

"I didn't say anything about children." Strange how he had come to that conclusion before she had.

"You should have said something." She studied him, searching for signs that he didn't understand. But they were none. He looked at her openly, and all she could see was sympathy.

"Yes, I should have. And for that I am sorry."

"What about this place? Your job?"

"Does it change things with my job if we are not together?"

"No," he laughed. He hadn't done that in a long time. "I think we are both adult enough to work together still." He sat at the table and let out a sigh. Not an unhappy one, more the type one would take before entering a storm. "So this is it, then. I knew all along I would never compete with this place. With him. You have too much history together and this house has a powerful grasp on you both."

"I did love you, Marcus."

He thought on this for a moment, then nodded in agreement. "Let's not make a fuss tonight. I'll head back to London in the morning."

"Okay. We can finish the champagne when everyone's gone."

He laughed again. "I hope he makes you happy, Lillian."

"This isn't about Nick." She was quick to correct him.

"I think all he has done is remind me of who I used to be."

Chapter 31

Ashlington, September 1814

Westbrook may have been dripping wet, but it didn't stop Henry from pushing past Bradley and embracing his friend. He held on to him as though the very presence of his steadfast lieutenant would erase all that was wrong in the world. "You should have sent word for us to expect you. I didn't think you were coming."

"Something is wrong?" Westbrook asked, as though he sensed Henry's turmoil.

"My brother was killed two days ago. Someone broke into the house."

"What can I do?" Westbrook's hand rested on Henry's shoulder, transferring a calm with its weight.

"We need to get you out of those wet clothes first." Henry looked down at the considerable puddle that had grown beneath Westbrook's feet.

"I shall have a mop fetched," Bradley said with an open resignation that in any other household would have him out on his ear. He took Westbrook's hat and dripping cloak, carrying them off at arm's length, his face dramatically wrinkled and nose turned up to the ceiling.

"Who did that?" Henry asked, noticing a scab on Westbrook's jaw.

"It's nothing. Picked a fight I didn't win, that's all."

Henry examined him for further evidence of his friend at war with himself once more. What had caused such pain now? "Did it help?"

Westbrook shook his head.

"Was that the door?" Louisa asked, leaning over the banister from the landing, preventing further interrogation.

"Lieutenant Robert Westbrook, my wife Louisa," Henry introduced them formally as Louisa descended the stairs at a trot. He doubted he would ever get used to calling her that.

"*The* Westbrook?"

"Yes."

"Really? He is here?" Louisa arrived before them in a swirl of long skirts and subtle scent of roses. Westbrook straightened his back, the way he did if Sinclair was telling them off.

"I am so pleased to meet you," she said, forcing her mouth, that had been down-turned since Danny had died, to smile.

Westbrook responded with a reserved bow and fixed expression. "The honour is mine, Mrs Durand. My apologies for not making it to your wedding. I was otherwise detained." He gave the last statement to Henry, though for once Henry could not discern the hidden meaning in the stare that followed. "You must excuse my appearance; it was a wet ride."

"I'm sure Henry is just happy you are here now." Louisa looked at Henry.

"It is good to see you, West," Henry said.

Westbrook smiled again. Fixed. No dimples.

A silence followed in which Henry imagined Danny descending the stairs, demanding an introduction, before recalling with a jolt that Danny would never demand anything again.

"I shall arrange for a room to be made up and a hot bath drawn. You'll call me Louisa, won't you, Lieutenant?" Louisa said, breaking the silence, taking on the role of courteous host.

"Robert," he said economically.

"Henry's parents are resting and supper is not for a few hours, so you can warm up and get settled in. I'm looking forward to getting to know you, Robert. I know we will become firm friends." She linked her arm into his, but crossing the hall, Westbrook untangled himself, and walked behind her, clasping his hands behind his back.

Louisa did not react to the frostiness of their guest and led him to the small parlour, where she gestured at a chair near the fire. She left the two men there, hurrying out of the room with hospitable purpose.

"She is trying to be nice," Henry hissed. "Why are you acting like a—"

"I am sorry I missed your wedding," Westbrook said with a strange emphasis on the word wedding.

"It was quite a day." Henry felt every bit as defensive as he sounded.

"I'm sure it was," Westbrook muttered.

"Is there something you wish to say?"

Westbrook shook his head and stared at the fire, steam rising from his clothes; leaving Henry with the distinct feeling he might be the source of Westbrook's current disposition.

Sometime later Louisa returned, announcing the bath was ready, and showed Westbrook to his guest room. Mr Samuels delivered his few belongings from the stables, and Henry pulled an outfit from Danny's wardrobe as a dry change of clothes Westbrook could borrow until his own had fully dried.

"Dry clothes and a new book I bought for you," Henry told him without bothering to knock.

"A new book?" Westbrook said with a splash from the bathtub that seemed to have improved his mood. Likely it was the promise of fresh reading material. The collection of tragedies Henry found in Winchcombe contained the sought after *Hamlet* Westbrook had been longing for.

"Did Sinclair's new leg arrive?" Henry asked, settling for a neutral subject as he placed the pile of clothes on the bed. Both men had travelled lightly, so every time his mother insisted on laundering his uniform, Henry had to wear the civilian clothes borrowed from Danny. He felt uncomfortable and starched in them. He longed for his favourite frayed red jacket that the years had moulded to his skin, currently lay in his trunk back at the barracks.

Perched on the end of the guest bed, he buried his head in his hands, wishing the two most important people in his life would get on long enough for him to bury his brother.

"He calls it his riding leg. Still worries about us

becoming irresponsible without him there to watch over us, and grumbles about being of no use to anyone," Westbrook replied, standing up in the tub, wrapping his lower half in a linen drying cloth.

Henry looked up. Were it not for the lingering memory of Westbrook's hand in his hair at Sinclair's, he would not have done such a blatant thing. Westbrook steamed with the heat of the water, his scarred torso its own list of battle honours, Henry able to name each and every one.

The bruises were new.

"What happened, West?" Henry stood, so he could inspect Westbrook closer. He did not realise his fingers had brushed the largest bruise by his waist until he heard Westbrook's breath hitch. "Exactly how many did you pick a fight with this time?"

"It's nothing," Westbrook said, head dipped, watching the indecision of Henry's touch. "Ended with my sister throwing my chamber pot over me."

"Whatever would she do that for?" Henry stepped away.

"According to her, I sulk. But I am more concerned with you. I am sorry about your brother. I know what he meant to you. How are you doing?"

Henry let him get away with the deflection, suddenly too tired to fight him anymore. Even war had been easier than the battles he faced here at home. "Doing what I have to do." Henry shrugged and sat back down. Doing what they expected of him.

Westbrook pulled on the dry underwear, then sat next

to him. "I mean, how are you really doing? In here?" He punched Henry gently with a damp fist on his chest.

"Lost. Alone," Henry said eventually, utterly clueless on how to further verbalise the enormity of what he felt.

Westbrook chewed his lip, and with the small lean that served to deliver the message that all would be well, he bumped Henry with his shoulder. "Not anymore."

"You should get dressed," Henry said, though it was the last thing he wanted. He stirred from thoughts of an alternative life, one in which he was no longer lost, no longer having to pretend. One in which his brother lived happily with Louisa and their child. "We shall be in the drawing room when you are ready." He rose to his feet, his intention to leave, but stopped short of the door. "About Louisa—"

"You always said she was not your girl." Westbrook frowned, arms folded, the pained expression back.

"She was in love with my brother and is expecting his child," Henry blurted.

Westbrook scratched under his eyepatch, tilted his head and cleared his throat. "So, you did not marry for love?"

Henry huffed. "No, West." He paused before adding, "I do love her, but like a sister. Danny was already pledged, and she was about to run away. Admittedly it was impulsive," this made Westbrook snort. "But I only wanted to protect her. Her and the child. I could not have put that in a letter, you see? It is very important to me that you like her."

Westbrook smiled then. It was a grin that lit up his face and caused the dimples to reform in his cheeks. "That's what we do," he said, standing, pulling the borrowed shirt over his head. "We protect the ones we love."

"I couldn't protect my brother."

"Does not make it your fault. We shall find out what happened, Henry."

"We?"

"Always." Westbrook gave him a serious nod, which caused Henry to smile finally. He walked back to his own room, feeling lighter and no longer alone.

Westbrook entered the drawing room dressed for dinner shortly after Henry and Louisa, the borrowed coat a fraction tight at the shoulders and his hair still damp. He seemed aware of the fact, doing his best to tame the curling ends with the flat of his hand. Tucked under his arm, he carried gifts.

"A wedding gift," he told Henry, presenting him with a long narrow parcel still damp from the rain. Henry thanked him with an intrigued incline of the head and lay the box on the side table to open it. Louisa moved to his side with a gleeful look of anticipation. When he pulled the lid off and pushed away the tissue paper, Henry stopped breathing. Louisa gasped.

"West, why it's magnificent!" he exclaimed, pulling out a curved officer's sabre complete with scabbard. His initials had been engraved into the scabbard's metal locket with twisting artistry. He drew the sword, noting the exquisite workmanship of the honed steel. The balance and grip perfectly matched to his hand.

"It is pure self interest, on account of you breaking your last one," Westbrook replied, scratching under his eyepatch. "I have something for you too," Westbrook whispered to Louisa as Henry ran a hand down the blade, marvelling at the quality. It was not lost on Henry that Westbrook's attitude to Louisa had changed markedly from when he arrived.

Westbrook handed her a much smaller drier parcel covered in an outrageous bow of ribbon. Louisa squealed. Her parents had rarely given her gifts. What few she had ever received had been from Henry. She gasped when she opened the box, sliding the silver bracelet straight onto her wrist.

"Thank you, Robert. It's wonderful." Unable to contain her excitement, she kissed him on the cheek. "Look, Henry."

Henry struggled to pull his attention away from the sword, but Louisa thrust her wrist before him, twisting the bracelet, showing him the intricate engraving on the band. "Look, it matches your sword," she told him, pointing at the crest near the hilt of his own gift.

Above her head Henry grinned at Westbrook in silent acknowledgement that their gifts not only matched each other's, but that of Westbrook's own sword, twin to the one Henry now held, and also carrying the leopard and jessant-de-lis of the Westbrook coat-of-arms.

"Thank you," he told him, all too aware of the catch to his voice.

"Hopefully it improves how you fight," Westbrook

said with his dimpled grin, diffusing the gravity of the moment. With a stage whisper to Louisa, he added, "It is truly terrible. I don't know how we have survived this long."

Louisa laughed. It was unguarded, and Henry noted the first time she had laughed since Danny died. Westbrook offered her his arm, winked at Henry and steered her towards the door where Henry's parents had arrived and expected introductions. Louisa handled these gracefully. Having known her all his life, Henry could see the cracks that losing Danny had caused her, but she was doing everything she could not to let them show.

Henry smirked as he heard Westbrook ask her, "Did he tell you about how I had to save him from that horse of his? What possessed him to spend a small fortune getting the monster back here, I shall never know. Henry was overboard for sure..."

Henry placed the sword back in the box, relieved that his people were now getting along. Sinclair's message about living as who we are without fear came to mind, together with the painting of the other Westbrook, James. Had their bond been more than that of friendship? No, Henry thought, his fingers lingering on the sword's engraved crest. He was simply desperate for any sign that a man such as Sinclair— the man that epitomised everything Henry wanted to be— could be the same as him. But, perhaps, loving another man did not have to live exclusively to such qualities after all.

The cook served dinner promptly, Nathaniel insisting things should continue as normal and muttering about the lateness of Christopher. Henry noticed Mrs Melton had included a dish of mashed potato and placed it within reach of his chair. The setting next to him, the one Danny would normally occupy, remained empty.

They confined conversation to the state of the weather initially, Westbrook having lots to say on the matter following his journey from his mother's house in Bath, then as the wine flowed Henry's mother finally asked what had clearly been on her mind since meeting Westbrook. "Tell me, Robert, how did you lose your eye?"

"The truth of it is very dull," Westbrook replied. "I got a face full of grapeshot. Nasty stuff."

Henry emitted a sound of amusement.

"Your son," Westbrook addressed Elinor with a wave of his fork, "has taken it upon himself to invent increasingly wild stories as to how it happened. Has half the regiment now believing it was skewered by the sabre of a French hussar who rode off with my eyeball still on the tip glaring angrily down at them all." He demonstrated by stabbing a carrot.

"How gruesome of you, Henry," Elinor grimaced.

Henry held Westbrook's gaze, remembering with acute detail the devastation of the actual moment and the weight of Westbrook's head on his shoulder as he later bandaged it.

"And what drew you to the army?" Elinor continued.

"My grandfather and then my father served with the Slashers, so you could say it is in the blood. I grew up wanting to prove myself to him and live up to his

357

expectation." Westbrook looked towards Henry's father.

Nathaniel drained his wineglass. Bradley re-filled it. "And did you?" he asked.

"My father died when I was eleven," Westbrook answered with equal bluntness. "So I will never know."

"I'm sorry." Elinor glared at Henry with a maternal expression that he interpreted as 'help me change the bloody subject.' But Henry's reaction got lost in thoughts of Danny again.

"Are you married? Is there a Mrs Westbrook?" Louisa asked, though Henry considered that topic equally fraught with danger.

"No. It is just my mother and my younger sister, Judith. She is engaged to a lawyer; a Mr Cross from Bath? Do you know of him?"

Elinor shook her head.

"It would seem I am to be surrounded by weddings; my mother has announced she is also to marry again. She has accepted the fervent advances of an old friend of the family's. This potato is as good as you always said it was," Westbrook told Henry with a grin.

"Everleigh?" Henry asked.

Westbrook nodded.

Henry let out a whistle.

"Sir Gilbert Everleigh?" Nathaniel asked, suddenly showing an interest in the conversation. Henry gave him a sideways glance. Everleigh had a substantial wealth his father clearly thought better used elsewhere than a soldier's widow.

"The same. Sir Gilbert had known my parents for a long time, and after losing his wife, well, as we all know," Westbrook said gesturing to Louisa, then Henry, "sometimes, friends fall in love."

Henry swallowed the remaining wine in his glass in a single gulp, distracting himself from that statement. It was while trying to gauge just how much wine Westbrook had consumed that Christopher entered the room accompanied by a cloud of sickly smelling cologne, reminding Henry of Christmas.

"You're late, Christopher," Nathaniel said, glaring at his youngest son. Christopher ignored him and looked at Westbrook inquisitively.

Westbrook rose to his feet, confirming Henry's suspicions by having to steady himself with a hand on the back of Louisa's chair. "Robert Westbrook," he said cheerfully.

"*The* Westbrook?" Christopher asked. "I've heard much about you. From Henry's letters." He shook the offered hand.

"Ah, proof at last. Henry can indeed write a letter." Elinor gave Henry a stern look.

"I'm Christopher, the youngest brother." The awkward silence that followed as they all felt Danny's absence seemed to Henry to last a lifetime. Henry's eyes fell to the empty place setting next to him.

"Robert was telling us he is from a soldiering family," Louisa said.

Christopher filled his plate and, reaching for the wine,

offered a top up to Westbrook.

"I've had plenty," Westbrook said with a shake of the head and a protective hand placed over his glass.

Henry sighed with relief.

Christopher took his time cutting his slice of baked pork into neat squares. "Did Henry tell you I nearly joined up myself?"

"Nonsense!" Nathaniel barked from the end of the table, pushing his plate away from him. "You wouldn't have lasted five minutes." Henry stared surprised at his father, wondering if this, just this once, might have been a veiled attempt at actually recognising the fact Henry had made a perfectly fine soldier despite his father's misgivings. Was the old man finally admitting to being wrong? "Though Henry has proved it is a career not altogether as difficult to survive as one might assume."

Henry coughed on the mouthful of wine he had just snorted. Opposite him, Westbrook put his weight on his hands to stand and protest, but Louisa touched him on the forearm and whispered something. He leant back in his chair and grinned at her before turning his attention to Elinor's end of the table, obliterating Nathaniel from his view on account of his missing eye.

"From the stories in the newspapers, your regiment has been in the thick of it," Christopher continued, either unperturbed or ignorant of the tension. Henry found it hard to judge which. "Badajos was a significant battle, was it not? Henry wrote that you both volunteered for the attack?"

The mere mention of the place made Henry shudder.

Westbrook pulled at his collar, then reached for the wine he had only moments before declined.

"Volunteered?" Elinor asked, her fork halting midway to her mouth.

"I think we'd all rather hear about London, Christopher," Henry said. "With all those debutantes to dance with, you'll probably be married next?"

Christopher laughed.

The mention of Badajos summoned Henry's demon as blatantly as if he had opened the door and welcomed it across the threshold himself. It found him buried as he slept that night. Bodies screaming as he tore at them. Men still alive piled above him, their gaping wounds splitting as he struggled against them, driven to find Westbrook.

Too much left undone.

The weight of his father's expectation pressing him into wet mud. His own burden of guilt trapping him there, sinking as the mud crept into his ears and nostrils.

The bodies screamed louder.

Henry screamed back, the struggle intensifying as the weight pressed down; what little air there was, rank with decay.

Where are you?

Then he felt him. Arms around him once more. The bastion of his body behind Henry; holding him fast against the madness, lighting the dark crevasses of his mind, throwing off the dead as Henry had once done for him.

"I'm here, I've got you. You are home," he heard

Westbrook say.

"A dream?" his mother's voice—scared.

"He said he didn't sleep well anymore. I could never have imagined this," Louisa—horrified.

A body rolled on top of him again, the greedy turncoat leering at him, licking his lips hungrily. Then Henry was carrying the body of the small boy from the convent, betrayed brown eyes asking, "Why didn't you get here quicker?"

The weight increasing, forcing Henry to his knees.

Danny replacing the child in his arms asking, "Where were you?"

Henry heard an inhuman scream. His own.

Westbrook's grip on him tightened. "Do not think any less of him," Henry heard him say. "He was buried alive."

"West?" he called out.

"I've got you."

"Don't let me go. Don't let them take me."

"I won't ever let you go," Westbrook whispered.

Chapter 32

Come Monday, true to her word, Olivia walked straight off the school bus to the manor. Nick heard Lillian let her in and their voices approach along the hallway.

"He's in his study. Go ahead, I'm just making some coffee," he heard Lillian say. "Want one?"

"Please," Olivia answered, then the door to the study creaked open, disturbing Nick's pondering of the phrase 'his study.'

"Hey Dad."

"Good day?"

"Not too bad. What are you working on?"

"Henry's time back here before Waterloo."

"Where do I start?" she asked, throwing her backpack into a gap on the floor. She looked around at all the boxes and piles despondently. "Eugh! Your filing system needs some work."

She was being brave. She had that restless look about her. Being back in the manor made her uncomfortable.

"What about homework?" he countered.

"Already done it at lunchtime and in my free period today."

Nick smiled. "Then that's your pile there." He

gestured at a box near the paned doors to the garden. "Fill your boots."

Olivia sat crossed-legged on the floor, plugged her phone into the wall socket, then shoved her earbuds into her ears. Nick could hear the music from where he sat. How it helped her study anything, he had no clue, but maybe it was more about dampening the emotional white-noise. That had always been her phrase, not his.

Lillian brought in a tray of coffee mugs she then handed around.

"Ollie, I told Lily earlier about what happened with Henry the night of the dinner," Nick said, having gestured for her to switch the music off.

"You don't think I'm crazy?"

"Actually, I rather like the fact it is not just me experiencing this," Lillian said. "I'm sorry though, that you got dragged into whatever this is, whatever is going on here."

"Don't be. I think I was meant to be here. I think he needed someone removed from it all."

Lillian raised her eyebrows as though she found this interesting. It hadn't shocked Nick. Olivia often came to conclusions with a wisdom beyond her years.

"What did he look like?" Lillian asked.

"A lot like the painting, perhaps a little sadder in real life than how conflicted he looks sometimes on canvas. You have very similar eyes. But there was something—nah— never mind."

"Go on," Lillian urged.

"It just seemed like he didn't fit there."

"Talking of Henry, Westbrook came to Ashlington after all," Nick said.

"He did? Good, he is exactly who Henry needed. Do you think they ever—wait—hold that thought, I need to make a phone call to my solicitor, let me go do that, then I want you to tell me everything." Lillian left the room with a squeak of excitement that made Nick smile until he caught Olivia watching him. He turned the smile into a yawn and continued typing.

"Aren't you sad she is selling this place?" Olivia asked, petting Holly, who had curled up against her legs.

"Hmm?" Nick said, pretending his attention was still on the monitor of his laptop, where he worked on a narrative for Westbrook's arrival at Ashlington. "What did you say?"

"Never mind. Are these all Louisa's journals? It is just as well she wrote, too. She covers lots of the gaps. Have you read this part about Danny's funeral?"

"Not yet. I am waiting for Lily to catch up. Something tells me we are only scratching the surface of Louisa's story. I get the impression she has more secrets to tell."

"I feel like we should order something to eat?" Lillian said, poking her head around the door an hour later.

"Indian?" suggested Olivia with raised eyebrows at her father.

"The one in Broadway? I've got a menu somewhere."

Olivia stopped her with a wave of her phone.

They ordered online for pick up in thirty minutes, and

Lillian joined them by seating herself in the armchair next to the fireplace. Holly lifted her head to judge if it was worth moving, but evidently decided against it and stayed put. Nick handed Lillian his laptop.

"Here are a few more pages to get you up to speed," he said, stretching. He sat back down at the desk and closed his eyes, resting them for a few moments, trying to work out what he needed to make headway on next.

Distracted by the little noises of interest Lillian was making, he cracked open one eye and watched her. She had folded her legs underneath her, leaning on one arm twirling her hair, which she had worn loose that day, as she read, engrossed. She seemed lighter, as though something had unburdened her.

He closed his eyes again. *Look at her Henry, if it were not for your actions, she would not be here. Were you my son, I would have been very proud of you.*

Nick opened the other eye, watching his daughter from the corner of what field of vision his secretive squint allowed. She, too, was deep into Henry's story, shaking it, searching for something. He should probably tell her more often how proud he was and look forward to the person she was becoming, not backward at what was gone.

"I'll go get the take-away," he said, rising to his feet.

"Okay."

"Um-hmm."

He was certain Holly was the only one to notice he had left.

When he returned with two carrier bags full of

steaming food that had given the Land Rover a lingering spicy smell he knew from experience would last a week, he called out to Lillian and Olivia, who joined him in the kitchen.

"You okay?" Olivia asked Lillian, who had gone quiet over her meal.

"I was thinking about the sword. I am pretty sure I have seen a sword like that here," Lillian said. "Would you be up for a rummage in the attic?" she asked Nick.

"Flirt," Nick said.

Lillian chuckled.

Olivia did the thing where she looked between them like she was watching a tennis match.

Having climbed the ladder into the attic, Lillian pulled the cord that switched on the light. The single bare bulb flickered into life, bringing with its illumination the smell of hot dust. Nick hoped the bulb would hold on as long as they needed it to. He didn't fancy being up there in the dark among the cobwebs.

"You Durands really throw nothing away," he said with his hands on his hips. "I'm surprised the attic takes the weight." The room overflowed with boxes, old furniture, and paintings. "Do you think there are more journals up here?" he said, stooping to search inside a promising cardboard box.

"Don't get distracted Nick, I know you, we'll be up here all night if you're not careful."

"I think this will take weeks. Look, there is another campaign chest. I can't tell who it belongs to. The lid is all scratched. That might be a twenty-eight again. I'd need better light to be sure. I'll come back up tomorrow with a torch."

"More of Henry's story?"

Nick shrugged, picking up a book.

"We're looking for the sword, remember?" she said. "Ah! Is this it, do you think?" Lillian rummaged around the foot of a coat stand that held an assortment of umbrellas and walking sticks at its base. She picked out a sword, curved like the officers would carry. The metal trimmings to the scabbard tarnished. The grip of the handle too small for Nick's hand. Perfect for a smaller man, more Olivia's size.

"Do you want to pull it out?" Nick said, his voice a whisper.

"No, you do it," Lillian whispered back.

He did, the blade scrapping against the scabbard's lining.

"It's beautiful," Lillian said. "How can a thing that takes lives be so stunning? It seems wrong."

Nick rubbed at the blade near the hilt. "Here," he pointed to an engraving. "I have seen this before. It's the Westbrook coat-of-arms, so must be the sword he gave to Henry. When you think about it, it is like he is saying you are family."

"I think he is saying more than that," Lillian said. "I think it was a declaration of love. Westbrook has been dropping enough hints. Henry is so wrapped up in hiding how he feels because of all the social constraints; he can't see what is right in front of him."

I see you, Nick thought.

Chapter 33

Ashlington, September 1814

Though Henry often woke in the night from the nightmares that plagued him to find Westbrook, holding him fast against the tide of madness, duelling with Henry's circling demon; never had Westbrook stayed in his bed until morning. He woke to find his mouth pressed against the nape of Westbrook's neck; amongst his dark curls, where he smelt of the heady combination of wood smoke, fresh rain, and dusty books. It felt like the end of all ends.

Henry shut his eyes again tightly, wishing himself back to sleep or for time to stop. His senses refused, and the clock on the mantle kept ticking. I really am going straight to hell, he thought.

"Are you awake?" Westbrook murmured some time later, voice muffled by the pillow.

"I am wondering what you are doing still in my bed?" Henry said, covertly moving his arm off his friend and attempting to turn away lest Westbrook detect how his heart was thumping.

"Bad dream. The terrible one. But you didn't hurt anyone this time." Westbrook rolled onto his back, closing the distance Henry had just created, and stretched. "Besides, I am not in your bed, I'm on top of it." He gestured at his shirtless skin and shivered.

Henry shifted and billowed the covers. Westbrook shimmied underneath and wiggled closer. For warmth, Henry told himself. "I suppose I woke the entire house?" he asked, propping himself up on an elbow. If he could only keep space between them, he might survive this encounter.

"Only your mother and your wife." Westbrook yawned. "They were concerned for you."

"I hate you seeing me like that."

"Henry, you are the bravest idiot I know. Now kindly shut up so I can go back to sleep." Westbrook closed his eye and swatted at him. Henry lay back down, head landing against Westbrook's shoulder. He felt Westbrook shift closer again, creating more contact among warm limbs hidden under the covers. No chance at all that Henry would sleep now.

He had done battle all night, it seemed. Why shouldn't he stop fighting now and finally surrender to what his heart wanted? Hadn't he done enough fighting? Had he not concluded that wanting Westbrook did not make him any less of a man? Not unless he continued to be a coward about it. The brave thing to do would be to tell him—to let Westbrook know the real him.

"Do you remember the march to Almendralejo? The winter we hardly ate anything. One night you asked where I would rather be," Henry said, emboldened by Westbrook's toe creeping its way around his foot.

"I remember."

"Well, it is here. This is where I belong—right here—

right now. With you."

The toe stopped moving.

Overcome by a sudden awkwardness, Henry wondered what on earth had possessed him to say that out loud and with more than a little hope that he hadn't. The silence that followed crashed around him, perfectly encapsulating how he felt. Like a blind man stumbling in the dark.

Then Westbrook moved, shifting away slightly so he could read Henry's expression with his remaining eye. "Please don't look at me like that," Westbrook said. "It kills me every time."

Henry looked away, heart sinking, the demon inside laughing at him.

But with a warm hand on his cheek, Westbrook pulled him back from the brink. "The look when you hate yourself for how you feel about me. It kills me, Henry, because I feel the same way about you."

Did he really say that? Did he mean what Henry hoped beyond all hope that he meant? He feels the same way? Henry frowned and watched a slow smile that made his heart skip, spread from where Westbrook bit at his lip, waiting for Henry to catch up.

"You knew? You know?"

Westbrook nodded.

There was too much Henry wanted to say, but did not know how or where to start. Instead, his free hand came to rest flat on Westbrook's bare skin, which had warmed considerably in the short time he had been under the covers.

Acutely aware that Westbrook's single eye could convey more soul than two of anyone else's, Henry dared to look directly into it, losing himself to the green. It returned his enquiry with such resplendence he thought if he did not burst into flames, he would willingly melt against him. Boldly, and with his hand steady for once, he traced his fingers along his friend's chest. Shut away from the world.

"I have been waiting for you," Westbrook whispered, pulling Henry to his open mouth.

Footsteps on the landing and a creak of the floorboard outside the door cut short any further exploration. Henry leant his forehead against Westbrook's in resignation, their quickened breath mingling in the chill morning air. The promised kiss abandoned.

There was a sharp knock at the door, then Louisa's voice. "Henry? How are you feeling?"

Westbrook grinned his ridiculous dimpled smile.

'How was he feeling?' Too elated to register the danger, Henry shook in Westbrook's arms that squeezed him tighter. How could he possibly explain?

For the first time, he felt like he belonged here at Ashlington, warm, safe, true. He felt elation—serenity. None of which he could admit to Louisa, at least not through the door. At the same time, he also felt utterly desolate that it couldn't be beyond the walls of this room and this stolen moment. He loved so badly it cut his soul. But despite feeling the purest thing he had ever felt, acting on it could be his death sentence. Having spent every waking hour for years doing everything to bury his feelings, he had almost lost himself, and losing the man next to him scared him more than anything. Finally, if the pressure below was anything to go by, he was fit to burst with frustration. Quite enough for one man.

"Much better, thank you." Inevitably, the words came out strangled, so he cleared his throat and tried again. "I shall be down to take breakfast presently."

Now aware of the threat to their safety, Henry watched the doorknob, willing it not to turn. It had no lock. Finding her husband in bed with a man this way would be disastrous for all of them. He had made her a vow only a few days before on their wedding day that he would honour her. The recollection of that vow made him look back at Westbrook, who had already let go of him and swung his legs out of the bed. Westbrook bit at his lip in thought, listening to the retreat of Louisa's footsteps. It was Westbrook's honour Henry had to protect, too.

They were not safe here.

"I know," Westbrook whispered. "Duty and honour." Normally, Westbrook would say such a thing with a look of pride and determination. This was said with sadness and a pained reality that creased his eye.

"We continue fighting and keep doing what we have to. Together?" Henry dug deep to maintain control and contain himself. From climbing on top of Westbrook, kissing and feeling every smouldering inch of him. From barricading the door and never letting him go.

"Always." Westbrook stood up, saving Henry once more. He pulled a blanket off the bed and wrapped himself with it, hiding his own frustration. "Henry, your house is bloody freezing. Would it kill you Durands to light a fire here and there?" He grinned, but the undimpled one. A show to convince Henry that he didn't hurt. Henry had seen it many times. Many of those occasions making more sense now. For how long had he been waiting?

Westbrook tiptoed for the door, where he put his hand on the doorknob, and hesitated.

During that hesitation, Henry crossed the room, taking Westbrook by surprise as he turned. Danny had let Louisa go; he now lay along the hall in his shroud, awaiting the rain to stop long enough for his burial, all his plans and dreams left undone. Henry would not allow Westbrook to leave the room in any doubt of how much he meant. So he kissed him hard, pressing Westbrook against the wall, all the while maintaining a foot against the bottom of the door to prevent further interruption. He remembered to close his eyes, and it far exceeded his imagination, Westbrook returning his kiss with fierce urgency and frenzied touch. Neither of them gentle through the need of each other.

"We can never do this again," Westbrook said, breath heavy with release, resting his head back on the wall, pulling Henry tighter against him. "Unless we find ourselves billeted in a room with a substantial lock," he added, with what Henry gauged to be a large degree of hope.

"I promise you, West—one day—somehow, we'll have more than this."

"Don't make promises you can't keep."

"I never do," Henry said, and kissed him with

deliberate tenderness. One aching last time, tracing the feel and taste of it to his memory. Not knowing when they would ever get the chance again.

Westbrook straightened his eyepatch, blew a stray curl off his face, and left Henry's room with feline stealth wearing an enormous smile.

Frustrations given temporary relief, Henry washed with icy cold water, dressed and sought breakfast where he found his mother, sat alone nibbling on toasted bread, reading.

"Good morning," he said, helping himself to Mrs Melton's finest bread, an egg and some cheese from the sideboard, unable to help the lightness in his step he immediately felt guilty about. How could he feel happy? He chastised himself. They hadn't even buried Danny yet.

But then it wasn't exactly happiness. More liberation at having been himself. For letting the real Henry Durand express himself to the one he loved. The guilt over his brother remained.

"Has everyone already eaten?" he asked, looking at the empty spaces around the table.

"You missed Louisa, she is in the garden. Your father has ridden to the Chiltons' with Christopher and your friend has not been down yet. Now the rain has stopped, your father says we shall bury Danny this afternoon." Elinor caught him with a fast hand as he passed her chair. "Does it happen often, Henry? The nightmares?" Her brow creased with a concern that Henry last saw before he had left Ashlington a lifetime ago. "You are my son," she said. "You do not have to go through something like that on your own."

"In the army you are never on your own." Henry sat next to his mother, leaning towards her to see what she had been reading. Something with a great deal of z's in the title, likely a romance.

"Is that why you like it?" She put the book down, not waiting for an answer. "I am pleased you have a friend like Robert there with you. He seems to know what to do to help."

About to take a bite of the boiled egg, Henry paused. He lowered it back to his plate. If she knew, if there was some maternal instinct that could read her son's secret, she was keeping it to herself. "We are there for each other. We put our trust in one another, with the entire company, our lives depend on it." He hoped she would poke no more.

"It will never stop me worrying for you."

"I am sorry I disturbed you last night." Deciding a swift exit was favourable to continuing the conversation, he stood. "I should find Louisa." He took the egg. It would only go to waste otherwise.

"You will be careful, won't you, Henry?"

His mother's question followed him to the garden, where he found Louisa among the herbs. His responsibility now. The warning from his mother pertained to returning to the regiment, he was sure, but it reminded him that Louisa had endured enough. He had always been honest with her. Their friendship built on their honesty. Hiding the truth from her would hurt her more than knowing such a thing, but however he broached the subject, he needed to tread carefully.

He watched for a moment, finishing the egg, before announcing his presence. She sang as she cut the stems with a small knife, her basket looped through her elbow. The melody, a sad one, began stripping away the layers of hope Henry had built that morning. The last layer—the heat of Westbrook against him—he clung to like a shipwreck, promising himself he would never let go.

He stepped behind Louisa and offered to carry the basket for her.

"Did you sleep well in the end?" she asked. Still grieving, her first words of the day were of concern for him. It broke his heart all over again.

"I did."

"I know I am not as worldly as you, Henry, but I would like to understand. We used to talk to each other about anything. I want you to know that hasn't changed. You know, if you want to talk about what happened in the war, what gives you such alarming dreams. Do you remember how you told me to talk to you about my father when he struck me? It felt better, though I am sure nothing compared to being buried alive."

"It was West. He got buried, not me." Henry said it without thinking. Not at all how he wanted to explain. His hand trembled, shaking the basket. He grasped it with his other, digging his nails in, hopeful the pain might stop the shake. It didn't.

She looked at him, pale eyes blinking, head tilted to

one side. "But you have terrible dreams about it and he said—"

"I imagine he said that because he doesn't want you to know it broke me seeing him that way. Louisa, it broke me because I thought I'd lost him."

"It's okay, you don't have to talk about it." She paused, then said, "Oh!" holding her mouth wide open. "You mean ..."

Henry nodded and waited for the look of revulsion, or worse, betrayal, that he might have only asked her to marry him to draw attention away from his genuine affections.

Instead, she glanced around, then took his arm, steering him away from the kitchen garden towards the sprawling oak tree where they could ensure they were alone. "You don't have to say any more, though it certainly explains a few things." She looked liked she might laugh, but bit at her lip. No doubt recalling the time he kissed her or just days ago when she had kissed him. "No wonder it felt so odd. You didn't like it?"

No matter how he answered, he feared he had just burdened her with an immense weight of shame. He considered not saying more, but he was all too aware that she might be the only person other than Westbrook himself that knew him well enough, that might understand, might help him understand.

"Do you remember me telling you that you were not like the other boys?" she continued. "There were no other motives to our friendship. It made me feel safe. I suppose that is why."

"Would you mind then, if I said more?"

"You can tell me anything, Henry."

"You should know, especially now, and yes, I suppose it explains a lot. I'm not supposed to feel this way, you understand, about him?"

Louisa nodded with a hint of "I'm not an idiot." "It puts you in great danger, Henry. Both of you. I understand." They reached the tree, where she lowered herself onto the old wooden swing. He gave her a push. "Tell me about him. The things you couldn't put in your letters."

"The longer we spent together, and the more I got to know him, I found myself doing anything just to see him smile. Every breath I took close to him was a better one. I did not understand what this was until the day he lost his eye, he put his head on my shoulder and it felt—"

"As though he fit there?"

"Yes! Like he had been made to fit there. From then on, every look, every touch of his burnt. I tried not to allow it. I really did, Louisa. I put up a wall between us, but he breached it every single day."

"There is something quite charming about him," she agreed.

"Eventually I tried to push him away. That was hopeless, too. All it did was hurt him. You see, for all these years I thought there was something wrong with me, that if only I could prove myself a real man it would go away." He stepped in front of the swing to face her, to judge her reaction to if he should continue, still expecting some flicker of disgust.

She squeezed his arm. It meant the world to him. A signal of acceptance and understanding that he did not think he deserved or ever dreamed he would have. "We cannot help who we fall for," she said, her voice small, the words almost lost in the enormity of their meaning. "You are more of a man than anyone I know, Henry."

"That wasn't why I asked you to marry me," he said. "It wasn't about covering up how I feel about him, I need you to know that."

"I know."

Comforted, Henry continued, the words spilling from him with his own awakening truth, and with none of the red herring he had earlier fed his mother. He told her of the crippling feeling of loss at Badajos and finished by confiding one of his darker moments into her safekeeping.

"When it all got too much, when the demons whispered that the world would be better off without me, it was West that stopped me." He took a deep breath, nose stinging with the threat of tears. "Because he always brought the meaning back."

"Oh Henry." Louisa's tears flowed freely, adding to her already stained cheeks. She wiped at his face with her sleeve. "You have loved him for years?"

Henry nodded.

"That is a lot to carry, Henry, even for you. Have you told him?"

Henry cleared his throat. "Not in so many words."

Despite the seven years' distance, she still knew him well. "I suppose you far prefer kissing him?" She said in a haughty tone, then smiled, so he knew she joked.

Henry nodded, unable to do anything about the grin spreading at the memory of how it felt, or the giddy heat rising in his cheeks.

"So you have!" she said.

"Only recently." The devastating combination of rough and smooth that had left him breathless and hungry for more.

"I think you should tell him you are in love with him," Louisa said, touching his hand. "If it were me, I'd have given anything for Danny to have said he loved me, no matter the circumstances. Just so I would know. To hear him say it."

The mention of Danny sobered Henry. "Danny said it. He told me he loved you—that he always had." Duty and honour, Henry thought. How can such noble intentions leave so many hurting?

"He said that? That he loved me?" An infectious smile spread across her face.

The corner of Henry's mouth twitched at the sight of it, and he nodded.

Louisa rubbed her pregnant belly. "You left quite a gap when you left, Henry. Danny and I both lost the person closest to us, so we filled that gap with each other. Had he ever looked at me the way Robert looks at you, then I wouldn't have needed to hear him say it." She shook her head, cutting off Henry's protest. "Robert doesn't make it obvious. But knowing this, what you have trusted me with, last night when he stepped into that room to comfort you, believe me, you were everything to him. I don't know—it was like you were meant to be together." She jumped off the swing and threaded her arm into Henry's, leading him away. "But there's more to it than honour and duty isn't there." She narrowed her eyes and turned him to face her. "You don't think you deserve to be happy, do you?"

She was right. Hearing her say the words brought clarity to some of the weight he carried. He had assumed he couldn't be happy because he felt different to the men around him.

"Oh Henry, you always did put everyone else first."

"We know what is at stake, Louisa. That includes you and the baby now. Neither of us would risk that. No matter how we feel about each other, nothing will ever happen between us to cause dishonour to anyone we care about." He did not count the moment he and Westbrook had shared that morning, deciding that belonged to them alone.

He spent further time sat with Louisa talking of Danny, doing his best to provide comfort despite doubting it helped at all. How could it ever be enough when she had lost so much? Then he made his way out of the rose garden and along the back of the house to the stable block. With Westbrook still upstairs, and expecting a turbulent day, Henry decided on a ride to organise his thoughts and keep him out of the way while they made preparations for the funeral later that afternoon. Searching the apple tree by the gate for an offering to Whisper, he found one high up. His favourite horse had seen enough of war; she deserved every bit of her early retirement at Ashlington.

It surprised him to find her tacked up, less so to find Westbrook's bay stood next to her. Westbrook himself ducked under the head of the bay, rubbing him down with a brush. Henry chuckled as Whisper nibbled at Westbrook's coat before giving him a forceful shove.

"Give over, you little brute. You had plenty of attention," Westbrook told her before disappearing into the stable and returning with his saddle.

"How did you know?" Henry asked, allowing himself to intrude on the scene. He was not altogether certain how things would now be between them and felt a sudden shyness.

Westbrook smiled at him, then glanced around them to be sure they were alone. "Because you are mine," he whispered.

Henry felt a welcome settling in his heart. "I am."

Whisper stamped a hoof smelling the apple, which Henry allowed her to take a bite of, risking his fingers so he could hold on to half of it to give to Westbrook's horse.

They rode out through the dappled woods among the foxgloves up the hill and onto the ridge where they let the horses have their heads and galloped. They took a few fences, one of which had always made Henry's heart thump in his chest as a boy, but Danny would encourage him to be bold and try. Whisper cleared it with ease, making him wonder if he had made the right decision to leave her behind. He would leave much behind this time. Not only his horse, but a wife and child. He reined Whisper back to a walk with a sudden fear that he wouldn't see Louisa again. Childbirth was dangerous, and he couldn't shake the dread that echoed around the place since losing Danny.

"West?" Lost in his own thoughts, it took Westbrook a moment to realise Henry had spoken. "Penny for them."

Westbrook reined his horse in next to Henry, their knees almost touching. "I was thinking of how things were in Bath with my mother and sister. Neither of them need me anymore." He looked away, and Henry could see his cheek muscles working as he clenched and unclenched his jaw. Composed again, he turned back to Henry. "I felt of no use, and I am not sure that is good for a man. Now I understand why it bothers Sinclair so much."

"I need you, West," Henry said, knowing it to be selfish. The honourable thing to do would be to encourage Westbrook to find someone to marry, start a family, be a father. But he couldn't. He had tried, God knows he had tried to do without him. "I will always need you."

"Even now you have a wife?" Westbrook said with a teasing grin.

"Are you going to tell me why your sister threw a chamber pot over you?" Henry countered.

"You do not want to hear about that today."

"I need the distraction. Tell me."

"It was entirely your fault."

"How so? I wasn't even there."

"I received your letter."

Typically blunt, it consisted of two sentences.

I am to be married Monday.
Please come.
HD

Henry wondered what his reaction would have been were he to receive such a message from Westbrook. He decided not to dwell on it.

"I got drunk in the first inn and more so in the second. The third had been quiet until I arrived. I picked the largest man, nudged him aside and drank his beer."

Henry winced. "You're an idiot."

"That's what my sister said. She broke up the fight and had my arm behind my back in no time, marching me out of the place. She is surprisingly strong for one so tiny, but then I was very, very drunk, you understand."

"I look forward to meeting Judy one day."

"You two would get on famously," Westbrook laughed. "Anyway, she bundles me into the carriage, twists my thumb back to get at your letter in my pocket—it still hurts—read it, then told me I should come, for the wedding. That you needed me. I said something about you having to go without what you wanted for once."

"It was selfish of me to expect you to be here."

"No, it wasn't, Henry. I had no claim on you."

"But that's the whole point. You did—you do—more than anyone."

Westbrook blushed, and Henry decided he liked the sight of it. Very much. "And the chamber pot?"

"We got home, and I retreated to my room. Your

wedding day came and went. Then Judy happened. Again. She stormed into my room, opened my curtains, blinding my only remaining eyeball, and moaned about the stench. Threw the contents of my chamber pot over me declaring, 'At least you have to wash now,'" this Westbrook said in a high-pitched voice. "She left me drenched in my piss, looking at my sword, deliberating the mechanics of how to fall upon it. Which is when I had the idea."

"I don't know whether to laugh or cry, West," Henry said, chuckling at such imagery despite the tears he chose for once not to hide. "What idea?"

"The sword I gave you yesterday belonged to my father. Sinclair held on to it after he died, had mine made to match it. He was almost as surprised as I was that you are married, by the way. Did I pass on his congratulations?"

Henry shook his head, still reeling from the revelation regarding the sword. He pulled Whisper to a halt and dismounted, putting his hands to his knees to counteract the dizziness.

Westbrook circled him on the bay. "The blade needed a great deal of work, to hone out the nicks and polish it. I did that myself and engraved it. Sinclair used to take me to the smithy when I was younger and broodier, but that really is a story for another day."

"Stop. The sword was your father's? It felt like it was made for me."

"I put on a new grip, too. It had to be enough, you understand." Westbrook also dismounted and advanced on him.

"I do understand. I will make it up to you for all that hurt I caused. And I will endeavour to deserve such a gift." He would do everything in his power to make sure he could.

Westbrook took Henry's hands, barely a whisper of air separating them, and leant his forehead on Henry's, his lips agonisingly out of reach. "You don't need to try, you already do. I knew the day I lost my eye that I was yours, that it was permanent. That's why I got so worked up about it. How could you ever like me damaged that way? But you never left. You stayed with me, patiently putting me back together, and I hoped for years you felt the same. When I saw it, that night of the ball where Roylance met his wife, remember? Your armour cracked multiple times that night, Henry—I also saw you weren't ready."

Three years had passed since Westbrook lost his eye.

They had hidden from each other for three years.

"I thought you'd hate me if you knew," Henry said.

"That's because you're an idiot," Westbrook declared as Henry's fingers fiddled one of Westbrook's coat buttons undone. "We should get back on our horses," he murmured in a gravelly tone that tickled Henry's ear.

Instead, Henry took a deep breath and lowered his head onto Westbrook's shoulder, resting it there, allowing himself to become heavier, wondering what he did to deserve such a man, and how he would ever get through burying his brother. He hadn't thought of Ernest Young for a while, but suddenly the image of his face near the campfire, laughing with Jackson, came to mind. Then Adams and Roylance killed at Toulouse. And Danny.

Brothers.

Westbrook wrapped his arms around him. "What do you need?" he breathed.

"This."

Westbrook nuzzled into Henry's neck, squeezed him tighter, then went perfectly still so that all Henry had to focus on was his heart beating.

He held Henry there until, ready to face what would come later that day, Henry finally moved. This coincided with Whisper stepping forward to nudge Westbrook out of the way and give Henry a lick on the cheek.

"Bloody horse!"

"She is jealous of you, West, that's all," Henry said, giving her a rub on the nose. "She has a point, though. Can you not look so damn charming for five minutes and give a man some peace?"

Westbrook laughed. His deep belly laugh, the one Henry could never help himself but laugh along with. He was still laughing when he pulled himself back into the saddle. That was part of why he loved Westbrook so much. He brought the light to any day. Even a day such as this, he might just get through because Westbrook would be at his side.

"I talked to Louisa. About... you," Henry told him, as their horses fell in next to each other once more.

"Don't tell me. Louisa took it all in her stride. She is a most..." Westbrook looked to the sky as he searched for a suitable word. "Remarkable woman."

"She also knows me very well. I'm not sure it came as

a great surprise. I have been meaning to ask you about the bracelet. It carries your crest too?"

"Louisa is the thing I did not expect. I did not know who you married, of course, your message lacking such vital detail. I presumed it to be that girl your father always wrote about. What I realised, however, is that whoever she is, I need her too because she is everything I cannot be for you."

Henry had not thought of it like that before, like how he had been what Danny could not be to Louisa. The three of them needed each other. The three of them might just be able to make this work.

"When I arrived here to find it was Louisa, *the* Louisa," Westbrook continued, "I was convinced I didn't know you at all. That everything I wanted was hopeless. Then you told me of the circumstances and the way you looked at me when I gave you the sword ... What I am trying to say is that maybe, one day, the world will not concern itself so much about whom we love, but I'd rather wait for that day with you than without you." He kicked back his heels and his horse responded, taking him away.

Whisper tossed her head, not pleased at being left behind, a feeling Henry felt much sympathy for. They caught them at the gallop. Westbrook, windswept and flushed, grinning across at Henry encouraging the race; an exhilarating race. The future lay before them, one where instead of dying in battle together, they might survive together.

Chapter 34

Ashlington, June 2015

Friday evening Lillian drove home from a haircut in Winchcombe singing to the radio. She glanced at the gate house cottage as she passed, then stopped the car and reversed onto the driveway. She knocked on the cottage door, which Nick opened wearing a kitchen apron with a matching tea towel draped over one shoulder.

"Sorry, looks like you are busy," she said. "Good look, by the way."

He brushed his hands down the front of the apron and stepped aside, bumping his head on a low beam as he did so. "Come in," he said, rubbing at the injury. "Your hair looks nice."

"Thanks. Actually, it was Olivia I came to see." She pried off her shoes and followed Nick into the compact lounge where Olivia sat on the floor, surrounded by an impressive array of textbooks and folders.

"Me?" Olivia snapped her laptop shut, curiosity widening her eyes.

"I know your dad is busy this weekend planning dig things with the professor, so I wondered if you wanted to come to London with me? I need to collect some of my things from the apartment and thought some company would be nice. We could do some museums, stay a night and I have two tickets for a show I booked ages ago. If that's okay with you, Nick?"

Olivia's eyes had gone even wider, though she immediately tried to hide it. She looked at her father, who Lillian noticed with amusement already looked uncomfortable at the suggestion of letting his baby loose in such a godforsaken place as London. She rather enjoyed the battle of glances that ensued.

"I'd love to!" Olivia said, victorious.

"I'm going to drive in so I can bring stuff back. I'll pick you up around eight so we can make an entire day of it?"

"You must get your study done tonight then," Nick said, perhaps clutching at the one thing that might bring the entire trip down.

"I've nearly finished, anyway. Thanks Lily, I'm so excited."

"Sorry, I should have asked you first," Lillian said to Nick with a grimace of guilt.

He laughed. "I learnt long ago that I have very little to say in what she does. Have you eaten? We have plenty to share if you want to stay." Nick gestured to the kitchen behind him.

She had skipped lunch and at the mention of food, she noticed the tempting smell of something earthy from the kitchen. "Are you sure?"

Olivia had already packed up her homework and disappeared upstairs, so Lillian followed Nick into the kitchen, where he offered her beer or wine. She took a beer and settled herself at the table while he finished washing the cooking pots. On the counter, under an upturned glass, a spider scuttled, searching for an escape.

"Want me to deal with that?" she offered.

"Would you? I normally get Olivia to do it."

She slid her hand under the glass, noticing Nick turn away with a shiver, and released the spider outside.

When she returned, he took a large gulp from his beer bottle. "Thanks. Marcus not back tonight then?"

"No, and he won't be again. It's over. We agreed we wanted different things."

Nick smiled. She wasn't sure what it meant, and he quickly changed the subject. "Dinner is just a veggie lasagne, nothing special."

"Well, it smells delicious." She probably held his gaze for too long, so looked away and took a long swig of her beer. She felt a pang of sympathy for Henry. How he had survived such proximity to Westbrook all those years without acting on it, she couldn't imagine. "Nick, if Henry and Westbrook finally got to express to each other how they really felt, why do you think he is stuck here? Shouldn't they be sitting on a fluffy rainbow cloud preening their angel wings together?"

"Optimistic of you to think they got a happy ending. Back then."

"Pessimistic of you to think they didn't."

"You said it yourself. Why else would he be here in this state of unrest? He is lonely. Even I can feel it."

Lonely. That is what Marcus had said about her. Only now she realised she had never felt lonely at Ashlington, even in the empty house. Surrounded by people in London, that was when she felt lonely.

"Want me to look after Holly for you this weekend then, or have you asked Mum?"

"She'd much prefer it if you had her, I'm sure," she said. Holly made no secret of the fact Lillian's role in her life had been reduced to provider of food.

Lillian made the apartment their first stop. It would be the last time she would set foot in what had been her home, and she expected to feel more, it marking the end of a four-year relationship with Marcus. But all she felt as she stepped off the lift was empty.

Marcus had moved nothing. She thought he might have boxed things up, but it looked like he hadn't been spending much time there himself. Scattered on the counter were business cards of estate agents.

Starting in the bedroom, she found her clothes still hanging in the closet. Olivia insisted on being useful, so she put her to work, taking things off hangers and packing them into the suitcase she had pulled from under the bed. Lillian methodically made her way through the apartment, filling a few cardboard boxes, surprised at how so many years could be reduced to such a few items. It felt very un-Durand like.

"It's just stuff," Olivia said some time later. Lillian hadn't realised she had been staring into the box.

"I just thought I'd have more of it. That sounds

frivolous, doesn't it? I thought by my forties I would have a house full of knick-knacks picked up around the world, each one holding a specific memory."

"Maybe you haven't made the right memories yet?" Olivia said with wisdom beyond her years. She chewed on her lip. "Talking of which, do we have time before the show to go to the British Museum? There is something I would like to see."

"I'm done here." Lillian scanned the apartment from where she stood, willing herself to feel something about leaving it and Marcus.

"You okay?" Olivia asked.

"I think I feel liberated," Lillian said with a shrug and a sigh she used to straighten her shoulders.

She sent Marcus a text letting him know she left the key with the guard. They checked into their hotel and from there took the tube to Tottenham Court Road, having agreed to have lunch before visiting the British Museum. It was over their panini, fries and general speculation as to what held Henry at Ashlington, that Olivia admitted she had never been to London before.

"Seriously?"

"Dad hates London. Too many people, and the tube alone is his idea of hell on earth."

"He has a point there." Lillian waved at the server and gestured for the bill. She later handed the server her credit card and Olivia thrust some cash at him, insisting she pay her own way. She checked her phone and rolled her eyes.

"Dad, checking up on us." She typed a reply, then

tucked her phone back in her pocket.

"He's protective," Lillian continued. "My father was the same. I guess when they do it all by themselves, they feel the responsibility more."

"You lost your mom when you were born?"

"Yes, though, my dad did a remarkable job of keeping her alive. He would tell me stories about her and kept reminding me how much like her I was, though I really think I was more like him."

Having settled the bill, they made their way out of the restaurant, Lillian steering them confidently in the museum's direction.

"Did you find it hard to make friends with girls?" Olivia asked.

"Completely. Your father was my best friend. I found the girls hard work."

"You? Are you finding it difficult at school?" It struck Lillian, not for the first time, just how much they had in common.

"I have a total of two friends at school. Annabel, she is new too, and Stefan. He's the nerdy kid I told you about who likes to think he looks after me. I'm not sure it's just school though, you know. I find making any connections hard. You go through all that effort and investment, then you are moving on again. After a while I stopped bothering."

"Well, when your dad makes you watch too much Harrison Ford or *Star Trek*, you can always call me." She put an arm around her as they walked, drawing her closer. "Even when I am back here, you would always be welcome to come up to London and hang out. That's what you young people call it nowadays, right?"

"Do you mean that?" Olivia stopped walking and turned to her.

"I do."

After a moment Olivia smiled, slightly lopsided like her father, and they began walking again.

Arriving at the museum, Olivia ignored the giant Greek columns and pushed a note into a slot of the donation station before entering the Great Court. She studied the map of exhibits, giving a grunt when she found what she was looking for.

"This way," she told Lillian and led her through the museum halls to a comparatively small exhibit room at the rear of the building. It showcased finds from Central America, overseen by three huge stone idols with their impressive headdresses that presided over the gallery.

"Dad found those." She said, pointing to a glass case against the rear wall of the room.

Lillian scanned the information plaque that sat underneath the display of smaller idols, intimidating masks, jade and gold jewellery. There she found his name and an explanation that the collection was on loan from the National Museum of Archaeology and Ethnology in Guatemala City.

"It was the year Mom died. I had left the dig early to go to the premiere of her movie in LA. It was the find of his career, but when Dad got the call from my grandparents, he dropped everything to come get me. I was in the car with her

397

when it happened. They say she died instantly. I was asleep in the back so didn't even see the accident coming."

"Olivia, I'm so sorry." It felt vastly inadequate.

"The thing is, he should have been basking in the glory, but he put me first."

"Of course he would put you first. One thing I know about your dad is that he would move the stars for you."

Lillian's phone chose that moment to vibrate in her pocket. She smiled at Olivia, expecting it to be Nick, summoned by their talk of him. But the caller id said 'Guy', wiping the smile away.

"Marcus told me you are in town. Why didn't you say something?"

"It is just a quick trip, really. In and out, getting my things from the apartment, look at a few places to rent while I wait for the tenants to leave my house in Camden."

"So meet me for dinner. I have a table booked at that little place you like."

"I would, but I have a friend with me, and we have a show booked."

"Oh—not the cleaner's son?"

"No, Olivia, Nick's daughter."

"Bring her along then. I'd like to see you, just a drink?"

They met Guy at the wine bar where they had spent many a Friday night. He waited at a table in the corner. Not exactly Friday night busy, but there were enough in the narrow bar to create a squeeze and for Olivia to turn heads.

Lillian waved at the barman, who recognised her and called that he would bring their drinks over. Guy had his laptop open and greeted Lillian with an air kiss to each cheek.

"With Warrilow out of the frame, we have so much more scope on the site."

Olivia flinched in shock, no doubt at Guy's use of the word 'site'. Lillian gave her a small shake of the head, hoping they could keep things businesslike.

"As you can see, my plans increase the potential, thanks to the housing."

"What housing?"

"This area here." He leant over Lillian, the sharpness of his aftershave tingling at her nose, and pointed to what was currently the lake and woodland. All part of the estate, yet also the landscape. "Don't worry about planning. I have that all sorted. My man on the council says it won't be a problem."

"What kind of housing?" Lillian asked.

"Five and Six bed properties. We can manage ten of them."

"So, not anything any of the locals could afford?" Olivia said.

"That isn't exactly where the money is, young lady," Guy replied harshly. "This is a business, not a charity."

Lillian gave Olivia another shake of the head, a message to not worry about it, not to take it personally. Lillian had learnt long ago not to prod Guy.

"So what do you think?" He asked.

"It is ambitious," Lillian said.

"Exactly. That is what we do well, you and I. We make a formidable team."

Swapping homes for profit. Making money and moving on.

"We do," she agreed.

Guy's phone rang and having shouted at it, he told Lillian he would take the call outside. She returned her attention to the laptop.

Olivia gave her a tilted-head Hawkins stare. "You are different here."

"You think so? I don't feel different." Lillian pulled at her blouse, suddenly self-conscious. "It is all just business, Olivia. I just play along, play the part he expects."

"Why?"

Lillian did not get time to think on it further because Guy returned with a face like thunder. She knew the look. He had likely been arguing with Claudia. "I heard from Claudia yesterday. She told me about Warrilow," she said.

"She did? I thought she would have been too ashamed. Selling out like that, to Warrilow of all people. She knew what that would do to me."

"She says it was what she needed to do." What Claudia had actually said was that her options were better with Warrilow and if she wanted to stay on top, then it was a small price to pay. She was also taking her long-standing clients with her. It was this that probably hurt Guy more than anything.

"Selfish cow. The minute it got rough, she couldn't handle it. Thankfully, you are made of sterner stuff. We will have the choice of the top contracts. You wait and see. Breaking up with Marcus will be the best thing you ever did."

Hardly a thing a friend should say about another, but Guy was hanging Marcus out to dry. She had once considered Guy a father figure but realised now they were two totally different men, after all. She felt Olivia's eyes on her, that astute teenager with the guts to call them both out, judging her. Lillian worried Olivia did not like what she saw.

Chapter 35

Ashlington, September 1814

The family graveyard was a peaceful place to the side of the house, under the reach of a willow tree hardly taller than the tombstones. Westbrook took station on Henry's left, as he always did. With matching swords hung at their sides, both men were dressed in the uniform they had arrived at Ashlington wearing. Westbrook smartly, Henry by his own admission, not so much.

Defying the usual form of only men being present for a burial, and because Henry had insisted, Louisa stood on Henry's other side; her arm linked in his, the anguish on her face his equal. When she emitted a sob, Westbrook broke post and caught her as she sank at the knees, unable to hold in her grief any longer. It was any wonder she had lasted as long as she had given the circumstances, Henry thought, guilty he had not been the one to catch her. Barely keeping his own emotions in check, he gave Westbrook a look of conflicted pleading.

"I shall take her," Westbrook said, unwrapping Louisa's fingers from the tight grasp they had on Henry's coat. "Come Louisa. Let us go inside out of the cold. I've got you." Henry felt his hand begin trembling until Westbrook brushed it casually with his own, imparting the message *I've got you too.*

Moments later, when he glanced over his shoulder, Westbrook was carrying Louisa back to the house. Guilt tumbled around in Henry's heart, forging itself with an overwhelming sense of shame that he had not been here to defend his brother. Again he had been self-absorbed and escaped Ashlington that night; escaped his family and responsibility once more. He could have sent Aunt Dot the cake with a messenger, or he could have ridden back that night. By the time Danny's coffin descended into the ground, the guilt had transformed into anger. Anger, he directed internally. His ravenous demon welcomed it.

Later, Henry found his wife propped up on the settee asleep against Westbrook (also asleep) who cradled an empty decanter of whisky and a half-full glass. Something had passed between them, and Henry found himself glad of it. Westbrook stirred as Henry sat down.

"Thank you, West, for being here." Westbrook passed him his glass, which Henry accepted and finished. "Our last words were in anger, Danny and I. He went to his grave, hating me for what I did. How can I have got it all so wrong?"

"Do you know what your wife just told me?" Westbrook whispered so not to disturb Louisa. "That it hurts loving you Durands. I agreed, naturally, but do you know what I also learned over the years knowing you?"

"What?"

"That we can't have one without the other. Love and

pain. You are hurting right now because you loved your brother. He knew that. You always said he was the smart one."

"You'll help me find who did this to him?"

"I have already made a start. But that will wait. For today, your family need you."

Henry leant his head on Westbrook's shoulder as he had done many evenings under the stars. At least there he had always felt safe and at home. He wondered if that was what Sinclair had meant when he said home is not always a place. Westbrook was home. He understood that now.

The peace proved fleeting. A clatter from the door and Bradley's voice giving orders to the staff announced the imminent arrival of the family back to the house. "Once more unto the breach, dear friends," he said to Westbrook, rising to his feet returning to duty. "Would you look after Louisa?"

Westbrook nodded and placed a protective hand on her head.

It was approaching midday the following morning when Henry found Christopher in the library sat with one leg crossed over the other, reading the newspaper. He decided that in looks, Christopher had grown to become a mixture of both his older brothers. He had Danny's lighter hair and rounder nose, but the larger frame and wider lips of Henry. Unlike his brothers, he preferred to dress according to the latest London fashions and was rarely seen without frills at his cuffs and some new silk neckcloth to bring out the detail in a patterned waistcoat. It occurred to Henry that, as the youngest, Christopher had been extremely successful in building himself into something that was nothing like either of his older brothers.

Without announcing his arrival, Henry lowered himself into the chair opposite, allowing his thoughts to settle around him. He and Westbrook had spent the morning riding round the estate asking questions, trying to jog memories among the household and the tenants. Resentment of their simple lives and their ability to return to normal so quickly when the quantity of loss he felt allowed him no such luxury had shortened Henry's fuse.

Westbrook had stepped in on more than one occasion, just as Henry's disenchantment with their lack of progress had threatened to boil over; calmly taking control of the conversation and endearing himself to those being interviewed. He had also offered to spend some time in the village, though Henry knew that likely meant the inn where he had taken an instant dislike to Louisa's father. Henry had to make him promise not to start a fight. This left Henry to return to the manor and reach out to Christopher, whom he couldn't help feeling had been avoiding him. They had barely held a conversation since the night Westbrook arrived.

"Your friend has been making himself at home," Christopher said, snapping the newspaper in half. "He has been interviewing the household."

"We both have." Henry straightened up in the chair, aware that despite having sought Christopher, he hadn't spoken to him since sitting down. "He is helping me investigate what happened to Danny."

"I thought Father had put it into the hands of the constable. It would seem he has more experience in these matters."

"It would surprise you what we have had to deal with over the years," Henry said.

"So did it prove useful, all this questioning?"

"Perhaps," Henry said with an incline of his head. "I am confused, though. Danny had no enemies; he kept a tight rein on this place financially. What reason did anyone have to kill him?"

"I thought it was a robbery? He disturbed them, they fought?"

"There is nothing of any worth in the study. The rents get banked on the day they are collected, have been for years. Your average burglar would be better off with the silverware or jewellery even, which leads me to think whoever it was had business in the study."

"I think you are over thinking this," Christopher said, waving away Henry's concerns with a lacy flick of a wrist. "Seeing ghosts where there are none. I miss him too, but none of this brings him back."

The soldier in Henry knew Christopher was hiding something. He only wished he could hunt it down. "What about justice? Danny deserves that," Henry said. The room fell silent, and Henry felt the restlessness of sitting too long consuming him, so stood and threw another log at the fire.

"I should marry the Chilton girl," Christopher said, causing Henry to spin around. So that's it?

He blew out his cheeks, letting the air escape with a whistle. "You're a braver man than I. Really? You would marry Ursula?"

"I know it is sudden, but my place is here helping father." Christopher rested his chin on his closed hand, rubbing at the underside with his thumb. "What better way than to take up where Danny left off? It should have been you, but you have made yourself unavailable, and you say you are returning to the regiment. This way everyone is happy."

"Even you? Is that what you want, Chris?"

Christopher nodded.

Danny held his motivations for all to see, each one meticulously calculated. Christopher had the face of a devious charmer, and Henry could not decide if he was telling the truth or not. Either way, he would take on a great deal. Henry felt some relief, albeit a guilty relief, that someone else would take on that responsibility.

"What about the man that was here the day you arrived? What was his name again?"

"You have no need of his name Henry, my business with him is not of your concern."

"Henry! Where are you?" The impatient cry of their father echoing throughout the house prevented Henry from pressing Christopher further. Christopher glanced at Henry with a flash of sympathy he had shown many times during their childhood when Henry incurred Nathaniel's wrath. Henry instinctively looked to the door which led into the garden, his only route of escape.

"Yes, Father," Henry called back, having decided to stand and face the enemy assault. "We are in the library." The brothers stood formally as their father entered with a look of impatience that over the years had transformed the countenance of his once handsome face.

"Your lieutenant is interrogating my household and I want it to stop!" he growled.

"West is not interrogating anyone," Henry sighed. "We have both been making enquiries to find out what happened that night. Nothing more. I apologise that I did not tell you—or rather asked your permission," Henry corrected himself with a sigh he kept internal this time. "But I understand you have had plenty to deal with. I want answers. I am only trying to help where I can, and this is something West and I are good at."

"We all want answers, Henry," Nathaniel snapped. "You have only been here five minutes and look at the trouble you have caused. You throw away the chance of a decent marriage, then you got the innkeeper's daughter with child." Nathaniel counted Henry's faults out on his fingers. "You have married her against my better judgement and as if that had not tarnished my honour enough, you are accusing people of being responsible for your brother's death. Exactly what did you think you would achieve by interviewing the Chiltons? People of standing! Their family have lived here for hundreds of years and some jumped up mere lieutenant from a soldiering family asks them what they had to do with it. I am beyond myself with shame, Henry, and once again you are the source."

Had a sober Westbrook been there, he would have given Henry a look warning him not to hit his father. A drunken Westbrook would have done it on Henry's behalf.

Henry decided on a deep slow breath to prevent himself from belting his father across his jowly face, then took one more because he was not convinced the first had worked. He noticed that Christopher had stepped out of the room at the earliest opportunity, the yellow-bellied coward. When he spoke again he was pleased to hear he projected the tone he used on the men.

"West and I were nothing but cordial and charming with the Chilton's and as part of our investigation have spoken with everyone who has anything to do with Danny, regarding their whereabouts that night." His own absence would haunt him forever. "That is—all but one." Henry straightened his back and looked his father directly in the eyes. "What about you, Father?"

He would never have the nerve to talk to his father in such a manner had Nathaniel not insulted Westbrook, who only still held the rank of lieutenant because he had passed up purchasing promotion so he could stay with the company. With Henry. "Tell me about the night Danny died," Henry said, sitting back down and gesturing at the chair recently vacated by Christopher.

His air of command worked, leaving Henry wondering why he had never thought to use it on his father before. The fury left Nathaniel's face, and he obeyed his son, sitting rigidly. For a moment looking every one of his fifty years, and something Henry had never seen before. Regretful.

"I heard voices, an argument. I sleep lightly these days," he explained.

Henry frowned. His father had not rushed to his room as his mother and Louisa had done the night he had screamed with the dreams of Badajos. Had he been awake and not acted because it had been Henry in distress? The fact he could consider the question left him empty inside.

"By the time I got to the top of the stairs there was a strange noise and I saw a figure run out of the study down the hallway."

"What did he look like?"

"It was dark, Henry, I don't think I can tell you much else. His clothing was dark, your size perhaps, but he had no cloak or greatcoat. I shouted for him to stop, but there was no way I could have caught him."

"He was young then?"

His father shrugged. "Fast. When I got to the study, I could see the candles were still lit, and I saw Danny's hand on the floor through the doorway." He looked up at Henry, brows creased with a rare hint of vulnerability. He didn't want to go on, but Henry needed answers.

"Go on."

"I rushed in to help him, thinking he had just been knocked on the floor or something—anything but—that. There was so much blood."

"Was he already dead when you got to him, or did he say anything?"

His father stiffened, eyes wide, then stood and left the room without answering.

Henry realised then that he had pushed too hard with insensitive questioning. What his father had seen had horrified him. His father might act with disdainful superiority on the outside, but inside he was the same as any other and, no matter how he tried to still convince Henry otherwise, Henry wasn't weaker than him after all. The thought came as a liberating spark together with the bittersweet realisation their bond remained far from ever being repaired.

Chapter 36

Ashley Spencer, straight from school if the chalky dust on her jacket cuffs was any indication, met Nick at the cottage a few days later precisely when she said she would. Which made Nick like her even more.

After helping lug the heavy bags of equipment into the cottage, he offered Ashley a cup of tea.

"I thought you might like to see this," Nick said, retrieving a cardboard box from his desk. Inside lay the pistol from the study. He wanted to learn more about the weapons Henry would have used. It seemed such a part of him he hoped it might unlock further understanding.

Ashley's eyes lit up with wonder. "May I?" she asked, hands hovering over the weapon.

"Be my guest," Nick said. "We were hoping you could confirm the era. I contacted Jim Kendall, but he tells me you are the expert around here."

Ashley cradled it gently as she looked it over, taking in every detail and stroking the smooth wooden stock. "It is original. Early 19th century. The engraving is worn, but I am certain it is from Lacy and Co. Any clues whom it belonged to?"

"I am certain it was Henry's, the man we are

412

researching from the Sinclair painting. It has his initials on the stock."

"Well, the period is correct." Ashley brought the pistol up to her nose and gave it a sniff. "It is in amazing condition. Would probably fire just like it did two-hundred years ago." She raised an eyebrow. Nick did not need telling what a kick she would get out of firing an actual period piece rather than the replicas she owned.

"I presume there is no danger of you killing yourself with it?"

"There is no damage, so it should fire true. We can start with what I brought you to try first though." Ashley placed it back in the box, laying it gently on the tissue with a sigh.

Tea drained, they headed outside, where Nick had dragged the outdoor table to the edge of the patio and suggested they fired down the garden bordering the woodland. Ashley looked around with approval and handed Nick a pair of spongy ear defenders. What must it have been like holding a line under fire? How frightening must standing in a square receiving thundering cavalry charges have been? What are you doing, Nicholas? He asked himself. You don't even like guns.

"I've brought a few of my favourites. Baker rifle being a woman of the 95th," she said, pulling the weapon from its carry case and laying it on the table. "And the Land Pattern musket."

"Brown Bess?"

"Very good, Nick. Range and accuracy not as good as

the rifle but still a devastating weapon when it hits its target. Your average foot soldier's bread and butter. Now, loading the musket is much the same as the rifle, so we'll go through it together."

Ashley handed Nick the musket; weightier than he expected and a tad nose heavy. He had never been comfortable around guns, so held it with trepidation and did his best to keep the dangerous end pointing down the garden.

"I presume you use blanks?"

"Yes, I make all my own cartridges, but I do make up some with musket balls for target practice. Okay, first cock the firing mechanism halfway, all clean in there, yes?"

Nick did as instructed, copying what Ashley was doing with the rifle, then nodded in agreement.

"Then we load using a cartridge like this." Ashley reached into the leather bag she had at her waist and pulled out a paper tube twisted at one end. "The ball is in the end of a live one, so you bite it off and hold the ball in your mouth. Tastes foul, I know."

Nick grimaced, having carefully copied Ashley's instructions; the powder bitter with a salty aftertaste.

"Then sprinkle a little powder into the pan and lock it off, just a bit. That's it. Next we pour the remaining powder down the barrel and spit the ball down. Scrunch the paper for the wad and ram it all home." Ashley extracted the rifle's ramrod with a practised flourish.

Nick pulled on the musket's ramrod, scraping it free from its notch. With a twist of the wrist, he plunged the end into the muzzle and banged it up and down just as Ashley had.

"Packing it all tightly down there condenses the blast and would make the shot more accurate. All done?"

"It seems long winded when you do it yourself, but they could fire a few rounds a minute, couldn't they? How many can you do?" Nick asked, trying to poke the ramrod back into the notch below the barrel. Ashley had made it look so easy with the rifle.

"By the end of the season I can manage three, but I am slowing with age."

"A problem I am all too familiar with," Nick grinned.

"Best off firing from the knee like this. There is a hell of a kick, so make sure it's wedged in at your shoulder," Ashley said, demonstrating.

Nick took a knee, then closed his left eye and looked down the sights of the musket, squeezing the trigger. Nothing happened. "Christ, it's—"

"Just pull harder," Ashley said, her voice disappearing in a loud crack as the musket fired. It thumped Nick in the shoulder and obscured his view with a billow of gunpowder smoke.

"Wow!"

"Right?" Ashley said with a grin, then fired the rifle.

He lost count of how many rounds they fired, but after what he supposed was half an hour, they both had black cheeks from the powder, and smoke hung in the air.

"Do you want to try the pistol?"

"Sure, I'll give it a quick clean down first, make sure everything is as it should be. The mechanism is sound at least," Ashley said, cocking the pistol and exercising the trigger.

Ashley fired it twice, proving it was indeed still in excellent condition, and offered a turn to Nick. Nick refused politely, deciding that to finish the session while he still had all his fingers and toes was the responsible thing to do. His ears were ringing despite the protection of the ear defenders. That was enough of black powder and flintlocks for one day, he thought.

Something banged on the garden gate, making both of them jump, despite the recent noise they had been making. The gate, a full height wooden one sunk into the high wall surrounding the cottage garden, shook as though some force on the other side rattled at it, desperate for their attention. Had they disturbed a neighbour?

Nick looked at Ashley, who seemed as surprised as he was at such an angry reaction. Nick opened the gate to find Olivia on the other side, on the ground, hands on her ears, panting, her eyes screwed shut.

"Olivia? What's the matter?"

"Stop it!" she said, keeping her hands firmly wedged on her ears. "Please stop it, he doesn't like it."

"What, Ollie?"

"The noise. It sounds like muskets."

"It was. Who doesn't like it?" Nick glanced behind him. Ashley was still where he had left her by the table, packing away. "Do you mean Henry?" He suddenly felt guilty. He should have thought about it, how distressing it might be for Henry to hear weapon fire, recognisable weapon fire. He would always act with reverence on an archaeological site. Why would he be so insensitive here at Ashlington?

"No. Not Henry. Someone else—someone angrier."

"We won't be firing any more. It's okay. Come on. Up you get."

He led her into the garden, carrying her backpack for her. She gathered herself when she saw Ashley.

"Hi Olivia. Your father and I have been firing some flintlocks," she said, as though it were an everyday occurrence.

"We were just packing up," Nick told his daughter, "will you be okay?"

"I'm fine now. It's gone," she fixed a smile for her teacher. "Hi Mrs Spencer, I'll go put the kettle on."

"Has she said anything about the scholarship?" Ashley asked Nick as she finished cleaning the musket. "She seems a little distracted lately."

Nick felt distracted himself. Still reeling from his insensitivity, acting like some gun wielding idiot, just what exactly was he trying to prove? His thoughts then focussed on what Olivia had said. Not Henry. Then who? Did they have two ghosts? He couldn't help but feel excited at the thought.

"To be honest, we have had something going on at home, so the distraction is my fault. As to the scholarship, no. She is still working it out."

"And you? Do you think you will stay or are you feeling the call already?"

The call had always been there, but now it had been replaced. With something stronger. An urge to stay.

"It was certainly my intention for this to be just a few years off while Olivia settles into school and uni', but the longer I am here, I realise I like it. I have been without a home for such a long time and with my parents getting older, perhaps it is time to enjoy it here for a while."

They ferried everything back into the cottage where Olivia was unpacking homework, had already raided the fridge for a snack, and graciously made Nick and Ashley cups of tea. Nick offered Ashley use of the bathroom so she might clean herself of the gunpowder, while Nick resorted to washing in the kitchen sink.

"You have been enjoying this project by the sounds of it. You say he died at Waterloo?" Ashley asked, emerging from the bathroom free of the powder on her cheek.

"We haven't quite got to the Waterloo part of Henry's story yet, but I am sure given the material we have, all will be revealed."

Ashley nodded. "The role of the 28th is well documented for that day, stalwart and valiant."

Nick did not doubt it, even though he knew that the documented accounts could often differ from what played out in the field.

***

Leaving her father and Mrs Spencer chatting, Olivia took to nature, searching for the unfamiliar presence she had felt. She wanted to comfort it. It felt more open than Henry. Rawer. She followed the boundary of the manor along the lane, then, at a lull in its prickliness, pierced its veil and climbed the stile, drawn to the lake.

Who was that? Olivia squinted. Dressed in period clothing, he was of a similar size to Henry. He stood by the edge of the lake throwing stones, not skimming them, just throwing them as far as he could. It gave him an angry bearing that made her think twice about approaching. He turned before she had a chance to back away and she saw he wasn't angry after all. It was more frustration.

"What in God's name are you wearing, girl?" he asked her bluntly.

"I could ask you the same. What are you trying to be, a pirate?" she said, putting her hands on her hips. "And don't call me 'girl', I'm sixteen."

His head jerked back with surprise, then he looked down at his attire with a frown which transformed into a wide smile and caused dimples to appear on his cheeks. "My apologies, miss. Robert Westbrook, at your service," he said with a flamboyant bow, confirming what she already suspected.

"Olivia Hawkins," she replied with the sudden impulse to pop a curtsey. "So you are *the* Westbrook?"

"Why does everyone keep saying that?"

He was different from Henry. Tidier, yet wilder. Like a big-game cat that would die fighting to protect its cubs. Her curse, however, was not because of his looks but more the fact it was happening again. Somehow she had crossed over between their times and was now having a conversation, just as she had done with Henry. Why did she get to see them and interact when others could only voice call, if that was actually a thing? The situation should have scared her and might have done, had she not got to know him through Henry's journals. Besides, where could she run?

"You know of me?" he enquired.

"Yeah, you're Henry's—"

"Lieutenant."

She gave him a sideways look and a slow nod with as much scepticism as she could muster. Boyfriend, more like and she had only read half the stuff on them. "Listen, we probably don't have much time, but I need you to give him a message. You are here after his brother was killed, yes?"

Westbrook nodded.

"Tell him to be careful, I don't know all the details, I'm still catching up with the research but—"

Westbrook's single feline eye had narrowed, and the frown was back.

She realised she was waffling. "It doesn't make sense, I know, but it feels like something bad is going to happen."

Westbrook looked out to the lake and sighed, managing to appear angry and sad at the same time. Olivia felt a familiar despair radiating from him, though he was not bothering to hide it as Henry tried to. Westbrook allowed it to flow freely.

"How much worse can it get? He has lost his brother."

"But he still has you," she told him with a raised eyebrow. "And Louisa."

"Yes." He folded his arms and shifted his weight. "He is a married man now."

"You know, West, where I am from, in my time, you can—"

"That's an odd thing to say," he interrupted, scratching under his eyepatch. "What do you mean when you say 'My time?' And only Henry calls me West." His hand flicked to his side. He wasn't wearing a sword, but Olivia imagined that was where the hilt might rest. The reach of the hand an instinctive reaction to the irregularities he had discovered. "Who did you say you were again?"

But before she could answer, he faded away.

"Ugh! I hate it when they do that." She stamped a foot, relieved to hear an aircraft overhead but frustrated she hadn't got the chance to tell him anything of importance. Then and again, perhaps it was best that way. If she meddled in the past, it could have disastrous consequences on her own timeline. Watching all that *Star Trek* had taught her as much. She pulled her phone out of her pocket and made an internet search under temporal paradox, to be sure.

Chapter 37

Henry found Westbrook lay on the grass by the lake; arm across his face, asleep. Like most soldiers, well practiced at snoozing, given the opportunity. For a moment Henry considered joining him, closing his eyes and shutting out the present. But Westbrook moved his arm and looked up, abruptly cutting off any of the more inventive ideas Henry was having on how to wake him.

"You should be careful. Little people might come and tie you up in your sleep." Henry joked.

Westbrook laughed. "The man-mountain needed a lie down."

"I have been talking with my father," Henry said, reining in his thoughts from *Gulliver's Travels* to the matter at hand.

"Tell me you didn't hit him?" Westbrook said, climbing to his feet, brushing down his coat.

"Not today."

"I'm proud of you, Henry. He cares about you; he just doesn't know what to do with you."

Touched that Westbrook would offer a different perspective, a door towards reconciliation perhaps, Henry also knew he did not feel quite ready for that yet. "I don't think he deserves your good opinion, West."

"He is your father. It counts for something. So how was it?" They fell in step together and made their way along the gravel path that led around the lake.

"The usual, really, but he said something interesting. That the intruder wore no greatcoat or cloak."

Westbrook raised an eyebrow as Henry thought he might.

"It had rained solid for three days even before you arrived. What sort of man would be abroad without a cloak on a night like that?"

"A wet one. Or one that did not have far to go."

"Christopher told me I was chasing ghosts," Henry continued.

"Ghosts?" The tone with which he said this made Henry study him closer. He watched Westbrook draw a long breath. "Would you think me deranged if I told you I think your house is haunted?"

"You mean more deranged?" Henry teased. "But you are serious? Are you seeing the faces in the dark again?"

"No, it was not like that at all. When I see them, I know who they are, the reason they pursue me. She was different. She doesn't work here at the house, nor have I seen her in the village. She seemed to come out of nowhere and disappeared in front of me. So what other explanation is there?" Westbrook laughed nervously. "She gave me a fierce dressing down for calling her a girl. She was down here by the lake, wore the most bizarre outfit and spoke in riddles."

"Did you say bizarre outfit?" Henry stopped walking,

his question pulling Westbrook up abruptly.

Westbrook nodded. "She called me a pirate!" he said, looking offended and amused simultaneously.

"A strange way of talking?"

Westbrook agreed. "Have you seen her too? Tell me I am not going mad."

"You are not going mad, West. I have also seen her. I don't know who she is, but our paths have crossed several times, and she is sometimes in my dreams."

Westbrook frowned. "She referred to me as West."

"Only I do that."

"I know."

"Well, whatever is going on, she is no ghost. She told me as much. But it's like we connect somehow; our time and hers. Strangely, I can't help but trust her."

"She said something about time to me—almost as though—never mind." Westbrook's smile dropped, and he shook his head. "She poses no threat other than to our sanity, which is already questionable. We have more pressing matters to discuss. I have more to share on the death of your brother."

"I wish you could have met Danny. He would have liked you," Henry said, happier thoughts giving way to the look of thunder on Danny's face when Henry told him he would marry Louisa. At the time, Henry presumed his anger had been directed at him, but now he understood it was likely Danny's anger with himself and the duty that prevented him from being with the person he loved.

They reached the boat house on the far side of the lake

where Westbrook leant on the wall, legs crossed at the ankles, and Henry paced the grass in front of him.

"You will not like what I found."

"Why?"

"Remember the man you described visiting your other brother. The day I rode here, I encountered such a man in an inn. He was collecting a payment from the innkeeper."

"Like a debt collector?"

Westbrook shrugged. "It's what I thought. I took an immediate dislike to the man."

"You would," Henry said.

"I wouldn't have thought much more of it had I not found this in Christopher's room." He reached inside his coat and pulled out some papers that looked like ledger entries. Henry recognised the swan seal on the bottom. He had last seen it in the study with Christopher and the man he had argued with. "I didn't like going through his belongings."

"It was better you than me."

"I asked around after he left. The man's name is Parish, and he was travelling north. His next port of call was Evesham. Is that far?"

"He has probably moved on by now, but we could be there within the hour." Henry nodded thoughtfully. It was their only lead after two days riding around the estate talking with anyone they could, trying to find any clue, any sighting of a stranger at Ashlington. Except for Westbrook's recent arrival, Parish had been the only unknown visitor.

"We also have this." Westbrook pulled something out of his pocket and passed it to Henry. It was a decorative cravat pin, a bright silver flower made of four petals at the head with a small emerald at its centre; left warm from its proximity to Westbrook.

"Bradley did not understand the significance until I asked if he had found anything out of place when he—" Westbrook squinted with the effort of being delicate with his words. "Cleaned things up. He found that under your brother."

"And you think ..."

"It might have fallen in the altercation; that it might belong to the man that killed Danny."

"Could it have been his, though? Danny's, and he dropped it earlier?" Henry twisted it in the sunlight, the emerald winking at him as though he had seen it before.

"They cleaned the room that afternoon. Bradley did not recognise it. He said Danny wore nothing like that. I double checked with Louisa. She agreed."

"No, but it looks familiar," Henry said, handing the pin back to Westbrook, his head swimming. He desperately needed action, not words.

They rode hard, Whisper glistening with sweat by the time they reached the small town. Perched within a great meander of the river Avon, the bustling market was alive with the noise of the animals in their pens awaiting their fate, and folk from the vale selling their wares.

Like Ashlington, not much had changed in the years Henry had been away. The tall clock tower from the ruined abbey still dominated the skyline with its ornate crown. The narrow streets and scent of refuse remained reassuringly familiar. They left the horses in the care of a boy at The Red Horse who promised to feed, water and give them a brush down. Henry tossed him a coin that more than compensated for his time.

"If all else fails, she likes apples," he told the boy, who barely looked tall enough to loosen Whisper's girth, but had a determined air about him.

Westbrook had already entered the inn and Henry found him sat at a round table with two tankards of beer. "I like this place," he told Henry as he joined him. With the market still in full flow, they were the only patrons, which would have been what suited Westbrook. Since Badajos, his dislike of crowded spaces had only grown. The barmaid, making the most of the lull in custom to wipe tables and sweep the floor, gave Henry a nod.

"I already asked," Westbrook continued, wiping the foam of the beer from his lip with the back of his hand. "She recognised the description of Parish but has not seen him today. She suggested we try the Northwick on the other side of the river. Ale not as good apparently, but their food is fair." The barmaid flashed Westbrook a suggestive smile with a glance at the stairs. Henry had never seen Westbrook take up such an offer and might have once put this down to his sense of honour regarding prostitution, but now he wondered if there had always been more to it. "Drink up, eh," Westbrook added.

The beer was a strong, hoppy, local ale that Henry felt going straight to his head. Westbrook seemed to have no such problem and had finished before Henry had drunk even half of his, and that was with his belly protesting.

Outside in the fresh air once more, they crossed the street and threaded their way through the bustling market, which is where Westbrook caught sight of Parish.

"There!" he exclaimed, steering Henry around a pig pen by the elbow. "Long coat, cocked hat and spectacles, if I am not mistaken."

"That's him," Henry agreed and barged his way through the crowd with Westbrook in close pursuit. It struck Henry that a cautious man might have slid through the crowd like Ernest Young would, un-noticed, but people had taken notice of him and Westbrook although neither were particularly big. He supposed it was the way they held themselves, that or the constant emanation of death they likely carried.

The crowd parted before them, making their prey all too aware of the impending danger. Parish turned and ran.

"You there!" called Henry, running down the street leading to the bridge that spanned the river Avon. Hoping to God he didn't trip on the cobbles, he vaulted a cart of carrots, doing his best to dodge obstacles, avoid the horse dung and keep Parish in view.

Parish darted right onto the road that lay next to the river and quickly turned left through the coach-gate to the Northwick Inn, where Henry caught up with him and thrust him against the wall.

"I know you," Parish said, struggling against Henry's grip. From the corner of his eye Henry caught sight of a giant of a man behind him, arms raised to strike.

Westbrook hit the giant at full tilt, knocking him down, and with a right hook that rattled the man's teeth kept him there. He put a foot on the giant's chest, shook his head and pushed aside his coat tail where he rested his hand on his pistol.

Henry held his own pistol shoved into Parish's belly. Not loaded, but the effect was the same. Parish stopped struggling and gave Henry his full attention.

"You *should* know me," Henry said, watching the fear in Parish's eyes as he looked to his fallen protector. "I told you if you wanted anything from my family, you had to go through me. Well, here I am."

"Durand," the man drawled, nodding in recognition. "Like I told your brother, when his account is clear, then I will happily have nothing more to do with your family."

"Did you kill him?"

"Kill? Who?" His eyes snapped wide in confusion. "Don't be absurd. My master plainly wants paying, we are not in the business of killing off our debtors. At the very worse we rough them up a bit and ensure they see the inside of a debtors' jail."

"Not Christopher, my brother Daniel." Henry gave him a shove against the wall, the bump of his head emphasising the name.

"I can assure you I have no interest in you or your other brother. I certainly have killed no one. That is not what I do. I collect debts. Normally just the mere presence of George," he tilted his head at the impressively big man, "is plenty enough to persuade any reluctant payment. Believe me, I have never even met—Daniel, was it? My only interest is with Christopher."

Henry felt Westbrook's hand on his arm. "He's telling the truth, Henry. There is no lie there."

"How much does he still owe?" Henry asked, pulling back his pistol with a sigh.

"Another fifty pounds," Parish said, straightening his collar and coat.

"My banker is here in town. I can take you there presently and settle the amount. I will want a receipt," Henry said gruffly, "and your word as a gentleman," it pained him to use the word, "that you will leave my family alone."

Parish bowed with surprising grace.

Westbrook hauled the bodyguard to his feet. The enormous George glanced at Parish, who, with a steadying hand, told him to stand down.

"No hard feelings?" Westbrook said, clapping him on the shoulder.

"Army?" the big man asked.

"Slashers."

"34th, honourable discharge." George knocked on his leg—wooden.

"Barossa." Westbrook pointed at his eyepatch.

Henry knew the army ran deep through Westbrook's veins and that he would relish the chance to chat with a fellow soldier. "Drink first?" he said to Parish, who was rubbing at his spectacles with his handkerchief.

"Hungry?" Parish countered.

Ten minutes later, Henry was biting in to a steak pie that oozed with salty gravy, one problem solved but the more disturbing issue still at hand. Westbrook and George were discussing battles in common and toasting their injuries. Henry kept half an eye on Parish, whose weasel like features twisted as he ate.

Parish dabbed at his mouth with a napkin. "Your brother has quite the reputation," he said.

"Danny?"

Parish shook his head. "Christopher. My master is not the only one he has owed money to."

"In the past?"

"Not necessarily."

Henry sighed. *What in the blazes had Christopher been doing?*

Chapter 38

Ashlington, June 2015

The chaotic noise of the students on the school bus forced Olivia to retreat into the music on her phone, earbuds wedged in deep. By convention, older students sat to the rear of the bus, but Olivia sat somewhere in the middle and gave up the seat next to her for whichever younger kid looked like they needed the moral support of a companion. When she stepped off, she felt like she could breathe again, delighting in her walk down the lane with the music switched off, the melody of birds and rhythm of nature the only soundtrack she needed.

She kicked at a pine cone, sending it spinning along the lane and bouncing onto the verge. It ricocheted, coming to a stop at the feet of a familiar, this time red-coated, soldier.

"Girl? Is that you?"

"Pirate."

Robert Westbrook pulled a face. "I'm not even in the Navy." He motioned at his uniform. "Can you really see me?"

"Yeah, I can."

"This isn't like the last time we spoke when you were the ghost."

For her, it had only been yesterday. For him, she did not know. "This is my time now. I'm sorry. You know it probably means—"

"I know what it means. It has been two hundred years. I have been here, watching them come and go, looking for him since." The sigh he gave was a long one, almost devoid of hope. What little he clung to had hardened his features.

She took a step closer, wishing she could touch him and offer some comfort. "Are you looking for Henry?"

"He said he had seen you back in our time. Have you seen him now? Here?" He looked around him frantically, as though searching for Henry was now hard wired. "I thought he would be here at Ashlington, but I can't get in."

Considering her impression of him from their first meeting, he now looked vulnerable and scared. More abandoned kitten than fierce big cat. "He is here and I think he is looking for you."

"He can't be. I would know if he were." He lunged towards her, leading with his remaining eye. "Is this my punishment?" he asked, his face close to hers, the despair and ferociousness back in an instant, as though if he could only fight something he might find the answer he searched for.

Olivia took an involuntary step backwards.

His shoulders sagged once more, and he apologised. "I did not mean to scare you."

"Why can't you find each other if you are both here? That does not make sense." Not that much of this did. Olivia thought. Least of all what connected her to these two soldiers other than the house and death.

"I made so many mistakes. You want to know why we are not together. That is why. It is my fault."

She felt it then. The anger he was holding on to. It was Westbrook that her father had disturbed with the gunfire. "All I know is that he never let you go, just like you never let him go."

He looked on the verge of denial. Some in-built reaction to all those years they had to pretend.

"Why do you think you still have your sword?" Olivia asked.

Westbrook tightened his grip on the hilt hung from his side and shrugged.

"I think it is important. You gave him one like it, didn't you? Your father's. You made a claim on Henry the day you gave it to him."

Westbrook blushed, her pirate a romantic old pussy cat after all. "How do you know that?"

"Henry told us. You know, if you lived here now, you could be together, marry each other and raise a family."

He looked at her blankly.

It was a lot to process, she thought. How could a man from two hundred years ago possibly reconcile what she was telling him? "You're not in Kansas anymore."

"What?"

"Forget it. I will have to work on my references, make them all Jane Austen or something."

Westbrook only looked more confused. "We would not have to hide how we feel?"

"Not here."

"Sounds like home." He closed his single eye for a moment, Olivia unsure if he were re-living a memory or trying to imagine such freedom. "I have been trying to keep Henry's family safe, like he would have wanted me to, but stuck out here, there is only so much I can do. Now I fear I am running out of time."

"I am going to help you find him. Will you trust me?"

"Only because he did," he said. His last words faint as he faded away again.

Chapter 39

Ashlington, September 1814

Henry and Westbrook returned to Ashlington, a change of clothes, then the fire in the library. Now more comfortable in his uniform, Henry complained about running out of time. They had to leave for the barracks the next day. Exasperated, his leg bounced with the vexing truth that he felt no closer to solving what happened to Danny.

Westbrook flicked through a book. Though Henry could tell he wasn't reading, he was sitting normally for starters, attention fixed on the flames of the fire. A figure passed the window that looked over the rear of the house, prompting Westbrook to stand and smooth his coat with a sharp tug. "Do you trust me?" he asked.

"More than anything."

"Then I shall return presently. There is something I wish to try."

"I could come with you?" Henry said, rising to his feet, thankful for the suggestion of action.

"If I am wrong, then it would be better you are not involved."

"Now that sounds exactly why I should come with you," Henry said, closing the distance between them, putting them dangerously close together should anyone see. He brushed a finger against Westbrook's hand.

"And is exactly why I asked if you trust me," Westbrook said pointedly, returning the touch with his thumb. He made his way to the door, turning to give Henry a dimpled smile, then left, leaving Henry with a churning in his belly not of steak pie.

As though he had been waiting for him to leave, Nathaniel entered the library only moments later, bringing with him his general air of disdain. "Your friend is up to something!" he declared. "I don't know what it is but we are going to find out."

"What are you talking about?" Henry said as his father grabbed hold of his elbow and pushed him out of the room.

"Don't you think it's coincidental that he turns up just days after Danny was killed?"

He may as well have just punched Henry for the shock he felt. How could he say such a thing when Westbrook had made every effort to be cordial with him and even sowed the seed of re-connecting with his father?

"What is he doing here?" Nathaniel continued hurrying Henry along the hallway. "There is something about him. He hides something, I know it. It drips off him so I can almost smell it."

Henry angrily grabbed his father's arm. "I don't doubt West for a second. He has saved my life more times than I can remember, and he is the very best of men."

Nathaniel shook off Henry's grip. "You haven't changed at all, Henry, you are still weak and impressionable."

Weak. A word that transported Henry to the summer he ran from Ashlington, timid and unsure of who he was. "I think it would surprise you, father, at how strong I am now. I left here a boy, and the regiment made me a man. One I am proud of. None of that had anything to do with you." Henry may as well have told it to the wall for all the notice his father took. Despite this, Henry felt something else settle on him. Pride. His own pride in the man he had become. Pride for facing his truth. Its value far exceeding that which he had coveted from his father.

"Let's see what kind of friend he really is. Christopher is in there. He is riding up to the Chiltons' to ask for Ursula's hand. If he hurts him..." Nathaniel growled, dragging Henry towards the stable block following Westbrook's route.

They stopped short of the door by the window where they could see the two men inside, Christopher facing the door, Westbrook blocking the exit. "Where did you get that?" They heard Christopher say. He took the cravat pin from Westbrook's outstretched hand.

"It is yours?" Westbrook asked casually. He dropped his saddle bag onto the floor.

"I thought I had lost it."

"Bradley found it under your brother's body. Whoever he had struggled with dropped it. It's over, Christopher," Westbrook said.

Morbidly, Henry watched Christopher gather himself. He saw it then, the guilt. Christopher carried it the same way Henry carried his own. Westbrook had seen what Henry had refused to. Deep down he knew he recognised the pin, but had buried that knowledge, not wanting to lose another brother.

"You stood there at your brother's graveside knowing the truth about what happened," Westbrook continued.

"He wouldn't let it go!" Christopher scowled through gritted teeth, looking more like their father than Henry had ever seen. "He was a clever man, Danny. He had the brains, Henry the heart, and I—"

"The ambition?" Westbrook finished for him.

Christopher laughed.

Henry looked at his father with raised eyebrows. *See?*

His father didn't have to reply. He put a steadying hand on Henry's arm, face twisting with denial. *Let this play out.*

"You do not know what it is like being the youngest, his youngest." Christopher rubbed at beads of perspiration on his forehead. "Being the nobody. All I have ever wanted is to be someone. Make him proud. To be wanted."

Westbrook said nothing.

"Danny discovered the investments." Christopher began pacing between the stalls. "I didn't think he would miss it, but—like I said," he tapped the side of his head with a finger. "He was a clever man. They assured me of a quick return. Machinery, they say it's the future. All I needed was a little more to cover what I had borrowed, so we argued. He wanted the money back; all Danny ever cared about was this bloody place and its reputation. I couldn't pay it back, I didn't even have the money to pay off Parish."

"The man Henry saw you with."

439

Christopher nodded.

"What happened, Christopher, that night with Danny? There was no intruder, was there?"

Christopher shook his head. A small part of Henry wanted to shout to Westbrook and tell him to stop. He didn't want to hear any more.

"We argued. Then we fought. He was strong. I had to hit him with the marble bust. I only meant to stop him yelling at me, as a threat to keep quiet, give me time to win the funds."

Henry still had his pistol at his waist from their earlier activities, what Parish had said about owing more elsewhere now worrying at him. He drew the pistol and quietly loaded it. Each step not only giving his hands something to do, but reassuring in the process. His father watched him, not trying to stop him. Frozen like a broken soldier on the field that had seen too much war.

"Win?"

"I have skill at the card tables."

Nathaniel groaned.

"I never wanted to kill him. I'm not a murderer!" Christopher continued.

Westbrook shook his head, unconvinced. "Just go Christopher, if it is more money you need, I shall give it to you. Do you have any idea what it would do to them if they knew it was you? It would destroy Henry. Take a ship somewhere, start again so they never feel the shame."

"What is it to you?"

"Henry is my captain, my friend." Westbrook took a

step closer. "There is nothing I would not do for him."

"If I go, I get nothing. Who are they going to believe? My father would not believe the likes of you over his own son. If I stay, I marry the Chilton girl and get it all."

"Did you not hear what I said?" Westbrook's patience was all but exhausted. "Henry already cleared your debt with Parish. That's the type of man he is. You only had to ask him. If you need more, then here—" he turned and bent to his saddlebag, his attention diverted.

Which is when Christopher struck.

Henry hadn't even seen the shovel in Christopher's hands. He had reached for it so quickly. The blade walloped Westbrook flat on the back of the head, throwing him forward with the force of the impact, his forehead hitting the wooden post of the stall.

"If you disappear, Henry will leave looking for you and will never come back." Christopher told Westbrook's slumped body.

"Stop!" Henry revealed himself as Christopher drew a knife from his belt and grabbed a handful of Westbrook's hair, pulling his head backwards holding the knife to his throat.

"I should have seen it before," Henry said. "How you have been acting this whole time."

"He threatened me, Henry," Christopher said, giving Westbrook's head a shake.

"No, we heard everything." Henry pointed at his brother, his voice lowering as his temper ignited. "You murdered our brother, you lie, and you dare to threaten the life of the only man who was willing to help you? West gave you a way out. You could have kept your name, your dignity, saved the heartache of our mother. He was willing to do all of this for you, and this is how you repay him? With a knife to his throat?" Henry took a step forward and forced himself to regain his composure of only for appearances.

His brother flinched, the knife piercing Westbrook's flesh. "What would you do if I took him away?"

"Don't! Don't you hurt him!" Henry said, teeth gritted, chest heaving with energy ready to be discharged. Henry did not need to search for an answer to his brother's question. The loaded pistol in his hand teased him with its weight.

"Henry," Westbrook said, his voice crackling like it had those years ago back at Badajos. He raised his head, straining against both the knife and Christopher's grip. His green eye stared straight into Henry's soul.

"He is your brother," he mouthed.

Henry disagreed.

In one smooth and rapid movement, he pulled up the pistol and shot Christopher.

The knife clattered to the floor, followed by Christopher, who clutched at his head. The shot had skimmed him, enough to shock but only a flesh wound.

"You shot me!" he said to Henry, who now towered over him. "Your own brother!"

"You're lucky I wasn't trying to kill you," Henry told him, then lifted Christopher by the throat to smash his fist into his face, opening himself and expelling all the anger and rage gathered on Danny's behalf. He was vaguely aware of Westbrook calling his name, but it was his father who pulled him away.

"That's enough, son," Nathaniel said, voice trembling. "I know. I know everything now. I shall deal with him."

Henry shoved his father off him, right hand shuddering as he hoisted Westbrook off the floor and, supporting his weight, led him out of the stable.

Bradley ran towards them from the house, alerted by the gunshot. Henry ordered him to help his father detain Christopher and send for the constable. Louisa met them in the hallway and took Westbrook's other arm under her shoulder, sharing the load until they deposited him on a settee in the parlour.

"What happened? Did I hear a gunshot? Does he need the doctor?" she asked.

Westbrook answered with a shake of the head. "Just a drink to stop the thumping in my head," he suggested hopefully.

"I'll get something to clean his wounds," Louisa told Henry as he paced the room. "What happened?"

"It was Christopher. All this time. He killed Danny."

She gasped. A hand flew to her mouth to catch it, then she screwed up her face, wrinkling her nose, and clenched her hands to her sides.

"I shot him." Henry wondered why he said that. Louisa did not seem worried if that meant Christopher was also dead.

"I'm sorry," Westbrook mumbled from the settee,

distracting her. "I was trying to handle it."

"You have nothing to apologise for. You were protecting me. Us," Henry said.

"You are my family."

Louisa gathered herself with a jut of her chin, ordered Henry to pour whisky and left them, returning moments later with a blanket and Mrs Melton in tow carrying a bowl of water and rags. Louisa knelt next to Westbrook, shook out the blanket and placed it gently over him. She allowed him a sip of whisky, then wrestled the glass back off him and began to clean up the cut on his head and the blood trickling down his face.

"You are going to wear the floorboards out, Henry," she snapped.

"There is no one to help father run the estate now with Christopher to be arrested." He locked eyes with Westbrook. "I shall have to stay. Resign my commission."

Westbrook opened his mouth to say something, but only a strange noise came out. Louisa pushed his jaw upwards, shutting it again with her fingers.

"Nonsense," she said, wringing out the cloth into the water, turning it bright red. "You and your father would kill each other within the first week of trying to work together. I shall help him."

Henry stopped pacing.

"I've already been more use to him than Christopher ever was and all the tenants like me. Providing your father can keep the books I can help with the rest."

"I don't doubt you for a second, you are most

capable."

"You don't want to be here, Henry, not yet. You need to be where you belong. Besides, who would take care of this one if you weren't there?" She patted Westbrook on the shoulder. "Then I'd have two souls on my conscience and that wouldn't do. We would have to talk to your father, but given the circumstances, if you speak to him quickly, I think he'd agree to anything you said."

"You would do that for me?"

"And me?" Westbrook added, halting the work of her hand with his own.

"And me," she agreed. "You told me to make myself a future here. That is what I will do. For me and the child. I'm not exactly tea party material, you know that, Henry. The Chiltons aren't done. They still want the land, but I sure as hell won't let that woman get her hands on Ashlington."

"I don't know, Henry. Maybe we should take her with us?" Westbrook winked. "She could turn a column with that fire."

Louisa prodded at his wound.

"Ouch! See what I mean?"

Henry smiled. "Ashlington will be in safe hands with you here," he said, pulling Louisa to her feet. "And this one," he put a hand on her stomach, "this one will have quite the mother to live up to. What are you going to call him?"

"What makes you so sure it will be a boy?"

"It is a Durand. It is usually a boy. Danny?"

"No. Danny didn't want him. We should name him after those that do. Robert and I discussed it yesterday. We do this together, yes?"

"Always," Henry and Westbrook said in unison. Henry laughed, knowing Westbrook could feel it too. A future they could work with.

"I should go speak to my father, see what is happening with Christopher," Henry told Westbrook, who shifted to get up.

"I shall come with you."

Louisa pushed him back down. "It won't hurt you to be separated for ten minutes. You have already bled over enough of the house."

"Has she always been this bossy?" Westbrook asked.

"I have been telling you that for years." Henry fixed his shoulders, took a deep breath and went to confront his father once more.

One last battle, then he would be free.

The commotion in the hallway increased with his approach. He found Christopher pacing the way Henry would, shouting at their father, nose all busted and blood trickling from where he now missed a front tooth. All Henry's work.

"It is your fault!" Christopher bawled at Nathaniel. "You did this! Danny would be here now if you had only given me a chance. The same chance you gave him. Your hands are just as red as mine. You did all of this! I only ever wanted to make you proud of me."

Nathaniel stood watching his youngest son, his damp eyes and hung head, accepting the blame without resistance.

Henry felt a slither of sympathy for the man, as fleeting as it was. Then he watched his father's mouth fall open and turned to see Christopher lunging forward with the knife. Had no one ensured its safety or had his brother carried two?

Henry didn't think further than that. He stepped into Christopher's path to protect his father, bumping Nathaniel aside, receiving a thump to his innards.

Christopher's astonished eyes met his with equal shock. "Henry? Why did you do that?" He pulled the knife out, wet and dripping, to stare at it as though surprised to find it in his hand.

He should have left it in, Henry thought. I would have more time.

Bradley took hold of Christopher, knocking away the knife, wrestling him aside as Henry crumpled, his hand ineffective against the flow spilling through his trembling fingers. Christopher might not have known war, but his stab had accurately hit something important between Henry's ribs.

People were shouting.

He heard his mother cry out.

Then Westbrook was there, holding him, telling him something. "We were meant to do this together, Henry. You promised." Westbrook growled, the soul inside that single green eye screaming at him again.

I didn't mean to leave you, West.

"Louisa?" Henry spluttered, feeling the blood now frothing in his mouth.

"I'm here," she said, pale eyes locked on his; that

brave, beautiful mind of hers, calculating what he might need.

"Don't let ..." He hoped she understood. His voice did not sound like his own and no longer worked now he struggled for breath. He could trust no one else with such a mission. He tried to squeeze her hand to let her know how much it meant. She looked to Westbrook, his hand reaching for the pistol at his waist. Henry watched her take it off him.

"I need you now, Robert," she told him sternly, fighting back her own devastation. "We both do. You claimed us too." She put a hand on her tummy. The message was clear.

Henry felt the relief wash through him as his life seeped away. She would keep Westbrook safe. Then Louisa was gone, pulling his distraught mother and father aside, leaving him with Westbrook.

Giving Henry one last gift.

Westbrook was right. It was not supposed to end this way. Henry had wanted to give him so much more. He had so much more he wanted to tell him, but the blood caught it all in his throat. All those words, the important ones, that he finally knew how and what to say were trapped with nowhere to go. He tried to use his eyes. Trying to tell Westbrook how sorry he was for failing, asking him to forgive him, but Westbrook wouldn't give up—his hands had taken over, trying to stop the blood with a frantic desperation.

"Don't go. Please don't leave me."

West, stop.

He felt Westbrook heave. Then his body moving. Westbrook pulling him onto his lap, resigned at last just to hold him. He felt Westbrook's cheek press against his. "I love you, Henry," Westbrook whispered, his voice cracking again, this time with the drawn out misery of grief. "Until the end of time. I should have told you years ago."

Chapter 40

Nick stopped reading and closed his laptop, looking every bit as shaken as Lillian felt. Not shaken, she felt like exploding. "They didn't get any time together?" she said, both angry for them and shocked. "They had the world before them, going back to where they belonged and it all got cut short." She passed a tissue to Nick. He looked like he needed it. They had spent most of the last twenty-four hours piecing together Henry's last journal entries and those of Louisa that corresponded. "Is that what is holding him here?"

"That he was brutally killed just as he felt a snippet of hope for his future? That he never got to tell the person he loved the words that had been eating him alive for years?" Nick sniffed. "Yeah, I'd say that qualifies as unfinished business."

"So why did we all think he died at Waterloo?"

"I think that is what they wanted you to think. It certainly explains why I could find no record of his death at the battle. No record of Christopher's crimes."

"What happened to Westbrook? Do we know?"

Nick shifted some papers and handed her a printout. One she had not seen before. "Thanks to the museum, we

450

have this. Recognise the date he died?"

"It's Waterloo. He died there, not Henry."

"We'll only know more detail if we continue researching, but I think we both know we are out of time."

Time.

The word hung in the air like swarming dust particles in a shaft of sunlight.

They *had* run out of time. The weather had warmed and Nick's commitment to the dig on the Fosseway would mean he would have little free time over the summer, and she would soon be back at work.

"There are more letters to Henry from Louisa here after he died," Lillian said, determined to keep to the matter in hand. "It seems like she did it often, she had been writing to him all those years, she carried on as though he was still there. I suppose it must have offered her some comfort, and it explains the one you found." She bundled those letters together. They would be filed away in poly sleeves and binders to protect them, to keep the memory of Henry and the others alive.

"Henry? Are you here?" she asked the room.

"I'm here," he said. "It brings it all back listening to you read about that day." Any shaking emotion in his voice only hinting at the distress he must have felt for the last two hundred years of separation. "The last thing he said to me was that he loved me, and I could not say it back. It shouldn't be so important—he knew, I am sure my actions told him so—but getting to say it was part of understanding myself. The last part, I suppose. To be at peace.

451

"All that time I wasted being ashamed. It was what he feared the most, being abandoned again, and I left him. I let him down, I let Danny down. I let them all down. If I hadn't run away and been there for Christopher, for Louisa..."

"Is that why you are here now?"

"It is the house. It allows me to be here like this. It wasn't immediate, more of a gradual thing. I tried to help you all over the years. Keep you safe. Comfort those that I could reach. It didn't work with everyone. When you came back, Lillian, together with Nick and Olivia, it felt different. More powerful somehow, it awakened something here, not only because of your emotions but also your history with the house. You are as much a part of its fabric as I."

"You kept us safe, Henry. We have found many examples. Like when my father fell from the window as a boy and you caught him."

"Caught who? I am tethered to the inside of the house." This he said with a fading hope. "I thought this was where he would come to find me, but it has been too long. I am trapped in here, like I trapped myself hiding from him, and he will never come. I shall be lost and alone forever. I can only hope he found someone who could give him what he needed—his own family."

The doorbell interrupted Lillian's defence of Westbrook before she began. Holly gave a snuffle of a bark as they heard the door open, then wagged her tail when she heard Olivia's voice.

"Anyone in?"

"Study," Nick called back.

Olivia entered the room flushed and out of breath as though she had been chased up the driveway. "He is here!" she announced, arms outstretched in a silent 'ta-dah.' She then glanced over to the fireplace. "Henry! You're here too. This is perfect. I thought it would be much harder than this."

"You can see Henry?" Nick asked.

"Yeah, he is walking up and down in front of the fireplace." She gestured in that direction as though it were an everyday occurrence. Lillian again marvelled at how unfazed Olivia was by any of this. "I've just been talking with Robert Westbrook."

"West? You must be mistaken," Henry said.

"Devastating curls, one-eyed kinda pirate look about him?" she teased.

"That's him! Truly?"

"Go to him, Henry," Lillian said with a shooing motion that felt every bit as absurd as the situation.

"I think he has. He's already gone," Olivia said.

"So why have they not just done that before?" Lillian asked. "Did Westbrook just get here or something?"

"He says he has been here since Waterloo."

He no longer startled her or came from nowhere. Instead, his presence grew around her. Blanketing her with a soft and comforting existence, making her realise she had felt it many times within the house over the years. She was also quite sure she had felt it outside, too. "Lillian?" he called as she climbed the stairs to bed that night.

"Did you find him, Henry?"

"No."

She thought she heard the hitched intake of a sob. "I'm so sorry. I wish we could help you in some way. Perhaps we can—"

"It was a fool's hope. We couldn't be together then, we can't now."

"Don't say that. Don't give up on him."

The presence left, leaving nothing but the icy chill of longing and the sound of her phone ringing.

"Henry?"

He did not answer.

The incoming call was Guy. She considered letting it ring to answer phone, reluctant to leave the past and have to face whatever current drama his call would invoke. But she answered it. He got straight to the point.

"I have always been there for you, Lillian. Right from the start. Now I need you." He told her with a hurried torment. "You are like my sister. You know that, don't you? You stepped into the role she left. Please don't leave me too. Don't make me go through that again."

How could she not listen to him? She had always listened to Guy. He had mentored her from the beginning of her career and got her to where she was. She owed him. To hear him in such distress on top of all the surrounding loss brought her to tears.

She had been through the figures. Her accountant had been through the figures with her father's solicitor. They all agreed. Financially, the development of Ashlington Manor and the sale of land for housing would leave Lillian far better off after the crippling inheritance tax. With the sale, she could keep her house in Camden and be a partner in the business. The success she had craved for so long was at her finger tips.

She asked herself what Henry would do. She did not have to look far for the answer. He had given up his own happiness to protect those that he loved. Guy and Marcus needed her. She had to act. She might not be in love with Marcus anymore, but she did still care for him.

"I am kind of in the middle of something here which needs my attention. Can you come here? Send your proposal for all of it; I will make sure I have my solicitor here. Tuesday? Midday?"

She then sent a text to Nick.

"Thanks for coming," she said, answering the door to Nick and Olivia the following morning, pulling them inside with little care for formalities. "It didn't work. Henry could not connect with him. He said that whatever power he got, it felt stronger when the three of us were together, so I think we have to work together on this. Olivia, do you think you can get Westbrook here?"

"We passed him on the way in, he is just outside the door. It's like he spends a lot of time there trying to find a way in. He told me yesterday he has been trying all this time. It is like the house keeps him out."

"I don't think it is the house." Lillian took a deep breath. She had hardly slept all night trying to make sense of it all, she only hoped she did not sound ridiculous. "I know this house. It wants its Durands to be happy. It is not the house keeping them apart."

"What then?" Nick asked.

"It reminds me of something Henry said in his journal when he first got home. Something about the angel in the graveyard."

"Tethered angels cannot fly. The ivy?"

"Yes, that was it." She knew Nick would have it all memorised. "Now stay with me. What is tethering them both? Not ivy, not anything physical like the house." She paced up and down. It was there, she could feel it on the tip of her tongue.

"Westbrook blames himself for Henry's death," Olivia said from the porch.

"Henry is regretful, also blaming himself for leaving Westbrook alone and for Danny's death. Like in his painting, he is sad but also angry," Nick agreed.

Lillian stepped into the porch with Olivia. "Robert?"

"He's here," Olivia confirmed.

"We are going to help you, Robert. Just stay there while we figure it out."

"I can feel it," he said, his voice a timbre deeper than Henry's. "The energy with all of us together."

"That's the key, we think. Olivia says you are angry. Would you tell us why? Lillian said.

"I am angry with him for leaving me alone."

Lillian glanced at Nick. They had both felt it with those they had lost. Nick nodded.

"But more than that, I am angry with myself for letting

it happen. It was my fault, you understand. It started the minute I let him leave Sinclair's alone. If only I had been here for the wedding, Danny might not have been killed. Then I was so concerned with helping Henry find some justice that I didn't see the danger of my actions. Christopher was only a threat after I confronted him. Everything I did here was wrong."

"It wasn't your fault, Robert," Lillian said.

"All you ever did was try to protect him," Nick added.

"There is more though, isn't there?" Olivia said, stepping outside, presumably closer to Westbrook's presence.

Like an audible click, Lillian felt it. She nudged Nick. "Do you remember what I said in the museum? About Westbrook and the others bringing Henry to life?"

"Their story is part of Henry's," Nick agreed. "He needs to tell us the ending. His ending."

"Tell us, Robert. Finish the story for us."

"The part you are really angry about," Olivia added.

"He said no one could know," Westbrook said with a bitter, deep venom that took Lillian by surprise.

"Henry?"

"No, his father. My next mistake that day was to show how much I cared. I wouldn't let anyone touch Henry. I sat there holding him for over an hour before anyone dared to come close. By that time, Christopher had been taken away, with arrangements for a significant payment to the constable to allow him to flee without charge. No justice, no honour!"

Olivia screwed her eyes closed and put a hand to her

temple as though his anger physically hurt her.

"Louisa sat with me eventually, and we agreed to take care of his body together. I carried him upstairs, and we did exactly that. Only those present knew what had happened, and Nathaniel wanted to make sure it stayed that way. That was the first thing he said when he came into that room to see Henry laid out. 'No one can know.' I couldn't hide it anymore. I had nothing left to give to keep it inside, so I let it show. I put Nathaniel against the wall with my arm across his throat. He should have been dead, not Henry.

"He saw me and I saw him. He saw that I was in love with his son, and I saw and smelt his fear. Fear that everything was falling apart around him. That his name and this noble house would be tainted forever by what Christopher did. And now he had just found a new hell to add to that shame. Me.

"He knew it, I knew it. I had to go. So I did. I left then to protect the baby. No one would know about my relationship with Henry, no one would know what Christopher did to either of his brothers. The name of Durand would endure. As far as everyone outside of that room knew, Henry left with me that day for the regiment. I took his horse. Do you understand? I left him. Didn't even see him into the ground. I left never wanting to set foot in this house again, and he will hate me for all of it."

"It was an impossible situation, Robert. You could not have done anything differently. What about the regiment? What did you tell them?" Nick asked.

"Nathanial arranged Henry's resignation. The colonel

was so busy with the arrangements for America it was not given the scrutiny it should have been. Then Bonaparte returned, and we embarked instead for Flanders. I did my duty. I took the company and then—"

"Waterloo."

"I thought I saw him at the end. Thought I heard him. But in the end I never deserved him."

"They told everyone that he died in battle. With you," Lillian said.

"That is how it should have been. But this is my penance. Trapped here, unable to reach him."

Olivia closed her eyes and held her head again in pain.

"Seems unfair to punish you when all you did was love and protect him," Nick said.

"The only one punishing anyone is yourselves!" Lillian said, suddenly most frustrated with her two ghosts. "Don't you see? You are punishing yourselves with all this anger in your souls. You are keeping each other away. There is so much of it, it physically hurts Olivia."

"She is right," Olivia said. "The anger only pushes you both further away from each other."

It suddenly seemed very clear to Lillian. "All those times you showed each other your vulnerabilities, all those times we read about, that is when you drew each other closer. Maybe that is what you need to do now."

"Henry is here too," Olivia said, gesturing to the hallway. "Over there, by the stairs."

"Henry, he is here. Robert is here, just outside the door," Lillian said.

"I can't see him."

"You have to reach out," she told him as Nick ducked into the study. "Stop feeling guilty about Danny's death, or about leaving Robert alone. None of it was your fault, either. It is like you said when you first contacted me. 'You have to tell him.' Now you can. There is nothing to stop you being together if you only forgive yourselves. It's time."

"Henry, this might help," Nick said, returning from the study with Henry's sword. "I found Sinclair's trunk in the attic when we found your sword. I got a little distracted the next day..." he gave Lillian a guilty glance, "and flicked through his journal. He wrote about Robert asking for his father's sword, that he put his heart and soul into mending it to give to you. His heart and soul, Henry. That's powerful stuff." Nick held out the sword flat in his outstretched hands. He had polished the blade so it shone in the shaft of light coming from the open door, and for a moment Lillian thought she saw the reflection of Henry in the steel. A pair of blue eyes like her own.

A hush descended on them and a cool breeze stirred her hair.

"What's happening?" Nick asked Olivia.

"I don't know. Henry touched the sword, then disappeared. Westbrook too."

***

Henry placed his hand on the sword and felt for the love Westbrook had poured into it. He had told him as much himself, that it had to be enough. Discarding the anger, reaching out like Lillian told him to, he reached for home; for Westbrook at his most vulnerable.

Let me in West. I still need you.

Then he saw him. Not at Ashlington. They were in another house, a library. A boy sat on the floor with his back against the bookshelf, books spilt around him, knees drawn up to his chest and arms wrapped around them, a mop of dark curls hiding his face.

Henry lowered himself next to the boy, his shoulder almost touching, and waited for the crying to stop.

"Who are you?" the boy asked eventually, looking up, one of his green eyes surrounded with purple bruising and swelling. The fighting had already begun. The drinking would be a few years yet.

"A friend."

"I don't have any."

Henry put an arm around him, ready for him to draw away. Or thump him. The boy did neither. He leant into the comfort offered, as though he knew it was made for him.

"Are you a ghost?"

"I suppose."

"My father is dead. He was a soldier like you."

"I'm sorry."

"My mother wants me to go live with my godfather. Says I make too much trouble here for my grandparents. That I am a bad influence on my sister."

Henry bit his lip to prevent himself from smiling. "It is a good idea."

"But what if he doesn't want me, either? What if he leaves me too?"

"He is the best of men. You will have many adventures with him. Lots of stories to tell, and more importantly, he has an enormous library."

"Really?" A splinter of interest.

Henry squeezed him. God, how he loved this man. "Huge! Plenty of Shakespeare ."

The boy wiped his eyes with his sleeve. "Doesn't sound so bad."

A familiar voice came from beyond the door. Sinclair.

"That's him," the boy said, straightening with a snuffled inhalation.

"It'll be all right, West."

"It's Westbrook," the boy said with a sullen frown.

"One day someone will start calling you West, and you will quite like it."

"Robert?" The man Henry expected to walk through the door was not this younger, blithe version of Sinclair, lighter and unscarred. Sinclair smiled when he saw Westbrook, releasing a familiar look of determination wrapped in compassion, that he would make this work or die trying. "There you are, my boy. Ah, finding some books to bring, I see. May I be of assistance?" Sinclair sat on the floor opposite and began arranging the books into piles. Ignoring Henry. He couldn't see him.

Wait for me, West.

Then Henry was at a battle. A huge battle. One he did

not recognise. One that his professional eye judged would soon be over with the French Imperial Guard in retreat. He drifted through the shroud of carnage, destruction, and the familiar stinging of gunpowder smoke, searching for the 28th , for his friends. His brothers.

Something warm and bright pulled him to one of the defensive squares recently hit by cannon. He found them, ranks bristling with bayonets. The major ordered the men out into line, less of a target for the big guns and the desperate last efforts of the French. "They'll run soon," Henry told him. "You've done very well."

Henry left the major and drifted to Jackson, now a junior officer, watched him cuff at his eyes, then take a letter from the pocket of his mortally wounded captain. Sergeant Cotton picked up the colours, and the company formed line with the regiment to surge forward. "Be safe," Henry said, weaving among the ranks like he used to.

As they moved away, he saw him. He knew to expect it, but the agony of seeing him hurt and lifeless devastated Henry.

He stretched out his hand for the fallen Captain Robert J T Westbrook.

To pull him up once more.

"It's time," Henry said.

"You promised me we'd do this together," Westbrook whispered.

"Always, West. You promised too."

Westbrook took his hand, and they were back at Ashlington, stood together in the hallway.

He felt him then; the press of that familiar form. Westbrook's arms around him once more, holding him fast against the madness, throwing off death as he had done through many nights doing battle with Henry's demon.

"I'm here. I've got you. You are home," Henry told him.

"I've been looking for you," Westbrook said with a sob.

"You really have been here with me all this time?"

He felt Westbrook nodding. "I don't do very well without you."

Henry tightened his grip, inhaling long days on the march, wood-smoke, fresh rain and books he always associated with the man he loved.

Tell him.

He took a deep breath. "I need to tell you something. West, I need to tell you that I am very much in love with you. I have been for as long as I can remember, before I even knew it myself," Henry said, the relief of it unburdening him finally, so that he felt himself smile. There was no demon in his soul, after all—only love.

"I should have told you years ago, trusted you. I should have known that even had you not felt the same, that you would have still been my friend." He loosened his hold, only enough to look Westbrook in that single emerald eye. "I wasted so much precious time being ashamed for being me, and I'm sorry I left you alone. I did not mean for it to happen that way."

"I have been so angry," Westbrook said, adjusting his own hold on Henry.

"What my brother did was not your fault, nor mine. None of it was. I would do it all again if it meant I got one more day with you. One more hour." Henry rested his forehead against Westbrook's, and the soul he thought he would never see again looked back at him and said *we are home.*

"Well, I'm not ready to go now. We missed so much," Westbrook said with a hint of humour that seemed to brighten the hallway.

"We don't have to go. Not yet. Shall we stay a while here?"

Westbrook nodded. "I have been dying to get my hands on Ashlington's library," he laughed at the implied joke, and the giddy joy Henry felt from such a sound let him know they would never be parted again.

"Home?"

Westbrook grinned in agreement and kissed him. The tender one. Like last time.

***

"Oh, they are back," Olivia said. "And—well—I am pretty sure they can see each other now."

"How do you know?" Lillian asked.

"Because they are kissing."

"Ghosts can do that?"

"Ours can."

465

"Wait, I can see them too," Lillian said, holding her hand to her mouth, blinking rapidly. They stood at the bottom of the staircase, as clear as she could see Nick and Olivia. It was only as they moved that she caught the blurring. Like a photograph out of focus, the smudged suggestion of another realm breached.

"Me too. I can see them," Nick said, unable to hide the wonder. He propped Henry's sword against the wall and Lillian felt his fingers grasp her own, saw him reach for Olivia's hand, too. "Ah, ladies, they have waited two hundred years for this. Shall we give them some privacy?"

Lillian hesitated. They were her family; she had only just found them. "You won't go anywhere just yet, will you?" she asked.

Henry looked over, Westbrook resting his head on his shoulder, their arms wrapped tightly around each other as though neither wanted to let go for fear of losing the other again.

"No, we thought we might stay," Henry said with a smile that reminded Lillian of her father.

"It's your home too, Henry," she said, unable to do anything about the brimming tears. "Both of you."

Chapter 41

"Louisa was right. They do look like they belong together," Nick said as he followed Olivia outside. She had to get to school and he to the university for a lecture.

"At least now they don't have to hide their feelings anymore," Lillian replied from behind him inside the porch.

Not knowing how to deal with that statement, Nick looked out across the lawn and the vale soaking in the contentment of the house, hoping it might change how he felt inside. "I'll start writing up his story for you. Up to you guys what you want to do with it then."

"Okay. Thanks, Nick. I'd never have done it without you. Either of you."

"I have to dash," Olivia said. "Don't want to miss the bus. Can I call in after school in the week? There is so much I want to ask them."

"Of course, thanks Olivia," Lillian said. She watched Olivia make her way down the driveway for a moment, then looked at him, something on her mind.

He held his breath.

"Why do we have Sinclair's trunk? Aside from Henry, there is no other link to him. And what about Louisa? You said there is no record of her death in the parish records?" she said.

It was not what he expected her to say. Not at all what

he wanted her to say.

"I don't know, Lily." He did little to disguise the annoyance in his voice, suddenly exhausted with the Durands. "If you need help with anything, the move, whatever, just let me know," he said in a kinder fashion, wanting his offer for further help to sound sincere, but all too aware of his emotions gathering force. They would get the better of him if he did not hurry and leave. Lillian had made her decision. There was nothing he could do.

When the vast oak door closed behind him, it made a noise like his own soul cracking in two. Nick moved slowly down the driveway, suddenly reluctant to leave, reluctant to turn his back on the place.

"You are going?" a voice said next to him. He expected Henry, but turned to find it was Westbrook.

"Durands can be very frustrating," Nick said, realising no one understood this sentiment better than Westbrook.

"It is part of their charm," Westbrook chuckled.

Easy for him to say, rentaghosting about the place, high on love requited, Nick thought.

"Don't give up on her."

But it wasn't that easy. Nick's heart was breaking. He was about to lose her all over again, and there was nothing he could do about it. He had to let her go.

***

On Tuesday morning, an hour before the solicitor, Guy, and Marcus were due to arrive, Lillian took some fresh flowers to her parents' grave.

The grief had not gone, but over the last few months, it had shifted. It now lay somewhere manageable; somewhere amongst her memories, shored up by all her new hopes for the future.

"You are very much like her, you know," Henry said, the blanket of his compassion enveloping her on the way back to the house as she walked through the rose garden. His generosity warming her before she could see him.

"Who?"

"Louisa. You look a lot like her, but you also have her strength," he said.

"You seem happier. Even if I couldn't see you, I can hear it in your voice."

"I am at peace for the first time. Sinclair said to me years ago that home isn't always a place. I knew at the time what he meant, deep down; but now—now West is here, I understand. He is my home." He glanced over to where Westbrook leant against the kitchen-garden wall. He waved at them, Henry's eyes kindling at the sight. Lillian watched as a contented smile stretched across his face.

"It was Robert that caught my father?"

Henry nodded. "He says you were all his family too."

"You both deserved a happy ending."

"So do you, Lillian."

"You didn't tell her, did you?" Westbrook said, lacing *his hand into Henry's as Lillian stepped inside the house. "That if she goes, our connection to this place is lost. That*

we move on, to whatever comes next. That without a Durand here—"

Henry stopped him and took hold of his other hand. "No, I didn't tell her. The decision is hers. She believes she is doing the right thing. Who am I to say otherwise? We'll just take every day that we get? And face whatever comes next together."

Westbrook nodded. "Always."

By the time the grandfather clock chimed midday, Lillian had set out a tray of tea and coffee in the dining room and fussed around as Stanley Heart, her father's solicitor, allowed Guy and Marcus to read through the contract he had prepared. She sat opposite them, re-reading her own copy. Its contents were largely as they had set out in their proposal; with a few additional caveats, such as ensuring the upkeep and security for those that rested in the small graveyard in perpetuity.

She looked up at the painting of Henry, searching for strength. Strength to go against what her heart really wanted, as he did when he married; strength to see it through like her extremely great grandmother Louisa had done at every turn.

It was next to the painting that she noticed a stained document. Someone had leant it against the bottom of the frame. An invitation.

"Read it," Henry said from somewhere behind her, sending a chill down her spine.

With the others busy at their laptops and contracts, Lillian walked to the fireplace and took down the letter.

Written in an unfamiliar hand, the writing was not as loopy as Henry's, more efficient, as though this person wrote often and took more enjoyment in the task.

Addressed to Theodore H R Durand—Teddy— Louisa's boy, the letter was dated a few days before Waterloo. Judging by the ragged edges, deep folds and tiny rips, it had been well loved and re-read often.

Dearest Teddy,

It will be up to your mother if she gives this letter to you when you are older should anything happen to me, but I realised that she can only provide half of your father's story for you. I consider myself fortunate enough to be keeper of the other half. Whilst I hope one day I can tell you in person, if I am unable, then it is important to me that you know who your father is to all the men who have fought with him.

Friendship can oft be an inadequate word. Brother does not seem to fit either. The word family comes closer, yet all these things do little to describe why I would gladly give my life for your father without hesitation. Maybe one day you will understand. I hope so. It is a wondrous thing to know.

I met him in a fight. My fight. Four men against me. Your father took it upon himself to intervene and make things a little fairer. I had been with the regiment a year already and not once had anyone showed me such generosity of spirit. Within weeks, we were inseparable and remained that way for the years that followed.

He is the bravest man I know, encouraging those

weaker than him, learning from those wiser, no matter their rank. He has a particular aversion to the sight of blood but will check the surgeon's tent after each skirmish or battle for our men and offer comfort and encouragement to the wounded when no one else would think to do such a thing. He would give his life for any of us, oft putting himself in grave danger for us. It is why we all feel the same about him.

Your father and I made friends and buried them over the years. We saw things that would send a man crazy with the horror of it. On the days everything seemed hopeless, and we questioned what we fought for, he would remind us of the answers.

With no heirs of my own, I have taken the precaution of naming you in my will. Though no Durand, I have a substantial sum that you may find of use. I understand large estates can be quite the burden.

I would suppose that this is the part where a responsible man would give some words of wisdom? Something about duty and honour, marrying well and raising heirs? But I think your father would want me to say this instead—test the boundaries and step over them every so often. Stand up for what you believe in. Protect the ones you love and love them fiercely. Do not waste a second. Tell them. Tell them you love them. Show them every day.

Your most humble servant,
Robert J T Westbrook
Captain, 28th Regiment

Lillian recalled Louisa's comment about discussing names for the baby with Westbrook. She had named him after those that wanted him—Henry and Robert. The name Theodore honouring the father they all deserved.

Westbrook's letter had provided Teddy and all those that followed with the well deserved heroic characterisation of Henry. Henry might not have been Teddy's father biologically, but no matter how undeserving Henry thought he was, the people that loved him made sure no one doubted his worth. That Westbrook had named Teddy as his heir could not be overlooked, either. Not only the financial stability this might have given Ashlington following settlement of Christopher's debts, but the emotional bond at play. He had claimed Teddy, too.

Then Lillian's extremely great grandfather had taken the words from Westbrook's letter and used it as a code to live by. Parts of it had been forgotten over the years. Important parts. Parts Lillian needed to listen to now. The parts Henry had been telling her about.

Tell them you love them.

She read the sentence again. More immediately, she had to stand up for what she knew in her heart was right regarding Ashlington.

Guy pushed the contract across the table to her. "Time to sign, Lillian."

But Lillian stalled.

"You need to sign," Guy said impatiently, thrusting the pen towards her. When she didn't pick it up, he moved around the table. "Please Lillian, do it for me." He gave a pitiful whine, gripping her forearm. She thought of Louisa and the bruises from her father, and shook herself free from his grasp.

"I'm not signing," she breathed.

"I'm not signing!" This time she said it louder for all to hear.

"What do you mean you're not signing?" Guy laughed, "Why the change of heart?"

How could he know? She thought. How could he know that her heart hadn't changed at all, it had just been found again?

"Lillian?"

"The soldier in this painting, Henry, died doing what he thought was right. Like him, I am going to stand up for what I believe in. I will not turn my home into a hotel development that ruins not only this house but the village, too. Don't you see? Ashlington is not just *my* home."

"Sentimentality. I always said it would be your downfall, Lillian. We agreed. We agreed this was best for everyone. Best for you!"

"But it isn't. It isn't best for me, Guy. It is best for you and the money you and the company would make. It is not best for the village, not best for the house, and certainly not what is best for me. I am sorry you all had a wasted journey, but I am not selling and I respectfully decline the offer of partnership. In fact, I will e-mail you my resignation by the end of the day."

"You can't do that, Lillian," Guy said. He looked at Marcus, expecting some back-up. "I made you what you are.

You owe me. Without this we'll be done."

"What are you talking about, Guy? Sure, we might have to tighten our belts, but we are far from done," Marcus said.

"Tighten our belts? We shouldn't need to tighten anything!" Guy flushed, fury riding its way up his neck to find a home among his frustration that no one was doing what he wanted them to. "We are supposed to be at the top. I needed you back in London where you belong, at my side."

"She doesn't belong in London, Guy. She belongs here," Marcus said. "I'm not sure I will ever understand it, but I can see it. This is your home." This he said to Lillian. Marcus might not have fought for her, but she was sure as hell he would fight for the company. He had that hungry look back in his eyes. He would be okay. He was back where he belonged, doing what he loved best.

She tore up the pages of the contract and handed them to Mr Heart. Who grinned at her. "You'll be selling your house in Camden then, Miss Durand?"

"Yes, that'll go some way to paying off the inheritance tax. I will have my own belt to tighten for a few years, but I'll be okay," she said. "Ashlington will be safe."

"You are not even of sound mind anymore. Marcus told me you had been hearing voices. How can you make such a decision in that state? Are you medicated right now?" Guy grabbed for her arm again.

With the cooling of her surroundings, Lillian felt Henry and Westbrook arrive either side of her. She gave them a slight shake of the head. Their assistance would not be needed. She would make sure Guy left, herself.

"This is all about your fear of being bought out by Warrilow? You knew what was coming, it was your pride that stopped you doing anything about it when you could. Swallow that pride Guy, take it from me, it is most liberating, and I can assure you all I am of very sound mind."

"You will be sorry. You'll be sat here in years to come with this house dying around you, then you will really regret what you just did!"

"I doubt that very much. I have never felt this place feel so alive."

***

Henry bit at his lip under Westbrook's crossed-armed scrutiny.

"I thought you were going to let her come to her own decision," Westbrook said with a shake of his head.

"I did—technically—consider the letter a nudge."

"Henry Durand, I thoroughly corrupted you, didn't I?"

Henry laughed. "And I enjoyed every minute."

***

It was Wednesday afternoon before Lillian saw anything of Nick and Olivia again. Holly's excited scrabbling at the door announcing their arrival before the doorbell did.

"We wanted to come and see how you are. Make the most of you still being here," Olivia said, still dressed in her school uniform. "Wow. What is that?"

"What?"

"This place feels—I don't know how to describe it—free? Happy?"

"Well, maybe the old place is happy because I'm not moving," Lillian said, giving Olivia a playful nudge as she shut the door behind them.

"Wait, you aren't selling?"

Nick said nothing. He stood there with his mouth agape, Holly jumping at his legs, begging for his attention. It gave Lillian a thrill to have rendered him speechless. He hadn't returned any of her text messages since the day Henry and Westbrook reunited.

"Nope. I am most certainly not selling. You missed all the drama yesterday. I sent them back to London. I'm going to keep the house, set up my own business," Lillian told them.

Olivia threw her arms around her and hugged for all she was worth. Lillian thought it was probably the best hug she had ever received and lifted the girl off her feet to spin her around before continuing. "Our two resident ghosts are already into mischief. One wants us to find out what happened to his wife. He has made a bit of a mess of your filing system by the way," she told Nick, "and the other is re-arranging the library."

"They are still here, then? I worried that reuniting

them might have moved them on, you know," Olivia said.

"They don't want to go. Not yet, anyway. If anything, I'd say what ties them here is even stronger now. Since reuniting their presence seems more powerful, hence the projection to your dad and I. Look at me!" she laughed. "Maybe I should start a blog."

"Can I go find them?" Olivia asked.

"Try the library. They are still getting the hang of moving stuff, so do keep an eye out for flying books. Maybe knock first."

"Well, it seems you have yourself quite the household," Nick said finally, having managed to find his voice. "I'm happy for you. Your dad would be proud."

"What about you? Are you staying?"

"I took the university job about a week ago. I didn't say anything because I decided that no matter what you did, this is where I needed to be."

"That is fantastic. What does Olivia think?"

"She is eager to spread some roots and her friend Demetrio is planning to visit. Like me, she has become attached to this place."

"Well, this might make what I am about to ask you easier then—" Lillian shifted and tugged on the bottom of her shirt. "With all that tax I have to pay, I have room for some lodgers, like an archaeologist and his teenage daughter. I mean, it might sound like an impulsive, sentimental Durand thing to ask, but there are plenty of rooms here if you were at all interested in moving out of that tiny cottage you keep bumping your head on?"

"Olivia and I move here?"

"You can pay your way. There doesn't have to be any strings attached, it's not a marriage proposal."

"Thank heavens!" Nick said.

"I just," she took a deep breath. "I got used to having you both around, you know? Henry says I should just come out with it and tell you what I really feel—he is quite the smug nag now—what he doesn't seem to understand is that only weeks ago I was engaged. It will take a bit of time to adjust."

"I can wait," Nick said with a small shrug. "As long as it doesn't take two hundred years, you Durands can be a bit slow at connecting with your feelings." He took a step nearer, confident Nick smiling back at her.

The house seemed to sigh, as though exhaling the breath it had been holding for hundreds of years.

Rowan MacKemsley

Excellent LGBT fiction and non-fiction by unique, wonderful authors.

Thrillers
Mystery
Romance
Non-Fiction
& More

Visit us at
www.spectrum-books.com
Or find us on Instagram
www.instagram.com/spectrumbookpublisher

Printed in Great Britain
by Amazon